THE ONE WHO WROTE DESTINY

THE ONE WHO WROTE DESTINY

NIKESH SHUKLA

First published in hardback in Great Britain in 2018
by Atlantic Books, an imprint of Atlantic Books Ltd.

1 2 3 4 5 6 7 8 9

A CIP catalogue record for this book is available
from the British Library.

Hardback ISBN: 978 1 78649 278 4
EBook ISBN: 978 1 78649 279 1

Printed in Great Britain by TJ International Ltd, Padstow, Cornwall

Atlantic Books
An Imprint of Atlantic Books Ltd
Ormond House
26–27 Boswell Street
London
WC1N 3JZ

www.atlantic-books.co.uk

For my sisters, kakis, masis, fais, mamis, faibas.
For my kız kardeş. For Harrow ba, for other
house ba. For mum.

MUKESH

Keighley, 1966

What stories will they tell about me?
Or will I have to give people my own history?

Mukesh Jani

Stasis

I have no reason to be anywhere.

I find myself in an in-between world, with no purpose, except to lean with my back against the wall, across the road from Nisha's amee and papa's house. Not like a stalker, yaar. No, instead, I am posed like the poet I am, my pen poised to make ink marks and etchings on an open notebook page.

So far, all I have written is Nisha's name: her first name, her full name, her first name with my surname, my first name with her surname, our names together. I write the openings of poems, but I never get past the first word of the first line. I have never written a poem before. I know that the first line starts with the word Nisha, though. Despite my lack of experience as a writer, her very existence inspires me, convinces me I was born to tell stories. Nisha means night. Maybe there is something in this for me to spin into poetry.

Nisha, tonight, you are…

Night.

I wear my best clothes because they're all I have that isn't my white pyjama lengha or my exercise shorts. And now that I'm not in school, I don't need to subject myself to the level of humiliation that comes with wearing short shorts.

The damp breeze reminds me that I am alone in England, in a navy-blue suit jacket that used to belong to my father, which I cannot button up. Amee tried to find me blue trousers that matched it, but failed. In the grey of Keighley, the difference between the two is extremely noticeable. I have two white shirts which, due to the climate, I can wear all day every day as there is never any chance of getting hot enough to stain the collar. I look down at my father's black tie, thin, with a pin that bears his name in Gujarati: Rakesh. I wonder what has happened to my wardrobe, now that I'm here. Amee has probably given everything to my younger brother. Because why take clothes invented for hotter climates to the wet and grey of England's green and pleasant land? Neha, you were born here, but up until my teenage years, all I knew was Kenya.

Nisha, are you my destiny?

I scribble over this nonsense and stare at the half-empty page. I hope I seem deep in thought. Especially if Nisha is looking out of her window. The trick is to arrive twenty minutes before she is due home from school and stay until five minutes after she leaves for rehearsals for the big Diwali show. I practise my pensive face every morning in the mirror above the basin in my room. My thoughtful look, my deep-in-thought expression, initially looked constipated. It then went through a phase of looking as though I might have squirted lemon juice into my eye. Now I look blank. It is the best I can muster but I prefer it to looking as though I am in pain.

I glance at my watch again – my father's watch; everything I own is my father's. I have to preserve these heirlooms to pass on to my younger brother. Until then, I am the head of the family, and thus inherit all his fancy items.

The watch says 5.30 p.m.

On the nose.

The British have funny expressions for things. 5.30 p.m. on the nose. Everything has a nose, it seems. Everything has human features and human responses. They did not teach me this in school. I learned about verb conjugations, about vocabulary, about pronouns, adjectives, adverbs. I was never taught vernacular. Slang. The entire English language is composed of idioms. I feel lost most days when overhearing conversations at breakfast between the owners of the house where I lodge.

I never say anything.

They assume it is because I speak no English.

Actually, it is because I do not speak their version of English.

I hear keys in the door across the street and stare more intently than ever at my notebook. I want her to notice me and yet I do not wish to be seen. I can just about see Nisha in my periphery. *Oh, Nisha*, I write, changing my style, not having Nisha as the first word. *Oh, Nisha, where is your head?*

I frown. What does it mean?

Nisha closes her front door. I scribble over the line and try again.

Oh, Nisha, what are we going to do with you?

I cross this out. It sounds as though I am her dad.

Oh, Nisha, let me in.

I cross this one out too, as it borders on murderous.

Poetry is difficult.

The door opens again and I look up from my book. Nisha is struggling to balance a bag on her shoulder and a bundle of sarees under an arm. I look down again when I feel as though she's spotted me.

Nisha steps out into the road and drops her keys. She bends

down to pick them up. I don't think she notices the bike coming along. Something overwhelms me and, fearing for her safety, I spring into the road, dropping my notebook and pen in my haste to get to her. I have to protect her. I have to save her. I have to stop her from getting hurt. I have to keep her out of harm's way.

The bike crashes into my side and sends me smacking on to the cobbles of the street, my head banging against a jutting stone. I hear my name being called. I hear someone call me a *bloody wog*. I hear the click-click-click of a bicycle wheel in a free spin. Before things fade to black, I try to remember my happiest moment, just in case this is the end.

Amee's aloo parathas could start wars. And they often did, between me and my brother. The trick to her aloo paratha was to slow-cook the potatoes all morning in water infused with ghee. That way, you could mash them with milk for a smoother texture. My younger brother and I fought over who got to have the first one, straight from the tawa.

I am sitting at Amee's table. It is my last meal with her before I leave for England. Though I should feel jubilant, I am mournful. Naman and Amee have both privately scolded me for leaving them with each other. They hate each other so much. He's at that difficult age where he's old enough to be desperate for his freedom but young enough that he still needs her to cook and clean for him. She's at the age where she would like some freedom from a teenage son who is old enough to cook and clean for himself, and responds to every request with an indignant groan like a cow being ushered from the middle of the road. They argue constantly.

I will not miss this.

I will not miss being the intermediary for two people who live in opposing camps. He wants freedom, fried foods, a football. She wants help around the house, a money earner, grades befitting a man of industry.

It's tough being the clever one. The funny one. I do not complain, though. I'm also the quiet one.

According to Amee I was always destined to go and study in London. She knew that was always the plan. Before Papa died, after Papa died. Even in the brief moments when he was dying, we all knew this was the plan. Now that we are here, she is not so sure.

She dresses up her concerns with barbed comments about Sailesh, who is my reason for leaving. If Sailesh were not leaving, nor would I be. I did not want to go on my own. Because Sailesh is coming to do things other than study, she is concerned I will be distracted.

She is right, I will be.

If Sailesh is going to be working the Soho clubs, performing to rooms full of sheraabis, eating dinner with white people every night, meeting white girls, hanging out with the Beatles and the Rolling Stones, am I really going to sit at home, quietly studying for my accountancy degree?

What Amee does not understand is that I can do both. I understand my responsibility: I just have to be twice as good as the other people studying to be accountants, so that I can have fun too. Why not? Why not have fun? Sailesh will be juggling for all these high-society people I've seen going in and out of the hotels in Mombasa, all wearing pearls and sparkling dresses or shirts starched whiter than an Englishman holding a milk bottle in winter.

Amee must know this, that as soon as I am in London I plan to have fun, to drink and party and meet girls and not study, which is why she puts the first aloo paratha, straight off the tawa, on to Naman's plate.

He is so surprised, he looks from his plate up to me and then back down again.

Amee drips ghee on to the paratha.

I look at her. She is avoiding eye contact with me.

'Bhai, would you like half?' Naman asks.

Those five minutes that follow – with Naman and me sharing the aloo paratha the way brothers should, while my mother is too stunned by his moment of generosity to protest – that stillness, when all you can hear is the churn of chewing, that is the happiest I have been in a long time. Certainly since Papa died. Who can remember what life was like before he passed?

I can hear my name bouncing around in my eardrums.

'Mukesh, Mukesh,' I hear, in Nisha's voice.

My half-conscious brain translates the tone of her voice as one of affection and concern, but as I open my eyes to the blindingly bright white clouds, I can see that she's angry and impatient.

'I'm late, Mukesh. You okay? Tell me you're okay. Not today of all days, bhai. Not today.'

I open my eyes, pat my hands up and down my body, feeling myself, just to make sure I'm still intact. She is frowning at me. Her face is partially obscured by curls, but she is definitely frowning.

'I'm awake, I'm awake,' I say and sit up, as quickly as I can.

I have never spoken to her before. She knows my name. How does she know my name?

She offers me a hand, to pull me up. I hesitate, but she jabs it at me insistently. I take it. Her hand is dry. Lukewarm. I pull on it, but I'm too heavy and overbalance her. She lands heavily next to me, swearing in English. She scowls at me, swears again and then begins gathering the fabrics she has dropped. I try to help but she yanks them from my grasp.

'What are you doing? I'm late,' she says.

Announcing his presence, the man who crashed into me straddles his bike and starts cycling away, shaking his head, muttering about *bloody wogs*.

I call 'sorry' after him.

He continues to shake his head as he cycles away down the middle of the road.

'Why are you apologizing to him?' Nisha asks angrily. 'He called you a wog.'

I haven't spoken to anyone since my first day in Keighley a fortnight ago. Not since my landlords asked me if I had any questions after they had shown me around my room and the facilities. I said no, added a thank-you as an afterthought and sat on my bed, watching them both go into their bedroom across the hallway. I heard the door lock, and when I heard them in hushed urgent tones discussing their impressions of me - harmless, teeth, smell, were the words I caught - I closed the door and continued to sit on the bed, hoping for some inspiration.

How did I end up here, 213 miles away from London? I hope Sailesh hurries up, I thought. This is not where I was supposed to be.

I didn't speak to anyone during my first week – not Nisha when I noticed I lived a street away from other Gujaratis, nor her brother nor her parents, not the people I bought eggs from, which I wasn't allowed to cook until I provided my own pans, according to Mrs Simpson, my landlady. (She was worried about the smell of curry seeping into her own pans. Did she think I ate fried eggs with curry?) I didn't speak to people I passed in the street, sat next to on benches, made eye contact with. I learned that I could be introverted when regarded as an alien by all who came across me. So I kept quiet.

In the evenings, I whispered certain words to myself that I had overheard during the day, to keep my English up to date. I whispered things like cummingwiv, outen, rutching, erwile, dook into my pillow, hoping that the more I repeated them, the more they would make sense to me, start to trickle off my tongue with ease. Down in London, when I eventually get there, I will talk like the locals, charm like the locals, make love like the locals.

'Hello?' Nisha is still looking at me. Her face is beginning to register concern.

I smile dumbly in response, showing all my teeth, nodding my head a little.

'Why are you saying sorry to that man? He ran into you. He called you a wog.'

'Sorry,' I say to Nisha.

I'm mesmerized by the way her nose twitches when she talks. I have not seen her speak before. I've not seen her lips move with such careful deliberation to avoid an accent. I have not appreciated how low her voice is, as though she is humming into the wide mouth of a foghorn.

'What is a wog?'

'Are you stupid?' she asks.

Nisha, my love, the object of my nightly fantasies and daily morning hygiene rituals, your talking voice is sending me into paroxysms of shivering explosions all over my body.

'Stupid, like dropped on your head as a child?' she continues.

I think I love her even more now that she is speaking to me.

'I got in his way,' I say.

'You were crossing the road. He should have been looking where he was going. Fut-a-fut he was cycling. He didn't see you. Or he did it on purpose. You never know with these English.'

'How do you know my name?' I reply, thrilled by the idea that she knows who I am. She knows exactly who I am.

'You're desi – we all know each other round here. And Mrs Simpson asked my mum if we were related to you. She pronounced it Mooooo-cash. Like she wanted money for a cow.'

She laughs. Her face changes. She has a smile that erupts from her chin, upwards, like a volcano of positivity. She has a serious face when she is thinking and a serious face when she is walking – I've noticed this in my various observations from afar. But this smile, it is utterly beguiling.

Oh, Nisha, you make me want to believe in destiny.

'I guess there aren't many of us here,' I reply.

'How did you end up in Keighley?' she asks, starting to walk, turning her head back so that I can answer her.

I assume she wants me to follow her. So I do. And because I haven't spoken to anyone in two weeks, and because it feels unnatural communicating, especially in the tongue I have been suppressing since I arrived, I tell her everything, much more than she needs to know, every excruciating detail. And bless her, Neha, you wouldn't believe it, but your mother listens to me. Or, at least, she nods her head every now and then as if she's paying attention.

'My best friend Sailesh, he's a juggler, one of the most famous jugglers in Mombasa. He has been playing the hotels for a few years now. His papa and my papa were best friends. But his papa died, you see. At the same time as my papa. It was a freak accident. They both drowned at the same time. No one saw it coming. They were trying to save my younger brother, Naman. And they swam out to get him. And they both... well, that's not the question you asked. My brother's fine, in case you are wondering. But my dad and Sailesh's dad died. And Sailesh threw himself into juggling, obsessively. At first no one noticed how talented he was, because – you know how it is. We all look the same. Especially to the British expats and holidaymakers. Eventually Sailesh became so well-known he was offered work in the clubs over here. "Come and see the mysteries of the dark country." He said yes because we've both watched movies. We know that this is the home of James Bond. Sailesh had to wait for his work visa to come through. He convinced me to come with him. I had always wanted to come to Great Britain to study. My papa had saved for years for me to study. And I applied to a college. In London. Sailesh's work visa didn't come through in time so he suggested I go on ahead and find a place for us both to stay. And he would arrive and pay for the rent and I could start studying. He told me that Keighley is a place near London that has lodgings accepting coloureds. He knows people who live here. So I came here. Here I am. In Keighley.'

Nisha stops walking and turns round to face me. She looks at my face, trying to read it, understand what is going through my brain. Then her lip quivers before that smile volcanoes upwards across the entirety of her face. She has a gap in her front two teeth that becomes more pronounced the closer it gets to the gum.

She giggles with the whole of her body.

I smile with her, not sure where the hilarity lies, waiting for her to fill me in on the joke.

'What's funny?' I ask about twenty steps later, stopping in front of a house and folding my arms.

She looks at me.

'Have you gone mad? Keighley is two hundred miles from London. What are you doing here? You can't get from here to college and back in a day.'

'I know,' I tell her.

I don't know how it happened other than that I got sucked in by Sailesh's enthusiasm.

Go to Keighley, he said. They take coloureds there. You will only be there a few weeks, a month, three maximum and then I will come and get you. And we will tear London apart looking for Tom Jones and Engelbert Humperdinck. Keighley is not that far. Your school does not start for three weeks after you arrive. You can wait for me. You have money, yes?

I said yes. It was the easiest thing to do. Arguing with this man is impossible. He talks like a machine gun. He will unleash a hail of words at you until you end up with your hands over your head, begging for mercy. Machine guns, they are bad for your health, bad for friendships.

I wish I had listened to my instincts and trusted my

to come here. Because the British would welcome me until he arrived.'

'You know what else is funny?' she asks. 'I know Sailesh. Shah, na? Sailesh Shah?'

'Yes,' I say, rubbing at my chin and scratching my ear. 'How did you know his name?'

Nisha laughs. 'He is my cousin. No wonder he sent you here. It's probably the only place in the UK he knows. I didn't know he was moving here.'

I nod.

'Yes,' I say. 'He's quite talented. Don't you think?'

'I have never met him,' she says. 'He's just a cousin I write to and send a rakhri once a year.'

I nod again. My responses are slow. I can't think of a thing to say to her. I feel as though every English word I've ever learned is useless because I cannot connect them together into a sentence. I've never spoken to a girl before. Even at school, I kept myself to myself. I let Sailesh have the relationships. I had the headspace. Sailesh could talk to anyone in any capacity. I was his mute sidekick.

I realize we are in a part of town I don't recognize. We have left Nisha's street and are approaching the church that dings a bell on the hour every hour, without fail. It wakes me up most nights. I'm constantly aware of the time, how slowly it is moving, how much I feel as if I'm in suspended animation.

'Where are we going?' I ask.

'Where are you going?' she replies. 'Good question, yaar. I don't know.'

'I think I'm following you to where you're heading. I don't know where that is. I'm sorry. I will go home.'

She exaggeratedly rolls her eyes, but then smiles at me.

'Will you come to our Diwali show tonight?' she asks.

'It's Diwali?' I ask, playing the innocent.

'Yes, bhai. It's November. We are putting on a show in the community hall. You were going to come to this, yes?'

'I didn't know it was happening,' I tell her, my body tense with an excitement I've not felt since leaving Kenya.

'Yes, bhai. Tonight. Seven p.m. People are coming from Bradford, from Huddersfield, to see our show. Did you not know about it?'

'You are the first person I have spoken to in two weeks,' I tell Nisha.

She laughs.

'I do not believe you, Mukesh. You know what I think?'

'What?'

'I think you want to be in the show. That's why you've been waiting outside my house for a week. You know I am organizing it.'

I stammer a protest. She has seen me. I thought I was invisible. I thought I faded into the white wall I've spent the week leaning against.

'It's fine, Mukesh. We can find a job for you. Maybe you can be the deer that Laxman kills? Or Hanuman's gada. We could wrap you in gold fabric and you could make a clank-clank-clank noise when Hanuman wields you. Yes, the way you defeated that bicycle, you can be the gada.'

Somewhere in me a ticking starts, a countdown timer to panic.

Nisha looks at me and laughs again, this time bending over, her hands on her knees.

'I'm joking, yaar. We can't make you be a gada,' she says. She pauses for dramatic effect. 'You don't have the body type.'

'Oh, okay,' I say, a little disappointed.

'Do you want to be involved?' she asks me. 'We need to finish sewing the backdrop together, someone to do all the make-up, someone to play tabla. All by tonight. It's a disaster this show, I tell you. A disaster. Anyway. What are your skills?'

'I am a poet and an actor,' I lie.

Trigger

Somewhere, somewhere, Nisha, my heart is in a box
A box locked with your hair locks
I listen to the roll and I listen to the rock
You are the hole in my sock.
My brain clouds.

'What do you know about the *Ramayana*?' Nisha asks me as she opens the gate leading to the back door of the hall behind the Catholic church.

I can hear the drone of a harmonium making its long elephant trumpet of desperation. The person playing it is clearly not an expert. A beginner at best.

'I read the comics of it back in Kenya,' I say.

'We are doing a performance where Sita dances for Rama, just before they return to Ayodhya. To show him everything she has gone through. Everything she has learned. Do you know it?'

'No,' I reply, then immediately regret it. I must say yes to everything. Ignorance does not make you needed. Knowledge does.

'I made it up,' Nisha says, smiling. She closes the gate behind me. I can hear the thump and pat of bare feet on parquet flooring. 'It is not actually in the *Ramayana*. But we only have girls in our community. And my brother. And Prash, but he's a bevakoof. So we had to come up with something. Have you met my brother? Chumchee? His name is really Chetan, but we call him Chumchee as he is always hanging around.'

'Yes,' I say.

'Oh, you have? Perfect, yaar. I am so glad I spoke to you. He will be less nervous having another boy dancing next to him. Are you happy to be Rama? He refuses to be him, yaar. We promised him he can be Laxman. Not Rama. You have to be Rama. If you do not do it, we will have to ask Suresh uncle. No one wants to ask Suresh uncle anything. You know about Suresh uncle?'

'Yes,' I say.

This is proving an effective strategy.

'Oh God, has he ever told you any of his stories?'

'Yes,' I say.

'Which one?'

I shrug my shoulders and smile awkwardly as if to say, *yep, that one.* Nisha frowns as she opens the door.

We walk into the school hall.

I expect to be transported to Dandaka Forest. Instead I am taken back to my childhood days. Benches that you had to sit on for assemblies if you were in the top year. Everyone else sat on the floor. Getting to the age where you were on a bench was an honour to look forward to, till you realized it gave you splinters on the backs of your bare legs. Bench privileges did not mean trouser privileges as well.

The walls are bare and once were white, but now they're scarred by decades of bored children picking off the paint, using it as target practice for flicked goongas, spraying it with shaken cans of soft drinks.

There are six people in the room. There is Chumchee. He is short and waddles like a penguin. He is pale and vacant, the type who would smile at clouds and old ladies. He looks like someone who cannot stop sweating. He smiles at the floor when we walk in.

There are three girls, dancing in a line, all dressed in sarees and wearing cat-like eyeliner, because each one wants to look like Mumtaz. They look like children playing dress-up with their mummy's saree box.

There is an old balding man in an off-white shirt and black trousers. He sports a sequinned waistcoat from a jubo lengha suit. He sits in the lotus position, murdering the air with a single-note drone from his harmonium.

There is also a white man armed with a butter knife, scraping off chewing gum from the bottoms of chairs. He looks harassed, as though he should be somewhere else. And he should. What a job.

'We have found our Rama,' Nisha announces.

Suddenly, I realize the enormity of the situation. Especially when Chumchee stands up to clap at me.

The girls stop dancing, put their hands on their hips in synchronized aggression and look at me, expressionless. As if they are waiting for me to say something impressive.

I wave.

'I am playing Rama,' I say.

This is an important role, playing one of the incarnations of Vishnu, and I feel like a trespasser in someone else's community. I am to stand up, in front of other people's families, and parade myself for their judgement. Mothers and fathers will be assessing me as a potential son-in-law. They will want to know what I am studying, who my grandparents are and what side of the heart disease/diabetes spectrum I fall into.

Both, as it happens. My family likes to have all angles covered.

'Him? He is playing Rama?' one of the girls asks suspiciously.

Nisha turns questioningly to me. She smiles. It is a smile that could launch a thousand ships. Which is a strange comparison to make. I know about Paris and the Greeks, but I still do not know why anyone would launch a thousand ships after a girl. We now have commercial aeroplanes.

She is beautiful. My hips ache. My toes burn. My mind turns from cloudy to fizzy.

'Yes,' I say, looking at her.

Chumchee appears by my side.

'Brother,' he says, smiling. 'My brother.'

I offer my hand for him to shake but he looks at it as though he would rather not be touched. Reluctantly he offers me fingers, which I pull on once. In the years I knew him after, I learned that it wasn't just me. Year after year, I saw him shrink when people approached, and stand two feet away from conversations, always listening, never part of the action.

He smiles, stepping back from me as quickly as possible, stumbling into some chairs.

Nisha, oh, Nisha, I would follow you anywhere.

She tosses something to me. It is a dhoti, green with pink sequins sewn into a makeshift paisley. It looks… big.

Chumchee hands me a domed crown, like the mound of a temple. It's gold foil over a safari hat.

I hold both the dhoti and the crown and I look around the

hall. The harmonium player has stopped playing his long endless note and everyone in the room is looking at me, smiling expectantly. The man removing chewing gum has disappeared. All eyes, however, are on me. I am here to save them all. I have to be their Rama.

'Get changed then,' Nisha says.

'Yes, bhai,' one of the younger girls says. 'We have to teach you your moves. We open the doors in four hours.'

I drop the crown.

'Four hours?' I gulp.

What do you mean four hours? I have just arrived. I have never been in a theatre production. I cannot dance. I don't know what anyone is doing. I don't know what I am doing.

'Mukesh bhai, are you sure you want to participate in this?' Nisha asks quietly, walking towards me, her hand outstretched to put reassuringly on my arm.

I wait for her touch. I will melt into it.

I edge forward, so that my sleeve reaches her fingertips that much sooner.

'Bhai saab,' she says. 'We need you to get changed. So we can teach you the dance moves and show you what you need to do. Where to stand. How to act. Who to look at. Yes? Is this okay? Can you do this?'

I take a deep breath.

'Yes,' I say.

This is not going well.

I was a quiet kid. I did not like anybody looking at me and sat in the classroom in the middle. Away from the clever boys at the front, away from the naughty boys at the back, away from the boys on the sides making hungama. The teacher never picked on anyone lost in the middle to answer a question. I would know the answers sometimes, but saying it out loud filled my heart with terror.

Talking in public was my greatest fear.

I grew up between a dust bowl and a blue sea. Where they met was an island, a booming port town called Mombasa. We lived there at an unremarkable time.

I do not believe in destiny. Not for our family. I do not believe in learning from the past. We live a life and then we die. I do not think there is anything remarkable about history. You know that, don't you, Neha? You are aware that whatever we learn about the past doesn't shape the future. We don't exist in loops of time. Nothing repeats, except human nature. Not events. Not mistakes. We're not pre-programmed to be dictated to by our past. All we can glean from it is that at some time at some point in some distant bygone era, someone will have done something to surprise you now.

None of this is by design. It is by circumstance.

My papa had the same routine every day. He and Amee rose at 5 a.m. for their yoga routine. This woke the rest of the house because they did sun salutations before clearing their nasal passages, one nostril at a time. This ak-ak-ak-akkkk noise signalled to the children that it was time to get up. Once yoga was over with and while breakfast was being prepared for my father, he did his calisthenics. He took a steel tray and balanced it on his head whilst doing hip rolls and knee bends. He stood on his head for a full minute and only then would he come to the kitchen for his garam chai and two sugar rotlis. Then, it was work – and work, for him, had to be hassle-free.

He had spent most of his life in the family haulage business in Nairobi, staring at ledgers and signing cheques and having lunch with the bank manager every week. It was a clockwork existence, and he wanted to be free from such regularity. So he left the trucks to his brothers and moved to the coast to have me and Naman. And a hassle-free job. He opened a kiosk. He sold cigarettes to white men and newspapers to everyone else.

But he still had an accountant's respect for numbers. He told me how his father had told him why it was important he understood them.

'I want you to understand every process, every minor detail of every number, son,' my grandfather had said to Papa. 'Then nobody can take you for a ride.'

'I understand, Papa.'

'Numbers are life,' my grandfather had continued. 'You understand that. Without them, we cannot survive. They create patterns in life. We exist in patterns. Without them, life is chaos.'

'I understand, Papa.'

As for me, the teachers told Amee and Papa, every time we had our school reports, *He has not made an impression in class. His written work is good. But he does not speak. And his maths is terrible.*

'Why do you refuse to speak in class?' Papa asked me.

'I do not need to prove to the class that I know the answers. I prove it to the teacher.'

He seemed unconvinced.

My father told me, 'You must never assume people know what you are talking about. You must never assume they even know you are alive.'

*

I ask where the changing rooms are.

Nisha smiles sheepishly.

'This is the whole room. Here. You can change on the stage and we can all turn away. Yaar, the thing is, we are going to see it all anyway, bhaiya.'

Chumchee laughs.

'I might look,' he says. 'We are brothers, after all.'

I don't want Nisha to see my frustration with the situation I have agreed to. I want her to think I am cool and breezy. Like Jimi Hendrix, man. That kind of thing. I want her to think, look at this guy. He strides into my life, hurling himself in front of a bicycle to protect me, and now he is saving my play at the last minute by playing the hero, because my bevakoof brother is being difficult – so I should definitely kiss him and cuddle him and promise him that, for ever and ever more, I will be his, whatever he wants me to be.

My girlfriend, I think. I want you as my girlfriend.

Oh, Nisha, Nisha, I unbutton my shirt.

Nisha, seeing I am doing her bidding, turns back to her dancers.

'Anjali,' she says wearily. 'You are not in time.'

'Come on, Nisha. It's a lot to learn. We only started this morning.'

I pause. This morning? Nisha, baby, darling, your organizational skills leave a little to be desired. I take off my shirt.

I stand topless, my hands planted on my hips, my shirt bunched in my fist. I am in hero stance.

No one pays any attention. Except Chumchee. He hovers in front of me, mirroring my pose. The little suction cups of my breasts tingle in the cool air. My nipples harden. I wish I had started from the shoes and socks and worked upwards. Disappointed in the lack of response, I start unlacing my shoes.

I hate being barefoot. Especially in places my toes are unfamiliar with. The ground feels crusty and unknown. My foot feels untrusting. I rock back on my heels, lifting my toes, keeping the surface area of foot-to-ground to a minimum.

I unbuckle my belt, watching Nisha instruct the girls, who peep at the wispy upside-down triangle of hair on my chest instead of following the choreographed steps. The harmonium player oozes out a melody, a slow droning piece, centred around three notes.

I start to pull my trousers down before I stop and realize.

I am not wearing underpants.

They are, the three pairs of them that I own, bathing in the basin in my room, waiting for me to beat the water out of them until they are dry.

I stop undressing and begin to edge into the corner.

One of the girls, seeing the bare curve of my bottom as I pull the trousers back up, sniggers. Nisha calls a halt to their rehearsal.

'What's the problem?'

Anjali points. She turns around.

I shuffle backwards in a panic but manage to stand on the hem of my trousers, tripping myself up and falling to the floor, bare bottom first.

'No, no!' I cry, protecting my modesty with my hands.

The girls burst out laughing. Nisha buries her eyes in a hand, her entire body shuddering with silent laughter.

Chumchee leaps to my defence, waddling over and attempting to help me shield my crotch. I try to bat his hands away but he is firm in his efforts and surprisingly strong.

I look at Nisha, openly laughing now, as if this is not the first time someone has exposed themselves to her.

I rue the day I decided to say yes to everything.

When the girls return, ten minutes later, smelling of tobacco and factory smoke, I have composed myself and changed into my outfit.

I wear the green sequin-and-paisley dhoti.

Again, I stand with my hands on my hips, my back ramrod straight, because if I move my head the crown will slip off.

I am formally introduced to the dancers - Anjali, Shilpa and Mala. I shake their hands and none of us makes any reference to what happened ten minutes ago.

I never remember the okay things. Only the good things and the bad things. They are what form me, what propel me through life. Surely, it is the okay, the mundane, the everyday that makes me more than the good and the bad times. When I first arrived in England, I was nervous, anxious all the time, panicking, because Sailesh was not here. He chose my path for me at all times. He knew our best move as a team. This was our dynamic. He would decide what was next for us and I would emphatically agree.

I haven't seen him for two weeks. I miss him. I have only my memories of our happiest times. I think about this a lot. Those happy times made me who I am. And yes, Neha, you will never know Sailesh. He made me into the person I was.

Without him, I would not have met your mother.

When he started becoming famous at the hotels, it didn't change him. I was worried he would leave me behind for a more exciting life but he remained my best friend. His dad was disappointed that he was straying from the family business. But, see? We had an end-game. Our ultimate goal was to head to Nairobi.

In the big city, we could be who we wanted to be. I had a cousin - Manish - who lived there, working in the family's maize business. He used to write me letters about what Nairobi was like. He told me about the girls, the music, the clothes and the freedom in general. Despite living in our family's compound, he said, there was a freedom in having access to the city. We were seduced. We wanted what he had.

Sailesh's career at the Casablanca hotel was entirely ruled by the assumption that one day we would move on to a bigger city. Nairobi. London. Certainly not Keighley, 213 miles north of London, the nearest place that advertised friendly lodgings for coloured workers.

I went a couple of times to watch Sailesh juggle. He would sneak me in through the kitchens and I would watch him stand in the centre of the room, an Indian, surrounded by the British Empire. This is something you cannot appreciate - I grew up while history was being made, during an occupation. I watched Independence unfurl before my eyes. I witnessed the last days of the British Empire. All these white men, eating and drinking as though they were destined to own us for ever. All those men, with their furry white chests and moustaches, their hats and their beige clothes, their young girlfriends and their strait-laced wives, all of it coming to an end. Man, it was a scene.

Anyway, I would stand in the door of the kitchen and watch the routines. Sailesh's look of concentration was a smile with a tongue in the left cheek. He wore one of Papa's old suits which had been discarded because of a tear in the left shoulder and wear in the crotch from overuse. Papa cast off the suit but Amee was resourceful and knew how to tailor it into something wearable. She re-sewed the crotch and worked the sleeves into something deliberately torn, to make Sailesh look like a dishevelled juggler. It was part of the act. He walked on stage - well, the centre of the room - playing a drunk hobo, with an empty bottle of beer. He pretended to trip, threw the bottle of beer into the air and as it reached the peak of its arc, he would remove another from his pocket, try to sip it, realize it was empty and then throw that into the air as well. He would juggle the two. Then a nearby waiter would walk past him with a tray carrying two bottles of beer; he would grab one, down the contents and fling it up to give him three bottles in the air. The third was a plant. It was half-filled with water. He juggled the three bottles, stumbling about like a drunk. People applauded. This was just his first routine, one that he savoured because it offered the maximum showmanship for minimum skill. It required no concentration - even though each bottle was weighted ever so slightly differently, muscle memory allowed him to throw them up with the precision of a master.

Things happened quickly after those first few performances. He was given a regular job at the hotel and left school to pursue the juggling. His father was terrified that Sailesh would never amount to anything. There was a quiet rule in his family: *a chance is only a piece of chance; hard work is worth more than chances.* It doesn't make sense but his father liked to think of himself as a philosopher. He wrote these motivational messages on the board outside Cheap Ration Store. Many times people would mistake his shop for a church.

Sailesh was granted an opportunity to come to London and work. He was contracted by the owners of the Casablanca hotel, who had interests in London, to play cabarets in Soho for a trial of one month, if successful extended to six months and then potentially permanently.

We had had dreams of Nairobi for so long that London seemed like a walrus; we knew what it looked like in books but assumed we would never see one in our lifetimes. Nairobi for us was a lion, a once-in-a-blue-moon sighting from the window of a car.

Sailesh was excited. This surpassed any expectation he had for his life, which had already been overtaken by his small success at juggling. We were expected to walk in our fathers' footsteps, to go and work in their businesses, continue their success, and survive to pass on even more to a future generation. We were not meant to live our own lives. Our desire to escape was real.

We wanted something more than what was on offer. Mainly because our letters from Manish showed what else was out there in the world, what life there was to be lived. It wasn't just the thought of girls, or the thought of drinking or anything like that. There was just this feeling that in Nairobi we would be free to explore our options. Maybe through the arts or through other people's businesses. It felt freer than where we were.

Nairobi, that's where I always thought we would end up. But

with no tangible plans to go, other than the general desire to escape, I started to feel as though I would live out my days running my father's kiosk and fighting with Naman over parathas. So when Sailesh told me about the London contract, he asked if I would come.

I said, of course, bevakoof.

When he broached the subject with his amee and I with mine, I had more success. This was because I presented it as a chance for further education. When I told my amee that Sailesh was heading to the UK to work and that I could go with him, maybe to study, maybe at a university, she practically exploded with happiness. She told me that before he died Papa had saved a special fund of money to give to either Naman or me should we want to continue our education. I would need to work to pay my rent, the caveat was, according to Amee, but I would be the first Jani boy to go to a university. A real university with professors and lectures and learning to better one's self. My father had wanted to get a degree in accountancy but instead had had to work for the family business. And that job, the stress of working with his brothers, nearly killed him. So he moved to Mombasa. Which did kill him. Because who lives by the coast but cannot swim properly?

Sailesh, on the other hand, broke his father's heart. We were two months away from finishing school and Sailesh's papa wanted to start taking it easy, while his son assumed more responsibility at the shop. Sailesh was unsure whether his father would let him go. But then the tide intervened and took our fathers from us.

This is why I do not believe in destiny, my child. Destiny has one single agenda: to force you to make decisions. Had Papa lived, Neha, you and I would be speaking in Swahili right now. Not this terrible English. Papa made a choice to run into the sea to rescue Naman. I made a choice to leave Kenya. I am not trapped by destiny. I command my choices.

I had to find something to study and I wanted it to be poetry. I liked poems. I liked reading them and the idea of writing them. Especially the rhyming ones. But I didn't think my father's money would be paid out for me to learn to write poetry. Naman was also encouraging me to go, saying, brother, you have to go and you have to get set up so you can bring me over. I want to walk through Leicester Square.

So I told Amee I would go to London to do my A levels and then I could pursue an accountancy degree. This made her so happy. She paid the money for my ticket – one way because, she said, when I was done I would be able to pay my own way to come back and visit.

Nisha leads me into the centre of the stage.

'Stand still,' she says. 'With your hands on your hips. Look like a hero.'

She counts in – ek, bey, thrun, char – and the harmonium blasts out a slow trance-like melody. The girls dance behind me. I can feel their shuffling steps, hear the jangle of the bells around their ankles.

I am bewitched by Nisha, playing Sita, my wife.

She bows her head slightly, looking up at me all innocent and doe-eyed. She smirks and then starts to dance.

'She is so submissive,' Nisha sneers, as she dips and whirls. 'Everything is about her husband.'

The girls behind me stop dancing.

Anjali shouts, 'She is the partner of our god Vishnu. How dare you.'

Nisha, without losing her step, keeps dancing. I can see the gyrations of her belly.

'Exactly,' she says. 'She is defined by who she is married to. I will never be identified by my husband.' She pauses. 'If I get married.'

Anjali rolls her eyes, and then chivvies the girls to continue dancing. She feels heavy behind me. I can hear her panting, trying to slow it down to disguise it as normal breath.

Sita, Nisha-Sita, steps towards me and twirls her hands up and down in front of my face and chest, never touching me, except for the wild fling of the odd bangle. I keep my posture as still as possible and I try not to move, I try not to breathe, I try not to be anything other than her stoic husband, returned from the jungle after an exile of fourteen years, ready to take his kingdom as promised.

I am Lord Rama.

Sita, Nisha-Sita, places her hands on my chest and rests her cheek on them. I can feel her light breath on my nipple.

I close my eyes, wanting to cry because this is the moment I have been longing for. Sailesh can wait for his visa for the rest of his life as far as I am concerned.

I hear the door crash open.

Something bounds into the room and announces itself with a booming voice.

'Nisha, I am here now. I will be your Rama.'

I open my eyes, startled. A muscular man, taller than me, fair skin with a thick moustache, stands with his hands on his hips, in challenging hero pose.

Nisha lets go of me.

'Prash?' She says. 'You came? I knew you would.'

He strides towards her. The air bubble of force around him pushes me backwards. I step on Anjali's foot.

He walks over to Nisha, loops one arm around her waist, leans her backwards and tries to kiss her but she recoils.

He stops and turns to me. 'You're wearing Rama's dhoti.'

I nod.

'*I'm* Rama.'

I gulp.

Quest. Surprise

I take my dhoti – Prash's dhoti – off, and hand it to him. He stands as close to me as he can, blocking Nisha and the girls behind him, almost as if to protect my modesty. He smirks and looks down at me intently. His eyes are brown going on green. I could fall in love with those eyes, collapse and cut myself on those cheekbones. Luckily, my fall would be broken by the comforting cushion of those lips.

Prash, my love rival, I am inferior to you.

I realize my trousers are three or four embarrassing strides away. Chumchee is sitting on the seat that I've hung them over.

I don't want to move. Partly I'm hypnotized by this Adonis. Partly I'm paralysed by embarrassment for my nakedness.

I shuffle backwards, cupping my lakri, and wrestle my trousers from the back of the chair. Chumchee, either revelling in my discomfort, or because he is a pendoo, doesn't move. He watches me struggle instead, absent-mindedly drawing circles on his thighs with his index fingers.

I wrench the trousers free, creased from being wedged between the plastic seat and his flabby back. I notice Nisha touching Prash's sculpted arm as he takes his top off. Anjali is staring at me, laughing, holding her sides to stop the shake of her jiggling belly. I keep looking at Prash and Nisha. He whispers something to her. I see her face crumple for a second, almost as if she is upset, before it returns to a smile.

Her resting face is a deep smile. It was the first thing I noticed about her.

That is a lie.

The first thing I noticed about her was that she was another desi and it was a comfort to know there was one so close. This is another reason why I do not believe in destiny, only in coincidence. It does not negate the fact that she was the love of my life. Had coincidence not led me to Keighley, had she not been the only desi I saw, had I not felt so isolated surrounded by so many goras, would we have fallen in love?

It's a strange thing. To be the only desi in a room. And yet, coming here, it has happened a lot. It is scary, looking out on to a sea of white faces, skin like plucked chickens, skin like alabaster walls. People look at you differently.

Mrs Simpson asked me on that first day, where are you from? I told her, Kenya. And she said, no, but where are your parents from? I told her, Kenya. No, but where are you from originally? Kenya, I told her again. I think she did not understand me because I was not saying India, the land of my forefathers; I am in an in-between world. It seems such an innocent question. Where are you from?

I don't know. Why does it matter so much?

I cannot talk to goras. I watch the way their heads tilt when they're trying to communicate with me, as though a sideways glance will make me seem more sympathetic. I will be more understandable askew.

I think about all of these things as I try to place one foot through the leg-hole of my trousers, and I topple over. I windmill my arms to try and keep my balance, but gravity takes hold and pulls me to the floor.

Chumchee jumps up and points at me, laughing. It doesn't matter – everyone else has already lost interest. The muscular Prash is in place, the music is playing and the girls are sashaying around him. He is a better Lord Rama than me. He oozes regality.

I look at Chumchee, pointing at my body, and he smiles at me. He bows his head, moves closer and nestles his forehead into my neck. I close my eyes and will myself to be back in my room, alone, practising faces in my mirror.

The show goes on.

Prash quickly picks up the steps. Ten minutes after my fall, I am reduced to a spectator. I pull up a chair next to Chumchee and sit with him as we watch the girls dance for their Lord.

I shift in my seat and think about leaving, but Chumchee puts his hand on my knee.

'I know you want to go,' he says quietly. 'Please don't. Please stay.'

'Why? There is no reason for me to stay. I am not in the show.'

'Do you like my sister?' he asks.

I don't answer him.

'Prash is a bevakoof,' he says. 'He will soon get bored and leave. Then you will be needed. You will save the show. Our hero.'

As Chumchee says these words, I watch Prash, as Lord Rama, sweep Nisha up into his arms. He spins her around and kisses her on the lips.

It must be unscripted because Nisha struggles out from under his mouth and the crush of his arms, and pushes him away.

She looks around the room, embarrassed. Then she touches her little finger to her bottom lip and rubs at it.

She glances at Chumchee and me.

'Again,' she calls out.

And the harmonium player considers his instrument for a moment before playing a sad, low note while the dancers readjust their positions.

Prash peacocks this time. His moves are more animated. He introduces hip thrusts and winks and clicks of his tongue, like someone calming a horse.

Nisha dances coyly. She flicks looks around the room, to gauge what people might be thinking.

When she meets my eye, she turns away.

'Please stay,' Chumchee repeats. 'It is boring sitting here by myself.'

I ignore him and stand up, picking up my blazer. Prash notices me and raises his hand to the harmonium player to tell him to stop. He walks towards me. Nisha asks him what's wrong. He holds his hand up again to shush her. It is not the time for questions. Smiling, he approaches me. He throws his arm around my shoulders, the weight of it like a python, squeezing me tight as he leads me towards the door.

'Where are you going, yaar? Kya jaay che? Where are you going?' he asks in English then Gujarati then English, just to confuse me. 'Bhaiya, stay.'

We are standing by the only exit. Prash places himself between it and me.

'Home,' I stammer. I've lost all my English, all my Gujarati.

'Nitaka nirudi nyumbani sasa hivi,' I say fluidly. In Swahili. I want to go home now.

He looks at me, confused.

'Home,' I say again.

It feels like an English word: it is plain, single-syllabled and with a long vowel sound in the middle. There is no letter to place stress on. It exists only as itself, not as a word you can mould and meld to make it your own.

Someone once told me that in Zimbabwe, children are often given names to annoy neighbours. So someone will be called Patience if the neighbour has a short fuse; that way, when the word Patience is bellowed, it means more than one thing to more than one person. In my family, we used to name our children according to the astrological signs. In England, they are named after their ancestors; memories are kept through the recycling of names. The man I lodge with told me to call him Harry even though his name is David. Harry was his father's name, is how he explained it to me, as if I would know what that entailed. But I loved the sentiment, of preserving memories through this recycling. Which is why your brother is named after my father.

Prash, short for Prashant, I think, means patient or tranquil. He was perhaps a quiet boy, born under a certain sign. His entire body language is the opposite of his name. He oozes aggression. He places his hands on the wall so that I am pinned between them. He bows his head closer to mine. I do not know where to look so I search for Chumchee, past his body. I can see the moist ripple of sweat on his perfect pectoral muscles. He must shave, because the closer I look, the more

I can see red bumps where the follicles are rebelling, growing back, searching for freedom.

'Where are you going?' he hisses, trying not to be heard, forgetting that this hall is an echo chamber. The best way not to be heard is to talk in your normal voice.

'Home,' I repeat.

'Where. Are. You. Going?' he repeats again, this time making each word its own sentence.

'Nowhere,' I say.

'Shabaash. Sit down. I cannot have you walking around the set while I am rehearsing. I am concentrating hard. I am trying to be Rama. You are distracting me.'

'Sorry,' I say. 'Sorry.'

He slaps the wall to my left. I look at it. He slaps the wall to my right. I turn to that.

'You, bevakoof, are not the star. I am. You do not distract the star. It is opening night. We have one performance. I have been practising for ten minutes. Maroo mathoo nahi ka. Okay? Bessi-ja. Choop-chaap. Okay?'

I nod.

'Okay?'

I try to wriggle out of his prison. I think about biting his perfectly toned arm.

'Hey,' calls Nisha from the other side of the room. 'Prash, challo.'

'You sit, you stay quiet, you watch, you smile, you clap, you love me. Okay? You are not Rama. I am Rama. You are not Laxman. Chumchee is Laxman. You are the audience.'

He finally pushes himself away from the wall and walks backwards, keeping his eyes in contact with mine so I know he is serious, that he is not to be trifled with or disturbed. He is amazing. He avoids tripping, walking into chairs, into people, into himself.

I want to drop to my knees, wring my hands to the sky and ask Sailesh why he has forsaken me here, of all places, 213 miles from where I need to be, 11,500 miles from home.

What I learned about performance, from Sailesh, is that it is a ridiculous thing, to stand up in front of people and try to entertain them. Storytellers, at least, I can understand. A story can instruct, can impart knowledge, news, history. A story can teach you about destiny, about family. Can dancing and juggling do the same? Or are they distractions?

When Prash dances, he does it so everybody in the room notices. He is not performing to entertain. He is performing like a peacock, attracting mates. Which makes me uncomfortable because Nisha is his mate.

I will break him, I think. I will use my mother's powers of tiny undercutting comments to make him feel bad about himself, and I will get him away from Nisha, the love of my life.

They stop dancing.

Prash strides over to me. I have not moved. I have been thinking about juggling. He pulls at my shirt and I feel the buttons strain. He drags me to where Chumchee sits, over to my vacated chair, and pushes me down into it.

'I told you to sit,' he barks. 'I cannot have you in my eyeline. You are disrupting this sacred dance. Sit down, bevakoof, or I will beat you.'

Staring at Nisha as I watch them rehearse, I remember falling in love with a classmate. It was some time after my one-sided romance with the maths teacher ended. There was one girl who always caught my eye, mostly because she was so small – miles shorter than her swan-necked gaggle of friends. She was skirting five foot tall, with a round face, thick severe eyebrows and toffee-coloured brown eyes. Her name was Sri. She smiled a lot which showed the slightest gap between her front teeth. Her lustrous black hair was always pulled into a messy ponytail or tight pigtails. She wasn't graceful and she wasn't clumsy. She wasn't naughty and she wasn't a swot. She just got on with things, had in-jokes with her friends and went through the routines of life demanded of her with a mixture of mediocrity and indifference.

I used to watch her kathak dancing classes because they took part during my free periods.

I was there when the small girl with the toffee-coloured eyes fell over a nearby dancer's outstretched foot and flopped to the floor in a tiny bundle, like a crumpled teabag.

'SRI...SRI CHAUHAN...GET UP NOW,' screeched the instructor. My lucky stars – spying was easy when teachers used the full names of your targets to berate them.

I saw Sri Chauhan leave school, walk out of the gate, punch Amitesh, the podgy quiet boy in the front corner of our classroom and sashay off towards the bus stop. Amitesh Chauhan...Of course! She was his sister! The stupid podgy quiet boy who bested me the whole time with grades and the favour of teachers. I had no choice. My route to Sri was through him. I had to make him my best friend in the entire world.

I assessed my hobbies, potentially transferable areas of interest I could use to barter companionship with Amitesh. He was definitely a fringe class member, more of a loner than me, more concerned with eating than bantering, more likely to whisper than to murmur, more familiar with retreating from social interaction than initiating it.

I could pretend I needed help with maths, one of his stronger subjects. Except I was better than him at maths and he knew it. We were classroom rivals, constantly aware of each other's scores and how they compared against our own.

The other option was just to make my intentions of being his friend clear. I walked home debating the best course of action. Coincidence, my old friend, winked at me once more because I saw Amitesh waiting, lost in thought, at the bus stop.

Approaching him was someone else, a face I can no longer remember except for glazed eyes and a teenager's wispy moustache; he made a grab for Amitesh's satchel, known to be stocked at all times with snacks. The mugger hadn't accounted for his victim's watchfulness, however, keeping the strap of the satchel across his shoulders so that, when it was grabbed, he was propelled violently forward, his round head crunching into the thief's nose.

This was my perfect moment. If I stepped in just as the thief got away with or without the bag, I would get points just for trying. I mistimed it, though. The mugger, blood flowing from his nose, wasn't leaving. Instead, he was still gamely trying to wrench the satchel from Amitesh. I squared up to him, defiant, despite inwardly cursing my premature entrance. I faced his glazed eyes and feeble moustache when – BOP – he punched me, hard enough to shake but not with any real conviction; he must have known that the battle was lost, because he then immediately retreated. I felt a trickle of blood ooze from my left nostril, as I watched some older kids decide now was the time to intervene and give chase, screaming at the fast-disappearing thief. My eyes brimmed with water, and my heart sank when Amitesh smiled thinly at me before boarding his waiting bus home as though nothing had even happened.

As he smiled, though, so did Sri - she was so small that I hadn't even seen her in the confusion. Her pigtails were tied with orange ribbons and she clutched some textbooks. She beamed at me, said 'thank you' loudly in English and got on the bus. She'd seen me take a punch. A punch that looked more severe than it felt, but my nose still stung when I tried to blow it.

I went home with a swollen face and a successful first impression.

Befriend the brother - it all makes sense.

I turn to Chumchee.

'Prash is very mean,' I whisper.

'But he is beautiful,' Chumchee says with a smile.

'Hahn-ji,' I reply. I look at Chumchee.

He is smiling vacantly in the direction of his sister and Prash. He sits with his back straight, his hands on his knees, his fingers gripping and rubbing them.

'He looks like an angry man,' I say.

'I have heard him shouting,' Chumchee replies. 'His cheeks go very red. He is lucky to be so fair-skinned.'

'How long has he been Nisha's boyfriend?' I ask.

'He is not her boyfriend,' he says in English. 'He is her naseeb. She said that to me. Naseeb. You know it? Destiny.'

I nod my head.

'He is that to her. What is your naseeb?'

I shrug. 'How do I know? You can't be sure until after the event. Anything could happen in our lives, and then we say it is destiny. I could fall over and say, I was destined to fall over.'

Chumchee laughs. 'Know what you want and go for it. That is destiny. Because then, everything you get, you had coming.'

'Why should we do anything in that case? I do not believe in destiny. It is a nonsense.'

'Look at him,' Chumchee says, turning back towards Prash, who is laughing at something Nisha is telling him. She is gesturing wildly with her hands, but the harmonium is still going. They get back into position, and begin the dance routine again. 'He does not need to try. His destiny is to get exactly what he wants. The universe has decided this for him.'

'No,' I say.

'And they call me the bevakoof,' he says.

'No,' I reply. 'They call you Chumchee. A spoon.'

He looks stunned, as if I have slapped him. Then he stands up and wails like a child who has dropped their ice cream on the pavement. The girls stop dancing to see what the matter is. Nisha throws her arms up to the sky in frustration. The harmonium player, eyes closed, lost in a trance, continues playing.

Prash shouts at the old man, 'Arre, bhaiya, ek minute.'

The harmonium player stops, takes off his glasses, cleans them and rolls his eyes at Chumchee.

'I want him to leave,' Chumchee whines to his sister, pointing at me. 'I need him to leave.'

'What is wrong?' she asks, looking at me suspiciously. 'What did you say to my brother?'

'Nothing,' I say innocently. 'Nothing, I swear. We were talking.'

Prash takes a step towards me.

'You were talking?' he asks.

I nod.

'Did I tell you to talk?'

I shake my head.

'Did I tell you to be quiet?'

I nod my head.

'Did you defy me?'

I nod my head again, then bow.

My mother once said, 'Namaste translates into English as "I bow to you". No wonder we were so ready to be colonized,' she told me and my brother, 'if, instead of saying hello, we show how subservient we are to other people. It is a Hindu custom, to serve. At the same time, it shows weakness. No wonder these mzungu mahdechods found it so easy to rule over us. We were too busy bowing.'

It is not difficult for her to say this as part of the diaspora, I realize now.

Language is important. We forget this because most of us don't understand its power. But language kills people. It hurts people. It colonizes people. I have lost count of the number of times I have seen on menus in those artisanal coffee shops your brother asks me to meet him in, 'chai tea'. It angers me, but, after a while, I just decided to order it, because it is delicious, and it is exactly what I want. I bowed to them. I let them corrupt our language with ignorance. They were my masters. What can you do?

Years later, your mother and I went to Indian restaurants, tandoori restaurants, balti restaurants with the fascination of tourists. This was food we had never experienced before, food that we had certainly never cooked or eaten at home. Yet it was being culturally packaged as our own. Our country had existed for only about thirty years at that point and already its cuisine was world-famous, despite it being unrecognizable to most Indians. So we went, like all the Angrezis, and we ate, ordering everything off the menu, asking for spicy hot, Indian hot, and the waiter sighed and told us the food wasn't invented for us, so it would be English hot. And we laughed incessantly about naan bread.

'Bread bread,' your mother teased. 'Bread bread, sir? Would you like some bread bread?'

That's why 'chai tea' used to upset me so much. Chai means tea. Tea is the English word for chai. The English call it their national brew. They had no idea of its existence before they took it from their colonies. You cannot go around the world taking everything and not only calling it your own, but also claiming it as a part of your national identity in the process.

When I bow to Prash, I know I am being weak in front of him. I can almost hear my amee tut at me.

I glance up, and he is already walking towards me. I almost know what is coming but I cannot move myself an inch.

I hear Chumchee breathing deeply, excitedly.

I keep my head bowed.

Prash pulls at my white shirt with one hand, wrenching me off the chair towards him, while with the other he slaps me three times across my cheek. One, two, three – firm, open-handed slaps, his aum ring turned inwards, its gold, coarse surface scratching my face. I bite my lip to keep quiet. I will not show weakness. I will not show subservience. He lets go with a shove and I fall over backwards, catching my kidneys on the lip of the chair and hitting my head hard on the floor. For the second time that day, it is as if a black saree billows over my eyes until I can't see anything.

'Wake up, bevakoof.'

I feel a tap-tap-tap on my cheek. I open my eyes.

Prash squats over me, gently slapping the side of my face with the offending palm.

'I…' I stammer, before realizing I don't know what else to say. 'My head hurts,' I tell him.

'Hahn-ji, get up, yaar,' he says, offering me a hand.

I maintain my dignity by refusing to take it.

'Mukesh? Are you okay?' Nisha asks me.

Her face is upside down, standing over me, her hair over her eyes like the dangle of a beaver's tail. My brain is spinning too much for anything more poetical.

Oh, Nisha, Nisha, my head.

I touch my hand to my cheek. I can feel the welt, the spectre of a larger, firmer palm. When I take away my smaller, bonier, shakier hand, I notice a smear of blood across it. From his ring. Aum. A sound so short and sharp that it drew blood.

'No, I'm not okay,' I say to Nisha. 'Your boyfriend slapped me to the ground.'

Prash grins.

Nisha blushes. Her mood turns defensive.

'He is not my boyfriend – why do you think that?'

From the way he kissed you, I want to say, but before I do, Prash glances at Nisha. 'Am I not?' he asks, hurt. 'Am I not?'

He is still squatting over me.

'I do not understand, Prash. What? No. I cannot have a boyfriend. We are not in London. I am not the lady on your arm. What do you mean?'

'Nisha,' he says. 'But Nisha.'

My spirits lift a little. With a few well-chosen words, I have caused a rift. *Boyfriend*. Definitions are important. Language is important. Not destiny. My path is dictated by the careless language of others.

He lifts his hands to her.

'Prashant, I have told you. My parents. Your parents. They have to meet. My mummy and daddy and your mummy and daddy. I know we like each other. But why are we talking about this? We have to do a performance. The show must go on.' She looks down at me. 'Are you okay, Mukesh?'

I shake my head.

Prash holds up both his hands and laughs angrily.

'You are making me look stupid,' he says to Nisha. 'You're making me look like Chumchee. Kuti. Why are you never happy?'

He pushes her.

Even though I am prone on the floor, even though I am terrified of him, I decide to get up and punch him.

I do not need to.

Your mother, Nisha, she stumbles, steadies herself and then leaps at Prash with clenched fists. She is fearless. She is the bravest person I have ever seen in my life. She springs at him and punches him in the chest. It is surprising and symbolic enough that Prash doesn't fight back.

He looks at me. Then at Nisha. She has both of her fists clenched.

I stand up slowly. Dizzy. Uneven on my feet.

'Nisha, you have a lot of energy for a person who is dying,' he says.

His tone is flat, the line delivered as though he is an assassin.

Nisha's face is emotionless for the second it takes me to realize that his words have destroyed her. She dashes towards the back of the hall, her bare feet pat-patting on the parquet floor like pigeons on tin roofs, and disappears through a door I hadn't noticed before. Another room? Where I could have changed? My skin flushes hot with my earlier embarrassment. Then I remember where I am.

Prash smiles.

'You are duttee, man,' Anjali says.

Prash pulls at the triangle fold of the dhoti and lets it fall to the floor.

He strides confidently towards his pile of clothes and begins to dress. He winks at Anjali.

Chumchee watches Prash's graceful body with a curious mixture of alarm and admiration. His eyes are fixated on Prash's muscles, visibly doing what they should be, moving him around the room with a power and a grace and a presence that only the strongest and most arrogant of us are afforded. Usually, they are white. Universally, they are men.

No one is going to see if Nisha is okay.

I walk, quietly, so as not to draw attention to myself, to the door at the back of the hall. I pause as I place my hand on the doorknob. As I start to turn it, I wonder whether Nisha needs me to run after her. Am I making any claims on her by following her? Am I encroaching on her space? Perhaps one of the girls might make her feel more comfortable?

Maybe, I think. But I love her, and this is my chance to be

seen as nice, if anything – and nice is the opposite of Prash right now.

I open the door.

It is a cupboard. Where sports equipment lives. Big enough for someone to change in.

Nisha is lying on a bench that can be turned upside down to become a balance beam. She is staring at the ceiling, her forearm draped across her forehead.

I walk in, announcing myself with a firm closing of the door.

The cupboard is small and dark. I can hear her breathing close to me.

'All right, che?' I ask.

'No,' she says. I hear a smile in her voice. 'Haven't you heard? I'm dying.'

Choice. Climax

Just as I am about to step out on stage, I have a sudden memory of being at home. Shammi Kapoor is on the radio. He is asking for the girl to come here, oh come here, in a stuttering sing-song way.

I'm standing in front of the mirror in the kitchen. I think I am in the house by myself. I want to see what I look like when I dance; there is a Diwali party later that night and Amee has told me there will be music and dancing. It makes me nervous. I am eleven years old and starting to realize people can see me.

I throw some shapes into the mirror, to see what I look like.

My hips jerk in every direction. I am emulating Shammi, which is what dancing looks like in my head. I shake myself around until my quiff flaps over my forehead. My hands begin by my sides, but they soon have the confidence to spring up to chest level, where they wiggle and writhe, until before I know it they're waving above my head, flapping wildly, like a distressed bird.

But I feel brilliant.

My eyes close. I am dancing!

And somebody is watching.

I feel a presence in the room. I turn.

Naman and Amee are doubled over in the doorway, stifling their laughter.

Embarrassed, with nowhere else to run in our tiny kitchen, I barge past them, pushing into Amee, as hers is the bigger betrayal. She stumbles backwards, calling my name angrily.

Now, standing at the side of the stage, two feet away from the front row, watching the shuffling of what feels like forty Gujaratis waiting for our performance to start, I feel that same melon-sized bulge of embarrassment in my stomach. I watch as Chumchee dims the lights from the switches by the front door and then runs up the aisle, hitching up his dhoti, his nipples shaking as he runs.

I glance across the stage to Nisha. She looks serious, nervous. Her eyes are closed. She is concentrating, shaking the tension from her hands. She cocks her head from side to side, stretching her neck.

The harmonium starts, a drone that hushes the crowd.

My first line is approaching. I want to vomit. It's not even a line, it's just one sound, but it has furred over on my tongue.

Chumchee looks at me intently as he waits for it to come.

I stare out at the crowd. I feel myself sweat. I sense my pores bursting open and streaming freely.

Chumchee nudges me. Nisha opens her eyes and glares at me.

My throat is dry, I can feel the sound I have to make slipping away from my lips, back down into my throat. I open my mouth in the hope that it will encourage the sound to come out. I begin to dribble. The harmonium is fading and the musician, sensing my stage fright, starts the note up again. It's loud and jarring.

I close my eyes. I see Naman and Amee laughing.

Nisha oh oh Nisha oh oh oh Nisha oh oh Nisha.

I open my eyes. I see Chumchee approaching. He finds this hilarious. He puts a hand on my shoulder and shakes me. He keeps shaking and shaking and shaking until…

'Auuuuuuuuuuuuuuuuuuuuuummmmmmmmmmmm mmmmmmm,' I intone, suddenly.

I just have to do the first one by myself and then the audience knows to join in automatically.

'Auuuuuuuuuuuuuuuuuuuuuummmmmmmmmmmm mmmmmmm,' forty tuneless voices repeat.

'Auuuuuuuuuuuuuuuuuuuuuummmmmmmmmmmm mmmmmmm,' they say again.

I mouth it the fourth time, my job is momentarily done.

'Auuuuuuuuuuuuuuuuuuuuuummmmmmmmmmmm mmmmmmm,' they all say, softer.

'Auuuuuuuuuuuuuuuuuuuuuummmmmmmmmmmm mmmmmmm,' we all say, the big finale, the primordial sound opening up the channels to the gods.

Then we all sing. And it is bad, let me tell you. It is tuneless, lacking in energy, characterless, but we do it.

Aum Bhoor Bhuwah Swaha, Tat Savitur Varenyam Bhargo Devasaya Dheemahi Dhiyo Yo Naha Prachodayat.

It's repeated four more times. I find the repetition comforting. Naman used to whisper this prayer every morning before breakfast.

Oh God, the Protector, the basis of all life, Who is self-existent, Who is free from all pains and Whose contact frees the soul from all troubles, Who pervades the Universe and sustains all, the Creator and Energizer of the whole Universe, the Giver of happiness, Who is worthy of acceptance, the most excellent, Who is Pure and the Purifier of all, let us embrace that very God, so that He may direct our mental faculties in the right direction.

I find it calming. I feel as though I'm at home. I almost forget that I am part of a show where I am playing an incarnation of Vishnu, a hero, a king, a strong-willed young man called Rama. A young man they will tell stories about for generations.

What stories will they tell about me? Or will I have to give people my own history? Neha, this is why I tell you all this. So you know my history. Because who else tells the great stories of the little people?

The play opens just as Rama has slain Ravana, the demon king.

On freeing his kidnapped wife, Sita, Rama asks her to undergo an agni pariksha to prove that she is chaste and thereby dispel rumours about her fidelity. When Sita plunges into the sacrificial fire, Agni, the lord of fire, attests to her purity. Rama and Sita triumphantly return to their kingdom, where they are crowned as rulers. This is the beginning of Ram Rajya, a golden time in which Rama establishes an ideal state with good morals.

This is who I am supposed to be.

Chumchee, playing the role of my most faithful warrior brother, and I are supposed to walk on stage with our bows cocked with arrows, searching for Sita. She will then appear and dance for me to prove she is my love. I will watch her dance before asking her to prove her purity. I do not understand the order of things. I do not understand why Rama thinks the first thing he should suggest to Sita after she has been traumatically kidnapped by a demon king is that she prove herself to him. Which, after all she has been through, seems like an imposition.

I am lost in thought and miss my cue. Chumchee pushes me on to the steps leading up to the stage. I trip and my arrow is released, disappearing into the darkness above Nisha and her dancers' heads. I duck even though it is flying in the opposite direction to me.

No one notices that I nearly assassinate my lead actress, or that I walk up the steps without an arrow. Luckily, I have a quiver with me and two arrows rattle around in it. Unluckily, I cannot reach them and walk at the same time. I wrench my arm over the top of my head, hunching my shoulder blades and twisting around to try and grab another arrow. They both spin in the quiver and elude my fingertips.

The more I twist around, the more I look like a dog chasing its own tail. I hear titters from the audience. I look ridiculous, whirling and wheeling on the spot, but it is important that I don't mess this up. I claw frantically at the quiver, and the titters become laughter, and just as I am at my most desperate, I stop.

The letter I received this morning comes back to me.

The letter I've been trying to hide in the depths of my brain.

As soon as I had read the opening line, I merely skimmed the rest and put it under my bed, heading out to wait for Nisha.

Sailesh is not coming.

I can feel the entire room watching me. Chumchee looks at me askance. I notice that his quiver has ten arrows in it. Mine, two. It's as if he has intended me to fail. He said it would make me look more heroic because I appear to have fired off more arrows. Now Chumchee pulls one from his quiver and hands it to me.

I realize I am standing stock-still in front of the audience.

They are looking at me, waiting for me. Some of them even have their hands in front of them as if they are unsure whether or not to clap.

I turn around. I cannot look at them.

Chumchee hisses at me, 'Come on, hero. We need you. Jaldi, jaldi.'

Sailesh used to make a quiet breathy *uh-uh-uh-uh-uh* sound when he performed, to help him concentrate and drown out noise from the people around him.

He juggled with his tongue lodged in his cheek.

He started learning with three soft red balls. They belonged to Mr Shukla, the owner of the bookshop where Sailesh worked, cleaning dust off the stock and keeping the shelves neat. He became fascinated with a book about juggling. When Mr Shukla noticed his interest, he produced the balls, and gave him the book for free.

'I learned with these,' Mr Shukla told him.

And when Sailesh had figured out the technique, and he was able to make the three balls stay in the air, Mr Shukla said, 'Those balls are meant for beginners. When you get too good for them, give them to someone else. Until then, keep them.'

He gave the balls to me so I could practise before he came. I haven't touched them since I arrived.

When he had mastered three balls, he added a pen, which made the rhythm difficult. The pen had a different centre of gravity to the balls and never arced in the same trajectory. Perfecting this awkward rhythm gave him the confidence to build on his skills, his hands becoming more attuned to every possibility and parabola, acting before his brain could process what was happening in front of him. Sailesh became obsessed with improving. Above Cheap Ration Store, there were three flats. We lived in one, Sailesh's family in another and the third belonged to Mr Shukla who worked so many hours we never saw him at home, only in the shop downstairs. They were all small and opened out on to a communal roof-top courtyard, where we dried clothes. Each afternoon, after school, Sailesh stood there and practised. No one but Sailesh was stupid enough to risk the intense burst of sun you'd be scorched by if you ventured into the centre of the courtyard. He stood there most afternoons and juggled till it was his time to go downstairs and help with the end-of-day chores in Cheap Ration Store.

It's important to remember these things, Neha. This is why I tell myself them again and again. So I do not forget.

And he huffed, that *uh-uh-uh-uh-uh*, repeatedly. It centred him.

'*Uh-uh-uh-uh-uh*,' I mumble now, my voice cracking slightly.

I feel a thump and look up to see Nisha banging on the stage and flinging her hand upwards to ask what is happening? I notice I have been holding on to Chumchee's arrow so tightly that it has snapped in my fist.

I'm reminded of the audience and I look out to them. I walk to the front of the stage and stand with my fists bunched on my hips. '*Uh-uh-uh-uh-uh*,' I whisper. I *am* Rama. I breathe in to say my first line when I hear the echoes of a noise outside.

'Wogs out, wogs out, wogs out, wogs out!'

I look at Nisha but it's as if she hasn't heard the venom in the voices. She gestures for me to continue.

I hold my broken arrow against the useless bow, almost as if to protect myself.

'Wogs out, wogs out, wogs out, wogs out! Go home, go home, go home!'

People in the audience begin looking behind them, just as Nisha and her dancers emerge on stage. I look at them. I say my only line quietly, because I am distracted by the noise at the doors. There is banging. The crowd inside grow concerned, shifting in their seats and murmuring amongst themselves.

Nisha, undeterred, moves into the centre of the stage.

Nervously, I intone, 'Sita, it is you. Is it you?'

No one is listening to me. People are barely watching us on stage.

Nisha, as Sita, dances for me. She snakes in and around me, so close I can smell the coconut oil in her hair and the sweat across her neck. She smiles, but it is a rictus; I can tell she is annoyed. The show is not working, not coming together. I want her to be happy.

The banging gets louder, a beat to accompany the chants.

Even Chumchee looks worried, and the boy has the vacant smile of a chicken with a chapatti, as Amee would say.

Nisha continues to dance.

The drone of the harmonium is making my sweaty skin itch. I want it to stop.

In the gloom, I see a man from the audience stand up and walk to the door to see what is happening.

Still Nisha carries on dancing, as if this is the only chance she will ever have to perform this show.

The man looks outside, through the frosted glass. I cannot see what he can see but suddenly he flings up his arms to shield his balding head, just moments before a brick bursts through the pane, shattering glass everywhere. It lands in front of his bare feet and he jumps backwards. The harmonium player plays a bum note and stops. Lights flicker on throughout the hall.

Nisha stops dancing and balls her fists in frustration. I move to stand in front of her, like a hero. I am still holding my bow, the broken arrow notched in the string, ready to fire. She pushes me aside and stands level with me.

The din from outside fills the hall. I cannot tell how many people are there.

'Wogs out, wogs out, wogs out, wogs out! Go home, go home, go home!'

Within that chant, there are the standard eys and raaaarrs of communal male shouting. The hole in the glass makes it all seem louder and closer. People are putting their shoes on, standing up, hurrying towards the stage. The harmonium player is wrapping a cloth around his instrument and putting it back in its box.

'Who is it?' I ask.

Nisha moves closer to me.

'I don't know,' she says. 'We received a note earlier this week saying that we had to cancel the performance. Signed by the League of Empire Loyalists.'

'Who are they?'

Chumchee leans in to me. 'Why don't you go outside and ask them?' he says.

'Do not do that,' retorts Nisha.

I smile at her and rub her arm. She raises her eyebrows questioningly and flicks my hand away.

'Of course I won't,' I reassure her.

'I don't know, Mukesh. I only met you this afternoon and on the day of performance you agreed to act in a show that has been rehearsing for three weeks, as the lead hero. You are either brave or a bevakoof. I don't know yet. I haven't decided.'

The doors rattle, shuddering against their hinges.

Now the lights are on and I can see that the Gujarati population of Keighley is smaller than I had realized. There are fifteen aunties and uncles in front of me, all barefoot and anxious. Slowly, they form a hub in front of the stage. The front door is the only way out and the only way in.

We are trapped.

Mounds of something brown are thrown through the hole in the glass.

Chumchee laughs. This time I can tell he is nervous.

'Will that door hold?' Nisha asks.

'What are they going to do to us?' I say.

'Why don't you go and ask them?' Chumchee responds.

We are scared, I think, but we are together. Sailesh won't be coming. I am here alone. These are my friends and family now. I cannot go home. I cannot afford a ticket. Will they send my body home if I die tonight? I feel so far away from Mombasa.

This is what I'm telling you now. Measure what you call micro-aggressions against a real fear like this. I cannot describe to you how I felt. You tell me about white girls wearing bindis at festivals and I will tell you about that moment, when I thought I was going to die and no one who loved me would even know.

I could disappear completely.

My biggest fear is that nobody will tell my amee what happened to me. I am here, by myself. The only times she will hear from me will be when I write her letters. What if there is no one to write to her about me? Who will record the violence against my body? History?

No one will mourn me.

What will happen to my body?

I drop my bow to the floor.

'Everybody,' I say. 'Get up on to the stage.'

'Kem?' comes the reply from the concerned hubbub before me.

'If we are a tight group, we stay together, whatever happens,' I say.

This makes no sense but it is empowering enough that everyone slowly joins us on stage. They stand behind Nisha and me. The harmonium player is hugging his instrument. We are together in our isolation – I have never felt more part of a community.

I am Rama.

My hands are on my hips, in hero pose. I turn to Nisha.

'What now?' I whisper.

'I don't know,' she says. 'This is not a regular occurrence for me.'

Chumchee pushes me forward. I turn around to glare at him.

'Go and see,' he says. 'Go and see if they will let us out.'

The door is shaking.

Why is the door even locked? I wonder. Were we trying to keep people out or in?

Gloved fingers poke through the hole in the frosted glass, trying to widen it.

A milk bottle, stuffed with a flaming rag, is dropped into the room and it rolls across the floor.

The flame snuffs as the bottle smashes across the parquet flooring, but it is enough to send squeals of panic through the gathered Gujaratis.

Another Molotov is thrown in, and this one bursts into yellow flames. One of the squeaky wooden chairs catches fire. This is how we are going to die.

Chumchee pushes me forward. 'You are the hero. Go and be the hero.'

I turn and grab him by the shoulders, his dry skin shedding into my hands.

'Choop,' I scream into his face. 'Choop re. Choop.'

I have to do something.

My mother will need to know about this.

I don't know where my bravery comes from. I ask a stranger for his shoes. He is reluctant, but gives me the shiny black brogues nonetheless, and I slip them on. They are warm and ingrained with the contours of someone else's steps.

I jump down from the stage.

'What are you doing?' Nisha asks.

'I do not know,' I say.

She jumps down as well.

'Come on then, hero,' she says. 'Let's rescue our people.'

I realize in that moment that I will never love anyone as much as I do her, so if she is not willing to love me, then I'd be better off dying tonight.

'What's the plan?' I ask Nisha, who is smiling.

'I don't know yet,' she replies.

We laugh at our lack of planning. I can feel people behind us bristle. But still we laugh. Your mother and I, for the first time together. I will remember that moment for my entire life.

I feel as though she has finally noticed me. Without thinking, I grab her hand. She tightens her grip around my fingers. We edge forward.

Other chairs are beginning to catch fire.

The shoes are too small for me. I need to cut my big toenails.

The feeling in the pit of my stomach is like a mango stone, trying to force its way into my throat. I want to throw up.

The banging on the door subsides as we reach it. It goes quiet. I cautiously peer through the hole in the frosted window. Figures in the dark are moving away from the entrance. I look at Nisha.

We shrug lightly at each other. Maybe they've got bored and are moving on, away, I think. I look at the flaming chairs; black smoke coils to the ceiling. The air in the room is being sucked into the fire. I am finding it harder to breathe.

I squeeze Nisha's hand more. She reciprocates. I go to open the door.

There is a roar and a cheer as something large and heavy flies through the smashed frosted glass and rattles to the floor. It's a bench. A whole bench.

Through the window frame, we can see two men using another bench as a battering ram. One, two and three loud bangs against the weakening doors before, finally, they accept defeat and smash open.

A group of men, five of them, stand on the threshold, fists clenched, balaclavas pulled over their faces, menacing.

I can see their chests heaving as they stand to attention.

They are waiting, perhaps uncertain as to what comes next.

'Paach che,' I suddenly cry out, surprising myself. 'Only five!'

We outnumber them and could easily overpower them if we act together as one.

I look behind me.

The audience members couldn't be further away from me if they tried. They are panicking about the flames and mutter to each other anxiously. They all look up at me as if I am Rama and must save them.

'Chalo, benchod na marr,' Nisha screams. She raises her fists like a boxer, dropping her chin to her chest.

This stirs our people into action. Each one moves slowly off the stage, skirting the flaming chairs and standing behind Nisha and me. I smile at how slowly everyone moves despite the peril. It reminds me of my amee and her slow shuffle.

I can see bricks in these people's hands, but it's too late. We are now committed.

Paki-bashing. I've heard whispers. Stories. When Sailesh told me about it, he laughed.

'But we are not Pakistani,' he said. 'We are not even Indian. We're Kenyans, bwana.'

'Will they know that?' I asked. 'Will they care?'

Sailesh died three days after I left for England. His mother wrote to tell me this. It was a perfunctory letter which arrived this morning. I read it once and left it in my room before I went to wait for Nisha.

Sailesh is not coming.

It did not register until now. I read the words but they didn't sink into my head. Seeing the Gujarati script made me feel as though I was at home, so I ignored the content, and kept the warm feeling of belonging inside me. You know that song? About keeping me in your heart? That is what I wanted to do with him. Keep him there, in my heart.

Sailesh isn't coming. And because he was at home, his mother could mourn him, tell his friends and family.

Me? In this burning little community hall in the north of England? I am not going to die here. I am not going to die on the soil of those who ruled over my people.

This is not destiny, I think. This is coincidence. Sailesh may not be alive any more, but I want to live.

A brick hits me in the ribs and I fall down, winded.

My chest feels caved in, useless. I struggle to breathe and stare at the ceiling. Nisha stands over me, shouting. I cannot understand her. I cannot hear her words though I know the intonation. I realize she is checking in. Am I okay?

My ears bleed into white noise. Everything slows. I can feel the brick, by my thigh. I put my hand on it. I close my eyes, then open them.

Nisha is looking towards the door, her fists clenched. I look up, noticing that the five men in masks have entered the school hall and are advancing, threateningly, on our position.

Sailesh is not coming.

I get to my feet, picking the brick up with me and hurling it at our attackers.

It strikes one of the men on his temple. He swears and crumples to the floor. One of the remaining four wields a cricket bat.

I look at Nisha. She cocks her head to one side and then shrugs. We run at them. All of us, tight and together. The aunties are in the middle, the uncles on the outside.

I glimpse Prash in the doorway. He catches my eye as he sizes up the danger, then turns and runs into the night again. Came back for his love. Disappeared when things got tough.

Nisha and I come face to face with a masked man, the one with a cricket bat. He swings it wildly, barely missing the top of my head as I duck and jump at him. Nisha and her dancers advance on another masked man, who is frozen still. He won't hit a girl. They pummel at him and he backs out of the hall.

The remaining two men are more effective and lash out at the fleeing audience. One manages to wrestle the harmonium player's box away from him and smashes it over his head, letting go on impact, so that both musician and instrument crash to the floor.

Two other men, uncles, balding, small and slight, help me fight the man with the cricket bat. He swipes at one of the uncles, the momentum of his own swing taking him off balance, which gives me the opportunity to push him over.

I hear a shout behind me and spin around to see the harmonium player about to get the imprint of a boot in his face. I run to him, tackling the attacker on the way. We tumble to the floor, and I land heavily on top of him. His mask comes off in the struggle, exposing his face. It's the man whose bike I collided with today. He is beneath me. Hours ago, I was under his bike. I pin his arms down with my knees and we look at one another. He looks at me with a mixture of pity and fear. My instinct is to punch him, but then I think of something much worse. I rub my sweaty cheek against his. He recoils.

Whatever happens, whatever victory we call this, I will still wake up Indian tomorrow.

'Benchod,' I hiss at him as I stand up.

He runs away.

In years to come, I will remember this night as the thing that made me feel afraid of white men and shiver in their presence. And whenever you and your brother ask me why I think you are both too Western, you'll tell me I have not integrated.

Why integrate into a country that wanted me annihilated, Neha? That wanted to beat my body with bricks and cricket bats until I bled to death?

But I cannot go home. I haven't enough money to get back. Besides, what have I got left there? I look at Nisha, helping people push through the door. She looks beautiful. No, I cannot go home. My body is rooted firmly here. With hers. In this green and unpleasant land.

Oh, Nisha, my Nisha

Your fists are like leather.

Outside, the night is crisp. The harmonium player, still a little groggy, looks at me and bows. He is clutching a cracked shard of his instrument like a blade.

The fires are dying out. The car park is empty, both the attackers and the victims already fled. My clothes, my only smart clothes. They are gone.

I am Rama now.

I look out into the night of Keighley.

Sailesh is not coming.

I let out a tear for my friend. He is not coming.

I walk home. Cold. Topless.

No one is around to see my shame.

'Mukesh,' I hear my name gently as I approach home.

I look up. Nisha is standing, leaning against the wall where I usually am.

She smiles.

'Hi,' I say.

'I'm glad you are okay,' she says.

Nisha, my Nisha, this is my heart. For you.

Reverse. Resolve

Falling in love is easy. Staying in love is the problem.

She is in my room. She sits on my bed and looks at my meagre possessions, judging me. She smiles, embarrassed. I am leaning against the door, until I realize this seems as though I am barring her exit, so I shift until I am propped against the basin.

My bottom is cold.

We do not talk.

The quiet reflective moment after the violence.

'My friend died,' I suddenly say, to break the silence. 'The one I'm waiting for. The one I'm moving to London with.'

'My cousin Sailesh?' she asks. 'I did not meet him. Sorry. I know he meant a lot to you.'

'He is family,' I say, uselessly.

'Yes,' she says, quietly. 'He was.' She pauses, unsure of what to say next. 'How did he die?'

'It was three days after I left. Always such a dangerous driver. I'd tell him, drive carefully. Why? he says to me. Other drivers are the problem, not me. And he was right. It was another driver. I wonder how I ended up in Keighley. So far from where I am supposed to be. The only thing I can think of, is maybe I am supposed to be here. It is written for me to be here. I do not believe in destiny. But what we saw tonight, that was a prelude to murder. They wanted to kill us. I could see it in their eyes. Why am I supposed to be here? I think it is for you. Maybe there is such a thing as destiny after all.'

I say this last bit looking at the floor.

She is quiet for a while.

'My mother tells me no one will want me,' she finally replies. 'I have pulmonary fibrosis, a respiratory disease in which scars are formed in the lung tissues, leading to serious breathing problems. It has a high-percentage chance of turning into cancer. I am broken. No one will take me, my mummy says. Even Chumchee will find *some*one, she tells me. Even that pendoo, Chumchee. Me? I will get a job, I will earn money, I will die financially comfortable, and my family will remember me as a failure. Is that my fate? Or is that just called one of those things?'

'We are both failures then,' I say.

'I think so.' She looks at me with kind eyes. 'Destined to fail together.'

'What about Prash?' I ask.

'What about him? Prash is only interested in my body. Nothing else. I think he showed his true colours two or three times tonight. Nah?'

'Hahn-ji,' I reply, smiling.

'You were very brave tonight,' she says, standing up. 'I need to go home now. Thank you. I think your bravery helped. We all got out safely. Well, except Mr Shah. He banged his foot on the door as he ran. He's in hospital. But the rest of us did, thanks to you.'

'Can I tell you something?' I ask.

She nods.

I pause. She scratches at her neck, impatient.

'My biggest fear was dying in a strange place and no one knowing where I am or how to mourn me. I didn't want to be forgotten. It made me angry. Who would write to my friends and family and tell them I had passed away, just as Sailesh's amee is now having to do? Is this selfish?'

'Maybe a little. But it is okay. Will you come to our house tomorrow? For Diwali? How are you celebrating?'

I gesture to the room.

'I am here.'

'No,' she says. 'After tonight, we should at least feed you some nasto, give you some rus, maybe some gulab jamun. It is important. Come to us tomorrow.'

I do not sleep that night.

All I can do is picture our life together. I come home from work. I put my hat on the hat stand, smell the hot dhoklas in the oven and crouch down to receive my children as they run gleefully towards me. I pick them both up and stomp like Frankenstein to the kitchen to greet my wife and my dhokla.

She is lying on the table, still, a garland around her neck, lifeless.

We are in black and white.

I wake up.

When your ba told you to believe in destiny, she did not know what she was talking about, darling. This is real life. We live, we love, we die, hoping we have left some love in the world. There is nothing else. If there was, why was Nisha taken from me?

This is why I only believe in coincidence. It can change your life, but it is not cruel.

Walking into her parents' house, I feel at home. With Rafi on the radio, the steel vadkis of water and the glass bowls of chakris and dhoklas, freshly made, I know that Gujaratis live here. I take my shoes off as I enter.

Nisha, dressed in a saree, serves me. I smile at her. She seems different here, in this space – she is not herself. She projects who her amee wants her to be. She's more formal. Deferential, even. I do not like this Nisha.

She does not speak to me but keeps her head bowed. She lets her father tell her to fetch things. This is not the woman I plan to spend the rest of my life with. Chumchee is resting in his room, Nisha's father tells me. He was so overcome by the events of yesterday, he is bedridden.

Her father asks about my family, where they are from. We talk about Sailesh, and how sorry he and his wife were to learn of his death. They talk of him as if he is an abstract. They have not met the boy. Instead, he is my friend and I try to show them how important he is to me. Because they are family, they have more of a claim to grief, yet they do not cry for Sailesh. Neither of them knows anything about him. We migrate across the world, removing links to everyone but those in the room with us.

Your ba looks at me, bemused, the whole time. She sits in an armchair and slices and dices potatoes into the palm of her hand. She must think I am funny. There is half a smile there.

Nisha kneels at her feet, ready to spring up should it look

as though my cup needs refilling or more food needs to be fetched and offered.

Eventually, after we have exhausted all conversations about Sailesh, we slip into silence.

I ask about cricket – there is a test series imminent – but her father does not follow it.

I ask Ba what she is making.

'Are you staying for dinner?' she asks by way of reply.

'I would love to,' I say, before realizing that it wasn't an invitation. It was a test.

Over dinner, I try to ask Nisha questions – about the show, about the men who came, about how she feels, about the League of Empire Loyalists. She is interrupted by her father.

'We do not speak of such things in this house,' he says, quietly.

'Those men,' I tell him. 'They wanted to kill us. I saw it in their eyes. We are lucky to be alive. So lucky.'

'We do not speak of such things. Such is life. Such is the way of this country,' her father says.

You never met him but he was eventually killed at a bus stop. By the same sort of people who wanted to murder us all that night.

I shoot a look at Nisha and she grimaces, as if to say, stop talking, now. I stop. In the silence, Chumchee calls out for water. Nisha places a hand on her mum's arm and stands up to take it to him.

The garden behind the house is a short stretch of concrete leading to an outside toilet. I'm nervously holding a small box of fireworks. Nisha and her mother stand in the kitchen doorway, waiting for the display. Her father appears behind them, leans over and hands me a lit incense stick. I have never done this before. I look to the upstairs window where Chumchee stares out, directly at me. When I wave he does not respond.

Diwali at home was brilliant. Because we had master showman Sailesh, and an open rooftop courtyard between our apartments, we could let all the fireworks off at once. I never had to do anything. All I was required to do was to ooh and aah and to say wow and so forth.

It was the one day a year we were religious. Diwali was a day to remember your roots and how far you had not come from them. Diwali was about singing tunelessly, my father leading us all in prathna. Diwali was about atoning for your lack of achievements and your lack of integrity. Diwali was about eating your body weight in gulab jamun. Diwali was about others, people less fortunate. Diwali was about staying out of your father and your uncles' way because that was the one day a year they would mix charras into their tobacco and churn it in their mouths till their eyes were red and glassy and their lips bled. Diwali was about family.

Standing here, in front of Nisha and her parents, is not Diwali.

I put the box down on the ground and select a tall thin firework. I twist at the crêpe lighting paper at its tip and place it in the empty milk bottle Nisha's amee has given me, as far away from the house as possible. I lift the incense stick to the firework and hold it to the fuse. The bottle topples over.

I pick it back up, to cries of encouragement from Nisha's dad, laughter from her and her mum. I lift the incense stick to the firework again, this time holding it upright with my free hand until the paper lights.

Red flares stream from the firework. It startles me and I drop it, jumping backwards.

I hear gasps from behind me. The firework shoots off like a snake on heat, zinging around the garden, ricocheting off the fence, spraying Nisha and her family with hot yellow sparks, careening into the toilet door. I duck for cover just before there is a deafening boom and a shower of red, white and blue fills the garden, twinkling like the American flag.

'My toilet's on fire!' cries Nisha's father. 'My feet are on fire!' he then screams. His socks are smouldering, and the outhouse is indeed flickering with yellow and orange flames.

I kick the door off its hinges as I try to put out the fire. Nisha appears beside me carrying a bowl of water and douses the flames with a hiss. The garden is quiet. Curtains twitch. Several neighbours peer out of their windows.

'Come inside,' Ba says wearily. 'I suppose we'd better all have a drink. I'll need one if I must now do piss in front of everyone.'

She laughs to herself and walks back into the house.

Nisha looks at me.

'Disaster follows you, doesn't it?' she whispers. I nod. 'Are you just unlucky or are you a causer of chaos?'

'I don't know,' I tell her. 'I love you,' I whisper a second later.

She laughs at me and puts a finger up to her lips. 'Pagal ho-gaya? What?'

'I love you,' I say, a bit louder, turning around and seeing her father, sockless now, standing in the doorway, watching me like a man with a loaded gun.

She sighs. It's a deep sigh, a frustrated one. She waits for a second. We watch the smoke curl from the burnt door. I hear her father shuffle away behind us. She is close enough that I can feel her skin causing the hairs on my forearm to prickle.

Suddenly, she puts her hand to the back of my neck, and quickly pulls me towards her. She kisses me on the cheek. Her lips are cracked, full, thorough, as they press against my stubble.

'You don't love me,' she says, quietly. 'Not yet you don't.'

NEHA

London, 2017

Maybe this is my manifest destiny.
Maybe this is my purpose.

Neha Jani

Denial

TUESDAY MORNING

GoTo: Bubblegum-Lung

It must be difficult for doctors to tell you that you have cancer.

They have to do it in the flattest way possible. They can't sound happy or sad. They have to sound realistic, bland, confident. You have to walk away from the encounter knowing that you have cancer and that it's not something to be sad about, because in your case there are no treatments available.

Also, there is nothing to be happy about.

Cancer is not a walk in the park. Which is not a great metaphor.

I don't walk other than for practicality. Walking gets me from A to B. Parks are cut-throughs. I have no use for this metaphor.

I have terminal cancer.

I keep expecting Dr Hamid to break into a grin in the meaningful silence that follows the delivery of the diagnosis. I want him to laugh. I laughed when Shilpa fai was cremated. Mostly because the singing at the service was woefully out of tune, simultaneously spanning every octave, major and minor key and note known to modern music. The smile crept on to my face, forcing my lips into a convulsion, revealing the grin's true intentions – a guffaw.

I don't find much funny.

Dr Hamid looks at me with all the goodwill in the world and there's something in his face, an earnestness that makes me want to strangle him with his stethoscope.

I cough instead.

Which appears to be my life now. The cough is empty – as though I'm trying to shift an immovable piece of bubblegum that's stuck down on the inside of my lungs. I can feel my diaphragm shudder, but it just won't shift.

I look at him through my watering eyes and he is poised with a tissue to hand to me, as though it's the simplest, kindest act in the world. I reach into my pocket and pull out some toilet paper that I'd grabbed earlier. I hack violently, hoping that something will shift whatever it is – the cancerous lump, the bubblegum of deterioration, the architect of my destruction – and I try to spit into the toilet paper, but only drool comes out.

I look up at Dr Hamid and smile.

'Well, that's that, then,' I say.

I ball up the toilet paper and put it back in my pocket.

'My mother did say there would be days like this,' I murmur.

I'm paraphrasing a song I hate, but in the moment it feels meaningful. As though I'm supposed to have some sort of golden moment of clarity that was passed down to me from someone I never met. I'm dying. Death is only a short time away. What song would I need to narrate it in the film of my life?

I thank Dr Hamid.

He mutters about some leaflets and referring me to the oncologist, the specialist of all things bubblegum-lung.

'Will it make any difference?' I ask him point-blank.

He looks down at his notes; the little pince-nez glasses he has on a shoelace around his neck fall off the bulb of his nose and he looks at me plainly. I know that he has delivered his death sentence effectively. I am neither comforted nor elated nor worried by his diagnosis.

'I'm sorry,' he says, closing my folder, placing it on an out-tray, picking up a glass of water and slurping it with satisfied wet lips.

I want to tell him I hate him. That he has ruined my life. I imagine mine is not the first.

I stand up and shake his hand, ensuring that I offer the hand still drenched in the evacuees from my bubblegum-lungs. I cough again, but I'm too busy shaking his hand to be decent about it and cover my mouth. I let pearls of my spittle settle on his sleeveless cardigan.

'Are you going to be okay?' he asks.

I shrug.

'No, Doctor. You've given me a death sentence. I have the rest of my life to live with that. You have the rest of this appointment to deal with it.'

I leave, knowing that this is a killer exit line. A movie gold moment. I wish my mama *had* told me there'd be days like these.

TUESDAY EVENING

GoTo: Messages from Beyond

Neha: egotist, hard-working, stubborn. Avoid these numbers: 16, 12, 9, 22.

I trace my mother's handwriting on the slip of paper. I try to picture the fortune teller who told her this. I try to picture my mother. I've only seen her in photographs, so giving her three dimensions is difficult. I don't know how her body moved. She was short, like me, just shy of five foot. Did she waddle or did she stride with purpose? Did she talk with her hands or with her mouth? Did she have the sort of nose that bounces with each word?

Maybe the fortune teller should have concentrated on the cancer in her lungs rather than the two foetuses in her womb. Maybe then I could understand the fingers behind the handwriting, the hand behind the fingers, the brain behind the hand. The waddle behind the short legs that went to the fortune teller in the first place.

Fortune telling: a bigger con than echinacea. A worse comfort blanket than yoga.

I don't know if I could have respected her if I'd known she dabbled in the dark arts of the stupid, thumbing her nose at science. But I might not have turned to science, had she been around.

There is no way of knowing. Ba told us that this was all written, all predetermined. She told us of destiny.

She is not here any more. She is a distant memory I barely feel is real. My mother is four photographs, each one of her smiling.

I don't feel bereft.

Why feel bereft for something you've never had?

It boggles my mind that part of me does look for these numbers: 16, 12, 9, 22. 16.22 in the afternoon. 22nd September. Lottery numbers. Phone number for the love of my life. Odds on horses. I notice them when they crop up. Because I'm aware of them. I know their significance. Their significance is through my powers of recollection. Not because 9.22 a.m. or p.m. on 16th December is going to result in a life-changing event.

Egotist. Hard-working. Who among us doesn't display these characteristics some, if not all, of the time? I'd have been more impressed if the fortune teller had nailed some of my deeper psychological defects - growing up without a mother, sharing a womb with a clown, being able to recite pi to seventeen decimal places by the time I was ten. Not caring in the slightest about any aspect of any sport, professional or recreational. Not being into music. Being a-racial, a-political, a-theological - these are the things the fortune teller should have gone for to really get my attention.

It's easy to apply a fortune teller's prediction, or a notion of destiny, retroactively, when you spot the pattern. That does not mean it was predetermined. Least of all, a second-hand prediction given by a fortune teller to a woman I've never met.

The fortune teller would have done better telling my mother that she and her daughter would die of the same thing before their thirty-fifth birthdays.

That would really impress me.

WEDNESDAY EVENING

GoTo: Tech the Tech

The other night, my brother told me he didn't understand what I did for a living. Could I explain it to him? I think he was fishing for material. One of the stand-up comedian's commonest tricks is to have pre-prepared jokes about people's jobs for when things are going badly, or for when they want a cheap laugh.

Who are you and what do you do? I've seen him go through this routine hundreds of times.

Good question.

I answered him honestly. I didn't try and put anything into layperson's terms. I laid out my life for him. What I do is:

1) analyse information to determine, recommend and plan layout, including type of computers and peripheral equipment modifications.
2) analyse user needs and recommend appropriate hardware.
3) build, test and modify product prototypes, using working models or theoretical models constructed using computer simulation.
4) confer with engineering staff and consult specifications to evaluate interface between hardware and software and operational and performance requirements of overall system.
5) design and develop computer hardware and support peripherals, including central processing units (CPUs), support logic, microprocessors, custom-integrated circuits and printers and disk drives.
6) evaluate factors such as reporting formats required, cost constraints and need for security restrictions to determine hardware configuration.

I've been in the same job for fourteen years. I use three screens, an ergonomic backless chair and four external hard drives. I'm the only one in my company who can do what I do.

There's a reason I've worked at the same place for fourteen years and have retained the same position I entered at. Raks laughed when I told him this but I gave him the truth.

'I'm not in this for glory,' I told him. 'Why get promoted? It takes me away from what I do best. Making things. People don't make physical things any more. They make things that exist inside boxes. I design the boxes that make what they do possible. Why do I want to manage other people doing that? You're just in it for the money, aren't you? I'm going to go down in history. And it will be for something I made. Not for something I was paid to make by someone else. This job gets 40 per cent of me. But that 40 per cent is better than 100 per cent of 90 per cent of other people.'

'I try and make drunk strangers laugh in the dark,' he replied.

'You're a national treasure,' I told him.

'I'm a national laughing stock.'

'Isn't that the point?' I rebutted.

'So what do you do exactly?' he asked, after a beat. 'Because your job description is nonsense.'

'I design computer hardware,' I sighed.

In the scripts of *Star Trek: The Next Generation* that I've downloaded, in instances where there is a computer malfunction or the warp drive needs fixing or the dilithium crystals are failing, the screenwriter has written, 'The tech is going badly', to which the engineer Geordi La Forge will shout out some technobabble. The script instructs him to 'tech the tech'. This is how my job description must appear to some people.

Star Trek hired technicians to tech the tech in the scripts to make them sound presentable. Often, when someone uses techno-bullshit in films or books, you read the words and nod, because nonsense or not, it probably sounds about right. So, to Raks, I tech the tech.

I head home from work, trying to think of an eloquent way to describe my condition. How would the greats describe it? How would the Bukowskis describe it? How would the Virginia Woolfs describe it?

I listen to a pink-noise app on the bus. It drowns out all unnecessary breaches into my brain. Drunk people's conversations, mostly. I've stayed late to finish things. Now that I'm dying, my biggest fear appears to be the legacy of unfinished projects. I'm struggling to concentrate. I look at the intoxicated commuters around me.

A middle-aged woman sits next to me. She's dressed in the drab grey suit of a powerful position at a big-but-dull company. She probably works in a bank or heads up a recruitment firm or something more mundane. She's swaying, clutching her bag and resting her feet on her shoes, where she pinches her toes. She smells delicious – the mix of old perfume, stale tobacco and sweet Chardonnay sweat from her pores. She has a pink cheek.

She's looking at a girl dressed for summer, short skirt, open-toed footwear, a white T-shirt, sheer over a polka-dot bra, her hair in a big twist out. She doesn't look that old. She looks as though she might be on her way to a gig by some young hip gunslingers in some young hip pub. Do people still say gig? Have they ever said young hip gunslinger? She looks like someone with not many responsibilities. The grey person is holding this against her. She looks at me every now and then and flicks her eyes back to the girl, to show me that she is disgusted with how she is dressed. And she wants me to be complicit in her disgust. Because I am dressed in black and I wear glasses and I'm much more interested in the screen of my phone, scrolling through lines of code that I need to troubleshoot when I arrive home from work, ready to work.

The stares build in tension until I feel her lean forward. She's going to say something. Why must people always say something? I switch off my pink-noise app, because she looks back at me to indicate that she requires an audience for what's going to happen next.

'Have some self-respect, love,' she says to the girl.

The girl looks at her and rolls her eyes. What? they say. She doesn't otherwise reply.

'No one needs to see *everything*,' the woman says, nudging me.

Then she stops nudging and looks at me.

'Eh?' she repeats.

She wants me to engage. She is desperate for me to validate her opinion. We are no longer spectators. We are either co-conspirators or antagonists.

I turn to her and take off my glasses and pinch the bridge of my nose for emphasis. 'She could be naked,' I say slowly. 'With the words "fuck me" written on her tits in lipstick, and it would still be neither of our businesses.'

I can feel my bubblegum-lung rattling as I speak. The grey woman with the grey life tuts at me and crosses her arms, leaning back into the seat with a thud. She begins to retort, but I talk louder, over her – it's the only weapon we have against white people. They fear a loud immigrant. It's easier to dismiss me later as an angry brown woman than deal with me in the present.

'I hope one of your stilettos gets trapped in a tramline and you get run over slowly,' I tell her through the coughs.

'She's the one dressed like a hussy,' she splutters.

I cough violently, my hands on my knees, leaning towards her.

I can feel the bus braking.

'Get off the bus,' I say. 'Now. No arguments. Get off.'

She grabs her bag and a supermarket plastic carrier with a *Telegraph* peeping out of it and stands up, pushing past the girl as she gets off the bus.

People look at me with admiration but I can feel the rattle of the cough. I spit into my hand and wipe the drool into her newly vacated seat.

The girl sits next to me, on top of my drool, seemingly unbothered. I can feel her naked knee touch my jean-clad one.

I cough repeatedly.

I cannot live like this.

'Thank you,' she says quietly. People around us nod as though I've been a hero. I smile vacantly, like I'm just doing my job.

WEDNESDAY EVENING

GoTo: Twice as Good

I sit on the bench of the bus stop near my flat.

The girl gets off the bus as well and looks at me strangely, as though she needs an excuse to engage. I'm coughing into my toilet-paper wad. My free hand is clenched white. When we were younger, my brother and I used to high-five using the backs of our hands instead of the palms. We called this 'brown five'. When Dad wanted us to choose a movie to watch, we'd reply with one of us holding out their white palm to represent the West and the other holding out the back of their hand to represent the East – because brown didn't just mean Bollywood. It meant martial-arts films and films from Kenya if the guy who drove an old mango box filled with VHS tapes around the houses of suburban immigrants had any that week. I look at my knuckles as I cough. I'm white underneath.

She sits next to me and her hand hovers somewhere behind me. She hesitates, caught between a comforting rub and a hard thorough smack, to help me through my convulsions. I unclench my fist and hold it up as if to say, stop. I'm fine.

I hack with all my might to shift the rattle. I manage a trail of drool and bloody mucus into my hands, the toilet paper disintegrated and fallen to the floor as my body shakes.

'Are you okay?' she asks, rubbing my back with what she thinks is comfort. I flinch and arch until she stops. 'Are you okay?' she asks again.

I'm regulating my breathing, slowing it down to a steady controlled crawl. I look at her.

'I'm fine,' I say, in a closed way, to break off the conversation. 'I may not seem it but I am.'

'Why did you speak up for me?'

I look at her and shrug.

'I don't know,' I say.

'I'm Yinka,' she says, holding out her hand.

'Neha,' I reply. I hold up my phlegmy hand and shrug.

I pause, realizing I have not spoken to anyone in hours. 'That woman really wound me up. She doesn't get to tell me who to disapprove of,' I say slowly.

'You didn't need to do that,' she says. 'I was fine to ignore it.'

Yinka takes out a vape pen and sucks on it, blowing smoke sideways, away from me.

I cut the silence. 'My dad sat my brother and me down – this was after my brother declared he was going to be a comedian and we had already had the standard freak-out about sensible careers versus hobbies – and Dad said to him and to me, look, if you're going to do anything in this world, you have to understand that we live in a society ruled by mediocre straight white people. They get ahead simply by their straightness and their whiteness and their ability to assimilate, which is encoded in their mediocrity. In order for you to get anywhere in life, you have to be, at worst, twice as good as all the mediocre straight white people of this world. All of them. Because you have to stand out. Got that? I really remember that moment. I was wearing a T-shirt that had Michael Jordan on it, which now feels too narratively perfect or something. But I did. It was a hand-me-down from a sporty cousin. My dad refused to buy us new clothes because we had growing boy cousins. God forbid I ever wanted to wear a dress.'

I cough, almost to stop myself talking. This is the most in-depth interaction I've had in two months.

'I had the speech too,' Yinka says. 'Except my dad said the opposite. He said it was best not to try and be better than your average mediocre white man. Instead just be the most extreme version of yourself you can. That way, you're only ever competing with yourself.'

'Your dad had less of a chip on his shoulder than mine, I guess.'

'Or more. Which meant he tried to game the system rather than play it.' She looks at me.

'I have cancer,' I say, closing my eyes and leaning back into her fingers.

'I'm sorry,' Yinka says. 'I almost don't know how to react. Why are you telling me?'

'It's easier to tell a stranger than your family, I guess,' I tell her. 'I'd feel weird if you felt sorry for me.'

We sit in silence.

'I guess that's why I responded to that person,' I say. 'I wanted to control something. I don't know how to control cancer. I can control her. I can, alas, no longer control my body.' I look at my watch, feeling tired and wanting to be at home.

'There are some things you can't control,' Yinka says. She looks at me strangely. It feels like I've met her before. Either she looks familiar or my brain is misfiling her. 'Your mind can outlive your body.'

'They haven't worked out how to reanimate brains without their meat carcasses,' I say. 'Yet.'

'Most people use this as an opportunity for a reset. A reason to change their environment. Do something for good. An act of kindness. A selfish project. Go to a place they've always wanted to see. Learn a language. Write a novel. Eat meat again. Trace their family tree.' She pauses. 'My dad died from cancer last year. It's all been on my mind a lot.'

'My mum died of it not long after I was born,' I say. 'I never knew her.'

'You know what he did before he died? He did all this

research into his family. He wanted to trace how it happened. How our family came to be. He found a lot of comfort in it towards the end. Maybe that's something you can do. Something worthwhile. Find out how it all fits together. Trace your family tree,' she says, standing up. 'Find the patterns. It's your destiny.'

'Destiny isn't real,' I say.

She pretends not to hear me as she slips headphones on and walks in the opposite direction.

THURSDAY MORNING

GoTo: Work, Loads

There's a note stuck to my screen requesting my presence in Miles's office as soon as I arrive. I peel the note off and use some screen wipe to clean the monitor.

I look around.

My desk is given a wide berth. I'd like to think that between the smell of stale smoke on my clothes, the three large and imposing monitors, and my general fug of disdain, there's enough of a reason for people to ignore me. I don't get included in tea and coffee runs, unless there's a work-experience kid in who doesn't understand the lie of the land. I refuse to sign birthday cards and eat cakes as though we're anything other than colleagues. And if it's a work-based query, what's wrong with email? Email is easier to prioritize.

I scrunch up the note and place it on a pile I'm collating, of passive-aggressive notes from Miles. If there was ever a man to be twice as good as, he's probably called Miles.

I head off in his direction, coughing as I go.

The office feels oppressive today in that it operates on routine paths, consistencies and a steady flow of electricity and exhaustion. I'm thinking about what Yinka said, especially about patterns. I can see them all around me now. Maybe Yinka was right. Find the patterns.

Dad once asked why I don't like spontaneity.

We were at Pivo, the bar across the road from my flat. He had turned up, unannounced, because he said he hadn't seen me in a long time. I told him that we had designated spaces to operate in. Anything outside of that induced chaos. I asked if he had considered whether I had plans for the evening.

'I imagine, if you did, you would have said you weren't free,' he replied.

'Father, what you need to understand is, I'm always busy. Whether I am conventionally busy because I'm at the opera or having a dinner party discussing the politics of the day or just on a date, or whether I am busy because my brain is on, always on, problem-solving, trouble-shooting, I'm always doing something.'

'Your mother wasn't very spontaneous either,' he replied. 'She made plans and she stuck to them.'

'You say that derisively,' I said. 'Like I should disagree.'

'You know words like derisively, but you could never be bothered to learn Gujarati.'

'It's a dead language,' I replied. 'Their word for computer is computer. The more technology develops, the more you have to understand that the future is in English.'

'I just wanted a quick drink with my baby girl,' my dad said. 'Is that so bad?'

'I would have liked some notice,' I told him.

'The Gujarati word for computer is kampyuṭara,' Dad sighed.

'You're late,' Miles says, as soon as I enter his domain. I nod. 'We're launching the beta on the Glendale project today, and you're late.'

'It's done,' I reply. 'I made it live while I was on the bus,' I lie.

Actually I pressed go this morning at 5.00, because I couldn't sleep. I finished the build two weeks ago. I've been using the spare time to read through a stack of digital vintage-era *Star Trek* comics I've torrented.

'You're still late,' Miles repeats weakly.

My perspective has changed. Late to him is closer to death for me.

'I have cancer,' I say, sighing quietly.

Miles looks at me.

'Right,' he says. 'This is a bit of a derailment of our previous conversation. How bad is it?'

'Terminal. I need to take some time off.'

He rubs at a spot on his forehead that he has over-squeezed – it has now scabbed over. He rubs so hard the scab peels off. I watch it intently.

'Well, then, maybe the best thing to do is keep busy,' he offers. 'I mean, how bad is it?'

'I said it's terminal.'

'Right.' Miles places his hand on his chin, rubbing at an imaginary stubble. 'I just think – and correct me if I'm wrong, but I'm not, because I've read about it in a men's magazine – the worst thing you can do in situations like this is take a break from your normal schedule. You have to keep to it, or the cancer wins.'

'I need to take some leave,' I repeat.

'How long?' Miles leans forward, straining till he can see the IN DEVELOPMENT board behind me.

He scans over the Post-it notes colour-coded blue. Blue means Neha. He smiles. He has a tooth missing in his bottom set. It went yellow and then black for eighteen months before it disappeared. No one talks about it. Not least because the new appearance gives him a sinister smile, as though he's about to shake your hand before tearing it off and chowing down like a barbarian at a banquet with a leg of lamb. I can see his pink tongue grinding away at his back teeth. I've done coke with him once before a meeting we'd both been up all night preparing a pitch for. He thought it would be a bonding experience. I can see that Miles needs a bump. Best not to prolong his craving.

'I need a month.'

'Sure thing. Let me know the dates, once you've had a proper think about how long you need. As long as they don't coincide with any rollouts or site launches, you're all right. It's coming up to school holidays. Everyone and their nut sack is off to the beach, am I right?'

'I need it to be a paid sabbatical,' I say, quieter, calmly, as if an afterthought.

'A whole month?'

'Miles,' I say, knowing that using someone's name to address them directly shows you mean business. It's something I only ever do when I'm angry or want something very specific. 'I've worked here for over a decade. My salary doesn't really reflect statutory pay increases in line with inflation. I've more than earned my bonuses. And I have never taken a holiday. Not even at Christmas.'

Miles rubs his tongue along his teeth, thinking.

'That's your choice. It's all your choice, at the end of the day. Your choice if you want to work here. Your choice if you want to take time off. Heck, it's your choice if you want to come back to a job or not.'

'A month's paid sabbatical. I could get it as sick leave through my doctor if I wanted. I have a note from him.'

This is not true. I declined a sick note because initially I planned to keep calm and carry on.

Also, because Dr Hamid was doing my head in.

Miles pauses.

'Cancer, eh? That's a fucking shame, my friend. A fucking shame. Email Trudi the dates, CC me in. See you in a month… I hope. Don't go and die on me.'

'I'll try not to,' I say, smiling for his comfort.

'Where you off to, anyway?'

'Home. Just home.'

I need to look into this cancer, the same one that came for Mum. *Trace your family tree.* Maybe Yinka was right? I should have seen this coming. Perhaps I would have done if I had bothered to look at my family history.

Miles has moved on, in his head, and is now swiping furiously on his phone.

I return to my desk to start clearing the decks before taking a month off. Yinka was right in her own way. *Find out how it all fits together. Trace your family tree. Find the patterns. It's your destiny.*

I need to take ownership of this cancer. I need to understand it, to see the pattern and establish whether it can be disrupted. Raks plans to have kids, one day. Can I save them?

Anger

THURSDAY EVENING

GoTo: The Kobayashi Maru

At Starfleet Academy, there is a simulated test for trainee crews called the Kobayashi Maru, named after a ship marooned in the Klingon Neutral Zone. Your job is to decide whether to try and rescue it, thereby risking war with the Klingons, or sacrifice it to collateral damage. It's a purpose-built no-win situation designed to show that sometimes decisions needing to be made don't necessarily have a clear-cut right and wrong road, a best course of action and a worst course of action. Some things you can't win – it's how you don't win that counts. If you're going to not win, then do it with style, integrity and aplomb. Not with misery, depression and defeat. Not by cheating the system the way Kirk did – by surreptitiously reprogramming the simulator so that it was possible to rescue the freighter. The irony is, he was awarded a commendation, for 'original thinking'. The Kobayashi Maru wasn't one for fancy semantic solutions. Nor was it for cheating on; that defeated the lesson to be learned. It was to prove a point. That you can't win 'em all, champ. How do you deal with that?

Mika, the barmaid in Pivo, is my Kobayashi Maru.

She's doing a psychology degree at the local university. She works four shifts in the bar to pay for it and she drinks whole milk out of a glass every night, instead of water or a proper drink.

She is, by rights, everything I hate. If I have to put a label on it, she offends my lactose intolerance, anti-sustainable farming stance (if you want to be really ethical, charge us less than the battery-farmed shit); she thinks she's cleverer than me because I rewire computer networks and she rewires brains, and because I loathe subtitled films – the disconnect between observing action and reading speech is so disjointed I can never immerse myself in the experience.

But there is definitely something, definitely, definitely something about Mika. Partly, it is that she is small and has a permanent half-smile. Is that a smirk? Like Bruce Willis in *Die Hard*. When he's wisecracking about not having any shoes and how a simple office Christmas party can never be a simple office Christmas party when you're a maverick cop who plays by his own rules.

Raks told me I was drawn to her because she pays me attention when we're in the bar. Because I tipped her. So she listened to my stories about PHP malfunctions and office politics and Miles's coke habit driving the needs of his company. She half-smiled at my stories and I poured pennies into the bedpans meant to be tip jars. Partly it was because someone had told me once, drunk, that I was a waste of a girl, because I had no interest in my own formidable tits. Mika, sighing, served ice into his Jack and Coke (only cuntish lads drink Jack and Coke, usually at the point of the evening when lager is going to give them hiccups, or they're bloated from too much wheat) from the bucket she empties the beer trays into. She's dangerous like that.

She wears clothes like a hipster, brogues and light summer dresses with her hair tied up in ribbons. She has a tattoo of a cat on her forearm. I hate brogues and I hate cats. Discomfort and vermin masquerading as tweeness, both can fuck off. I have a tattoo of the Starfleet insignia (original series iteration, not *The Next Generation* or other) just above one of my formidable breasts. I like the comfort of knowing I can call Scotty to beam me up when needed.

Not that he has ever said those words.

Whenever I walk into Pivo, which is every evening after work, I worry that I am in love with her. Raks thinks I confuse love and friendship because I've never had either. I tell him he confuses humour and desperation. Either way, whatever I decide about our relationship, she is my Kobayashi Maru.

If I venture any further into developing a relationship with her, I might ruin the most human relationship I have with anyone outside my machines. Not to put too fine a point on it. Also, her manager might intervene and ask her to stop working there. He wouldn't bar me. I spend too much money there. The manager of Pivo, this particular suburb's premier Czech-themed bar, has a strict policy about his bar staff dating punters – so it's a no-win situation.

There isn't any way to cheat and reprogram the simulation. Mika is a problem to which there is no solution so maybe I can beat it instead of solving it. I Twitter-stalk her – she occasionally repurposes topical jokes I have told her – I click the viewable profile photos on her Facebook account; I find, after going back through her entire timeline, a Tumblr that belongs to her, that hasn't been updated in eleven months, called

Mika's Cats. I know everything about her and everything about her annoys me.

Is it love if it's born out of revulsion?

I sit at the bar, watching her serve a couple who also come in every day. They bring a small yappy dog. She drinks a glass of white wine and he a Guinness. Her lips have disappeared into her face but she persists anyway with thick red lipstick, and red nail polish covers her advancing cuticles. At half five every single day, she eats a plate of prawn cocktail, dipping individual prawns into a small silver bowl of orangey-pink sauce. She jerks the wine glass to her mouth in a sudden burst, gulping away, banging her dentures each time against the rim. He stares at a crossword he never comes close to completing.

Every evening I watch them and try to imagine my life with that amount of dependency. That level of routine. That amount of mercury. It makes me feel nauseous just thinking about it.

Those patterns.

THURSDAY CONTINUOUS

GoTo: Mucous Mud. True Love

My cancer has become a condition I've attributed colours to. These range from mucous-mud green through to sunny-day yellow.

Raks and I haven't spoken about it. I haven't heard from him for three months. Other than a favourite of a tweet I wrote linking to a video I'd made about PHP rankings. When he's on tour, we don't speak. We're close and we're not. We both acknowledge that the real twin for both of us is our different careers, and that's what we inevitably bond over, a shared work ethic. I just think what he does is ultimately pointless, even though I know stand-up comedians think theirs is the truest art form.

I remember seeing Raks doing a set which he ended by doing that bit of crowd work I loathe - who are you and what do you do? He picked on one of the only brown people in the audience, which considering I was also there, meant it was a particularly diverse night for him, and he asked if he had met her on shaadi.com.

Pathetic. Poor girl.

So when he faved my tweet about PHP malfunctions, I bet he did it sarcastically. As if to say, stop filling up the internet with highbrow tech. The internet was built by highbrow tech. But it was built for dick jokes.

I think about Mika. Watching her body wrenching down on the lever for the Guinness as though she is a machine deploying some sort of crusher, I feel my stomach fizz. Her half-smirk as she stares into the decorative condensation on the tap makes my throat feel dry.

I worry that I am in love.

I've never been in love. It was not part of the plan.

I find a guide to knowing whether you're in love, written by Justin Bieber. His songs are all about love, so it stands to reason that he probably knows a bit about it.

He describes the symptoms for knowing whether you're in love as: clammy hands, inability to talk fluidly, a heightened heart rate.

My hands are dry. Lukewarm. An inability to talk fluidly? I spend large portions of my day in silence staring at lines on a screen - I don't think talking fluidly is possible for anyone of my ilk. My heart rate is slower, fuck you, fucking cancer, so that too can be discounted.

I read on.

I apply the rest of the schema to my situation. *Have I completely forgotten my ex?* Well, seeing as I've never had a girlfriend, a boyfriend, an other half, a significant other, a pal, a fuck buddy, a thing, a bae, before, that's definitely a no. *Can I not stop thinking about her?* Apart from work and shows I'm currently watching, like *Breaking Bad* and *Fringe*, she does occupy a lot of my thoughts. If I had to quantify - maybe 10 per cent. But that's significant, given that 60 per cent of my thoughts are subconscious, at least 10 per cent is work, 15 per cent is on the shows I'm watching and 5 per cent is probably on miscellaneous stuff it's not worth individually listing because it's not significant enough to warrant its own line item. So suddenly 10 per cent seems like a shit-load. *Do I care about her?* This seems vague. Of course I care about her – I wouldn't want her to get rabies or be savagely mugged, but I extend that right to most of humanity, MOST of humanity, but caring for someone seems subjective. I don't want to just sleep with her; instead, I want to share laughs with her, know what she's thinking. *Do I find her quirks charming?* Seeing as she represents everything I hate about the world and I'm still interested seems, to me, to show that I am indeed willing to tolerate - tolerate being the operative word - her quirks. *Do we have great chemistry?* Between a technologist like me and a psychologist like her, we're bound to have great chemistry...

I laugh to myself. She looks up from the wine she's pouring.

I stare intently at my phone, flushing red.

Once the couple have paid, she walks over to me.

'What's so funny, Spectacles?' Mika says, using a nickname she's tried a couple of times to disguise the fact that she doesn't always remember my name.

'Oh,' I say, flustered. 'You know.'

'Tell me. God, I'm bored. Make me laugh, Spectacles.'

'It's nothing, Testicles,' I reply, using the nickname for her I am also road-testing. Partly as a way to associate the nickname I hate with balls so she'll have a Pavlovian response and stop calling me Spectacles. Maybe she'll also come to hate testicles themselves through my conditioning. Thus far, she hasn't objected. She wouldn't, though. She may not like the nickname but she will enjoy the fact that I am a very generous tipper. 'I've just thought of something funny,' I say.

'Teeeeeelll meeeeee,' she says, leaning on the bar trying to place her face between mine and my phone.

'You had to be there.'

The article continues. *Do I notice other women as much?* This depends. I think most people are stupid so I tend to hardly notice anyone. Not for any reason other than that I'm not sure I need to. I notice her because I like her. *Do I love spending time with her?* Jesus, Justin, could you be more generic? Well, I ensure I make myself present at every one of her shifts. *Do I mind compromising sometimes?* Tolerating her various quirks is one big compromise. *Do my other priorities take a back seat?* No. *Do I think about the future with her in it?* I don't have a future, I have a cancer. I am only thinking about the present and about working on the past.

That's that. Too many nos. I'm not in love. I have cheated the Kobayashi Maru test. I throw my phone down on to the bar in triumph.

I hear my mobile making a shrill noise and look down at it.

I must have accidentally hit the YouTube tab because a Bollywood song is playing. A woman in a black sequinned dress is dancing and singing even though she holds the microphone at arm's length. People applaud. A man in a red tuxedo tries to get her attention. The song sounds familiar.

I can't quite place it.

SATURDAY AFTERNOON

GoTo: Data. Sets

My mother died of the same cancer that I have.

It infuriates me that I didn't see this coming.

Physiology has no coincidence. DNA has patterns. Established ones that run the helix of time. I'm trapped by my own genes. By the consequences of who fucked whom.

I don't really understand why things like my cancer weren't predicted. It's as though we assume that leading a healthy life, having a balanced diet, eating your five-a-day, exercising regularly, making positive decisions, staying happy is going to free you from your genes. It won't.

It's not hard to spot the patterns. I have lung cancer onset by pulmonary fibrosis and scar tissue forming in my lungs. So did my mother. I don't think Ba did – she told me once she would inevitably die of a broken heart.

My dad has diabetes. Raks has diabetes.

Patterns.

Trying not to notice them is tough.

How did I not see this coming? It's a blind spot in my knowledge. I knew of my mother's condition, but my need to know as little of her as possible, to keep her as a spectre, meant I was blinkered. My efforts to forget that she ever existed because she has had zero impact on my life made me misplace even the simplest details about her: the tragic cancer, her murdered father, her run-over brother, her ridiculous husband, her dying early, her twin children who were motherless. If I had seen it coming, I would have tried to have different goals in life. I wouldn't have ploughed so much time and energy into this company. I probably wouldn't have travelled any more – I would have retired early and made films, written scripts, recorded that acoustic comedy-songs album I planned after I drunkenly wrote the lyrics to a song called 'Rubber Girlfriend', about having a sex doll as a life partner. Imagine Raks's face. If I was the funny one. It would be worth doing just to see his reaction. That would be the ultimate comedy.

Heading home from Pivo one night, I stub my toe tripping over the fountains in the pedestrianized town centre. They're rancid stagnant ponds that look deep enough for a child to drown in. The step down into them is low and they are deep. I miss avoiding them because I'm thinking about something. These patterns. They're bothering me.

When I get home, I clean the whiteboard that I've put up in my living room and write down the names of any family members I can think of. I realize, halfway through, that I'm using a Sharpie, a permanent marker, instead of a dry-wipe one.

'Oh, well,' I say to the room, to the picture of me and Leonard Nimoy framed above my monitors. 'I'm dying so who the fuck cares.'

I can only think of ten people, which is ridiculous. I get to the point where I'm writing down things like Snaggle Tooth Auntie; All the Gold Rings Uncle; Cousin Who Has Definitely Sexually Assaulted Someone Because He Boasted About It to Raks and Raks, to My Surprise, Didn't Tell Him What a Cunt He Was (I write him down as Grope Cousin); Wig Auntie; Wig Uncle; Wig Uncle With Bad Breath; Pharmacist Uncle; Very Vocal About My Childlessness Auntie; and on and on. They're a blur of masas, masis, fuvs, fais, mamis, mamas, faibas and kakas and kakis. I know them by salutation only.

And Ba.

No one knows what happened to her. She just disappeared. I wondered about her. She was kind to me and Raks when we went to see her in Kenya. She kept telling us the entire trip it would be the last time anyone saw her. She was ready to go. And soon afterwards, she stopped writing, we stopped writing and our link with Kenya was cut.

She showed me kindness. She tried to get me to relax into life. She tried to sell me on destiny. She also tried to convince me to let go a little, that everything was pre-written, which is laughable and unscientific. Raks bought into her narrative and took from it that he was owed something. She had had such sadness in her life – I suppose the idea that life was pre-written meant that at least someone was watching over her; that she hadn't quite lost everyone.

The relatives who are alive are written down in green. The ones who aren't are in red.

I put Ba in red. There's no way she can still be alive.

Then I sit at the computer and start typing the names, along with their alive-or-dead status, and what they died of, to the best of my knowledge.

I should phone my dad and check some of these details. Probably all of them. I'm not the most up to date on the movements of the Jani family.

At some point, I fall asleep in my favourite position, curled up on the two-seater leather sofa I spent nearly one thousand pounds on because it's so comfortable, even though I can't stretch out on it fully.

The flicker of the television screen showing sitcoms from a dedicated comedy channel, together with the frenetic whirr of fans in my computer tower and the space-flight twinkling stars of monitors, soothe me into a deep sleep.

In the middle of the night, I think I hear the Naseeb song come on the television again. I'm discombobulated and don't know if I'm imagining it.

I wake up the next morning to find that, drunkenly coughing in my sleep, I have hacked up a thick slug of phlegm that hangs from my mouth like a fish hook. The television is off.

MONDAY MORNING

GoTo: Doing Drugs with Your Boss Creates an Uncertain Work Environment

Miles calls me.

'You can't leave,' he says firmly, masking panic, I assume.

'I can. I have. Thank you. For the memories,' I add, in case he thinks I'm being sarcastic.

'When did you clear your desk?' he asks.

'This morning. I came in at six. I couldn't sleep.'

'What about the Robertson project?'

'Debugged…'

'The landing page?'

'Working now...'

'The...'

'I'll save you some time, Miles,' I say. 'I finished them all last week and over the weekend. I have cancer. I'm dying. As you know. I don't like unfinished business. And I could go at any time. So I thought I'd finish up my projects so I don't have you rueing my name as I head for the afterlife.'

'Aren't you an atheist?'

'Even atheists repent on their deathbeds. Hedging their bets. Just in case.'

'You can't leave,' Miles says. 'You just can't. We need you.'

'I am fully aware of how indispensable I am to your company. But this is a good thing. Maybe you'll find someone else to nurture for the next fourteen years. Or you'll find someone to have a less co-dependent relationship with.'

'Neha, look, I've never told anyone this...' He pauses.

This is it, this is the moment he professes his undying love for me and I tell him what a disgusting turd he is, how his constant sniffing, inability to iron shirts, daily lunch of Babybels and cold cuts of meat is enough to make me vomit. That when he touched up my knee when we were doing that bump in the disabled toilet before the pitch, I wanted to take his hand and break it over the cistern before shoving it as far into the U-bend as possible before flushing and kicking him in the nuts with Tracy from HR's stilettoes.

'If you leave, I can't give you your profit-share points. I can't cash them.'

'Why?' I ask.

'They don't really exist. There hasn't been enough growth

in the company for me to be able to pay them. And I imagine you could initiate legal proceedings, but you have to ask yourself, do you have the time? With your condition?'

I hear him laugh – a quick ha-ha.

'That's fine,' I say slowly. 'Remember the ten-thousand-pound equipment budget you gave me?'

'Yes.'

'I'm keeping it all. I've already taken it. You can have it back when I die.'

I hang up the phone and smile.

Smiling makes me cough.

I wish I had a permanent scanner attached to my lung, projecting its image on to one of my monitors, so I could observe the cancer, get to know her. I've called the cancer Nisha.

My phone rings.

Assuming it's Miles, I let it ring out.

I look at my phone later. It's my dad. I haven't spoken to him for three months now. Sometimes I don't even miss it. Those are the days when I remember I haven't spoken to him or he tries to get in touch. The rest of the time, he doesn't figure in any of my thoughts.

I call him back.

I need his help.

TUESDAY LUNCHTIME

GoTo: Fathers Always Pay

Dad meets me in Pivo.

He comes with a plastic bag filled with my favourite snacks from the Gujarati shop opposite his house. He goes there most mornings to get deep-fried breakfasts, freshly cooked samosas and milky sugary masala tea. I'm surprised I haven't had a phone call in the middle of the night saying he's had a heart attack.

I know it will come one day. Although his father drowned. Who knows whether the pattern of circumstance replicates? Between diabetes, a bad diet and the threat of drowning, my father has not got long left.

He has taken to bachelor living with the verve of a student.

Still, this simple act of parenting, feeding a child – though I will throw all the food into my already-overflowing bin when I get home – charms me in its quaintness.

He walks with a hunch now. Because our meetings are sporadic, I see the change in him. He looks older each time. Which I know isn't an insightful thing to record. That's just how time works. He doesn't look as though his body is embracing, or even coping with, the marching-on of life. He limps when he walks. He's wearing open-toed sandals today, with a thick cushioned sole. One of his big toenails has turned black, readying itself for an imminent departure. His fingers tremble as he hands me the bag of food. We hover, both wondering whether the other will embrace. It begins to get awkward so I take the lead and sit down. He sits down too. I stand up again.

'Pint?'

'Please,' he says. 'And nuts. Salted. Not dry-roasted. Maybe they could cut up an onion to mix in? And green chilli?'

'I'll ask,' I say, knowing I won't.

As Mika pours the pints, I look at her forearms. They are splotchy today. As though she's had an allergic reaction to something.

'What's up with your arms?' I ask.

'Oh, you noticed,' she says, without breaking eye contact with the taps of lager. 'It's a new make-up I'm wearing called cheap cleaning fluid that my skin is allergic to...'

She eye-rolls at me.

'That sucks,' I say, in the absence of any way to solve her problem either practically or emotionally.

'Your father?' she asks, nodding to my dad who sits with his eyes closed, head bowed, asleep probably.

'Yeah,' I say. 'Tuesday lunchtime seemed like a good moment for a family reunion.'

'I hope he doesn't sleep through the whole thing,' she says, handing me the lagers.

I tell her to add them to my tab. Part of me, now that I'm unemployed, wonders if I'll live to pay it off. Another part of me hopes I do. They've been good to me here. Well, except for the bouncer who told me on Saturday night that he wouldn't let me in wearing trainers. Dress sexier, I was told. It's Saturday night, for fuck's sake, I was reminded. I pointed out men walking in, one even wearing the same trainers I was, more battered than mine. Yeah, but this is Saturday night in Watford – we have appearances to keep up.

Dad has placed a five-pound note on my side of the table.

I push it back to him. The movement causes the uneven table to wobble and spill lager where his hands rest. He opens his eyes, casually, as though he has been playing possum.

He picks up the five-pound note and waves it at me.

I shake my head. 'I put it on my tab.'

'Take it,' he says aggressively. 'What else do I have to spend money on? Other than my children.'

'A fiver doesn't cover the round, Dad. It's fine.'

He extracts his wallet and pulls out another fiver. Folding one into the other, he places them next to my pint glass.

I leave them there.

'So, my beautiful daughter,' he says, clasping his shivering fingers together. 'You know that Manish is having a janoi next week? Shall I pick you up on my way?'

'Sure,' I say. 'Dad, listen. I need your help.'

I realize, the second those words slip from my mouth, that they're badly chosen. Asking for his help rather than demanding the information I need is the easiest way for him to try and slide into my life again. I start to retract.

I don't want him to know about the cancer. It's nothing he can help me with. And the last thing I want is his sympathy because that sympathy will be laced with a mournful regret about my dead mother, rather than any genuine concern for me.

'It's no big deal,' I add, trying to play the whole thing down. 'I just need information.'

'How can I help?' Dad leans forward on to the table until he occupies the entire space between us.

'I'm building a database. For a medical company,' I lie.

He doesn't understand what I do. I can make him think it's database design. He probably doesn't even know what a database is.

'I need test data. Can you email me the names of everyone in our family going back as far as you can, both your side and my mum's side? Their relation to me. What they died of. What age. What country. I might require more filters and more information but I won't know till I sort this initial data set and see what it tells me.' I pause. 'Please,' I add, hastily.

Dad leans back the moment he realizes this help I need requires work from him.

'Impossible,' he says. He looks around, for an invisible audience waiting for the punchline. 'I've forgotten the password to my email.'

He laughs and slaps himself on the thigh for emphasis when he sees his joke hasn't had the desired effect.

He and Raks have a long-running competition to see who can make me laugh. It's been running for fourteen years. So far Raks is winning two to one.

The numbers are so low I can tell you exactly what each one did to make me laugh.

Raks fell over trying to tickle my father.

My father fell off the toilet reaching for another toilet roll.

Raks prank-called my father and pretended to be the bank foreclosing on Dad's photocopying shop.

I sip from my drink and look around the room. Mika is leaning on the bar, head resting on hands, eyes closed. There is no one else here. Dad stops laughing and I turn back to him.

'So?' I say.

He shrugs. 'Sure. I can do this for you in a few weeks. I'm really concentrating on booking a holiday at the moment. Lots of research. What do you think? St Lucia or Dubrovnik?'

'That's your either/or?'

'For the prices I've been quoted, yes. It has to be all-inclusive. You think I will stay at a self-catering apartment? I would forget to buy milk for my tea all the time. Supply my own toilet rolls. There would be no one to talk to except for foreign television channels.'

I pull out a tablet from my bag and place it on the table.

'What's wrong with right now?'

'You want me to show you the places I'm thinking of?'

I pause. I nearly laugh in his face. This man is so ridiculous. This is why we don't talk. One of many reasons. The great storyteller, in love with his own place in a story.

'Let's start with Raks and me, and our cousins, and work backwards from that.'

Dad gets up and stands, hovering by the table for ten seconds or so. He looks around Pivo, for some reason fixating on the lighting.

'I'd better go and relieve myself. This is not a quick-pint conversation.'

'I just need a list. Not their life stories,' I say, looking at the time.

'Never stay the full whack, do you?'

The phrase 'the full whack' stings. I think about my cousin Bhima. One of the smokers in my family, my first enabler because I used to steal cigarettes from his room when he was at work. Raks and I would pay his mum a surprise visit. She lived down the street from Dad. One of us, in rotation, would talk to Auntie about schoolwork, about Bollywood films, and the other would sneak upstairs, into Bhima's room, and steal his fags. He probably knew. He probably didn't care. He had made the long hard journey in our family from secret-shame smoker to open smoker, so didn't need to count, ration or be careful about concealment. Growing up, we had an abundance of family functions. Every Sunday, for they were always Sundays, to accommodate the ones with shops, there was a function, in someone's house, a community hall, a school hall, a park. Raks and I would rather be anywhere else. We thought ourselves independent sorts who wanted to smoke cigarettes and repeatedly browse the aisles of video shops and record shops just in case that week was the week Portishead or Radiohead released an album we hadn't heard about. We put in the time with those functions; just not much of it. We'd show up late, in time to have twenty minutes to say hello to family members (a hello in a problematic accent or a Hari Aum, sometimes a Jay Shree Krishna if we were feeling fancy) before food was served. Raks would load up a plate. I grabbed a samosa and a kachori. We ate and ran.

One day, Bhima, smoking outside, saw us as we left. We were good at not saying goodbye, only hello. That way, we didn't have an extra twenty minutes of 'Why you leaving, you just got here, have you eaten?'

With a cigarette in his mouth, which was at the time the coolest thing in the world to me, he said, 'Why are you going?'

Raks stared at the ground. I smiled.

'Homework,' I said blandly.

'You know, sometimes you have to stay the full whack,' he said, before turning back to the conversation he was having with another of our cousins whose name neither of us knew.

There was disappointment in how he turned away. He knew we were phoning in our appearances, not interested in spending time with our cousins.

We were found out.

We thought we were so slick but he knew. He knew everything the entire time.

Being seen, it was so mortifying to me as a teenager.

The full whack.

*

'Why do you want to know all these things?' Dad asks, returning from the toilet. I cough, trying to keep it sounding as calm as possible.

I shrug. 'For work,' I say again. 'And Ba, tell me about Ba. What happened to her?'

'Ah, yes,' Dad says. He takes a long slow sip of his lager. 'You want me to tell you the story of how your mother and I fell in love, do you not?'

'Not again, Dad,' I say, pleading.

'Not a problem,' he tells me.And he begins. Starting as he always does, with the leaning against the wall.

'I have no reason to be anywhere,' he says. 'I find myself in an in-between world, with no purpose, except to lean with my back against the wall, across the road from Nisha's amee and papa's house. . .'

And like always, I listen, hoping for a clue to how I got here.

Bargaining

TUESDAY EVENING

GoTo: Research. Development

I stare at the records for these seventeen family members and their bios. I scan over the A3 sheet of paper with the family tree I sketched out when I got home from Dad talking at me. There's a daunting number of names of people I don't know, mostly male; the women all seem to have the same name but the salutation after it, faiba, masi, mami, etc., makes them crystal clear in my brain. I realize how many men in our family I call uncle rather than kaka, mama, fuva, masa, because I don't know their actual names.

They never want to talk to you if you're female. At functions, you're expected to serve them while they sit in silence, occasionally relaying the contents of a letter from 'India' to each other. It's as nebulous as that. The letter is from India. Not from a named person. Sometimes, there will be cricket chat. Other times, they will discuss problems they are having with builders or workmen.

The hardware I build, the systems I facilitate through the boxes I make, they make all of their lives easier. I am of equal status to them and thus sit with them. I have no interest in cackling and gathering in the kitchen with the women, to perform the servile tasks expected of me. And yet their names are the ones I retain. Not the sea of miscellaneous uncles, wearing thin white polyester shirts and navy blue trousers, chewing tobacco and arguing about who hates Muslims more.

I stare at these names.

I like to be process-orientated, even when building a project from a small scale up to its full potential. I love every part of the process, from the innocuous beginnings of data collection and building subsets, through to pushing the information to reveal new and interesting things.

These names correspond to a folder on my desktop called 'Photos of the Janis'. The file name for each picture is clearly labelled with the names of its subjects. I'm trying to build a piece of functionality that can marry a visual representation of the family tree with corresponding head shots of my family members: the cousins, the second cousins, the uncles, the uncles of uncles, the first wife, the second wife, the grandparents, their servants, the nieces, nephews, the alive, the dead, the forgotten about and the ostracized, everyone, no exclusions.

Any photograph that isn't a portrait will correspond to a date and event in the timeline. Every photograph will correspond to a location in the world, because the family spans India, Kenya, Aden, London, Leicester, Canada and Wales. Every photograph will correspond to an approximation of the date it was taken in the timeline. Once I have those parameters, I can start to measure what role cause of death plays in our lives and vice versa. Once I establish the landscape, I can spot the patterns within it. I can already see, though, that this is just not enough. I know it's not sufficient simply to upload these photos with no context into some functionality with no function. That would just be Facebook.

What happened to Ba? The stray thought itches my skull.

It's an easy enough task but what does it do? What sense of my family does it give? Who does it celebrate as its characters, who lived, loved, fucked, argued, made up, poked fun at each other, poked fun at themselves? This is the problem with history. There is no way you can contextualize anything with a series of photographs. Everyone is frozen in time as a statistic, not as a person.

I file through the seventeen records I've already created.

I know nothing about these people except when they were born, when they died (if they're dead), how they died, thanks to Dad, and how they're related to him, and thus to the grander structure of the entire family.

It's a small set of data but it's a start.

What did they like? What did they dislike? How did they really view their fellow family members? They can't all have got on. I remember arguing with Raks about him being sick on my sofa and not cleaning it up, just going home and leaving me to deal with it. He didn't feel guilty. He thought it was funny and it ended up in his stand-up. I am material for him. My need to show him how to behave like a functioning human.

So we can learn. We don't know anything about the past, we don't care, we look back only to romanticize. We never learn anything. We only reminisce.

I tell Raks his stand-up is about nostalgia. About looking back on the past with no real analysis. No need to try and understand it and what impact that has on futures. If I can prevent the next generation of Janis from getting these genes, these disgusting ailments, the diabetes, the heart disease, the angina, the high blood pressure, the cancer, the fibrosis, then maybe they can stop making our mistakes. How much of that is about the secret lives of immigrants, what we did when no one was looking, as well as when they were?

Accessing some dark websites, I try to flesh out these records, see if I can find news stories about these family members, like local news documents of when he won this spelling contest and when she won that football tournament, these will help.

I hack the records office's Mobile Gateway. It isn't even a cloud network like I initially assumed. It works on an outdated system that's pre-Cloud, meaning that all the computers in the local area are hooked up to the local authority's network and you effectively have two desktops. You have your normal one, which works as fast as your machine works, and your Mobile Gateway desktop, which you, as a local authority employee, are expected to use; it's exceptionally slow. You share the bandwidth with everyone else using the remote desktop and the further you are away from the server, the slower the thing works. I mirror an email address and request a replacement password.

Every record, every scan, every microfiche is logged in this system. I can find anything I need. I don't need newspaper reports or anything like that, yet. I'm after facts to begin with, so I can build a framework. Once I have facts, I can move on to profile-building with education results, health records, criminal and civil disputes, logged complaints. Some of these would involve a deeper hack into the local authority's system.

I look for news reports on the aftermath of the Diwali show.

I find a couple of stray references that I download to review later.

I create search terms around the family tree. I check through names on the list then delete the file paths, realizing that because my family is largely unimaginative and thus repeated a lot of the names for their children and grandchildren, I can't just port over records and expect them to match up to the right people. I have to do this manually for each branch of family at a time. It's annoying to see that two Manishs attended the same university and did the same course, getting the same degree. It may have been decades apart but still it makes it difficult for me to allocate these records to a home within my framework.

SUNDAY AFTERNOON

GoTo: Rest. Relaxation

My energy wanes and each evening, I find myself in a new pattern. I watch episodes of *The Next Generation* and think about death.

I drink wine by myself.

I make my famous egg-fried rice. Special ingredient: sugar.

I take the bins out.

I read. I stare at words until they blur. I Google Image search photos of cancerous lungs, print them off and leave them around my flat. I think about smoking. I visualize myself smoking. I mime smoking. I drink coffee and my hands do the air cigarette. I get into deep searches looking for information about whether e-cigarettes work with the ol' cancer.

I start referring to my ailments as the ol' cancer.

Out of breath? The ol' cancer.

Council tax late? The ol' cancer.

No milk? The ol' cancer.

I develop a character for it. It's a smoker, with a raspy, fast-talking 1920s New York reporter/gangster voice.

Nowlistenhereseewhatsthebigideaigotascoopforyouyou-gotcancercancerItellsya.

I feel lost. I sleep a lot. I don't reply to emails as much. No one emails me now I don't have a job.

I long for sleep but it eludes me. Frustrated, night after night, I wish for death.

I look up ways to relax online. I trawl through lists of local spas, potential hobbies, social groups and cinema times. Nothing is working.

I watch episodes of *The Next Generation*. I watch as Worf and Troi go from colleagues to lovers with almost no signposting. I marvel at how much taller than her he is, at how, for all its utopian diversity, *Star Trek*'s creative decision to make her wear such a degrading skin-tight outfit is both genius and appalling.

I don't feel relaxed.

I track down the song that's been haunting me. It's from a Hindi film called *Naseeb*. It's the title song, about destiny. The plot of the film sounds flimsy. In it, four friends win the lottery and two of them get together to murder a third member of the syndicate, and frame the fourth for it. Years later, his three estranged sons come together to exact revenge. Naseeb means destiny. The title song, pretty repetitive, pretty disco, presupposes that all of this has been written by someone else, probably God. Destiny, it suggests, is being written by others, not us.

Are you written to be with me or not?
Am I written to be with you or not?
Are you written to be with me or not?
Am I written to be with you or not?
This isn't something we can know, only that person knows
Who has written everyone's destiny.

I can hear this song, playing on a transistor radio, as a sea breeze blows past palm trees and through the open door of a one-room house.

I am six years old, maybe eight. I can't quite remember. I am with my twin brother. We are staying with her, with Ba. The song is playing on the radio.

Now it shows up everywhere – on YouTube autoplay, on the radio, from passing cars, looping endlessly, as though it is sending me a message, from Ba, that all of this was pre-written. I hear it in its original form, remixed, sampled into bhangra and hip-hop, whimsical slow white-girl acoustic cover version, chopped and screwed, with an obnoxious big-beat backing.

Each morning, I return to writing this algorithm. Initially, before my energy surge comes, I feel slow to start.

No, a voice in my head says. You're about to cop it, cark it, die. Cos of the ol' cancer. Make the most out of life.

I hate walking. I hate socialized institutional eating. I hate dinner-party conversations, team-building games, ice-breakers, presentations, speeches, discussing art, making art, talking in any language other than C++ or Dothraki – what is there to do with life?

Spend time with loved ones.

I look at my brother's tour schedule. I smile. He's in Bracknell tonight. The big time, I mouth to myself. I have no interest in seeing my father.

I stand up and walk to the window that looks out on to the high street. I peep behind the curtain and the net curtain. Pivo is open. I long for it.

My tongue feels dry.

Every online source tells me I need to drink more fluids.

I think about water.

It offers no comfort. I grab a hat, slip my feet into my shoes and pick up my house keys, jingling them. I head out for a drink.

SUNDAY NIGHT

GoTo: Patterns

I return home from Pivo, drunk, my eyes half open as I stumble around the flat. It took a pint I couldn't finish and two shots of rum but I am blotto. I return to find the door open and my keys in the lock. I thought I locked up. I'm too pissed to dwell on it and I enter my flat, calling out for Ba, in case she has come to see me.

Silence.

I sit down at my desk. Relying on my overfamiliarity with my keyboard, I perform a manual export of information about all of my family members. For each one I pull out date of birth, location of birth, date of death, cause of death as these have the parameters I can base all my pattern-mapping algorithms on later.

I port over eighteen of my family members, with thirty-six to go. I learn nothing new about any of these people. They remain names and basic details on a screen. The only thing that sticks out to me is how many of the females have the same genetic condition.

I am suddenly not as individual as I thought.

I pour myself a whisky, from a bottle I was given as a Christmas present from work. It's cheap and largely goes untouched, except for when I'm this drunk and need to sip something that slowly brings me back to consciousness. Each sip is like a jolt of electricity to my cerebral cortex. I'm weak in this moment. I know where I've stashed a pouch of tobacco. I see a stray rolling paper on my desk, poking out from under my keyboard. I pull at it, as carefully as I can in this state of inebriation, so as not to rip it. I tear some card from the top of the box the whisky bottle came in, and I roll it into a cylinder. It is my glossy roach. The fumes from the embossed foil will probably do my lungs more damage than inhaling the smoke filter-less. With an expertise and practised steadiness from two decades of drunkenly rolling cigarettes, the only level of Zen or calm I have ever attained in this state, I make myself a fag. I light it and listen to the paper crinkle as the tip glows amber for 'get ready'. I inhale, exhale and think about the ol' cancer. The tobacco forms a protective fuzzy shell around my entire body. I feel blessed to be alive.

The numbers don't lie. It seems as though it was always inevitable I was going to die of cancer. The numbers speak for themselves. The probability is too much to ignore. I know it's a small data set but the repetition of DNA patterns in a bloodline is inescapable. I'm bewildered, I don't understand why I'm discovering this now. If the small data set of my family is anything to go by, this should have been obvious to me. A thought pops into my head – if the numbers don't lie, I can map the cancer correctly. I can find it in genetic code. I can predict the occurrence of cancerous cells. I'm God. I'm a cartographer, building a map of the future. You can't beat the numbers, there is no way. Good data does not lie. And good data can tell stories, lead us through difficult times, map out our lives, give us life itself. And take it away.

If you can't beat the numbers, the statistical inevitabilities, that pepper history, is there ever any point trying to live your life? Would you pursue your same hopes and dreams if you knew, statistically, you would end up childless and unmarried, or would that spur you on to be the best you could be in that particular inevitability you were cursed with? It becomes a rod for your back. I don't know if my family members have the brain space to handle such information. It's like time travel.

I think of that moment in *Back to the Future*, when Doc Brown talks about the catastrophe that awaits anyone who meets themselves in the future. Or in the past.

'I foresee two possibilities. One: coming face-to-face with herself thirty years older would put her into shock and she'd simply pass out. Or two, the encounter could create a time paradox, the result of which could cause a chain reaction that would unravel the very fabric of the space-time continuum and destroy the entire universe.'

Destroy the entire universe, I think. I smile. Now there's a legacy I can live with.

But then Yinka said to find the patterns. The patterns are important to recognize. We can only break them once we are aware of them. They are important to disrupt. Let's imagine this: if out of the eighteen people I've looked at so far, six of them have had this condition, that means, in our family, one third of us is afflicted by this bad DNA. If we then analyse the medical records of those who have the same condition outside my family, what does this mean for us? Can we trace the condition back to the source? Can we identify it in children before it manifests itself and have it prevented? What I'm considering is bigger than me, perhaps. Bigger than my family.

My ba believed in destiny, my father believes in coincidence, I believe in patterns and consistency, and my brother believes in the manifest destiny of his own male ego.

This isn't destiny and this isn't coincidence. This isn't the male ego. This is a pattern. I can do something for the world.

All those years I hid at my desk, building hardware systems to improve voice recognition for cinema booking systems, to improve remote cellular tinkerings when your smartphone goes bust, to make the algorithm on Shazam faster and more accurate, and I thought I was doing good. Maybe this is my manifest destiny. Maybe this is my purpose. To identify every child in the world who will have this condition, and get it identified early.

Save the universe. Doc Brown, I need to save it, not destroy.

START: MONDAY MORNING. END: FRIDAY EVENING

GoTo: Phase 1 – Montage

My daily patterns emerge; my cough worsens. Data is successfully entered by hand and virtually ported; I scope out a plan to track cancer locally, then regionally, then nationally, then continentally, then internationally, through various hacks to medical and insurance databases; my breath gets shorter and shorter. There are four answerphone messages from work asking for help with bugs found in the Glendale rollout. There are two emails from my dad asking for dinner. There is food ordered through websites, which goes uneaten. There is no one else I contact aside from this. I spend four days on phase 1, which is the basic data sets, and they all contain enough information to build a framework. I lose weight. I attempt a hack into more records held in the local authority database. I'm able to access library records, council tax records, school records and health records. The latter is easier to get hold of than I realize because doctors, it would appear, didn't think too much about their passwords. I lose my appetite. The idea of chewing food feels revolting. I order some protein shake powder from Amazon. I dream of Ba and I think about calling my dad but don't. I find oral accounts of immigrants moving on to the same four streets our family lived on in the early days. I match up quantitative remembrances with facts and cross-check them with other data paths to ensure I'm not assuming things, that I am entering only fact.

The family tree is built. Every breath I take is now audible. I have everyone who lived in the UK entered. I have photographs associated from specific ages for all: two years old, twelve years old, twenty-two years old, and older where relevant, up until current age. I note with interest that my generation has been childless. The Jani family is dying out and there is nothing to stop their tale of mediocrity and immigration from being forgotten by a history that prizes only news and big wins.

I half remember a proverb that I think Ba told me.

Until the lion learns to speak, the tale of the hunt will glorify the hunter.

I search for Kenyan proverbs trying to find this one, but I can't. Instead I come across one that simply says, a man without a donkey is a donkey.

I think about a donkey called Little Vijay that I met in Kenya. How much I loved it. I can trace my feelings of coldness towards people to that donkey's demise. Whatever kindnesses Ba and Raks showed me in the aftermath of the incident pale in comparison to the memory of a relative beating that animal to death.

I widen my searches. I start hitting increasingly fragmented search results hoping for more than just listings of names or caches of articles.

And then I find one about my dad making history in 1968, years before I was born.

SATURDAY MORNING

GoTo: Shock. Awe

I dream that I'm asleep and I can't breathe.

I don't subscribe to dreams being anything other than a warning from your body.

I dream literally. That's fine. I don't need to swim in jelly to know that I'm anxious about something.

I wake myself so I can sit up and breathe.

Once I've caught my breath, and my survival instinct has stopped pulsating, I think about my dad.

I pick up my phone and look at the scanned newspaper clipping again. It's still on my browser.

Dad, you tiny goat.

In 1968, he tries to buy a house, is refused sale on account of the colour of his skin, is convinced by the newly formed Commission for Racial Equality to bring the case to court, making it the first-ever case to be tried under the recently instituted Race Relations Act.

He loses.

On a technicality. According to the news story, the potentially landmark historic case was lost because lawyers were so quick to bring it to trial, to try and showcase the powers of the Race Relations Act, that motions weren't filed correctly, a key witness was not interviewed, and crucially, the barrister was not fully briefed. And so they lost. My father lost.

He never told me about this.

I don't subscribe to the theory that, being children of immigrants, my brother and I are any different from anyone else and owed more or less. I want and expect the same. I create and uncreate my own opportunities. I am afforded the same, legally protected potential for advancement as everyone else.

This case, my father never talked about it. It feels important. This is the burden of immigrants, to be good immigrants. We only become the good type once we've transcended the stereotypes of benefit-scrounging and job-stealing. And we can only do that by being successful at sports, or winning national talent shows, or by baking delicious cakes. I am not a good immigrant, because my skills aren't transferable, in a broad sense. No one is standing over the coders of tomorrow saying, well, this young South Asian coder, she is a good model for her people. I can never transcend.

The more I think about it, the more I realize that I wish not to outstrip race. I can never truly reach a point higher than the one that belongs to my skin tone. And that is enough.

Even though I was born here, I can never be a good immigrant. My father, if he had won this case, would have stayed a bad immigrant. Because he was challenging the system by showing that sometimes people aren't afforded the same safe space to create and uncreate their own opportunities. Instead, my father was highlighting societal, institutional barriers in place to stop us from running the same race with the same trainers and the same conditions and the same training. The best thing he could have done in that situation was not let anyone know he had even been involved in such a challenge.

I used to wonder why these insular communities and networks of immigrant families spring up and why they never want to integrate, let alone assimilate.

Now I completely understand their mentality.

Why put your head above water? You're not wanted here. The systems are there for equal opportunity and for social mobility and for the advancement of man, but not you.

It's like a secret life of immigrants. We create magic and pretend it's mundane. When Raks told me how much he was offered to do an advert for an Indian lager as opposed to a regular one, I wanted to tell him it was worth selling out over. My brother has principles, he says. He doesn't want to be seen as an ethnic comic. When I explained to him that ethnicity is irrelevant in this context, that everyone is ethnic, his reply was, we're not talking about ethnographic sociodemographics here, Neha. We're talking about the language people use to attack you and make you feel shitty.

I read through the *NIB* about my father again.

I start to imagine what my father could have changed. Maybe we would have been brought up in a better house. I could have grown up not the type to want to run off and find my own space as soon as possible.

I try to imagine my father as anything other than a buffoon.

Raks once asked why I hate our dad.

'Because he never asks questions. He always tells us stories. He's more in love with himself as this great storyteller than his own children,' I told him.

'He's just an oddball,' Raks said. 'He's ultimately harmless.'

In the news story, I see something in my father that I've never understood before become clear. I understand his need for invisibility. He told us that we had it easy, that things like racism were now unsaid, so at least you could pretend the world was on your side. He had the scars on him to show that it was worse in his day.

I feel a tear.

I don't cry.

As in, it's not something I do. I don't think human emotion should be allowed to be manipulative like that.

I stare at the faded glow of the monitors working away in the next room.

The rattle is back. In my right lung. It feels like a thick wet piece of bubblegum, stuck to my bronchioles.

I fall forward till I'm on all fours, kneeling. I force a cough.

SATURDAY EVENING

GoTo: Accident. Emergency

Waking up in a hospital feels like opening your eyes inside a coffin. You realize the lack of air flow very quickly. The stray beeps of machines in the near distance is calming at first, then suddenly alien. People move with such grace and quiet, they could be ghosts, harbingers.

Waking up in a hospital and not immediately knowing how you got there is even stranger.

We open our eyes expecting familiarity. This is why I can never sleep in hotels. They're anonymous carcasses with the occasional dash of indistinguishable humanity, a television, insipid art, the buzz of other rooms.

In movies, people open their eyes in hospital with a jerky start, seconds away from ripping the tubes from their body, their nerve endings coarse with survival mode.

In soaps, people open their eyes quietly, because there is usually a revelation happening in the room, between the doctor and their wife, husband or parent, and they'll need to reveal they knew that information in fifty episodes' time.

In this moment here, I take a second to work out where I am and five more to remember how I got here, before my brain can acknowledge that it's encased inside a body in considerable pain.

I remember calling the ambulance, I remember pocketing my phone and my charger.

I remember lying on the floor.

I remember the paramedics walking in through the open front door.

But I don't remember opening it.

I realize I am holding something.

I hope it's my phone.

I look down, hoping my eyes will focus.

I'm holding a hand.

I look up to its owner but my eyes take a second to refocus. I'm not wearing my glasses.

The smell of starch and cleaning fluid hits me.

It smells comfortable. Like home.

Like my home away from home, for want of a lesser cliché.

'Mika?' I ask, stupidly.

Are you to be written with me or not?

'Oh. You're awake. Spectacles, I was just about to leave. I have a shift. Now you're awake, I suppose I can't go. Oh, well. Maybe you can tell my boss.'

'Sorry.' I cough.

'You okay, Spex?'

'Water,' I croak.

'Always a barmaid,' Mika sighs.

I watch as she lets go of my hand, lifts it up and drops it on my chest. I have no muscles to stop it slapping down on me. She pours water into a plastic cup, lifts my arm off my chest and places the cup in it, squeezing till I grip. I lift the water slowly to my chin, touch, and then lift it to my bottom lip, ensuring it is pouring into my mouth. She stands, watching, impatient.

'Glasses,' I say into the bubbling echo chamber of the water.

I manage a tiny sip down my throat. The rest trickles either side of my neck.

I gulp frantically as I feel the cool liquid soothe my hot neck.

I let go of the cup when it's empty. My pillow is soaking. I turn my head sideways so my cheek can be cooled by the damp material.

Mika puts my glasses on me when I return my head to neutral position.

'Thanks,' I say. 'Should you call a nurse?'

'I guess.'

She stands to leave.

'Don't be late for your shift,' I whisper. 'Your boss is a massive cunt.'

'Can I ask you a really depressing question?' Mika asks.

I nod.

'Why is Pivo your in-case-of-emergency number? What about your dad? Don't you have a twin brother? Your local pub? Spectacles, that's crazy.'

'You're the closest to me,' I say. 'Geographically. In an emergency, you'd be first on the scene.'

'It's not in my job description.'

'They called you?'

'Yeah, said you were stable. But when they found you, they said you were pretty weak.'

I watch her push her glasses back up to the top of her nose and I have a memory of Ba doing the same thing to me, pushing the glasses up my nose, and smiling kindly, as we left the donkey Little Vijay to die. I'm remembering all these simple things. You tend not to remember the smaller things. Only the big ones. But watching Mika push her glasses up her nose makes me remember. It makes me realize.

I'm not ready to die.

My ba may not exist any more. But I do and I have things left to do. We accepted her lack of existence as easily as we accepted her as a relative. My father experienced so much anger and destruction in the years he was here. He fought for things I didn't know about. He watched his wife die, knowing from the second he met her that he would outlive her. My ba watched Bapuji die and returned home to escape the demons of his violent demise.

And me, what have I done? Who have I saved? Who did I fight for?

Peter Glendale and his cinema ticketing project? Miles?

No. I have work to do.

'Do you want me to call your dad? I can,' she says, looking at her fingers.

She has black ink on her right hand. She licks at her palm and rubs at it.

'No,' I say.

'Why won't you call him?' Mika asks.

'Because,' I say, 'I don't think he would care that much.'

'Why?'

'Because he's more invested in the ideal of his dead wife than his living children. This is my dad's folly, to relive the past, night after night, picturing every scene, every spoken word of dialogue, every moment, like it's a Bollywood film. He plays it back in his mind's eye, as he listens to Lata and to Kishore. We're burdens to his perfect memory of his beautiful amazing dead wife. My mother, supposedly. Though I know nothing about her other than the story he gives us every time we see him, about how they survived a horrific attack and fell in love at Diwali. My twin and I remind him of her imperfections.'

'He'll still want to know. You're his kid.'

'No,' I say. 'He killed me just by having me. He doesn't get to say goodbye.'

Depression

WEDNESDAY EVENING

GoTo: Initial Rollout

The beta test is complete. The initial projections come back, throwing up some errors.

I knew there would be some issues around Ba's disappearance. I can account for everything except the date and cause of her death.

I assume she's dead.

We haven't heard from her since we were in Kenya. Dad let that side of the family fade into obscurity. No love lost. He told me that we reminded them all of what they had lost, not what they gained.

We wondered about Ba through the years. That week Raks and I had spent with her was so life-changing for me, that I couldn't understand Dad's resistance to contacting her. Raks and I wrote her letters, but as the months piled up, we stopped. Years later, as teenagers flicking through a photo album, Raks found a photo of us on that Kenya holiday, and asked Dad what happened to her.

Dad told us a long story that didn't go anywhere, about how Ba was born on a dhow to a mother who drowned, then left for the UK where she watched her husband and children die, before moving back home because she wanted to be near where it began. I stared at the photo. I tried to see myself in her but I couldn't. All I could see was someone who was fading in my memory till she became a still image. And my mother was a still image. I hated that. How quickly time slips away for us. We forget. Things cease to be real other than in the moment. Dad was convinced that Ba died the year we came to visit. He suspected she killed herself. I barely knew the woman, but it feels like an adequate explanation.

Now, all she is to me is an anomaly in the data sets.

Maybe she did kill herself. Or maybe she died of cancer, as the rest of the women in this family line seem to. If she had the same cancer as my mother, that her mother had, then my algorithm would be more complete. Currently, she is a problem I have to wonder about.

Now that she is part of my work, I can't stop thinking about her.

I haven't tasted her sugar rotlis for over twenty years and I can still feel the sweet grains on my lips.

What happened to you, Ba?

The cancer is causing me to make mistakes in the code. I'm not usually this sloppy. As time slips away, so does my patience with being right. The stakes are lower now that they will outlive me.

Before entering the rollout, I take out the records for her date and cause of death. I don't want to run it with bad data. If I am to try and expand the data sets increasingly till I can help the entire world, it has to be iron tight at the source.

I feel as though the code and I don't agree. We are fighting, in tension with each other. I write lines. Each one seems to delete itself before my eyes. I squint at the screen, unsure at what I'm seeing.

I go to bed and dream in lines of C++.

I wake.

I look out of the window at Pivo. It's dead on a Wednesday night. Barely any cause for a bouncer, but one stands sentry all the same, hoping for some trouble to justify his presence.

Everything is about justifications.

I look at Raks's entry, shifting the sleep from my eyes with a fingernail. At first, I'm not sure what I'm looking at. Also, I was coding until the second I fell asleep and then dreamt that I was continuing to write lines so I cannot now differentiate between awake me and asleep me. I'm not sure why I'm seeing what I'm seeing.

There is a new line added to his plain-text entry.

I open up Dad's entry on another screen.

He has the same new line too.

The extra line predicts how they will die.

In text, it looks remorseless. Just as death should be. Plain. Just as death should be. Like Dr Hamid's delivery. Simple. Not emotive. Clear, in order to manage expectations. It does not bother me in the slightest that he will die on a bus. It makes sense, actually. A man constantly running backwards to his past instead of to the destination of now, dies in transit. He'll probably be facing backwards.

I don't know if these are real projections or projected fantasies. I don't know where the code has come from. I don't even know what I'm building any more.

Do I want my brother's work to kill him? Do I want my father to be alone and in transit at the end? Did I write this?

Did I create this or is it something divine? Is destiny talking to me through my machine?

These are patterns I cannot fathom.

THURSDAY NIGHT

GoTo: Deterioration. Fortune

I have to sleep propped up.

It's the best way to let air pass in and out of my lungs. In the days that follow the found fag, I purge my house of cigarettes, bidding goodbye to my favourite friend. I can no longer draw enough breath to pull on one. I buy a second-hand oxygen tank and a comfortable armchair, so I can sleep. I set up my laptop as a proxy for my main computer. This way, I can work in my armchair, without too much movement, taking in oxygen if I need to. I have no appetite.

I cash in some ISAs because I don't know what I want to do with the money I've saved over the years but feel it should be readily available in case inspiration hits. Before the week is out, I have more money than I know what to do with. I sell my collection of DVDs and CDs to a website that repurposes second-hand goods, netting me another £1,000. I sell my collection of comics to a collector, for £2,000. I keep my *Star Trek* memorabilia. It feels comforting to have these close to me.

I can feel the end approaching. And these things are just things.

And this is just distraction from carrying on the algorithm. I haven't looked at it since I saw Dad and Raks's entries. I peered into the code and saw a heap of lines I don't remember adding at all. It scared me, if I'm being honest. It suddenly seemed as though I was out of control. I felt like maybe I'm better than I give myself credit for – somehow, my code is divining patterns and projecting likely outcomes.

Someone I went to school with, his Twitter bio, while giving nothing away about him, says boldly, Beat cancer twice. I might change mine to, Even cancer couldn't stop me being a genius.

I stream old episodes of the original series.

I mouth quotes to myself:

'It is illogical for a communications officer to resent the word frequency.'

'I examined the problem from all angles, and it was plainly hopeless. Logic informed me that, under the circumstances, the only possible action would have to be one of desperation. Logical decision, logically arrived at.'

I jig and I re-jig my will.

My net worth, my fortune and my savings have grown at an exponential rate. I have banked six figures. I sell all my furniture, including a nearly-new massage chair.

Strangers come and go, taking my washing machine, my bed, my decks from the three months I thought myself a DJ, my table and its corresponding chairs. Watching these faceless nobodies come and go, as I sit in my armchair, I realize that this is my fortress of solitude. The only person who has ever breached its walls was Raks, and all he did was complain about how dirty everything was.

I am softening. I can feel my mind softening as my body weakens. I feel the tinge of regret: regrets about wasting my considerable talents on things other than great, regrets about never going back to Kenya, regrets about never taking much interest in my family, regrets about Ba – the anomalous bad data of her is haunting my dreams. I see her death, in its many forms, unfold in my mind's eye, each one tantalizing me with its potential truth. I've wasted my adult life working, and what have I learned, what can I do? Being an expert at hardware design for communications tools and voice-recognition software is cool, but what does that mean, really? Anything I developed just threw down the gauntlet for someone younger and smarter and sharper to develop something better. Because they have ambition whereas I view it as art.

I can feel my body deteriorating. I dream in Spock-isms.

'The older the victim, the more rapid the progress of the disease.'

'You haven't the right to be vulnerable in the eyes of the crew. You can't afford the luxury of being anything less than perfect. If you do, they lose faith and you lose command.'

THURSDAY NIGHT

GoTo: Home. Truth

I wonder why I don't want my brother to know I'm dying.

I used to revel in the idea that twins worked in code that couldn't be hacked. That there was something in our DNA that allowed us to share things telepathically. As a teenager, I read whatever I could find in the library's science section about twins. Nearly every pair can relate a story. Sometimes, one twin experiences a physical sensation of something that is happening to the other (such as labour pains or a heart attack). Other times they will find that they perform similar actions when they're apart, such as buying the same item, ordering the same meal in a restaurant, or picking up the phone to make a call at the exact same moment. It was proven a few years ago that conjoined-twin telepathy exists. But for Raks and me, non-identical twins, we couldn't even come close to finishing each other's sentences.

I rarely understand him. Sometimes his ego drives me crazy. While we can amiably talk about everything other than something real, we don't have to be emotionally close. He and I invent in-jokes, silly little games, new shorthands for communication instead of talking about anything that *matters*. I don't want him to see the pain I'm in. Especially when he's on tour. This is his big moment, the time he will transcend into the greatness he was destined to have. Ba told him that. That he was destined for greatness. I didn't believe it at the time but now, if she's trying to communicate with me, I must heed her words. I cannot derail him. I cannot ruin it. Am I feeling empathy? Is that what this is?

What I do not understand about my brother is society's impetus towards forcing us to relate to each other. Whatever that means. We have to get on. We have to share things. We have to love people, and each other, unconditionally.

I ask myself why a lot; whenever I feel social pressure forcing me to send him a text to ask how he is.

But without those expectations, I suppose we only think of each other when we're in the same room.

I text him: *Would you want to know how you were going to die if there was a way of finding out?*

He replies instantly, as if he has been waiting for this question for a while.

Yes, he texts back.

THURSDAY NIGHT

GoTo: Early Adopter

I send Raks the log-in to the site.

I've password-protected it and hidden it on my server. I have neha.com. To all intents and purposes, though, it isn't a live site. It's where I test little projects.

The North Essex Housing Association once offered me £1,000 for the URL. I said no. My name is my name. Their acronym is a short-for.

One of my favourite little projects is Beam Me Up.

I have every episode and film of every iteration of *Star Trek* loaded up into a program on here. I have analysed and codified all the vocal patterns and scripts so that you can speak into the microphone and have a conversation with one of your favourite characters. I always choose Spock. The program manipulates their vocal patterns so that they talk back to you. Currently they speak in fragments of script. I'm still working on the intelligence bit, and now will probably never have a chance to finish it. It is all a massive infringement of copyright in any case, so I hide it away.

I've also hidden the script of my family tree. I've disguised the whole thing as a piece of family history. It has photos of people, all the information I've collected about them and references to where they appear online.

It was interesting finding the newspaper *NIB*, scanned online, from the *Daily Mail*, about my father's case. Though he lost it, he still made history. The first person to bring a case under the 1968 Race Relations Act.

This secret past.

History is filled with dates, events, things that happened, important moments that shaped the world, meetings, deaths, births, wars, peace, negotiations, acts of kindness and terror – these lay out a modern history we can understand. No one remembers the tiny things, victories and losses, the personal triumphs and failures. I have become constantly impressed by the stories of my immigrant family I've found online – the local news stories about my bapuji being murdered at a bus stop in Wembley; others surviving an attack; winning the baking competition with a shepherd's pie, Indian-style; climbing Mount Kenya to raise money for an orphanage; being the first person of South Asian descent ever to be nominated for a best costume-design BAFTA – these things. Again, I must be softening as I get weaker, because these stories make me cry. A new pattern emerges. Person moves to new country, triumphs over adversity, has a small success, gets on with life. It makes me realize how hard they had it. I think I was given the space to have my career free of the barriers of immigrating and then immediately being asked to integrate in a society that didn't want me here. I didn't live through the paki-bashing; the no blacks, no dogs, no Irish; the race riots. I lived in their aftermath. So I had the space to try and be my best self. I think. My inherent privilege talking here, but it's my dad's striving for mediocrity, to be comfortable and not to be seen, hidden in the depths of the middle classes, that gave me the space to just work. I know this is not a privilege afforded everyone. I am talking only of my own experience. In my dad's desire to hide, I flourished.

I wonder if Raks has logged into the site. I almost want his take on it before I continue. I need to know what it is I've done.

I need him to tell me it's real. So I text him.

He replies and asks if I've been hacked.

I tell him no, just log into the site, check it out.

He eventually replies and says he's logged in but he's not clicking on it. He's thought about it and doesn't need to find out. I want to know what's happened between that text and this.

I wrote a script for the log-in screen before I sent him the text: *Do you want to know how you will die? Yes. No. Don't know.*

I log into my admin screen and check his usage, his behaviour flow.

Logs in: 13:42

Ends session: 13:42

He didn't even consider the possibility for a full minute.

The beta test has failed because it has to measure itself against human frailty.

FRIDAY MORNING

GoTo: Feedback Loop. Set 1

I remove the screen between log-in and the records page. Maybe the question is too candid.

I decide to carry on working on the algorithm. Maybe people should be allowed to know how they will die. If life is patterns, if families are patterns, if history is patterns, maybe anomalies don't exist. Wouldn't you want to know how long you have, so you can plan and maximize time and be efficient?

I am aware I haven't looked at my own record yet. It seems too inevitable to do so. The ol' cancer, you'll be the death of me.

I carry on adding lines of script to the code, to try and work around what I'm referring to as the Grandmother Problem. I work all night. I stop for two slices of pizza and a Fanta. I can barely breathe, barely chew, barely sip I am so tired but I can feel the end of the project approaching. I know what I have to do. Every profile is assigned a space on the family tree. This blog is made live. The software I've been working on is uploaded. I have created a death predictor for my family. In the future, all you will need to do is add any newborn children's birth dates, sex, birth weights and it will calculate their cause of death. There are lines of code I don't understand. I am weak and my eyes frequently blur so perhaps, with all this screen time, I'm just not reading them properly.

The death predictor. Every now and then, I think it's not real. In my hazy state of mind, I think I am destiny, manifest, the predeterminer of your death based on established patterns within our family.

I need more time to expand the data sets, to bring it out wider. I am ready to rest for the moment. I fall asleep at 1 a.m. and wake up at 2 p.m. the next day.

SATURDAY MORNING

GoTo: Napoleon Dynamite

The *Napoleon Dynamite* Problem is this: the film itself is so divisive, people who should like it - nerds, outsiders, goofballs, fans of comedy - don't always rate it. And the people who should hate it - jocks, dicks, bullies, arseholes, management consultants - consider it their favourite film. Thus, it has a ratings score of 2.4, because you either love it or hate it.

What does that mean for algorithms designed to make

recommendations based on what you like and don't like? If you like a film an algorithm doesn't account for your liking. Can you beat the code?

If I'm trying to find a pattern for this cancer, and I don't know how Ba died or when, and whether it was from cancer, or from other things, then what does that mean for my algorithm? She is my Napoleon Dynamite.

The anomaly in the algorithm.

SATURDAY AFTERNOON

GoTo: The Game

Raks texts me.

The text says, *I lost.*

I smile.

I reply, *Me too.*

Two minutes later, I text him again.

I lost.

He replies, *This game is infuriating.*

Over text is when I feel affection for my brother. His presence in a room irritates me as we have previously established. However, it's these occasional text flurries, usually based in nostalgia, that endear him to me.

We've been playing a game for the last fifteen years. We invented it on our way home from my ba's house in Mombasa. The journey was long – we had to travel by coach from Mombasa to Nairobi, and the road was so bumpy, neither of us could sleep. Dad was listening to a tape of his and Mum's favourite songs on a Walkman. We had nothing to do. It was too shaky to read.

So Raks invented this game.

The aim of the game is to forget you're playing it. If you remember you're playing the game, you lose. You have to then tell the other player, I lost. Then you start again. The amazing thing is, for the five minutes after one player loses, the other will inevitably lose, because it's still in the front of their mind. So you automatically lose.

Playing it on that bus, when the game was all you could think about, it was a legendary match.

Raks texting me that he'd lost – this makes it 86–72 to me. The last time either of us lost was four years ago. It was me. I was drunk and sitting at the bar of a pub, nursing a pint, trying to remember something else, I don't even remember what. And something bizarre happened in my brain. Instead of recalling the thing I needed to recall, it reminded me that I'd lost.

The game is infuriating.

The game is much like life. You forget you're living. And it's only in the brief moments after you remember to cherish what little time you have, that you do anything to take life by the hands and dance as though no one is watching. Ten minutes later, you're watching episode after episode of whatever show you're into on Netflix and eating a whole tube of Pringles, because that is really what life is.

SATURDAY EVENING

GoTo: Text. Refresh

The text chain with Raks continues for the rest of the day. Eventually, he asks me what the site was that I pointed him to.

I tell him, *It's destiny.*

Destiny, he replies. *I'm only interested in her progeny.*

My brother, ladies and gentlemen, a maker of jokes when things really matter.

I don't reply.

Eventually, he texts, *What about destiny?*

I ask if he remembers Ba.

Not much. Like, I have a very fond memory of her. What about her? What about destiny?

She believed in it. She really believed in it. It was her most Hindu trait. I've had some unexpected life news recently and I decided to set out to prove whether she's right or not. Can you believe it? I'm trying to prove the existence of destiny.

You weirdo. What unexpected life news?

I hesitate, before replying, *I quit my job.*

I love my brother and don't want him to worry.

Good, he replies. *It sounded really boring.*

SATURDAY NIGHT

GoTo: System. Reboot

Ba phones me.

'I am here,' she tells me.

'Where?' I ask.

'Where you left me,' she replies.

She sounds distant.

'In Mombasa?'

'Will you visit me soon?' she asks. 'I know you will. He's here with me. He told me where you all went. He's here.'

'Ba, what are you talking about?'

'Hum˙ premal˙a mitro tamara badha dusmano kanvart˙a thase.'

'I don't understand.'

'Jay Shree Krishna,' she says.

The phone clicks off.

I'm staring at the ceiling of my bedroom. I don't feel as though I've been asleep. I don't feel like I'm awake.

I know I'm not holding a phone.

SUNDAY MORNING

GoTo: Bug Fix

The first thing that bothers me when I wake these days is the feeling that someone else is in the flat with me. I'm unsafe. I am vulnerable.

My space has been invaded.

I try to ensure that my monitors are all off when I go to sleep, and my laptop is shut.

But the monitors are always on, things are happening on the screen, bits of code, bug fixes I don't remember writing.

I start to worry that I'm sleep-coding. I don't even think that's a thing but I look it up.

Every morning, though, strings of code are appearing in the algorithm. Ones I don't remember writing.

When I look in mirrors, objects so familiar to me before, a poster of Spock, a cardboard cut-out of Starbuck, a bust of Darth Maul, all become confusing presences, people, physical entities, invading my space. I am no longer alone.

No one tries to communicate with me; they just let me

know that they are there. My solution is to have the curtains open and the television on while I am awake.

I sit and drink a clear tea, looking at some of the bug fixes written overnight. Nothing looks particularly anomalous, extraordinary or dynamic. The fact that it has been written and I don't remember doing it unnerves me.

I want to go for a walk. The flat feels oppressive. But the tea is the right temperature and my feet need elevating. I stay put.

I think about texting my dad. I'm weakening to the idea.

I think about the money. Who I might leave it to.

Maybe I'll give it all to the donkeys.

Apparently, it's a British thing – the reason why a donkey charity receives £13 million every year – because what's more humiliating to a family than a person's fortune being given to a bunch of asses over them?

I spill my tea. When I return from the kitchen with a cloth to wipe down my desk, there is no trace of liquid.

I brush my teeth incessantly, but my mouth never feels minty. Instead, it feels furry and stale.

I lose.

I text Raks.

I laugh. I actually feel lost. For the first time in my life, I am aimless. The project is complete, but I'm beginning to wonder about the ethics of it all. Should we know these things? Do patterns offer us comfort? Does knowledge of our destiny give us agency? Would telling my family how they are going to die help them avoid it or would it happen regardless? Is knowing the manner of your death a blessing or a curse?

I feel haunted today. I keep seeing black spots in the corner of my eye, turning around and finding nothing there.

I decide to check my name. Out of interest. Out of confirmation.

I click on my name. It opens up with a photo of me from the staff page of my old job. It lists some basic facts, links to some industry awards I've been associated with.

I've been avoiding this. Not because I was scared of what I might see, but because things are obvious – I have cancer-filled lungs. There's only one way out for me now.

I read through my record. It tells me things about myself I already know, functional things.

It then tells me I am going to drown.

I stare at it. A mistake, surely. Surely?

Is there a bug? Is this because of bad code? I know Mum's grandmother drowned, and so did Dad's dad. But me? I don't get it. This doesn't make sense. Is it bad code or is it real? Will I decide I'm done with this world and jump off a bridge? Will I fall asleep in the bath and be too weak to pull myself out? Will I be water-boarded because of my development of the Death Predictor, which then goes worldwide?

Drowned? It makes no sense.

SUNDAY NIGHT

GoTo: Someone Else's Code

I wake up to that song.

The singer is so shrill and coy, it drills into my brain.

I open my eyes. Slowly. Trying to work out if this song is in my head or somewhere in the room.

My laptop is open, on my thighs, keeping them warm. My music player is also open and a song is on loop.

Tere naseeb…mere naseeb…I know the lyrics off by heart now.

I wake till my eyes focus, pick up my glasses from where they've fallen on to my lap and give myself a few seconds. I leave the song playing. It's soothing. It's comforting. It's like the last song I will ever hear. Perhaps it is something I should ask to be played at my funeral. I can see Ba making rotlis as this song is on the radio, me watching her, a *Star Trek* comic book open in my lap. As if no one is watching, she shimmies a hip at the chorus.

I smile at the partial memory.

I don't remember pressing play on this song, nor do I remember procuring it, legally or illegally. I certainly don't remember looping it.

I press stop.

The flat suddenly feels like mine again. Everything belongs to me. I'm unnerved so I close my laptop and struggle my way to standing. I waddle over to the kitchen where I pour myself some water, sip and think, leaning on the sink for support. My clothes are baggy on me now. I have to punch a new hole in this belt. I hold my trousers up.

Who keeps playing this song?

I sit back down at my computer and look up the lyrics to the song. I don't understand Hindi so I put them all into an online translator.

Ye hum kyaa jaane, ye wahee jaane, jisane likhaa hain sab kaa naseeb.

What do I know, only he knows, the one who has written the destiny of all.

This is the bit that was looping. Like a stuck record, trying to tell me something. Ba communicating from wherever she is.

She is trying to tell me something.

What do I know? Only he knows. The one who has written the destiny of all.

I look at the date of release of the song.

Stray fragments from the trip to my grandmother's keep coming back to me. Sugar rotlis, museums, learning to eat mangos the proper way, learning to swim, long bus journeys, donkeys.

Ba, I miss you. Little Vijay, I miss you.

Ba? Are you trying to communicate with me?

Little Vijay? Is that you?

MONDAY MORNING

GoTo: Processing

I go for a walk.

The plan is to walk across the road to Pivo, drink a clear tea and walk back. I want a beer. I cannot sustain a beer. Not in my condition.

My eyes sting with the natural light. It's colder than I remember now I'm in an unregulated atmosphere. I've not been wearing cushioned shoes and the backs of my feet, my heels ache when I try and press them into the pavement. I cannot do heel-toe, heel-toe. I walk like Frankenstein, one clunky whole-footed stride after another. I should have showered.

I see a man, sitting cross-legged next to the fountains between my house and Pivo. He wears a long puffy raincoat over his jubo lengha. I stop and wait for him to look at me. He's

Indian, not uncommon for this area, but he looks elaborate. He has a white U painted on his forehead; a severe red line of powder runs down the centre of it. He has flower petals in his lap. His eyes are closed, and he is mouthing something to himself.

Sensing my presence, he opens his eyes. He doesn't stare at me but I can tell he knows I am there. I stop walking. He stares blankly in front of him before turning his eyes to me.

He is young, in his early thirties, thick black moustache freckled with white, a severe face with a puckering, small mouth. He wears round glasses.

He looks at me blankly. It's only for a second, because then he peers at his watch. He looks at me again and closes his eyes once more.

I walk past him as quickly as my weak legs will allow.

MONDAY AFTERNOON

GoTo: Pivo

Mika tells me an interesting fact.

'Pivo,' she says, 'is Czech for beer. And piwo is Gujarati for drink. Weird, eh?'

I nod placidly.

'Do you believe in destiny?' I ask.

'I'd need to, working in this place,' she says. 'It has to be my community service, before the big time. Before they find my blog and give me a TV show.' She pauses. 'You ask funny questions, Spectacles. Everything you say leads us down a surprising path.'

'Is that your dream? To be on TV?'

'Isn't it everyone's?'

Mika pours a beer without me ordering anything. I accept it.

MONDAY EVENING

GoTo: Cheating the System

Is that what I've done? I wonder. Have I tried to cheat a higher power by attempting to emulate it? Is my computer a rival for a god? Have I offended him or her? Is this what happens to atheists at the end?

Rational thought makes way for a fear, reverence and religiosity, in the hope that, just in case there is a god and I need to keep the guy onside, just on the off-chance? I didn't think I was that easily led.

I am the master of my family's destiny, and the captain of their soul. I laugh, remembering having to learn the poem I'm paraphrasing by heart at school.

The master of our destiny. I could not control the cancer but I can now control its detection. That's what people say about lung cancer, specifically. Early detection saves lives. I hope Raks has kids and I hope he has twins, and I hope they live a long, happy, fulfilled life.

My father, my brother, they both need to know about their fate, about the algorithm. Its predictions. They can save themselves in ways I cannot.

I may have cheated the system, I may have told death I can see its patterns.

I've created something that can tell your destiny. A digital palm-reader?

*

My brother is more selfish than me.

We're both self-obsessed. But he is more so than I am. His career dictates that. He is on stage telling people his version of our lives, hoping for laughter, aiming for laughter. He has no sensitivity to what parts of our lives can be material for him.

I'm tired. Tired of mining the past to try and figure all these things out.

Weighing up our failures against each other.

What do our respective failures tell us about who is the better twin? My failure to not escape my mother's genes versus his inability to be noticed by our father. To be fair, our father didn't notice me that much, either – he was always too busy obsessing about his perfect memory of our mother.

We are our parents, sieved through.

The glass of beer in my hand is cold, comforting. I look around the empty bar, scanning for Mika, to remind myself that I am present.

I want to hear my ba's voice again. That phone call, I know it wasn't real. Just some sleep-deprived hallucination. Was it? I feel as though she is near me now. I get a pang of homesickness. Home doesn't exist any more. My father sold it when Raks finally moved out. He lives by himself in a one-bedroom flat above his shop. We cannot be accommodated there. We do not do the joined-up family thing unless it's at a pub, and even then, we're hoping our phones will give us an escape route.

I sip my pint.

My family, they need bringing together. And I need them, I realize. It's time to let them know what's happening to me. Maybe they can take me back to Ba?

I text my brother, I text my father, I ask them to meet me at the pub the following day. Raks replies quickly and asks for a change of location nearer to him – he has an Edinburgh preview later. I decline and insist it's Pivo or nothing. *I have something to tell you,* I write. *It'll be easier near my house.* He says he's busy. I do not hear back from my father.

I cannot breathe.

I long for death. I've had enough now. Come on, let's see if there's an afterlife. If there isn't, I won't know any different.

I do not drink the beer. And I leave when the room feels oppressively unlike the cocoon of my flat.

TUESDAY MORNING

GoTo: Setting Fire to Destiny

If the one who wrote destiny is looking for a fight, then come for me. If the one who wrote destiny doesn't want me to peer into its code, then come for me. If the one who wrote destiny believes in their own existence, come for me. Either way, I'm not afraid of what I don't believe in.

I wake up, sitting on the toilet.

In my hand is a picture of my ba holding my mother. Dad gave it to me once, when I was asking about Ba. He said it was the only photo of her he had. This was when I was a child. I haven't seen this picture in years, and I don't remember looking for it but I must have done. I don't even know where I would have found it.

I leave the toilet, looking back to see exactly how I ended up there.

My monitor is flashing. I stumble over to it.

Are you sure you want to delete destiny.xml? Y/N, it asks.
I don't remember trying to delete the site.
There is someone else in this flat. I feel unsafe.
Maybe destiny has decided to come for me.

Acceptance

WEDNESDAY AFTERNOON

GoTo: Paperwork

My father's birth date is wrong.

He phones me up to tell me this.

'Hey, kiddo,' he says, in his jovial voice, begging to be liked.

My father has always wanted to be popular. It's pathetic. Who wants to be liked? It gives you an uneven personality, private and public, anxiety tearing you apart as you debate new ways to be. If people cannot accept your flaws, they cannot be your friend. I keep a tight net for this reason. I will not change myself.

My father's biggest failing, apart from his romantic ideal of my mum, is thinking that what you think is more important than what he thinks. It will be the thing that kills him. Or a heart attack. The prevalence of heart disease, angina, diabetes, in his family, according to my algorithm, will give him a heart attack at sixty-six years old. He is a goner in two years' time. He will outlive me.

Ba lasted longer than both her kids, and her husband.

Raks, he'll live for ever, even after he dies on stage in several decades' time. He is content now. Immortalized in joke. And YouTube. YouTube is the cockroach of the internet. Indestructible.

'I realized something last night,' Dad says. 'You will find this funny. You wanted to know all about our family history, and our dates. For your database. And I remembered – before I came to the UK, I had to apply for a passport. I did not have one. And they want to see your birth certificate but I do not have one of those either. I was not given one. Nor did my amee have a birth certificate.'

'Right,' I say.

'But Sailesh, my old friend and I, we decided to make up my birthday. We didn't know how long I had been alive. Amee could not remember. She gave me two different dates, two different years. We do not celebrate birthdays. This is a Western thing. We did not mark another three hundred and sixty-five days of living. We only mark when we are born and when we are dead. Everything else in between is gift enough. What I am trying to say to you is, when I was twenty-three, and I returned home to bring my bride to my amee and papa, we met my cousin. Who had a birth certificate. And Amee told me I was born in the same month as him. She'd remembered and had a letter to prove it. And she told me, this is the month and year you were born. So I am one year older than I thought. Can you believe it?'

'Okay,' I say.

He continues, 'I never changed my birthday because I don't like hassle. And it becomes your birthday. Every year. Because English people tell you to celebrate the day. I do not like marking occasions. I think about the date I met your mother, the date I asked her to marry me. The date we went to register the wedding. The date of the civil wedding, the vidi, the sanghee, the Hindu wedding. I remember all of those dates. But not my birthday. I think I am a year older than I originally thought. I am sixty-six. Funny, eh?'

'Father,' I say, 'you have ruined everything.'

'Are we still meeting later?' he asks.

'You are no longer welcome,' I tell him.

WEDNESDAY AFTERNOON

GoTo: Rage

My rage is short-lived.

I smash a wine bottle in the kitchen. The way the metal of the sink sheens through the red liquid feels comforting.

I go to swig from another bottle but I cough at the first sip and spit the wine down the plughole. I clutch the sides and hunch over, trying to control my breathing through the coughing.

My father ruins everything.

My entire program is useless now. I have all the wrong data. Dad's woolly birth date is inexact. Ba is still an anomaly. I have been working on too many wrong assumptions for my work to have any meaning. My legacy is redundant.

Destiny and patterns cannot coexist. Not when humans are left to police them.

THURSDAY AFTERNOON

GoTo: Last Stand

I cannot think in this flat. I decide to go out to Pivo. I dress in a black T-shirt and jeans, put on my tweed blazer, slick my hair down with warm water from the kitchen sink. I look lost in all my clothes, like a goth MC Hammer.

Before I leave, I take as many deep breaths with my oxygen tank as I can. I don't need it all the time. It just makes it easier for me to breathe when I am sedentary, working on computer screens, ignoring my body, trying to forget I even have one. I am so angry. Only a drink can quench the thirst of my rage. Months of work, my entire legacy, fucked up by my useless father. The only good thing he ever did was move to this country. I look at myself in the mirror, switch the oxygen tank off and leave the flat.

And where is Ba?

How did she die?

It haunts me.

I feel the fresh breeze in the open-air corridor caress my face. Like recirculated aeroplane air. I gulp at it. I walk down the three mini stairs from my front door to the building's main front door, one lump of a foot at a time, slowly, holding on to a cold handrail that sends a pleasing tender shiver up my arm. I reach the bottom and hobble out on to the high street in my suburb of my city for the first time in a few days. It is bright. All the grey dust particles gleam like diamonds. It hurts my eyes. I close them and wait for my eyeballs to stop throbbing. I open them.

I cross the road and wonder what I've been missing all these years when families shared stories and reminisced and talked about the good ol' days. I have no good ol' days. I only have now. And that's just how I've been ever since I was a teenager. When your earliest memory is some creepy dude in a nappy squeezing your hand till it hurts, and a beloved animal being beaten by a stranger, you decide not to retain things. You make new memories. You overwrite bad code.

My father is in the pub, with two pints and a packet of crisps in the centre of the table, on his phone, texting. I told him not to come. Yet, just hours later, here he is, oblivious to my wishes. We sat here only weeks ago, at the same time, at the same table in the window, when he regaled me, once more, with the heroic story of how he met my mother.

I feel engulfed in my coat, wondering whether I can disappear into nothingness.

Seeing his stupid smiling face reminds me of how angry I am with him. That I am related to him bewilders me sometimes. Replaying those memories over and over in his head. Grief can do funny things to you, but sometimes you have to be in the room.

I do not want to see this man. I cannot look at him without feeling as though my destiny machine has failed.

I try to take a deep breath. I can hear the crackle of immovable phlegm in my lungs. Much as I hak-hak-hak up what I think of as disgusting snot, it will not budge from my bubblegum-lung.

Mika notices me as I enter the pub. I acknowledge her with a swift nod of the head. She smiles that crooked smile, adjusts the straps of her spaghetti top and carries on wiping down the bar.

I acknowledge my father and nod at him too, walking over as purposefully as I can without my breathing aid. I am sweating with the effort. I haven't done any exercise for a month and my face stings with sweat, my lungs ache. My dad rises to greet me with an outstretched hand followed by a one-shouldered cuddle, the badge of greeting for the male 'in touch with his feminine side'. I plop myself down on the seat as quickly as I can, managing not to keel over. There, I place my forearms on the table in front of me, lean forward and draw in as much oxygen as I can. I close my eyes and wait for the wave of nausea and weakness to pass.

'You okay, Neha?'

'I'm fine. Under the weather. That's all,' I say without looking up.

'You don't look well. Eating okay? Your famous egg-fried rice?'

'I've been busy.'

'How is the test site coming along?'

'It's ruined,' I tell him. 'Databases are only as good as their data.'

'Oh, Neha,' my dad says, pushing my pint closer. 'You mean, my birthday? What a silly thing to forget. Funny, na?'

'I need to start the whole thing again. You interconnect with me, Raks, Mum, our grandparents, your grandparents – don't you get it? If your birthday is incorrect, it ripples out; it affects everyone around you in the system. Your mother didn't have you when the program thinks she had you; you weren't doing what it thinks you were doing when she died; you weren't at the point in your life that it thinks you were at when I was born. Everything is out of sync.'

I rub my shoulder blades against the back of the chair, sitting up straight, then allowing my body to sag into comfort. I can feel the room fizz and throb around my father. I look at the premium-strength lager in front of me and gesture to ask if it's for me. My dad signals for me to help myself. As I do the thirst takes hold and I neck half the pint in a gulp. I hold the glass to my cheeks, first one and then the other, and close my eyes. I am thirsty, out of breath, and a cold lager poured from a keg is the stuff of beauty John Keats refers to. It is a joy for ever. I only know that reference because of the film *White Men Can't Jump*, which Raks made us watch incessantly in our early teens, because he wanted to be as wisecrackery (or black, as I ribbed him) as Wesley Snipes and as good at basketball as Woody Harrelson.

'So,' my dad says, elongating it until it's practically a sentence of its own. 'I think you are mad at me.'

'I am mad at you. I told you not to come, Dad.'

'Let me make it up to you, kiddo. Why don't I...' After a long pause he says, '...tell you about the time I met your mother? You love that story.'

I laugh. 3–2 to Dad.

Amazingly, he manages to cut the tension.

This is the pattern that is most consistent in my life, this story that Dad always tells me. It suddenly feels like a comfort. The room is spinning, the beer smells horrible, I can feel my arms shaking. Everything in me is weak and shutting down. Of course I want to hear this story. I've always found it tedious. But today, now, in this moment, it's the pattern I need the most.

My dad, this is the only thing he can give me. A GIF of the past.

'Okay then, Father. I'm game. Tell me everything,' I say. 'I don't want the glossy details you always give. I don't want the yadda-yadda-yadda omissions. I want every detail. I want to feel like I could walk away from this and know enough to have a conversation with her. I don't want you to think any detail is too sordid or horrible or unnecessary. I want to know everything. Don't get anything wrong. Don't make this story the tragedy that is your birthday. If your legacy to me is this story, tell it to me in a meaningful way.'

My dad pauses.

'That much? That sounds like hassle.'

'This family exists in patterns. I want to see how she fits in, so I know how I fit in. Don't tell me anything is a hassle, Father. You being my father is a hassle. You cannot keep trying to pay for things with the credit card of losing the love of your life. At some point, you have to remember that your children are people, and we've been in your life longer than she was. You hold on to this story as if it's the most important thing. Tell it to me like it's the most important retelling.'

My dad drinks his pint. Slowly, a smile comes over his face.

'Was it destiny that brought you two together?' I ask.

He must see the ghost in me because he puts the pint glass down and leans forward.

He takes a deep breath. He is nervous. He looks at me and smiles, as though this is the first time ever he has told the story of him and her and them. The story of who he was and the story of his best friend, the love of his life. The one who only exists in memory now. There are connections to be made, patterns to be established, genetic code to be analysed and interrogated.

'I have no reason to be anywhere,' he says. 'I find myself in an in-between world, with no purpose, except to lean with my back against the wall, across the road from Nisha's amee and papa's house. Not like a stalker, yaar. No, instead, I am posed like the poet I am, my pen poised to make ink marks and etchings on an open notebook page...'

*

He tells me everything. He spares no detail. He tells me how he met my mother. In one long stream of excitement at reliving the memory. He assures me constantly, this is exactly how it happened, because he replays the scenes every night in the video tape of his head. So he does not forget. Memory can trick him. Muscle memory cannot. So he plays the story out in his head every night.

He tells me the story of immigration itself, of him and my mother, and he leaves nothing out. He looks at me with concern. I must seem desperate and drained, like someone with nothing left. My dad, over the course of the next three hours, four pints, several packets of crisps and the innings of a one-day international being projected on to the back wall of Pivo, tells me everything I need to know.

As he tells me the story, I revel in its familiarity, and surprise myself by being nervous at some points about how it'll turn out.

He starts to make sense to me. The line of code he represents in the algorithm in my life is to tell me this story.

Finishing it, he tells me more - about our birth, the first weeks grieving for his wife and looking after us, the confusion, the support from my mum's brother Chumchee, the endless nights walking us both up and down the street he lived on, me falling asleep with a thumb in my mouth and Raks on his chest. All these remembrances confirm his fatherly feelings towards me, that he does things for a reason, and I am here for a reason. And that is love. Love is a code that cannot be written. I make no notes, have no reaction on my face to indicate happiness, relief or a sense of closure, but I listen to everything my dad says, and when he finishes, I say the one thing he has never said before, to anyone, because people think that I think I'm always right and that I have no empathy.

I realize that this is the story of when my father was happiest, and I cannot begrudge his happiest moment not featuring me. He must relive it. In that moment, I want to be as happy as him when he lives in that story again. I want to not always be right. I want simply to be happy.

'You and Rakesh look just like her,' he says. 'Well, Rakesh looks like her with a beard. But you do. Every time I look at you both, it's all I can think about. The family I could have had. Which upsets me. Because I have that family. You are here, right in front of me.' He wipes his eyes. 'And all this stupid fool can think about is what he lost.'

I see tears in his eyes.

I look at him and smile and say, 'I'm sorry, Dad. I'm so very sorry.'

THURSDAY EVENING

GoTo: The End

Dad leaves an hour later. Telling me the story has brought all manner of things up for him and he wants to go home and listen to Rafi and think about Nisha. I let him go. I feel at peace with him for the first time in ages.

I think I am nearing the end. The ol' cancer is beating me. I am weak. I've done the thing I thought I would never do – forgive my dad for his endless grief. Will I drown? I need to finish reworking the program, to expand the data sets and to prove that patterns exist. Logic requires consistency. Life must have patterns. If we are to be logical beings, we need consistency and patterns.

However, as Spock says, Insufficient facts always invite danger, Captain.

Mika walks over to my table.

'How are you doing?' she asks.

'I'm doing well,' I lie. 'And you?'

'I'm okay. I feel like I'm wasting my life here, as ever.'

'You should leave.'

'So should you,' she says. 'You don't look well.'

'Thank you. That's good advice.'

I gulp down my pint even though I don't want it. It tastes metallic in my mouth.

'Mika,' I say, as she starts to edge away from my table. 'If there was a way to know, would you want to know how and when you'll die?'

Mika thinks about it for a few seconds.

'No,' she says. 'I love your weird tangents. I don't know where they come from or what they mean, but they give me life. No, I wouldn't.'

'Why?' I ask.

'Imagine the pressure of knowing how long you had to get the most out of life. Not knowing keeps us moving forward. Would you?'

'I thought I did,' I say. 'I thought that in order to understand our purpose, first we had to understand our patterns.'

'I don't know what you mean,' Mika says.

'Neither do I, as it turns out.'

Ba, I think, is the key to everything. I text this to Raks. *She is the anomaly in our pattern. She taught us so much in that one week we were with her. She formed us as people. She pushed us towards ourselves. Subtly, maybe. I have regrets about forgetting about her for so long, about throwing myself into my career.*

That slip of paper written down by Mum, that I saved from that Kenya trip. *Neha: egotist, hard-working, stubborn, avoid these numbers: 16, 12, 9, 22.* I am these things. Is that destiny or a pattern? Ba said Mum was an egotist, hard-working, stubborn. I wonder what Raks's fortune was? Am I my mother? Am I her image? Is that why my father struggles with me? Because I remind him too much of what he lost. He has never told me I look like Mum. Ever. I don't see it in the few photos I have seen of her.

To exhibit the same traits as my mother. There is no scientific basis for this, only that it is a learned behaviour. But if I never knew my mother, how could I become her?

Mika is right. We should not know these things. My father is right. We have ended up where we are because of coincidences. I wanted to believe in destiny as a way of mitigating my diagnosis. I wanted to believe that there was a pre-written path. I think coincidence and patterns can coexist. But destiny is retroactive.

The algorithm told me I would drown.

I stand up. I feel drunk. I need to go home and delete the algorithm. I need to go to Kenya and trace Ba. I will then return to Lamu and visit the donkeys that I loved so much. This is how I will spend the rest of my days. In Kenya.

The room is spinning. I must go home.

I stumble towards where I think the door is. I walk into tables and chairs and squint as much as I can to see through the tears filling my eyes. I feel confused all of a sudden.

My vision is blurry and my mind feels like the inside of a vacuum cleaner – white noise and dust particles. I take my glasses off to see if I can focus. I reach the front door.

Outside, the breeze is cold but my head still reels. I stumble home, struggling to breathe, gulping down as much air as I can. I trip over the foot of the Indian man in the puffy jacket, and as he smiles at me, I try to recollect where I know him from and I tumble into the fountains, feeling the cool splash of murky slick oiled water around me as I submerge head first. I can hear Ba calling to me, I can feel the impact of the alcohol, I can feel something tugging at my body, while at the same time, a pressure is pushing me under. I try to make myself weightless. Let whatever fate claim me. I let someone else drive. I hand over keystroke control. I remove myself from the admin list. I am drowning.

It is as it should be.

I try to relax my muscles despite them tensing, fighting what's happening.

A loop closes. History repeats and repeats. My father has seen all of this before. It's not even the cancer that will kill me.

It's the water. Ironic, given how dehydrated I feel.

'I am done,' I say into the water. 'You were right.'

This was my destiny.

I think of my brother. And my mother. And my ba. And the ol' cancer. You cannot combat fate. It is the override code.

Goodbye. One day you will die. Until then, goodbye.

I try to empty my mind, but I feel a tug at my back. A pain in my shoulder. And I am rising, violently. Being pulled at.

There is a sheen of white noise all around me. The vacuum-cleaner sound is deafening.

I feel myself fall to the floor. I look up. Mika stands over me, her arms and front soaking, panting heavily.

'Spectacles, are you okay?' she asks.

I am alive, I think. I have broken the pattern and I am alive.

RAKS

Multiple. Now

Colonialism, what's up with that?

Raks Jani

'A Flea Can Trouble a Lion More than a Lion Can Trouble a Flea'

Laila. London

She masturbates with tears in her eyes. No nudity but good facial expressions needed.

Not for me, I think. No thanks. I log off the casting-calls app and open my phone's camera. I practise what I imagine are good facial expressions for wanking. Biting my lip seems forced. Scrunching up my face and smiling makes me look as though someone has placed a vinegar-soaked rag under my nose. I close the app and look to make sure the bus hasn't gone past my stop.

I know it hasn't, I'm too familiar with the area to let that happen – the event's in a house opposite my old school.

I can't do wanking face. I won't be applying for this casting. I didn't study for three years as an actor to take jobs where a fee constitutes £5 contribution towards my travel and a sandwich lunch. All for the artistic satisfaction of simulating wanking *with good facial expressions.*

The men get the castings where they need to be a good-looking nerd, or a superhero, or the type of guy everyone wants to fuck. If I'm lucky, I get to play one of the girls who gets to fuck the guy who's the type of guy everyone wants to fuck rather than the girl who doesn't get to fuck the guy who's the type of guy everyone wants to fuck.

I close my phone and put it in my pocket.

I get out the printed-off email with information about today's gig. I look at the photo of the guy who I'm supposed to act for. I recognize him. A comedian. I've seen him perform before. He's okay, seemed too nervy to get his jokes out, which were funny, could have been funnier with better execution. Comedy is, ummm, errrr, what is it? That thing, what is it again?

I look at his face, tracing the froth of his curly hair with a finger.

Timing.

Comedy is timing.

This is the weirdest acting gig I've ever had. But it beats masturbating with tears in your eyes.

The door to the house is wide open so I enter. I take my shoes off and blend in.

These types of wake I remember well. They're often an opportunity for family to catch up, so relations descend on the house to show their faces and offer condolences, eat the lukewarm khichdi and leave. You either sit reverentially in the room where the prayers are happening or natter in the kitchen with the aunties.

This is the first time I've been to a Gujarati wake in a cramped flat above a photocopier shop, though.

People will look at me and assume I'm a cousin, probably Prabhula masi's daughter. Every Gujarati family has a Prabhula masi.

You imagine these occasions to be sombre. People sit in front of the mandhir and sing tunelessly, for thirteen nights, going from sad to more sad to depressed to bored to numb to sad again.

This wake is much more alive.

The hallway is the battleground for a four-way Nerf-gun fight, girls versus boys; the girls, at the top of the stairs, are obliterating the boys who fight relentlessly, too stupid to realize that if you have the high ground, moral or physical, you win the war. The kitchen is brimming with aunties, kakis, masis, mamis, fais and granny bas, all shrieking in Gujarati and cackling through the sides of their teeth. The men sit in a circle in silence. B4U is on. Shah Rukh plays coy with Kajol. I remember the song well, though the television is on mute.

I feel at home. With the men in the front room and the women in the kitchen, I try to find somewhere to compose myself.

I move into the dining room, which appears empty, where snacks are laid out in steel bowls. I take a samosa and let it crunch into my mouth. There's too much garam masala on the potatoes but it is warm and tastes exactly like the pre-made samosas my mum buys and deep-fries. I haven't been home for months. The train to Leicester costs the same as twenty-two bottles of cheap wine and I enjoy getting drunk more than seeing my parents.

It's hard to feel like an intruder when the house seems familiar. The clear plastic table cover, the huge Hanuman painting on the wall, the statue of Kali stamping fools' heads off, the steel bowls of samosas, bhajias and chutney, the music.

It takes me a second to realize. It's a song from the film *Naseeb*. Hema Malini, in a shimmering black sequinned dress and ridiculous fringe that's also a quiff, sings with the microphone at arm's length, while Amitabh Bachchan plays the happy-go-lucky waiter in a red suit, John Jani Janardhan, falling in love with her from across the room.

'Naseeb?' I say, to an empty room, hearing the Nerf-gun fight descend into boy tears.

'Yeah, I think so,' I hear from a small voice to my right.

I jump in shock and turn to face the chair.

It's him – Raks Jani. Sitting in an ill-fitting black suit with a black tie that's too thin, wiping clean his glasses as he squints at me.

'Hey,' he says. 'You okay?'

'I'm sorry about your sister,' I tell him.

He stands up, putting his glasses back on. I steel myself to do the thing I've been paid to do. Here he is. I can do this job within five minutes of arrival, with a bonus samosa in my belly, and go straight home to invoice for the £750 fee.

It's ridiculous. I don't understand it.

He tries to smile.

'It's okay,' he says. 'I mean, it's not. I just mean, thank you. Thanks for coming, right? You're, errrr…' He hesitates, trying to pluck my name out of the same roster of Gujarati cousin names that we all live through, hoping to land on a girl's name.

Manish, Dipesh, Sailesh, Rajesh, Sita, Rita, Manita, Kajal, Radha, Dipti, Vimal, Vipal, Bipal, Minul, Minal, Rinum, Manan, Minan, Minay and Karthik. Maybe Manita, Tina, Naina, Bhawna, Amee, Mira, Mina, Bina. It's in there somewhere.

My nerve breaks.

I do what I'm paid to do.

I reach out my hand to his.

Instinctively, he reaches his out to mine too. I keep my face frowning and serious, as instructed. One foot back. One foot forward.

I thrust my hand into his and shake three times, firmly, up and down definitively. I look him in the eye and his sightline darts between our hands and my face. When the hands have shaken three times, I draw mine back in a wiggling-fingered explosion.

'Good. Bye,' I say firmly. 'Good. Bye. One day you will die. Until then, good. Bye.'

Raks hesitates, then he looks at my hands again, surprised. Almost robotically, he replies.

'Goodbye,' he murmurs. 'When I die, I'm bringing you down with me. Goodbye.'

I can see his face tense up, as though he's holding back a well of tears. I can feel his body trembling. He snorts as a tear falls down his cheek. He hunches and puts his hands in his pocket, frozen.

I let go, grab another samosa, turn quickly and walk out of the room. My cheeks sting. My head is bowed.

I do not look back at him.

A passing masi offers me a, 'Hello, beti, how's your mum?'

'Fine,' I stammer, high-pitched, desperately searching amongst the rubble of open-toed sandals and black Clarks shoes for my Converse, wishing I'd chosen shoes that you could slip in and out of, instead of having to stop somewhere, put the things on and tie up the exceedingly long laces.

I see my beaten formerly-white Converse with the biro marks on the left shell toe from a long boring train journey, and I pick them up, rushing out of the door towards the front garden. I can sit on a wall and put them on.

I feel like crying. What was I doing in there?

I still don't understand the job.

£750's a lot of cashola when you're a jobbing actor, especially a woman who has to deal with castings involving your body, nudity, humiliation and dressing like you're well up for it.

Busty female. We require a scene where we spray fluid on you and you make out with a small old man.

Thugs will try to grab your butt so I need you to wear something enticing but conservative-ish.

You will be caressed in a subtly erotic way by a deformed pig-man.

Needs to be okay that we glimpse her butt in the shower and comfortable with the 'rape' scene.

'Excuse me,' I hear, a few houses down as I lean against the brick side wall of a garage and try to wrench my sweaty half-a-size-too-small Converse on to my flat feet.

The film contains some tasteful allusions to sexual assault.

That last one, that one nearly lost me my agent – sick of me saying no to parts with mostly one line, one nipple, one butt cheek, my agent took umbrage with this one – it was a feature, with a semi-famous director, if your *Mastermind* specialist subject was British directors with derivative gangster film knock-offs to his name.

I told him I was holding out for the main part in the Mae West biopic. The timing was canny. The next day a Mae West biopic was announced in the trade papers. I sent my agent a picture of myself in a blonde wig, with the caption, 'What time's the audition?' and it must have charmed him enough not to dump me. I mean, he's a shit, the industry's a shit but having an agent is better than years without one, like I had. At least I can say I'm represented.

I turn to see Raks, running down the road.

He stops, panting, in front of me as I do the standing-up lacing of my trainer. He is sweating. He takes off his glasses to clean them again. His right eye is slightly off-centre; his pupils beady, intense, as though they're searching for something and if he can't find it, he'll cry. I know nothing about this person but I feel sorry for him.

'What the fuck was that?' he asks, putting his glasses back on. 'What you just did. What the fuck was that?'

'How do you mean?'

I'm not sure I'm supposed to say what I was doing or why I did it. My agent didn't specify the way to behave if confronted, or how much I could share about why I was there.

'What you did. Wait,' Raks says, stopping. 'You're ummm… you know… The…'

He mimes the handshake, pulling a face as though he has smelled something rotten.

'What?' I ask, my shoes on now, ready to flee.

'You're not related to me, are you? I know you, though. Who are you?'

I smile. I can't believe he doesn't remember, though I'm sure he's done the joke time and time again – and I bet he cringes every time.

When I asked my friend Mike – who had been up that night too, trying out a five-minute set, his third attempt at stand-up, blagging his way on to a bill with more established up-and-coming people like Raks – to explain what had happened, he said crowd work was essential for when your jokes weren't landing. In the case of people not finding your pre-prepared stuff funny, you could rely on taking the audience on and making fun of their hair, jobs, general appearance, choice of companion or place of birth.

'Haven't I seen you on Shaadi dot com?' I say.

When he said the same words to me, it was a cheap shot. Like I was the only Asian in the room apart from him, so hearing a culture-specific reference to a crappy marriage site was weird. He was doing badly that night, sweating his way through the set, begging the audience with his beady eyes to love him, and they just weren't responding.

I was his first crowd work of the evening – I was three rows back, and, to all intents and purposes in the dark, but he pointed at me, and made me feel exactly what I was – the only brown person in the room. He didn't count. He had a platform. I sat amongst the white people of the Amersham Arms and let him reduce me to every conceivable stereotype, jolting him from laugh to laugh. 'Maybe our mothers should meet. Wait – what caste are you? I'm Shaggy caste. They call me Mr Lover-Lover.' It wasn't even funny – people were creasing, though, because he was confirming all their expectations of our culture. Because if you acknowledge that the stereotype might be based in reality, boy, does it make white people more emboldened to laugh. Not like they find it funny. But that they are revelling in how superior they are.

'Oh,' he says.

He remembers. I smile at him. The impact of what I've

done to him, for him, has gone and I'm angry again. Just as I was when I blogged about it the next day on my 'Chai Tea is Tautology' blog.

'It's cool, man. Laters, yeah,' I say, walking away and cringing into my coat collar.

He runs after me.

'Why did you do that?' he asks.

He talks softly when he's not on stage. Like a librarian worried about the noise levels.

'Do what?' I ask, not stopping.

'Why did you do that handshake, say those words? How do you know about that? Who are you?'

I want to tell him that following me down the street is no way to get a woman to answer him. I don't owe him anything while he has a threatening attitude.

'Laters, man,' I whisper.

'Wait,' he says, more urgently, loud, pathetic. 'Please. Why did you do that? I need to know.'

This is the park where my friends and I used to come and watch people play basketball. Someone would have a Walkman connected up to some battery-powered speakers playing tinny RnB and gangsta rap. We'd sit on the grass next to the nets and watch the game. No one really knew the rules, and those around what constituted travelling were enforced arbitrarily. I'd bring theplas and bhajias made by my mum so that I didn't have to spend money on snacks. My friends brought cans of Coke and cigarettes stolen or cadged from elder brothers and we watched basketball. As though it was our nation's pastime. The park was thriving then.

Even though the swings look brand new, the park is empty. The netting around the basketball courts has been torn down and the grass tennis courts are now a meadow. The public toilets are boarded up.

We sit on the swings.

I'm swinging freely while Raks remains rooted to the spot, his arms slumped around the chain to keep him from falling face first on the ground.

'I was paid, through my agent, to go to a funeral and do that handshake and say those words to the brother of the deceased. You. I don't get many offers of work at the moment that aren't playing the wife of a terrorist or a girl with her tits out, and seven hundred and fifty notes is seven hundred and fifty notes. So I did it. Sorry if it upset you.'

'It did,' Raks is looking at the ground again. 'You know, my sister and I used to come here and play tennis for hours. Back when she did exercise. Look at the courts now. It's like a rainforest. Almost extinct. Verdant but nearly extinct.'

'I'm sorry for your loss.'

'My sister, my twin sister, that was our handshake. We've been doing it for years, decades now, since a trip to Kenya when we were kids. It was our thing. Good. Bye. One day you will die. Until then, good. Bye.'

His voice cracks. He presses his lips together tightly, hoping that if he doesn't open his mouth he won't cry.

I look at him sympathetically and slow my swinging.

'I didn't know.'

'We never told anyone,' he says, before he lets out a sigh, low and rumbling, like a Tube train beneath my feet.

His shoulders shake and he twists his heels inwards and

out, into the wood chippings. I notice he's wearing flip-flops with black socks.

'Only my ba saw it,' he says. 'We invented it when we went to visit her. It was our thing. Her and me. Only us. Not even my dad knew about it. How did you?'

'I'm just a jobbing actor, dude,' I tell him. 'I read the script, I say the lines, I get paid. Maybe it's like a message, beyond the grave, from your sister.'

He looks at me and takes his glasses off.

'But why?' he asks. 'Why would she do that?'

'So she has a chance to say goodbye, I guess. It's quite beautiful.'

Raks turns to me and slips off the swing, falling on to the chippings below. I laugh, without meaning to. He stands up and pretends to slip on a banana peel, falling down again.

When he stands again, it is directly in front of me. He smiles. There are dark circles under his eyes and a tear hanging from a beard hair.

'Can I see you again?' he asks.

I meet him outside the off-licence. He is holding up a blue bag of Red Stripe tins. I open my handbag and show him the nice-but-cheap Tesco wine I read about in the *Guardian Weekend* magazine.

He wants to kiss me on a cheek because he bends slightly when I offer a hand, which he takes, before the bow. I offer the whole of my cheek, to avoid a straying on to my lips (it's happened before) and when we release, he goes in for a second one. My face is so far over, that as I relent and switch cheeks, our lips graze.

I can't help it.

I laugh.

He kisses my other cheek.

'That's very continental of you,' I say.

'It feels like how they do things in the movies. Believe it or not, this is my first ever date.'

'Do you usually just get drunk in groups of people and snog whoever you're closest to who's single? Then you end up dating them for six to eighteen months?'

'Yeah. You?'

'No. I don't know that many people. Actors are always fucking, though. The work is so antisocial, the only thing to do is just get drunk and shag people after filming or whatever.'

'Really?'

'No.'

'Stand-up's the worst for a social life. You spend your entire career being as social as humanely possible. Chatting to people, making them laugh, drinking with them. And then you competitively socialize with comedians afterwards, getting pissed and trying to be the funniest person in the room. It's exhausting. You realize how much of your life you spend viewing yourself through the lens of other people. You realize you care less about how you think of yourself and more about what others think of you. And that professional life, it becomes your sense of worth. I don't want to socialize in my free time. I want to eat pizza in dark rooms and watch films. And sleep off my daily hangover.'

We fall into a weird silence as we walk to the restaurant. There's a pressure to keep talking on dates, as a silence will assume you're boring each other. I think of something to say.

We arrive at the restaurant – a scuzzy-looking kebab shop that from the outside looks untasty, unhealthy. But if you're brown, you know it has the best £2 kebab rolls, and you always get the dhal too. I can see Raks's smirk when we enter. The place is my choice and I haven't warned him. On the wall there are posters of pehliwan strongmen in their leopard-print pants, standing next to gadas to show how strong they are.

'What's good here?' he asks.

'Avoid the curries. Kebab rolls, kathi rolls, dhal. Only.'

'Sign me up,' he says. 'What's a kathi roll?'

I look at him incredulously, one eyebrow arched, the diagonal opposite corner of my mouth upturned in a Bruce Willis quizzical smirk.

'I don't eat Indian food much,' he says.

'This is Calcutta food.' I point to the sign: *Sweet'n'Spicy – Kolkata cuisine.* 'Don't be that guy. The one who conflates all of South Asia into generic Indian.'

'Sorry,' Raks says, almost embarrassed. 'I just find the food too heavy, you know? It smells amazing, though.'

We sit. I thump down on to my plastic seat, deflated with the thought that I've chosen poorly with this restaurant.

Raks takes his glasses off and cleans them. It's a particularly annoying nervous tic. He looks distracted.

'What you been up to today?' he asks. 'Any more ridiculous castings?'

'I've been rehearsing for a play.'

I explain its premise. I'm playing an ayah to the daughter of a British soldier and he becomes obsessed with me. I use his obsession to bring home some truths about the occupation of India. Neither of us wins and in the end I die by letting him stab me because I won't sleep with him and because my brother has joined the resistance. The stabbing is a dreamscape metaphor for sex, dealing with themes of otherness, about bodies and the violence inflicted on them and being a woman of colour. Or at least that's what the playwright told us. We're still trying to work the themes into the script. It's going to Edinburgh. I ask if he's going.

'Yeah,' he nods. 'My show is just - well - it's okay. I'm struggling with it. I don't really know if I can do it now.'

'What's it about?'

'It was about my family. About my sister, about twin shit, and about how we both hated being Asian growing up, and rebelled against anything Asian because we were desperate to be white. It was going to be called "A Lovely Bunch of Coconuts" or something. But I dunno - now that she's passed, I'm not mad about the idea any more. Nothing is being said about a living breathing person. It's being said about a dead person. There's almost too much tragedy in it. It's just not working. I don't know.'

He sighs.

'It sounds good, I guess. I mean -' I pause. 'Yeah, so I guess we'll be stuck together for a month. This'd better go well. You'd better fall in love with kathi rolls, my friend.'

'I only dine at the Tempting Tatty in Edinburgh,' he says softly. 'You were going to say something about my idea. But you stopped. Tell me. I need a sign whether to do it or not.'

'How truthful do you want me to be?' I ask, weighing up the options in my head of how to give headline feedback to a headline idea.

'Really truthful,' he says, looking at his can of Red Stripe, lifting the ring-pull and snapping it back and forth repeatedly.

'Don't bother, dude. "A Lovely Bunch of Coconuts"? Who the hell wants to listen to that? I mean, being British Asian isn't a binary thing – it's complex, layered, nuanced, there are many types, tropes, archetypes – but what even is a coconut anyway? It's outdated, dude. I don't know. Just be you, you know?'

He looks disappointed, takes his glasses off again and cleans them.

'The thing is, that is me. That's my story.'

'Fair enough.'

'Yeah,' he says. 'My sister told me I was being too self-hating. I didn't really think I was, and irrelevantly so too. I never thought about any of this stuff growing up. Race shit. Suddenly everyone's talking about diversity and you start to notice it and then once you notice it, you can't unsee it. Suddenly I'm obsessed with it, and still figuring it out. And I'm starting to wonder what I've let slide 'cause I just never thought about it before.'

'I don't mean to pick you up on it. You've only really given me the blurb for a show you're still writing.'

'I always thought that talking about race was lazy, before. Like, I just wanted to tell jokes, to large rooms of people. I want to make arenas piss themselves. That's okay, isn't it? I don't imagine myself getting there by doing the Indian thing. But now that my sister's died, and I've started thinking about family, I've realized she's the thing I wanted to talk about. Us, our journey. I'm struggling with articulating it because...'

'You've never really thought about before?' I'm trying not to get angry and/or throw my kebab roll at him. 'I get that it's important to you to talk about it. But does it still need to be said? It feels like we've moved on. Also, your show should be about you and your sister.'

I pick up my paneer kathi roll and bite into it so we can turn our attention to the food. It's too hot.

'I don't know,' he says, spooning some dhal into his mouth. 'A few months ago, I was trying to tell jokes. This is delicious, by the way,' he adds as consolation.

He unfolds the kathi roll and removes the kebab and onions from it. He reaches for the sachets of sugar, tears them both as one and sprinkles the grains on to the kathi, before re-rolling it and eating it.

'The closest I can get,' he says. 'My ba used to make the best sugar rotlis.'

'What happened to her?'

'I don't know. We drifted apart. She was in Kenya, we were here, in London. We were too lazy to write letters. It's sad. I really remember her. Maybe my show should be about her and my sister and me – we spent this week together, where it was like, I don't know. My dad left us with her, a stranger, and we'd never met her before, and we all just had to get on. We were in Mombasa, we didn't speak Swahili or Gujarati, and she didn't speak much English. It was wild. My sister fell in love with a donkey called Little Vijay, and then it got killed.'

'That sounds more fun than "A Lovely Bunch of Coconuts". Write *that* show.'

I stir my dhal to cool it down and watch as he lifts the can of lager to his mouth, letting it hover for an excruciating ten seconds.

'I'm really sorry,' he says flatly, before taking a long slow slurping sip of his Red Stripe. 'I'm not amazing company at the moment. I'm trying to write this show and be hilarious and also my sister's just died. And I want to tell jokes about her, but it feels too soon. I didn't even know she had cancer for the longest time.'

Raks eats more dhal.

My kathi roll is cool enough to eat. I do so in three silent bites, letting the grilled paneer and pepper squeak against my teeth. Raks checks his phone. He finishes his makeshift sugar rotli and pushes the plate away, holding his can of Red Stripe in one hand and his phone in the other.

'My sister was like a *Big Bang Theory* character,' he says. 'She was quite bizarre. I never quite got how to be with her because she would judge me whatever I did. And I needed that. She, in her own way, was pushing me to be better at everything I did by showing me how unimpressed with my choices she was. Our mum was like that, apparently. According to my ba. Constantly making you seek her validation. It's genius, actually. The ultimate tool for ambition-building. I just...' He puts the can of drink down, and scrolls mindlessly at his phone. 'I saw her will, and her final wishes. She hired you. My sister hired you from beyond the grave. It's all so strange. She died suddenly. We found out she'd been diagnosed with cancer for two months or something and hadn't told us. And she had this accident, where she nearly drowned. She confessed everything to our dad. We moved her into his flat and I looked after her. I stopped doing gigs and previews for a bit, and we just hung out. Me and my sister. And it was just so funny. Being twins, you have these silent reference points and in-jokes and it's where you feel most complete, like yourself. I thought I could write about her and me and how we were and how we are and how we ended up. Because we came back together. She died while we were watching *Star Trek 2*. We were slumped on Dad's sofa, and he was ordering pizza. Our heads nearly touching, her hand resting on mine. She whispered, this is the happiest I will ever be, and cried. It was such a sombre moment that the film became heavy and sad. At the end, just to make the moment lighter, I yelled KHAAAAAAAAAAN like Kirk does, and looked at her, but she had passed. The happiest she will be, she said.'

'I'm really sorry. It was a strange will request. But the more I think about it, it's really beautiful.'

'Yeah, she wrote so specifically in her will, like she knew you. And knew she was dying. That's just her. Find someone who looks like her to come to her funeral, and do the handshake we've been doing since we went to Kenya when we were kids. And it would freak me out. But it was her way of saying goodbye.' He sniffs. 'It's beautiful, actually. She just wanted to say goodbye. I always thought she thought I was a prick. But she must have thought enough of me to ensure she said goodbye. Thank you.'

I nod. I reach my hand out to touch his. I remove it when I realize how oily they are. I wipe at his wrist with a napkin.

'Do you think I'll be a sell-out if I do "A Lovely Bunch of Coconuts"?' he asks.

'What?' I say, admiring the old photo of Gama the Great, a pehliwan wrestler from the Edwardian era, on the door of the men's toilets. The women's toilet has Hema Malini as Basanti dancing for her life on broken glass to save Veeru from being shot by Gabbar Singh; her arms are crossed above her head, her chest is pushed out and she looks demure but anxious. She may have been a shrieking victim in that film but she was also strong, independent and nuanced. The men get a strong silent type in Amitabh Bachchan's character. The women get a heroine who dances to save a man's life.

Maybe I should try my hand at Bollywood. My Hindi's not terrible.

It's a better idea than this morning's offer – *naked, covered head to toe in silver paint, wearing an elephant mask and having gravy thrown at you.*

'Do you think I'm a sell-out?' he asks again, assuming I'm thinking very hard about the answer and not wondering what I'd look like naked with silver skin, and whether getting paid £50 plus breakfast is worth it to satisfy my curiosity.

I deflect while I think.

'Do you think you're a sell-out, Raks?'

He laughs. 'Of course not, I think I'm fucking hilarious. I feel like this show is not a good idea.'

I sigh. Why must everyone I go out on dates with turn romance into advice-seeking? Can't they read books and online blogs when they want to learn something about themselves? It's what I do.

'You don't need to be anything,' I say, picking the kebab off his plate and biting into it. 'You certainly aren't required to be self-hating. You don't play to the white crowds any more. You play to a new world which is slowly realizing that non-white people are also nuanced. You don't need to be the voice of all the brown people any more. There's enough of them around now that you don't represent all of us. We don't only have *Goodness Gracious Me* any more. We can admit that *East is*

East was problematic. We can say *Bend It Like Beckham* was a cheesy white man's wet dream. We can say that Cornershop didn't need the validation of Fatboy Slim. Why do you think you need to be the spokesperson for us, the ambassador to white people? Why even tell them things? You think I tell white people places like this exist? No way, man. This is our secret. This is the secret spot that you keep sacred so the balti houses and tandoori houses can thrive. We, us, the brown people, take our business where it belongs. Don't ever think you need to be the voice of a generation. Because that is the quickest way to being a sell-out.'

'I think I get what you're telling me,' he says, smiling. He takes his glasses off and places them on the table, then looks at me, with sad eyes, as though we're really seeing each other for the first time this evening. 'Whatever I do, it has to be real to me, not just a trope. No big statements. Just me.'

'Just you,' I say.

'But funny…'

'That's kinda important,' I reassure him.

I order a kulfi because I know he wants to go. We sit in silence and admire the artwork. I notice that the tiles around the room are the exact same ones used in my family home's downstairs toilet. I stare at the uneaten food on his plate and wonder whether I can finish off the rest of the kebab.

'A Man's Actions Are More Important than His Ancestry'

Mukesh. Edinburgh

I watch my son take selfies with fans, and sign his DVDs, and I feel proud that he is doing what he was always meant to do. He reminds me of Sailesh. Sailesh loved the attention but at the same time wanted to hide from it. It was too much for him. It's amazing what you remember, the more you play it in your head. The same goes for Rakesh. I sip my pint and wait.

Rakesh eventually walks towards me. As he does, three people congratulate him on a brilliant show.

'What did you think, Dad?' he asks.

'A show about a donkey?'

'It's a show about Neha,' Rakesh says. 'I wanted her to live for ever.'

'It did not have many jokes.'

I did not mean to offer this criticism. I could hear people laughing all the way through, chuckling, big laughs here and there, but I did not find any of it funny. It was all the truth. It was all about us. There is nothing funny about us.

'I didn't expect you to laugh, Dad,' Rakesh chuckles. 'A show called Little Vijay, all about the time you abandoned your kids with a stranger in the middle of Mombasa, it doesn't exactly paint you as father of the year.'

'Stranger? Eh,' I remind him. 'That is your ba you are talking about. She is family, not a stranger. You are very sentimental.'

'I know,' Rakesh says.

Two more people approach him and say they loved the show, interrupting me. One says that it made her cry. I want to talk to Rakesh about his sister. I have not seen him since the funeral and I want to tell him about the day she and he were born. It is just us two now. We have to stick together.

'Shall we go somewhere else?' I say, interrupting their conversation.

'Sorry,' Rakesh says to the people he is talking to. 'This is my dad.'

'Your son is fucking funny, mate,' one man says to me. His girlfriend nods. 'So fucking funny, mate.'

'Thank you,' I say. 'I taught him everything he knows.'

We are in another pub. It is quieter, near our hotel, near an Indian restaurant I would like to try. I ask Rakesh what I can get him.

He puts his hands on his hips and thinks.

'Okay. I was going to head to another spot at the Stand at midnight. Can't drink too much.' He looks at his watch. 'Okay. Sure, I guess I have an hour before I need to be there. I mean, what sort of drink are we talking? Is there a price limit – are you, like, beers, wines and soft drinks only? Or am I allowed a whisky chaser? If so, can I go for a decent whisky, given that we're in Scotland, or do I need to go for a high-street whisky? What if the wine I want is served by the bottle only? There are so many variables.'

'Rakesh, beta,' I say. 'I am your father. I will buy you whatever you want.'

He orders an ale. I order a vodka and soda. We sit at a table.

'Where shall we eat, bwana?' I ask, rubbing my stomach and winking.

'Dad, I have to do another set tonight. I don't know if I'll have time. But we'll get breakfast tomorrow before your train, yes?'

'I came here to spend time with you. We need to spend more time together.'

'Yes,' Rakesh says. 'We do. It's just, it's Edinburgh. It's kinda like the busiest time of the year for me.'

'You are hiding here,' I say.

'What do you mean?'

'I have not seen you since the cremation.'

When Rakesh left the wake, I followed him, to try and get him to come back. I saw him talking to a girl I did not recognize, and I watched them walk off together, to the park. My son has been broken by the loss of his sister, I know this. They did not realize how similar they are.

Rakesh takes after me in that he is a storyteller, and a funny one. Sometimes. While Neha was like Nisha, stubborn, headstrong, right.

Seeing this boy succeed here makes me happy. I did not think he could take this life. Growing up, he was so sensitive. Especially to criticism, particularly from Neha. She would never let him have it easy. If it was wrong, she would tell him it was wrong. If it could be better, she would tell him how to make it better. If it was good, it was not good enough.

When Rakesh told me he was going to be a comedian,

I added up in my head the cost of sending him to university. The amount of money it cost me to get him to find out that he wanted to tell jokes to strangers.

A girl approaches Rakesh. She looks familiar. She smiles at me as he rises. They hug.

'Hi,' she says to me.

'Dad, this is my friend Laila,' he says.

'Pleased to meet you,' Laila says.

I remember her from the funeral; the girl he chased after like a madman.

'Friend?' I ask.

'Friend,' Rakesh says, nodding.

'Raks, man, that show, it was perfect.'

'Thank you, that means a lot,' he says. 'I have you to thank.'

I watch them talk for a few minutes and look around the room. One of the things I still find strange in the UK, even after forty years, is how it feels to be the only brown people in the pub, yaar. I immediately worry that Rakesh and his friend are talking too loudly.

I remember when Rakesh was a little boy. Watching him run around the house, with a T-shirt on and no nappy, it was the cutest sight. Neha sitting and reading. And Rakesh running and running, wanting me to look at him.

Before Nisha died, she said to me, about these children, 'Be kind to them, always kind.'

And when I collected them from their ba, she said something similar: 'Both of your children can change the world. They have that in their destiny. Support them. Be their father, not their friend.'

Everyone had so much advice for me. All the time, advice.

Every day, new advice. as though they knew how to raise two children with no help.

Rakesh notices me as he says goodbye to his friend.

She says goodbye to us both and leaves, smiling.

'You hungry?' he asks me. 'I need to line my stomach.'

We are sitting in a chip shop, with a jacket potato in front of each of us. They are drowning in beans, covered by a thick layer of cheese.

It is my son's Edinburgh tradition.

Go to the Tempting Tatty. Get the jacket potato with cheese and beans.

'How often do you eat this?' I ask.

Rakesh tries to answer but his mouth is full. I hold my hand up to say stop.

'I do not want to see the contents of your mouth,' I tell him.

I reach into my overnight bag. I am lucky that my train was delayed and I did not have time to leave my things at my hotel before Rakesh's show.

I pull out my small glass container that used to contain cinnamon. Now it has chilli flakes.

I sprinkle some on my potato. Rakesh stops eating and looks up at me. He pauses, slightly disturbed by my action, and looks around. I put the container down between us. Then he slowly breaks out into a smile, picks it up and sprinkles it all over his potato.

'I've got chilli flakes in my overnight bag, swag,' he says.

'Pardon?' I reply.

'It's a Beyoncé thing. This is amazing, Dad. I love this. I love that you travel with this. Ready to chilli everything. The chilli man.'

'Your mum used to call it Indian-style,' I tell him, laughing. 'When we were out, and I added chilli to something, she'd say, chicken burger Indian-style. Or cucumber sandwiches Indian-style. Or jacket potato Indian-style. It always made me laugh.'

'Dad, you are hilarious,' he tells me. 'This is really, really funny. Anyway, it's good to see you. Thanks for coming up to my show. I can't believe it. I think this is the first time any of my family except Neha has ever seen my act. And what a show to come and see. The one about you. I mean, it would have been less awkward for me if you'd seen the one I did last year, about how I became an internet meme, but there you go.'

'I listened to the show on your website,' I tell him. 'I still do not understand what a meme is, but did you ever think to tell those people that you are not Muslim and therefore using your face as a way of describing angry Muslims is offensive to you?'

'No. Like I say in the show, whether I'm a Muslim or not isn't the infuriating part. It's that they thought I was an angry one. You have to show solidarity. Those people don't give you the benefit of nuance. So you have to stand side by side.'

'I have stood side by side,' I tell him. 'It is not a place I wish to be again. Have I told you about the story of how I met your mother?'

'Yes,' Rakesh says, looking down at his potato, shovelling a big piece into his mouth.

'Let me see. I have no reason to be anywhere. I find myself in an in-between world, with no purpose, except to lean with my back against the wall, across the road from Nisha's amee and papa's house...'

This show is different from the earlier one. This time the comedians, who are drunk, come up to do five minutes of material about the politics of the day. We are in a pub. The stage area has been dressed in a big black curtain. A man is talking about the Prime Minister and people are booing. There is chatter from the back of the pub. Rakesh is sitting next to me, shaking his right leg furiously. I put my hand on his knee to steady it. He must be nervous.

He takes out his phone and looks at something on the screen, then looks around him.

When his name is announced, he bounds on to the stage. I do not know how he has this much energy. I can feel the bottom of my stomach swimming with baked-bean juice and melted cheese. I feel heavy.

Rakesh's energy, on stage, is that of someone who has just been electrocuted and has five minutes of intensity before falling over. He is shrill. He talks in a voice I have not heard before. Normally, his voice is like mine, slow and mumbly. On stage, he is shrill, loud, a fast-talker brimming with nerves. His voice goes quickly up and down from falsetto to loud and assertive, sometimes in the same word. He is someone I have not met before.

'Colonialism,' he says. 'What's up with that?'

People laugh. I smirk. Colonialism was silly.

'Thanks for the railways. I always have to say thanks for the railways, it seems. Forty per cent of the country said colonialism was a good thing. Forty per cent? I don't understand it.

That's a lot of people who think that the systemic rape, pillage and resource-mining of countries across the world, enslaving whole generations, forcing them to be Christian – then when some countries fight back, giving them the illusion of democracy and dividing the people – is a good thing. A positive thing. Well done, the Brits. Wasn't colonialism great? It was shit. I know it was shit. My dad knows it was shit. He grew up during the British Empire, did you know that? The British Empire. And he thought it was shit. And the forty per cent of you who thought colonialism was a good thing – if you'd been alive at the time, it wouldn't have been like *Downton Abbey* for the majority of you fuckers. No, you feudal serfs would all be dead of scurvy and syphilis. How's that for white privilege? Everyone wants to go back to the good old days, no matter how shit their place in society would have been, because at least they would have owned the coloureds. Am I right, ladies and gentlemen? Colonialism, what's up with that?'

'Fuck off back to where you came from then…'

The audience gasps. I look around me, angry. How dare they interrupt my son? Go back to where he came from? My bloody son is from Harrow.

Rakesh freezes. He looks out into the crowd, a hand on his hip, and sighs. He doesn't know what to say. The audience is waiting for his response. He has none. Whispers start.

I stand up, trembling with the same combination of anger and fear as I did all those years ago, when Nisha and I stormed the community hall doors.

'Who said that?' I shout to the crowd.

'Yup,' Rakesh says. 'I brought my dad and he's going to beat up the dad of whichever fucker said that, so goodnight and always punch a Nazi and see you in the car park. I'm bringing my dad.'

The entire audience bursts into laughter. They clap. Some stand up. People pat me on the shoulder. My face slips from anger into laughter.

Rakesh jumps off the stage.

'Let's go,' he whispers.

'Why?' I say.

'Because I've just challenged someone to a fight and I want to go in case they actually accept.'

We have a drink in my hotel bar. People approach Rakesh and say well done. One of them, a desi with round glasses, smiles at me as Rakesh signs his DVD.

Rakesh is distracted. He is looking through social media. Someone has uploaded a video of the entire encounter and people are either calling us heroes or dismissing the whole thing as a set-up.

'Dad, man, I was going to be angry about you interrupting me and embarrassing me, but people are really rating this online. We're getting so many retweets. I think this might go viral.'

'What is a retweet?' I ask.

'A lot of people are talking about it online, let's just say that.'

'Is that good?'

'Yes, definitely,' Rakesh says, sipping at his gin and tonic. 'It means more people will come and see my show. Maybe they'll expect to see you. Should you stay? No. Okay, look, it was very funny. Just don't do it again. I can handle that sort of shit.'

'Why didn't you?' I ask.

'What do you mean? I was just working out what to say to him, and then you interrupted.'

'No, you stood there for so long in silence, the audience was getting nervous. I had to say something. You cannot let people talk to you like that,' I say. 'You cannot let them tell you to go home. This is your home.'

'Thanks, Dad, I appreciate the support. But that's my job, tearing down those ignorant dickheads. You didn't give me a chance.'

'No,' I say. 'You do not tear them down. You tell them this is not acceptable. No excuse, no racism, no laughter about racist jokes, no letting them getting away with it, no debate. Never. I told you the story tonight of how I nearly got beaten to death defending your mum.'

'You fought together.'

'We fought. For you to stand in silence, and let that man tell you to fuck off back to where you came from.'

'It's not that simple, Dad. I get a lot worse in nicer places, in worse places. You have to be able to take a joke. People say horrendous things to non-white comedians all the time.'

'And you think that's okay?' I ask.

I finish my pint and stand up, walking over to the bar to order two more drinks.

When I sit down, Rakesh is still staring at his phone.

'What's happening?' I ask, trying to imagine his online world and what it means.

'Ricky Gervais said it's a set-up, but cute. Piers Morgan has retweeted it. People are calling me a fake, saying it never happened.'

'You should take it down.'

'I can't,' he says, sipping at his next gin and tonic and running his hand through his shaggy hair and then his beard. I wish he would shave.

'We need to talk about Neha,' I say.

'I don't want to talk about Neha.'

'Why not?'

'Because, Dad, it's painful. And I need to do this month where I stand on stage and talk about her for an hour, and I just can't dwell on the death too much. She would have wanted me to do this show and not mope about her.'

'She is your sister, beta. You have to think about her. It is unfair to think that you can ignore these feelings. To her memory, and to your health.'

'Dad, I am committed to this theatre and this show for one more week. Every day, I see people, I talk to people, I tell jokes to people, I make people laugh, people tweet about my work online, people rate me, invite me to do paid gigs, invite me on the radio, I'm even due to go on the telly soon. It's all exhausting. Being so public, especially when something so private is destroying me. But it is what it is. When this month is over, I am doing as promised in her will, and I am taking her ashes to Kenya so she can be near Ba.'

'Why does she want to be near Ba? Besides, Ba might not even be in Kenya any more.'

'Where is she, then?' Rakesh asks.

'Why do you both keep asking me this? I don't know the answers. We lost contact. She is probably no longer alive.'

'I want to go and look for her. When I'm in Kenya.'

'Why?'

'Because she's my ba.'

'Son, I am sure she is not alive any more. She was old. It has been nearly twenty-five years since you were both with her.'

'I need to find her, Dad.'

Then I lose Rakesh to his phone again.

We finish our drinks and I can tell that my boy is ready for bed. I want to go up to my room and listen to my music and talk to Nisha.

'Shall we call it a night, bwana?' I say.

'Sure,' Rakesh says, standing up. 'We're having breakfast tomorrow, aren't we?'

'Of course. Will you meet me here?'

Rakesh nods. He gives me a hug.

Someone approaches him. A girl, she waves at him.

'Oh, hey, Raks. Oh, and this is... are you really his father?'

I blush. 'Of course I am.'

'What you guys did tonight, showing that heckler that racism is unacceptable here, I love it. Love trumps hate,' she says. 'Well done.'

'Thanks. We're just smashing racist fools, one person at a time.'

'Your dad is, at least,' she says. 'Not all superheroes wear capes. Anyway, have a great rest of the fest.'

She walks off. Rakesh looks at me and shakes his head.

'Of course,' he says. 'Of course I'm not trending on the internet. It's you, not me. Life is ridiculous.'

'Son,' I tell him, 'I love you. And you must not take shit from anyone. Not about this. Promise me. You're British, Rakesh

Jani. You are a British man, and it is your right to be here. If anyone disagrees, punch them in the face.'

'Dad, I'm a joke-teller.'

'Punch them in the face, Rakesh beta.'

'This is your fatherly advice to me? Punch people in the face.'

'You know what we went through to give you a life here. And now you have to ensure that life is preserved for those who come after you.'

'Thanks, Dad.'

'You deserve to have great things happen to you, beta. Many, many great things. I am sorry I did not give you much time when you were a child. I have been thinking about it since Neha died. Since she told me this. You deserve only the good things. But remember, only take them if they are good. Do not take opportunities that come with bullshit.'

'I won't, Dad. Look, I know I'm destined to be great. Ba told me when I was younger, and I'm certain good things will happen. I know that. But that has to be my focus, Dad. It really does. Especially if I have to work twice as hard.'

'Son,' I say. 'I don't have much advice to give you…'

'Untrue,' he quips. 'You've been advising me all night. Carry on…'

'Once you are great, remember that people look up to you and you cannot do any of this in isolation.'

'I can feel my ego tingling, the amount of times I've called myself great. I need to stop.'

'You should have said something to that man,' I tell him, pointing my finger into his chest. 'You should have said something.'

'I know. I'm going to go. I can jump on another late-night set. You know, you're internet-famous now, Dad. They're calling you #rakspops.'

'It should have been you who is internet-famous.'

'See you tomorrow,' he says, turning towards the door.

'Bye-bye, beta,' I say, to my son, the comedian who will change the world.

As he leaves, I take out my smartphone and look for his Twitter account on the internet. #rakspops, that's me.

He has more followers than I thought. He must become a leader.

'All Cassavas Have the Same Skin but Not All Taste the Same'

Rakhee. New York

The first time he comes in, he lectures me about our menu, telling me that calling it a 'chai tea latte' is cultural misappropriation. I smile, thinking he's joking, but then he launches into a whole spiel about it, and I'm like, dude, I just work here.

'You know chai tea latte is a redundant phrase, right?' he says. He's from London. He might think that over here, we're all gonna be fawning over his accent but no chance, buddy, this city? This city is full of tight-asses just like you. 'It's cultural misappropriation. Chai means tea, right? So you're pretty much serving tea-tea, like tea-flavoured tea. I'd like some tea – what flavour, sir? Tea-flavoured tea, please. And anyway, seeing as you mean masala chai, not chai chai, so I guess a spiced tea, you know it's made with mostly milk, right? Half milk, half water, probably. Or if you're being really luxurious, all milk, all day. So having a masala chai latte is redundant, because it's already made with milk? What are you going to do? Add milk to the tea-flavoured tea that's made with milk? Mmmmm, delicious.'

I can't help but smile at him committing to the bit. Like, he really wants to own this moment.

'And what can I get you?' I ask.

'I'd like an Americano coffee, please,' he says, laughing. 'Surely, if it's American, you'd just call it an American coffee, right?'

'One Americano,' I call out. 'Would you like it in or out?'

'In, please.'

'For here,' I shout.

Behind me, I can feel Maggie pretending I'm invisible again. So I call it out a second time.

'I fucking heard you,' I hear her mutter.

I take the payment and carry on serving. Serving's better than the alternative. If there's no customers, there's the code of the barista: if you've got time to lean, you've got time to clean.

Hard-ass boss, I mean, this is Brooklyn, I should be sitting with my feet up, reading the book of Zadie Smith essays I brought to read on the L. If I've got time to read…I must be an essayist and writer living in the most saturated place for essayists and writers in the world, serving up coffee to them.

I watch this guy sit in the window and stare outside. He's brought a magazine but he doesn't touch it. He's got his phone on the table but he doesn't touch it. He goes into a deep stare with the crosswalk outside, watching the borough throb.

The second time he comes in, he orders his Americano. He's quieter. Less showy.

'Sorry for being an asshole yesterday,' he tells me.

I shake my head. 'I fed your feedback to the owner. Wait – can you feed feedback?'

'I think you just feed back.'

'No, but I was feeding back your feedback.'

'So you fed back to the owner that I had commented…'

'Wait, no, because you had feedback, that I relayed. Yes, I relayed your feedback to the owner.'

'And…'

'He thinks you're an asshole,' I say, laughing.

'That's fair.'

'I think you're fine. You're okay. Americano? Or as the Americans call it, coffee?'

'Please, thank you. Can I have it to go?'

'Sure,' I say. 'No people-watching today?'

He doesn't reply. A call comes through on his phone and he takes it, listening intently as he pays, juggles with phone, change and wallet, and goes to wait for Maggie, the slow-ass, to pour him a fucking coffee.

The next customer tries to give me his number. I decline it. He drops it into the tip jar anyway, winking at me. Fucking creep.

The third time he comes in, he asks if I want to get a cup of coffee some time.

'Or,' he says, 'maybe something different. You're probably sick of coffee, right? What about baos? I could really go for some. You like baos?'

'Baos are fine,' I say, laughing.

I look around. Maggie's listening. This coffee shop has a strict no-fraternization policy. I think it's because some bigwig hot-shot bullshit whatevers come here and they've said to the owner that people keep slipping them their scripts and head shots and manuscripts, and they're like, I just want my one-drop vanilla macchiato or spiced pumpkin latte in peace.

'I get off at seven,' I say quietly.

Noting my secret squirrel nod, he nods and mouths, quarter past, out front. I smile.

I get asked out for a date every single fucking day.

He's the first one not to say I look exotic or ask if I'm related to Riz Ahmed or Mindy Kaling.

Look, it's tough being Indian in the most hipster parts of this fucking place, okay? I remember, a guy said namaste when I walked past a yoga studio, and I was like, guy, what the fuck man, you wanna say hello to me? Say hello. Don't think you're being all spiritual and shit. Fuck you, buddy.

I was carrying a tiffin filled with my lunch. Four layers – dhal, bhatt, shaak, rotli – and I think he thought, oh, look, a desi girl with her spiritual food carrier, how exotic and quaint?

Fuck you, buddy. It keeps things separate. It's practical as fuck and when I come home late at night, it makes me feel safe to know I'm carrying steel with sharp edges. It's not exotic. It's daily life. My dad took one of these to work with him every single day. He told me once that a security guard searched it for a bomb. He worked at that same damn hospital for thirty years and they still treated him like a terrorist.

I wore a kurti one day. And people were like, oh, is it Diwali or some shit? I was like, Mr Mayonnaise, please, it's fucking ninety degrees outside. You think I want to wear a T-shirt made of synthetic bullshit, or do I wanna wear breathable cotton and look ek dum first class, you tell me?

But this guy, British desi guy, he seems okay. Plus, he's right about the chai tea latte thing. I looked it up.

I changed the menu that night after work. It's chalkboard, so whatevs. I changed it to 'masala chai'.

The owner didn't notice. Neither did Maggie.

'What name do you want on the cup?' I ask.

'Raks,' he replies. And he doesn't spell it. Because I should know.

I pick up a cup. And I write R-A-X on it. I add a winky face emoticon so he knows I'm joking.

He smiles and the break of white through the unkempt beard and messy curly hair is a beacon of hope.

Seven-fifteen, I mouth.

He nods and walks along the line to collect his waiting coffee.

I nearly dance on the spot but there's another customer waiting. She's staring at her phone, and orders without paying attention.

I give her the best customer service she will ever have in her life. And she doesn't even know it.

There are some benches navigating a flower bed outside our coffee shop. They're not supposed to be there, but the tree in the flower bed offered such magnificent shade, people started sitting there in summer with their cups of coffee, to watch the world go by. Except their fat asses kept breaking the fence. My manager took the law into his own hands, literally, by building the fences again, this time with seats made from floorboards that have been in our basement for the longest time, just lying against the wall, taking up space – from before, when this was another Brooklyn coffee shop under a different name.

Raks is waiting for me. He has changed into a plain white

T-shirt, a navy blazer and some brogues. He's wearing the same khakis.

'Date clothes?' I ask.

'Oh, yes,' he replies. 'I forgot how you Americans love to label everything a date. Want to go to the movies? Sure, it's a date. Hey, I'm hungry. Let's grab dinner. It's a date. Who are you dating at the moment? A bunch of people. I went on a date to buy a stapler, a date to post some mail, and a date to see one of the new Marvel films. Which one? I don't know, I was too busy making out in the back row. Because it was a date.'

'I wholeheartedly feel like the British should avoid saying "making out".'

'I agree. It sounds like I'm telling your mum on you.'

'So what do you want to do?'

'What does one typically do on a first date?'

'Get coffee, I guess.'

'I bet you're sick of coffee.'

'You used that line before.'

'I did. Sorry.'

'So,' I say, placing my hands on my hips. 'This is a date?'

'I guess so,' Raks says, extending his hand. 'Official date introductions then: I'm Raks.'

'Rakhee,' I say.

'Wait, I asked out a girl called Rakhee? This is amazing. This has never happened before. I've literally been waiting for this moment my entire life,' he says, standing up. He gestures with his hands to the sky like someone receiving manna from God. 'This is the best news.'

'Raks and Rakhee?'

'Rakesh and Rakhee. We are equals.'

'Define equal,' I say, smiling. 'You're still a man. That makes you pretty much in some other level of fucking food chain, you know.'

'Yes, Rakhee, but we're both Indian. So in that respect, what trumps what? Dick or pigment? Because if pigment trumps, then we are equal. If dick trumps, well, I mean, that just sounds very funny.'

'Let's go for a walk,' I say. 'We're kinda just riffing in front of my work at this point. And I'm tired of this place.'

'Beer,' Raks says. 'Let's get a beer. We need beer. See, this is what the British do on dates. They don't date. They go somewhere that serves alcohol, let that cut through the awkwardness and inhibitions, and then they get off with each other, or they find something political to disagree on. In my experience, anyway.'

'Get off?'

'It's like make out, but it sounds way more handsy, don't you think?'

'A beer would be lovely,' I say.

Raks pauses as if to remind me it's my neighbourhood.

It's been hot today. I can see that from the number of people standing in the shade of the buildings with cold coffees. I probably made half of them. I haven't been outside once today. Workday A/C blinkers. I can feel the middle of my back slimy with sweat now I'm exposed to the elements.

I walk Raks to a bar that has a shaded courtyard. At this time of the day, the sun perfectly splits the street in half down the middle. Both banks have thick shade. The sun gives the street that strange *au naturel* Instagram filter you associate with New York City. Actually, that thing you associate, it's a

Brooklyn thing. You wouldn't get this much axeing of light in Manhattan.

I feel anxious for some reason.

Raks has a nervous energy about him. Not in a way that makes me feel unsafe. Just in that he seems to talk a lot, he keeps a lot of thoughts spinning, and if he let these thoughts fall to the floor, he would have to start dealing with life.

I spy a table in the courtyard and skip over to it, exaggerating my steps, so that any other interloper knows the wild moves I put in to secure a seat.

Raks joins me in my bound; he skips towards the table as though he's doing the running man. I spin round and moonwalk to the table.

'That's the worst moonwalk I've ever seen,' he says.

'Hey, buddy, no negging on a first date, write that rule down for sure.'

'I'm not negging you. It genuinely was terrible.'

We sit down. I wipe off a fleck of lettuce from the surface of the table. It leaves a single sesame seed. I flick that off too.

I look up at Raks. He has put on sunglasses. Even though we're in the shade. I can't see him now.

'What do you do, Raks?' I ask.

'Why do Americans always ask that first? Defining the parameters of engagement, as though our careers are social status. It feels so labelling. It's like, my first question to you would be, how are you doing? What's been happening with you? I think that's not necessarily British, but all I can think of is that the British say, how do you do? And the Americans say, what do you do?'

'Do you think you're British?' I ask. 'I mean, I'm American.

I get that. My national identity is clearly defined to the point where I have a cultural understanding of where I'm from, where my parents were born. But Lord above, I pledged allegiance to that damned flag every damned day for so many years at school. I'm American. Every desi from the UK I meet is always like, my dad's from this village in Gujarat, my mum grew up near this village in Kenya, or whatever.'

'We have this cricket test thing in the UK. Well, it was a thing. Maybe it wasn't. Anyway, there was this politician, pretty old-school, and by old-school, I am implying he was probably a racist, but you know, don't sue me. Norman Tebbit, he who invented the saying "on yer bike..."'

'I've never heard that saying,' I laugh.

'He once said he didn't understand how people don't have jobs. Every morning his dad got on his bike and went out looking for work.'

'So what's on your bike?'

'It's like, get out of here, do something useful.'

'Right, cool. And the cricket test?'

'Norman Tebbit was annoyed that all these immigrants were coming over here and not supporting our sports teams. Instead they were supporting those of their countries of birth, and worse than that, their children were not integrating, because they were following their parents' sports teams, and not England. So, if you want to be English, you support England. Or fuck off back to India.'

'Wait, wait, wait,' I say, nodding at the waiter to indicate that I am thirsty. 'A major politician is telling you that integration is all about sports teams. Sports, sporting teams, people playing sports. Sports are stupid. I know that is the most un-American thing I can say, because society views you with the utmost suspicion if you do not like sports in this country. But how can you make such a declaration about your sense of self, your sense of identity, your sense of nationalism, according to who you support in sports?'

'It's dumb, right?'

'The dumbest.'

'And here's the ridiculous thing – I did some gigs in India, and I was doing material about this very stuff, about being supposedly Indian but my dad being from Kenya, and growing up in an England where people wanted me to canonize Ian Botham over Kapil Dev – they're both cricketers – and instead, all I wanted to do was listen to New York 1970s garage punk and watch Wes Anderson films. And you know what everyone said?' I shake my head. 'Nothing, not one laugh, not one acknowledgement of relatability, not one amen. Someone came up to me afterwards and said, my friend, stop living in a world that wants you to feel post-colonial and know that the feeling you have is post-colonial colonialism, that shit never dies. So just get on with life. So I stopped. I stopped doing stuff about race for a bit. Because it's not important to everyone. It's only important to the children of immigrants. And we're spoilt anyway.'

'Wait, so you're an electrician?'

Raks laughs, quietly, but it's still a laugh.

'No, I'm a comedian. I'm here doing some gigs.'

'Oh, cool. That's *what you do.*'

'Indeed it is.'

We order beers.

The waiter lingers in case we want food. I shake my head.

'You know, I haven't laughed once,' I tell him.

'Yes, it's a truth universally acknowledged that stand-ups are either unfunny morose obsessives or desperate for your laughs. Sorry.'

'I'm joking, dude. But seriously, it's sad that you didn't want to do stuff about things that are important to you.'

'My last show was about race, I guess. It was about me and my sister, and our place on the brown scale. And how, when we were growing up in London, it was so much more binary than it is now. And actually, I kinda wish I was growing up now. I wouldn't have been ostracized by my cousins for preferring Radiohead to Safri Boys. And how frivolous it is to self-define by what band you like.'

'All this stuff, it's important.'

'Only in the sense that it can make people universally comfortable or uncomfortable. Material without maximum relatability or shock doesn't work.'

'True. Yeah, the reaction to the show was strange. People laughed, sure, but there was a lot of crying. It was very, very personal. About my sister who died, and the things that made us different and the things that made us the same. Through the lens of a weird trip we took to Kenya once and how our ba told us both what our destinies would be. People really went for it. They kept saying how universal it was. And I was like, I'm glad you saw the universal stuff, but don't forget the specific stuff about culture and heritage. I guess you're right.'

'I'm sorry about your sister.'

'Thank you. The show was my way of dealing with it. I wrote it in like two weeks before Edinburgh started. I went on this weird date and got told off for my original idea. When we texted after, she was like, just write something personal. And I did.'

'That's cool,' I say. 'So what did your ba tell you about your naseeb?'

'She told me I would be great.'

I laugh.

Our beers arrive. I take a sip. Raks takes off his sunglasses and squints at me while he sips his beer.

He sneezes.

'Bottled beer, man,' he says. 'I'm definitely allergic to whatever gas they squirt into this stuff to keep it bottle-fresh.'

'You want something else?' I ask, looking around for the waiter. He shakes his head.

After a pause, I say, 'I think it's interesting. That in India, our struggle to belong is completely bewildering. It's like, my cousins, my desi ones, whenever they come here, they're just, like, I'm squatting here but actually I belong in India. I couldn't live there.'

'The fact that we're even talking about it would infuriate them.'

'What else is there to talk about?' I ask.

'What do you do?' he says.

I think about the question. I think about how to best self-define. It feels uncomfortable, untruthful, even, to say anything other than that I'm a barista. My Liberal Arts degree. My blog. The one article I put up on Medium. All of them feel like things I did when I wasn't working.

To be a barista.

It's a growth industry.

The thought of being a writer, worse, an essayist, as a career terrifies me.

What would that life look like? Remember when you got up at your own tempo, dressed in your favourite tweed and went and sat outside a café all day, filling your notebook with sketches that would eventually become your novel, watching the ebb and flow of those toing and froing between their jobs and homes, you thinking, I am living a waking dream right now. I am exactly where I need to be.

No. Me neither.

There's nothing worse for the modern writer than the reminder of a time when we got paid, a reminder of the times of the boozy lunch, a reminder of the time when we were the main source of home entertainment. Now we're competing with video games, streaming television, the internet, we have to work harder. And hey, we have to work. Someone tweeted this article in the English *Guardian* recently bemoaning the death of the novelist's life. There was an author who couldn't afford to build a writing shed because he couldn't write in his house. Wah wah wah. If you can't afford to write your next book, get a job. It's not hard. The publishing industry is shrinking while the craft coffee experience is expanding exponentially. The world needs baristas. It makes financial sense to train up as a barista. There's no shame in it. It's a trade. The world loves coffee. It's an experience that can't be replicated on the internet. Where's the shame in working a job?

I am a good barista.

'I'm a writer,' I say.

*

Our check arrives.

The gentleman, Raks, takes the folder and looks at it. He pulls a shocked face and returns it to the centre of the table.

'I always do that joke where I pretend to be horrified by any bill. But I stacked it because I was worried you'd think I was one of those men who automatically assumes they'll pay for the company of females and issue an edict of power.'

'I'm a struggling writer,' I say. 'You can pay for me.'

'I'm a comedian doing a night in Brooklyn,' he replies. 'We're a long way away from the *Tonight Show*.'

'But you're destined to be great,' I say. 'You may not be able to afford two beers now. But when you hit manifest destiny, you'll laugh about this moment.'

I take the folder and open it to look at the bill. $17. I get out my wallet and scan down the items listed, to make sure we haven't been screwed. I'm just like my dad. The accountant. With his own calculator. His own diligence at ensuring that nothing was being sneakily added to the total.

The man assumed the entire world was trying to take advantage of him. I assumed, for years, it was because of the way our family had left Uganda. Then I realized it was his nature. He wasn't suffering from a longstanding grief of exile from the country of his birth. He was naturally paranoid.

We're good.

Table 13, I note. Underneath, it says Mr and Mrs Apu.

I look up at the waiter. He's innocuously tattooed, a patchwork quilt of maritime and '70s cartoon references snake around his forearm, like a cast of characters, lining up to say hello. He wears a Miami Heat basketball top and he wears his hair in a man-bun.

Apu. From *The Simpsons*. Us. Really.

Raks raises his eyebrows at me. I grimace.

Thank you, come again.

'What?' he asks. I push the folder towards him. He opens it and scans the receipt. 'That's expensive, innit? It's just bottles.'

I tap on the offending section of the receipt. He looks at it, then he looks up at me. He looks around. There aren't that many people in here. He looks at the waiter and back at me before rolling his eyes.

'Fucking hipsters,' he whispers.

'Right?'

'He's not getting any tip.'

'He's not getting any of our money either.'

'He probably thinks it's cool.'

'Is that okay? Is that good enough?'

Raks thinks hard about his answer. He pauses. He scratches in the epicentre of his mass of curly hair, searching for the crown.

'No, I guess not,' he says.

The waiter walks over to us; he's removed his cap.

'You all set?' he asks.

I stare at him. He has bleached blonde hair, with no roots. That, coupled with his very pale skin, the sallow Draco Malfoy milky-skin look, the hollow small eyes and omniscient smirk, it angers me so much.

'What the fuck, man? Apu?' I hold up the receipt to him.

He goes to grab it.

'What's that?' he says.

I pull it back.

'Oh, no, I'm holding on to this one. I'm going to make it internet-famous. Apu? Thank you, come again? Is that how you distinguish us? As Indian? We came here to drink a beer and you racially abuse us and charge us seventeen bucks for the privilege?'

'I – I'm sorry,' he says. He throws his hands up as if to absolve himself of any guilt. 'Look, I'm no racist. I'm from Virginia. That's just how we talk down there. I'm sorry. I didn't think you'd see that.'

He makes a grab for the receipt.

I stand up to face him. I look down. Raks has placed his thumbs at the top of his nose and is pressing down, looking up at our confrontation, almost embarrassed.

'You didn't think I'd see that? Is that really your idea of an apology? I'm sorry you saw my racist receipt. You weren't meant to see my racist receipt. So because you saw the racist receipt you weren't meant to see, I mean, that's on you. Is that your argument? Is that what you're telling me? That's just how we talk down there? How does that have any impact on my life whatsoever? You telling me that your common racist parlance in your state of wherever-the-fuck is acceptable everywhere else? I mean, how dare you? How dare you blame me?'

'I'm not a racist,' the waiter begs.

'I didn't say you were,' I tell him. 'I did not tell you that you were a racist. I said you wrote a racist thing. Do you even know the difference between the two?'

Raks starts to stand up, to leave. I look at him until he sits back down.

'Can you call the manager, please?' I ask.

'I am the manager,' the guy says, looking around at the two

or three other customers, hoping for allies, instead getting back a whole lot of stink-eye.

'Well, you should be ashamed of yourself, then,' I tell him. 'I will be making a formal complaint, buddy.'

I don't know where this is coming from. My cousin told me I had become increasingly confrontational since working in the coffee shop. Like I had all this pent-up rage from smiling at people all day and treating them like they are always right. And this was making me project all my frustrations on to things I could control. I told him it was the worst thing he could do, to tell a woman of colour she's being irrationally angry, like not only does she come from a subservient culture, but her womb is stopping her from acting in an appropriate fashion.

We walk out of the bar.

I keep the receipt.

We're walking towards the end of the block.

'Can I take a photo of the receipt?' Raks asks. 'I want to put it on my Facebook. I reckon there's something funny I can do with this.'

'Why didn't you say anything?' I ask him.

'What do you mean?' he says, confused.

'I argued for our people. And you sat there.'

'I didn't want to talk over you. Everything you said was perfect, actually,' he offers limply.

'You could have agreed more forcefully.'

'Yes, I could have. I'm basically a coward.'

'You're a comedian. You're supposed to be the bravest of the lot.'

'Comedians have a thick skin. And a thin skin. On stage, when we're in control, it's perfect, and when we're not, we're getting better, stronger, harder, faster.'

'You're not turning this into material,' I tell him. 'This is life. Promise me.'

He nods.

I look at my phone, wondering if I can find myself an excuse to leave.

I go to see his stand-up show.

He opens with a bit about American sitcoms and the omnipresence of what he called 'the wanking foreigner'. How everyone who is not American, from somewhere foreign, another culture, will be caught jerking off somehow by a beautiful Westerner.

The frustration at not being able to get it on with the beautiful Westerner, the complications arising from adjusting to city life in Western society, the omnipresence of cleavage – it proves too much for 'the wanking foreigner'. 'The wanking foreigner' will be impotent in front of women; these white girls will be the subject of their wanking fantasies. He says the word 'wank' so many times that it's really funny, then funny, then really funny, then unfunny, then tedious, then more tedious, then the funniest thing in the world.

Even though I've lost respect for him, I can't help laughing.

'The wanking foreigner,' he says. 'This is what America wants to tell itself – that its girls are "for internal use only", that they don't want to leave or to marry or fuck people from other places, that they exist purely for American dicks, and the only way to disempower the allure of the dusky foreigner is to turn him into the wanking foreigner, pathetic, and privately living out a perverse fantasy of unattainment.'

The audience is with him, waiting for the punchline.

'We are impotent, and hard,' Raks says. 'It's confusing.'

I laugh. The audience erupts, whoops and claps and belly-laughs.

He's good.

He asked me to stay and wait for him after the show but I leave as he says goodnight.

The audience applauds enthusiastically.

He bows.

I sit up off my seat and stand. I wait until he's not looking and then I walk towards the door.

Outside, men thrash away at plastic containers with drumsticks. The city is a cacophony. Even on its quiet streets, you can always hear cars and the squelch of sneaker on concrete. You can feel the buzz of electricity and wi-fi in the air. You're breathing in the cloud. I stand outside and look around the intersection, either for a dive bar I can decompress in for an hour while I read my book, or a subway stop.

I don't know Crown Heights too well.

The people walking past all look as though they work in publishing. Between the bookish totebags and Warby Parker glasses, the brogues and pressed chambray shirts, I might as well be suffering at a Jonathan Franzen reading with all the white people in the city.

'Hey,' I hear. 'Rakhee.'

I turn around. It's Raks. He's smiling apologetically. I smile back at him. I'm tired. I don't want to stand here.

'It was so hot in there,' I say.

He nods his agreement.

'You were great,' I assure him.

He smiles. Like a baby, a baby dog.

'I'm going to go home now,' I offer by way of peace.

He cocks his head to one side.

'I'll see ya,' I say.

'Wait, Rakhee,' he says. 'We didn't get our baos.'

He points across the road to a bao joint that has a service window.

Three guys in vests and baseball caps lounge outside, smoking. One of them has a shirt draped over his shoulder that's the same colour as the signage. Slow night.

'I'm going to go,' I say.

'Is this because of that bar manager? That dickhead?' he says.

I want to tell him yes, that it is everything.

That not saying anything, that smiling and either accepting the systems that oppress us or using them to tell a story to a bunch of strangers, where you get to control the narrative for maximum impact, it's disingenuous and weak. We are gods. And we are treated like animals. For years we thought we were the problem. For years we were made to feel like we were being too confrontational, too sensitive, too unassimilated, making us feel guilty when we weren't the problem, lying to ourselves that these things were in our heads, that no one else could see them.

And then you're handed a receipt that calls you Apu, and you find yourself explaining why the word is toxic, and you're back where you started again. Alone, because it's only ever you who calls it out. Everyone else counts on your bravery.

'No, Raks,' I say. 'I've got to be at work tomorrow. And you have an adoring audience to charm again in an hour. Have a great rest of your trip.'

He grimaces. 'I fucked this up, didn't I?'

'You did,' I tell him. 'It's okay. You can turn it into material when you realize your destiny of greatness.'

'A Donkey Will Always Say Thank You with a Kick'

Uncle Dave. London

The number of times I have to write 'It's just a joke' in an email, I should have it as a template. These bloody over-sensitive left-wing comedians never get it. Your job is to be funny first.

Funny first.

No one is watching my show for my politics. They're watching it for the jokes.

I look at the bio of this guy and try to remember why we decided to put him in the show.

Box-ticking exercise from upstairs, probably. More women, more coloured people, more disabled people. Do you fucking know how hard it is to find a Bengali paraplegic lass? I mean, don't even try and ask for her to be gay as well.

It's exhausting.

I'm trying to put on a weekly topical news show. Box-ticking should be for council meetings. It has no place in comedy. Funny. Is. Funny. How many times do I have to fucking say it?

Raks Jani – not even nominated for a Perrier. Not even. And still here he is, refusing to say one of the many jokes we've given him.

Racist, apparently.

He should think himself lucky. He is killing comedy. He

may not realize it but he is destroying the fabric of the funnyman industry. First, he thinks he's owed a place in my show because he's a minority. Secondly, think about the word, minority. Who does he think the majority of our audience is? Fucking Mr Patels up and down the country.

Sometimes this shit forces the racist out of me. Just because I'm so fucking furious at having my fucking show meddled with. It's a comedy show. It's not supposed to put representation above funny. Funny is funny.

He's not even done a major tour yet.

I'm so angry, I don't even reply to Simon with something bland like, he's free to suggest alternative jokes, as long as we get takes of both. Both Simon and I know what'll end up in the edit. I don't email that back.

Instead, I'm pacing my office, looking out through the glass at my production worker bees. A quick headcount – Sri, Ming, Ore, Paul, Mo – yeah, we're fucking representative here. Those guys, fucking hard workers, that's why they're here.

Box-tickers like Raks make things twice as hard for those here on merit.

I storm out of my cubicle and stand in the main office. People look up at me. They feel my presence when I enter a room.

'Are they still in rehearsals?' I ask Sri, who has a live camera feed straight to the studio. She looks up from one screen to another, then shakes her head without looking at me.

I walk towards the stairs, trying to see, in the reflection of the glass door, if people are looking at me, knowing that someone is about to get bollocked.

*

I met Raks on Monday. He was booked already but came in with his agent, darling Dotty, to come and meet me. She probably told him I'm a kingmaker and he needs to pay his tribute to me. Eat the man's shit, she said to him, and you'll be rivalling Jack Whitehall for saturation point.

I'm not going to argue. It's a fair assessment.

I've eaten enough shit to know that shitting it back out the other side and feeding it to someone else – well, that's where the power lies. If there's no one lower than you to eat your shit, you're literally the bottom of the shitheap.

He made me laugh. He said, due to the traditions of his culture, he now has to call me Uncle. Uncle Dave, he called me. Thank you for the opportunity, Uncle Dave. I laughed.

He talked a bit about his Edinburgh show, how he found it, his second full hour, a personal show about the death of his twin sister. Barrel of laughs. Grief is only funny years later. He talked about the show like I had seen it. He talked about the show like I knew everything about him and his comedy. I stopped him.

'Raks, I know a lot of your sort.' I paused, to let him think I meant Asians. 'Up-and-coming comedian is the break-out star of Edinburgh. You're heading for big things fast. And you want it all now. You want *Live at the Apollo*, you want panel shows, you want meetings about the sitcom loosely based on your life. But being the break-out star is only the first due you have to pay.'

Raks nodded like I was giving him the keys to the car that'll drive him to the kingdom.

'That's true, Uncle Dave.'

'This isn't advice, Raks. This is a warning. I've seen too many of you lot crash and burn and die on your fuckin' arse too many times. Don't die on your arse, my friend.'

'Good advice, Uncle Dave,' Raks said, like he was patronizing me. Like he knew.

'What's the best bit of advice you've ever been given?' I asked, throwing him a curveball.

'To be honest, Uncle Dave,' he said, 'my dad's advice was always, stay away from white people, they want to murder you. So at this point, what you told me, even if you meant it as a warning, it's now single-handedly the most important piece of advice I've ever been given.'

'Your dad sounds like an interesting man.'

'I mean, most white people *do* want to murder him. He's a dickhead.'

I laughed.

I have to walk through the studio to get to the green room and the dressing rooms. It's just the guest presenter and the two regular hosts who get dressing rooms. The other two on the panel, we shove 'em next to the bowls of dry-roasted peanuts, sweets and ply them with coffee and alcohol and hope for some sort of jittery high-octane performance. Also, if they're politically opposed – like Raks and this *Daily Mail* columnist – then hopefully they'll either want to fight or fuck by the time the cameras roll.

Television, you do make my dick hard.

Today's guest presenter makes my dick hard too. Maybe because the way he travelled round India on those railways and managed to remain posh and British was so utterly charming. Who am I kidding? I love a posh knowledgeable bloke with a strong chin.

Charlie told me that my dad has a strong chin. Maybe there's something in that.

Raks is on his phone when I storm into the green room. He looks up and smiles, nervous. He knows why I'm here.

The *Daily Mail* columnist looks up from his paper - the fucker is reading his own fucking paper - and nods at me.

I beckon Raks with my finger. My index finger. I will not give him the benefit of words. The stupid curly-topped arsehole. Just one look at his tired, bearded face encased in a cauliflower of hair and I want to break him down into tiny little pieces.

He gestures to himself. Who, me? he asks.

'Of course you, who the fuck else am I pointing at?'

The *Daily Mail* columnist lowers his paper on hearing the word 'fuck'. I see a smirk. Raks stands up and follows me as I leave the room.

I don't tell him where we're going. We're silent as we walk the corridors. When we reach the stairs I head down to the basement.

I can hear him behind me. Almost skipping.

In the basement, there's a screening room, empty and soundproofed.

It hums with the dampness of foam walls and heavily cushioned chairs.

'Whisky?'

He hesitates.

He's working out whether this is something he wants to do. His big telly break. Circumventing the usual route of smaller appearances and going on one of the big guns. And I'm offering him alcohol when he needs his brain the most.

I'm not stupid, son.

'Join me,' I say.

I turn to him. He nods. His entire head of hair shakes when he does. I walk behind the bar and fiddle about in the cupboard till I feel the neck of a bottle at the back. I pull it out.

Secret supply. Everyone else gets bottled lager and boxed wine. This is for me. For emergencies.

Noting that it needs to be replenished, I pour two fingers each of the Talisker in plastic cups and put the bottle down. I hand one to Raks.

I like to wait, to see where they sit, what they do, how they react. I hover behind the bar.

Raks stands and waits for my lead. He is scared.

'Take a seat,' I tell him.

Raks leans back on to the arm of one of the folded chairs. He looks at me and waits. He shifts till he is straddling the armrest like a bike saddle. He puts one foot up on the folded chair it's attached to.

'Indian-style, eh?' I tell him.

'Sorry?'

'That's how Indian uncles sit, right? I had this guy tell me that he had to ban his kids from sitting Indian-style at the dinner table. He's Indian too. Said it was rude.'

'Dunno. It's just comfortable, sorry.'

He puts his foot back on the floor.

'Apparently all Indians, even you, have elongated tendons in your heels, helps you with that squat that you all do, while you're talking, or cleaning, or shitting or whatever.'

'Wow, I never knew that.'

I wait for the interaction to sink in.

'Tell me a racist joke,' I say.

Raks stands up.

'Sorry?' he says, confused.

'Remember when you came in for a meeting with your agent? And I gave you that warning.' I nod to prompt. He looks confused. 'And you said you'd only ever received good advice from me.' He nods. 'Trust me. Tell me a racist joke.'

Raks looks at his shoes, then brings the cup of whisky up to his mouth. He sniffs it, touches the rim to his nostril, then places it on his bottom lip before tipping it.

'What was that?' I ask, as he baulks at the taste.

He doesn't answer me. Instead he murmurs, 'I lost.'

'Raks, mate, what are you talking about?'

'Sorry – pardon?' he says. He looks confused for a second. As though he's just woken up in a strange market in another country.

'The thing with your nose?'

'Oh,' he says. 'That. My twin sister taught me that. I always spill drinks down myself. There's a blob of wet on most of my T-shirts that looks like Boris Johnson's head. And she said it's because I pour the drink before it's arrived at my mouth. I need to ensure the glass is at my mouth before I pour. That's my problem. So she said, touch it to your nostril, then to your bottom lip, then you can tip it. Now it's like a nervous tic.'

'Right,' I say. 'Okay. I'm sorry about your loss, by the way. I heard she…'

'Yeah,' Raks says, nodding. 'Thanks. Thank you.'

I pause. Enough for it to not seem like a heartless segue.

'So, now tell me a racist joke.'

'Why?' Raks asks. 'I don't know why. I don't even know if I know any. Like, are they racist? To who? To me? To you? Am I trying to find an aren't-white-people-the-stupidest joke? Am I supposed to kick another race? I don't get the brief.'

'Tell me a racist joke,' I say. I'm starting to lose my patience with this guy.

'The British Empire, am I right? What's the deal with the British Empire? Am I right? Am I right, ladies and gentlemen? Remember to tip your waiter.'

Raks shakes his drink at me and smiles.

I say, 'My regular Indian taxi driver picked me up whilst singing along to his crappy Punjabi music at the top of his voice. He smiled when I pulled out my set of new earplugs. "Looks like you've come prepared this time," he said, laughing. I smiled back at him and replied, "Yes," as I put them up my nostrils.'

'Whoa, Bernard Manning, okay. Why?'

'Raks,' I say, coming out from behind the bar. 'What's ten foot long and wrapped round a cunt? A turban. What do you call a good-looking Asian? Asif.'

'What do you call an Englishman farting? British Gas.'

'Go deeper. Go more racist.'

'I feel like I'm on a hidden camera show, man. I mean, Uncle Dave. What is this?'

'No one has called you a paki while you've been here, have they?'

Raks looks at me weirdly, as though I'm talking in code.

'No,' he says. He shakes his head again, just to emphasize it. 'No. Definitely not. What?'

'Have they or haven't they?' I stand in front of Raks and put a hand on his shoulder. 'You can be honest with your Uncle Dave, my friend. You can always be honest with me.'

'No,' Raks says. 'They haven't. Everyone has been lovely. Everyone has been super nice. This is a dream come true. Thank you for the opportunity. It means so much to be here.'

'You're welcome, you know. Not enough young comedians show us the proper respect we deserve when they come through here. Instead it's all, what does this mean for my career? Where am I going to go to next? How do I get to be a regular on a show like this? No one actually thinks to say thanks. A thank-you goes a long way. You see? Indians are very polite. I've always thought that. Polite. Very polite. Namaste – it means, I bow to you, right? It's nice that when you greet someone, you show your subservience to them, your politeness by bowing.'

'No wonder we got invaded,' Raks says. 'We're always bowing to people, showing how weak we are. Something my dad once said.'

I laugh. It throws me off the speech.

'What I'm trying to show you, Raks, is what racism actually looks like. So that you might stop being a massive fucking paki and just say the bloody fucking joke that we have written for you.'

Raks looks up. I have his attention now.

'Say the fucking joke,' I tell him. 'It's funny. It'll get a laugh. People will think you're a nice self-effacing Indian. Okay? You will say the joke.'

Raks looks at the door. Yup, you're right, mate. There is no one here.

He says nothing.

'Look at me,' I say. I stand close to him. I finish my whisky. 'Repeat after me. Uncle Dave...'

'Uncle Dave...'

'I will read the script...'

'I will read the script...'

'That you graciously wrote for me...'

'That...you...*graciously*...wrote for me...'

'Because...'

'Because...'

'I want to work in television again after today...'

'I want to work in television again after today...'

He is meek in his repeating. It makes me want to laugh in his stupid fucking face. I hope he realizes he will never be on any of my shows again.

'Do you understand now?' I say. 'Do you understand now what a racist joke is?'

He nods. 'I didn't say...'

'Pardon?' I say, poking at him. 'What did you say?'

I poke again.

He looks up at me. 'Do I need to do the accent?'

I shrug. 'Well, that's up to you. Depends if you want that racist joke to get a laugh or not.'

I leave him in the room. I consider locking it until after we've filmed the show.

He is silent as I walk away from him.

My favourite part of the recording day is the rehearsals. It's a chance to see the comics' natural reactions to our scripts before they get anaesthetized to them. To see the guest presenter giggle his way through the first run-through of his opening monologue and the put-downs he has for each member of the teams as he introduces them. To see the non-comedian, in this case the *Daily Mail* columnist, get his comeuppance time and again, until the point where he is immune to all the insults hurtling towards him, so that he'll forget what a figure of hate he is for the duration of the recording. He'll think they're all together, the last gang in town. And then he'll check his social media on the way home, and see what we all think of him, as the public have their say. I get to watch the improvisational genius of the long-standing team captains, their ability to segue seamlessly between politics and pop culture, their back and forth, the will-they-will-they of their on-screen relationship, the do-they-really-like-each-other-or-hate-each-other of their off-screen relationship.

I'm glad there are no girls this week. They try to bring gravitas to the show. And how fucking unfunny is that.

I return to my office and nod at Sri. To say, he's doing the fucking joke.

I switch my monitor on to the CCTV cameras and watch the green room, waiting for Raks to come back, see what he's like. What is his body language saying?

I worked on this sitcom in which we got a guy called Michael Jenkins to brown up to play a Muslim neighbour. He had one line per episode. Usually, towards the beginning, he would come into the shop and make an increasingly bizarre request. It was funny. But what really sold the joke was getting Michael to play him. I don't even think we gave him a name. He was just the Mossie in scripts. We tried it with an early Prash Shah role but he didn't test too well, and though he did okay it never got the laugh we needed. It had to be one of the signature guffaws at the start.

Michael, browned up, sold it every time.

Don't tell me funny's not funny.

Raks enters the green room and sits down. He reaches for a towel, opens it up and buries his face in it.

I eat an apple and ring Sri on the intercom.

'Sri,' I bellow, wanting to laugh. 'Get some poppadoms for the green room, and a massive bowl of mango chutney. Sharwood's. Not Patak's. It has to be Sharwood's.'

The second run-through stalls because the *Daily Mail* columnist doesn't like the constant references to his newly-dyed hair. I bet he's done it because he's about to run for office or use this to do more telly work. It's very arresting. It would have taken about ten years off him if his actual face didn't look ridden by gout. He keeps his right hand under the desk at all times.

When we met I went to shake his hand; I led with my right hand, as you do. He kept his in his pocket and then lifted the disgusting ham fist to me – scaly, bloated and so red, like a dry serrano ham.

'Gout,' he said, before shaking my left hand.

Dyeing your hair is the least of your problems, brother. You need to think about your health. Maybe eat less cheese, dine out on the blood of Syrian refugees only two days a week, eat a salad. Bloody hell.

Anyway, the guest presenter keeps referencing it, and I might have to tell him to stop. Because there is a massive difference between a repetitive joke and a call-back reference. This isn't Stewart Lee. He built his whole annoying shtick on one funny joke, overtold till it's not funny and then retold till it's funny again and then thrown away to be brought back at the end. That's fine, Stewart, you talk to students for three hours for £50 a night. I'm in the comedy fucking business, mate.

Repetitive does not work.

And a call-back. On a television show with a tight editing process that cuts to script – it'd better be the best fucking call-back in the world.

They take a rehearsal break – five minutes, for comfort. The euphemism for pissing is now comfort. Jesus fucking Christ.

I head down to the studio to watch.

Raks is still in his seat when I arrive on set. He's looking at his phone. When I walk over he glances up at me.

'All okay?' I say. I look around. People are in earshot. I smile at everyone who walks past.

'My twin sister told me, just before she passed away, that it was written in the stars or whatever that I would die at work. That was my destiny.' He looks at his fingers. At the phone. 'I didn't get to tell her. Comedians die on their arse all the time. And if you don't die on your arse, well, you won't get better. She said it, as we watched films together. She had worked on a thing that she reckoned would predict the future. She wanted me to get better. And in order to get better, she told me, I had to die. On my arse. It's the gigs that suck, the jobs that sap your strength, the times you aren't the funniest sad clown in the room that make you better. If I'm not driven by my failure, if I'm driven by success and ambition, why the fuck am I not a management consultant?'

He looks up at me.

I go to put a hand on his back. I don't.

'Raks, you need a few minutes to compose yourself?'

'I am going to die,' he says. 'Every night.'

'Dying is easy,' I say, quoting the old adage. 'Comedy is harder.'

'Real comedy doesn't make people laugh and think. It makes them laugh and change,' he quotes back at me. We're in a strange quote-off.

I go for the big guns. 'Humanity has unquestionably one really effective weapon – laughter. Power, money, persuasion, supplication, persecution – these can lift at a colossal humbug – push it a little – weaken it a little, century by century, but only laughter can blow it to rags and atoms at a blast. Against the assault of laughter nothing can stand,' I say. I have the quote on my wall and stare at it most days. It was a present from my mother-in-law, and bloody hell, she'd give me shit if she knew I thought about chucking it in the bin every single day. 'Mark Twain said that.'

'Is the joke funny?' Raks asks. 'I don't even know any more.'

Me neither, I want to say. Me fucking neither.

The run-throughs are a strange environment. The crew is instructed to laugh as loudly and as emphatically as they can, to create the illusion that the jokes will have the ha-has, but also to help with pacing and timing, to ensure that we don't tear through a script without leaving space for chuckles. Who knows what gets applause these days too?

When it's time for Raks to say the line, to do the impression,

I watch his eyes. He knows it's coming and there is a terror about him.

He looks off camera. There is silence.

When the set is cleared, I sit in the presenter's chair and look out into the camera.

'You could just not be on the show,' I tell him.

'It feels like a betrayal. I've never done an accent. For anything. Well, I used to, but that's how you get by when you're an immigrant kid. You do the voice, in your most 1980s sitcom way. You go full *Short Circuit*. You try to fit in and make yourself more palatable, more open to integration or assimilation by thinking your parents talk funny in the same way your so-called friends do. Do you know what code-switching is? It's like a speaker alternating between two or more languages or language varieties, in the context of a single conversation. Multilingual speakers of more than one language sometimes use elements of multiple languages when conversing with each other. Like when you have an Anglo-Indian, such as myself, in the room. I have three voices. I talk in Guj-lish, my normal voice and white comedy party. I don't know whether my normal voice, in which I feel most comfortable, most safe, even feels like me any more. I've splintered into different personas. This is the trick of living publicly online with increasing watch and scrutiny by others. When I first started out on Twitter, I had ten-odd followers, all people I knew in the real world, people I could be myself with. As my following increased, I had to become less of myself and more of the public perception of me as the writer. And it made me lose track of who I was and what voice I spoke in. Nowadays, I ensure that whenever I tweet about comedy things, I add the odd "fam", "bruv", "cuz" or "innit", just to ensure the execution of my thought comes with the necessary rooting in my background. Do you get me? Uncle Dave, I am not that guy. This is not my fight. You need a *Citizen Khan* or a *Goodness Gracious Me* up in here. You have brown Stewart Lee. At least, that's what I hope. So, in good conscience, I'm not telling that joke. I've written three alternatives. None of them show any political bias. They're all dope, cuz. Get me?'

I get up and I walk out of the studio.

I stand in the disabled toilet for five minutes, timing it on my watch. I am so very fucking tired. I've had a Kirin cooling in my fridge since Tuesday. It will be at the optimum temperature to watch the show with. Simon's out tonight anyway.

I come back in.

'Raks, we're done,' I say. 'Get up, we'll find a replacement.'

We've interrupted the start of the rehearsal and I can hear one of the team captains say for fuck's sake. I shoot him a look to remind him that my name's the last one in the credits, and the one we linger on, so he can fuck the fuck off.

Raks stands up like a naughty schoolboy. He pauses. I think he realizes everyone is looking at him. Not at me. At him.

He holds up his hands and looks at me.

'We're fine, Uncle Dave,' he says. 'We're fine.'

If it wasn't the time it was, I would have pulled him out anyway, to sweat him. But this is enough.

'We're running late. Set needs to be cleared in forty-five minutes for tech run-through.'

Raks sits down.

*

When the joke comes, he gives it a self-conscious shot, and the loud laughter from the crew is enough to send me back to the screening room for another dram of the Talisker.

I watch promos for our new season of comedy with the door locked.

I walk past Raks in the corridor. He takes his phone out and pretends to be talking.

I watch from my office. I like to gauge how the laughs fall through the speakers – it helps to hear the jokes that land. Because in the room, everything sounds funny. No one will be watching in the room when it's broadcast on television, though.

I get a text from Simon. It says *U R MY SPACEMAN*. I don't answer. I don't know what he's referring to. He's probably fucked already. I promise myself I won't wait up for him. It's like you're priming yourself for an argument for hours so that when it lands, you either go aggressively or so limply there was no point bringing it up at all. It feels like it's nearing its inevitable end.

There's an email from Raks's agent thanking me for the opportunity. I delete it without replying.

There are three more emails – one is a press release for a memoir, another has some suggestions for next week's guest presenter, as though we don't book this up months in advance, and the third is from one of the writers with some last-minute joke punch-ups. Too late, dickhead.

I watch the feed of the live recording. It's warm, and the

guests are so-so. We are lucky to have such practised team captains, who are able to steer and punch and subvert and comment and lead, allowing our guests the space to give facts to answer the question.

The jokes about the *Daily Mail* editor's hair dye make it in. People laugh, then sigh-laugh, then laugh again as the references come thick and fast. Raks improvs a bit about junior doctors at a rave that has the whole crowd applauding. The guest presenter leads from the front, utilizing the script for every laugh, every single joke, every pause, every giggle, titter, groan. Thank you, me, I think.

Thank you, me.

I'm flicking through Broadcast when I hear Raks do an Indian accent that's so perplexing, it sounds like a Welsh crow. My feet fall off the table and I lean forward. He is going for it. He is utterly going full throttle at the accent and the joke.

It's glorious.

Well done, mate. I think. You heeded the warning.

What follows is silence. Only silence. A single guffaw.

I make a note to fix this in the edit.

A Man Without a Donkey Is a Donkey

Ingrid. Lamu

La-la salama, Raks sings to himself as he tips his sister's ashes into the Indian Ocean. He's parroting the boy steering the dhow who started singing it. I ask what it means.

'Sleep well, now,' the boy says.

I rub Raks's back as he cries. He grabs my hand and pulls it to his face and my fingers are wet with his tears.

He puts the urn on the floor of the dhow. The boy asks if he can have it. I nod.

The song rattles around my brain. As the dhow cuts through the water, the sun glinting off the waves like television static, giving it the shimmer of bad reception, John plunges the urn into the ocean and swills out the last particles of Raks's twin sister. Once he is satisfied, he places the urn under the bench.

'Everything in Kenya is recycled,' John says to me. 'It is good for carrying water. Pole-pole. Slowly-slowly.'

I smile at John and look out at the horizon. Everything is blue. It is a bright, sunshine-filled day, and despite this act that I have borne witness to, I am feeling at peace.

Raks takes some deep breaths and looks at me.

'Thank you for coming with me. I don't think I could have done this alone.'

'You aren't alone.'

'I wasn't supposed to come here,' he says. 'I was meant to wait for my dad in Mombasa. He wanted to be there when I said goodbye to Neha. But I felt she would have liked to come here. She loved it that time we came as children. It felt like the right thing to do. Plus, I had to deliver that cheque for the will.'

'You don't have to tell me things,' I say. I know I have a face that looks as though it can be trusted with secrets.

'She has fond memories of this place,' he says.

The boy steers us back towards the shore, our job done.

'She once sent me a message, just before she died. It said, *Find Ba. She is the key to everything.* Sorry, I'm babbling. I haven't spoken to anyone, really, since I left the UK. And my job involves talking for a living, so it... I'll shut up.'

He doesn't, though. Raks goes on to tell me that until he received that message from his sister, he had barely thought about his mum's mum for the last few decades, that visit of theirs a distant glimmer. And she repeated this on her deathbed, saying, 'Our destiny is linked to hers. If you want to understand how we came to be as a family, you need to find out about her. What happened to her. She loved us both so much, and she didn't need to.'

Raks is bewildered by Lamu. He doesn't really remember much from when he came here as a child. The landscape is meaningless. I can see that on his face.

It's an island operated by donkeys. There is no other transportation – it's either foot or saddle.

We met hours before, in a bar. He was sitting with a beer, watching people get on and off the island in the harbour and he was worrying about money. He left a suitcase of things at the hotel where he's staying in Mombasa, things he wouldn't need on a weekend trip to Lamu. He left his passport. Kenyan bureaucracy, liking an element of authority, makes it very difficult to withdraw any money without a passport. There are no ATMs. He would have had to go into the branch, show two pieces of ID to the bank manager along with his bank card, and sign three pieces of paper. But it's the weekend, so they're shut.

I sat at the bar, sipping on a tropical fruit punch, trying to think about the evening. Some days, I just want to watch a film, but with the time I have left, it feels wasteful to waste hours on television.

I lit a cigarette and he approached me, asking for one. I lit it for him.

He lingered.

'I don't usually smoke,' he said.

'What changed?' I asked, wondering if he could see me rolling my eyes through my Ray-Bans at the corny line. I could see him looking intently at my face, probably admiring, I would hope, the Jackson Pollock of freckles covering my cheeks.

'It's a good conversation starter,' he said.

I sighed, expressing my annoyance.

'Sorry, I just haven't spoken to anyone for a while. You're the only one in here and it felt like a thing you do when you're travelling – bum a fag, make friends for life, wonder in seven years' time why you're still connected on Facebook. Thanks for the fag.'

'Pleasure,' I replied.

'German?' Raks asked.

'Yes,' I said, pulling out my book from my bag. It's usually a good way of signifying the end of a conversation.

He persisted. 'I'm English,' Raks said. 'But don't hold that against me.'

'You don't look English,' I replied. Which surprised me as I said it. I meant to say something else, something bland.

'I'm Raks.'

'You sound Indian.'

'I am. What's your name?'

'Ingrid,' I said, sighing, looking around for help. I angled my body and head away from him, meaning I'd have to turn around uncomfortably to answer further questions.

'Like the Bride of Dracula,' he said.

I grinned, then turned back to face him.

'Yes, as a matter of fact. I'm named after Ingrid Pitt. My father was a fan of *Hammer Horror* films.' I laughed. 'People always say Bergman. Not Pitt. I'm impressed. What did you say your name was?'

'Raks,' he said. 'I'm not named after anyone famous.'

He reached out his hand to shake mine. It was dry and small. 'Maybe a Bollywood star you've never heard of…'

'Rakesh Roshan, maybe?' I said.

They love Bollywood films in Kenya. I've seen my fair share in recent weeks.

Raks laughed.

'Touché,' he said.

His laugh, shrill and contagious, involved him clapping and letting out this high-pitched squeal from the back of his throat. It was lovely to see. The most happiness I had experienced in weeks.

I asked him to join me.

'What brought you to Lamu?' I asked.

'It's the opposite of technology,' he said. 'I thought I could disconnect from the world.'

'They have free wi-fi at this bar.'

'Yes,' Raks said. 'Thank God.'

'What do you think of the donkeys?' I asked.

Raks thought for a moment, almost as though he needed to have a big symbolic opinion about them. Only later, when he told me he was a stand-up comedian, did I understand that his slow responses were him trying to formulate jokes.

'A man without a donkey is a donkey,' he said. 'I saw that on the wall of a donkey sanctuary I visited earlier.'

I nodded.

'I know,' I replied. 'Those of us who face our burdens alone, we're doomed to a life of misery.'

'Exactly.'

Raks described for me how he took a donation cheque to the donkey sanctuary this afternoon, causing chaos by arriving with unsolicited money.

'Yeah, it was a weird vibe. A faceless figure, standing on the balcony, threw the cap of a beer bottle at me as I opened the gate of the small sanctuary and fought the donkeys to get into the courtyard.'

'Why a bottle top?'

'No idea, but I told them I was in possession of a sizeable donation. So I was pointed to a woman wearing a lab coat, tending to a donkey. You can always trust a person in a lab coat, right? She smiled at me as she pulled out a mobile phone and sent a text without breaking her smile or her eye contact with me.'

'What happened next?' I asked.

'Moments later, someone called Mrs Bridge arrived and made me sign the cheque directly over to her. She showed me around the donkey stables and asked some questions about where the money had come from. It's a donation in my sister's name. She died recently. Cancer.'

My cheeks flush hot. I smile sympathetically.

'I was telling her all this stuff about my sister, like how amazing she was. But I ended up self-editing. 'Cause death is the best reset. Dying gives you the Wikipedia page you want. No one wants to remember anything bad about you. So be the biggest arsehole you can and do one nice thing. When you die, that is what people will remember.'

'What did Mrs Bridge do next?' I ask, almost knowing the answer, hoping he hasn't been played for a fool.

'Aaaah, you know her then?' I did. All the mzungus know each other here. He continued, 'Mrs Bridge, interesting lady. She took my cheque, then showed me into an enclosure to meet another donkey, called Mala. She told me to pet it and I did, and it blinked. Mala had a dribbling nose. One eyelid was half-closed. She was panting. I blew on her nose like I was told, to show I was friendly. I approached her from the side as instructed. As I blew, she shuddered and walked forward till my eye and nose line were square with her bottom. Mrs Bridge shrugged and told me she's having a difficult day. I asked if she meant her or the donkey.'

'She's an interesting lady for sure,' I said, laughing.

'I know. I've just handed her a cheque for a heap of money

and without realizing it, I spent two thousand more shillings on a T-shirt and a water bottle. I'm skint. I have enough money to pay for a dhow trip I need to take. But that's it.'

I laughed. 'Sounds like you are also having a difficult day.'

'I can't get any money out,' he said. 'I went to the cash machine and they wouldn't give me any cash. There's only one cash machine on the island...And it's a bank manager.'

'Everything is through cash,' I said, smiling: I've been stung by this myself. 'What are you going to do? Unless this is you asking me for money. Which would be uncool. Slick, but uncool.'

'I haven't spoken to anyone, really, since I left the UK. As I said. I feel weird.'

'I am your entertainment.'

'Is that a question or a request?'

I laughed and leaned back in my chair.

'Seriously,' he said, ruffling his hair. 'Don't feel like you have to talk to me or hang out with me. I'm just passing the time with a beautiful woman. Terrible way to spend an evening.'

We talked for another hour, before the subject of his sister came up. He held back tears as he told me about his mission, to scatter her ashes off the coast of Lamu, where she felt she'd been most happy in her life. I'm similarly here, to live out my days. The story resonated.

When he told me that she died of lung cancer, I knew that something more than synchronicity was in place. We had come together for a reason.

He cried, finally, when it came time to head out on the dhow. I told him I would accompany him.

*

When we disembark from the small boat, I feel tired and hot and bothered.

'Let's go swimming,' I suggest.

'Sure,' Raks says. 'I have time to kill.'

'I want to show you a secret spot on the island, where paradise lives.'

We walk along the promenade, away from the boats. I am silent, reflective, giving space to Raks to confess the things that are clouding his mind.

He talks, in jagged stories, about his sister, about his family, things he did and should not have done.

There is no point to him telling me these things other than that he needs to externalize them. I listen without judgement. Having lived with my own thoughts for so many weeks, it is nice to hear someone else's.

Raks left his home town the day after his sister's funeral, to go and attend a festival for a month. He hasn't spoken to his family, except for his dad, since the funeral. He is upset that no one, not his cousins, aunties or uncles, has thought to check in with him.

Raks wore a bow tie to his sister's funeral because he wanted to stand out. Not that he'd admit it, but he wanted his family to look at him and think, wow, that Raks is one stylish dude.

He had the eulogy in his pocket. He was going to read Puff Daddy's verse from 'I'll Be Missing You' and say some things about Neha's genius. Standing in front of his family, being the conspicuous one in a bow tie, the one who had organized everything, he didn't account for the flurry of emotion that came with realizing everyone was looking at him and the room was silent for the first time in days.

This was not like doing a tight five above a West End pub, he said to me.

He read the first line of the rap and sat down, crying.

His cousin Veena had to read his speech out and she missed all the inflections, emphases and jokes, speaking in a dreary monotone. Raks sat in a foul mood, upset he hadn't been able to deliver the memorable set he'd planned.

When it was over, Neha was committed to the fire and they all went back to Raks's dad's house for some food. At some point, Raks suddenly disappeared.

People assumed he'd gone to do some stand-up.

The day after the funeral, he woke up with a hangover. He'd left the wake to spend the night at his sister's, going through her things and drinking his way through old bottles of Neha's wine-club delivery he'd found next to her bed, which stank of old cigarettes. No one had been in the flat since she'd had an accident and been moved to the family home – it was musty and smelled of death. He managed half a bottle of white on an empty stomach before he was blotto and had to lie down on the sofa. The particulars of Neha's will dictated that everything be given to charity unless Raks wanted anything.

He kept reading the message she had written just for him. A message from beyond the grave. Alongside a handshake at the funeral. It was just bizarre.

Raks took the books, mostly programming textbooks he didn't understand, to the charity shop. Neha's clothes went to a clothes bank and he was left with an impressive amount of alcohol, an empty functioning Smeg fridge, DVD box-sets and computer equipment.

In the flat by himself, he looked around at all the things

Neha surrounded herself with in order not to feel lonely. The toys, the box-sets, the wine. Everything in the flat pointed to the computer and the space where a plasma screen mounted on the wall used to be. When Neha wanted to watch things, she'd load them up on the computer, turn the plasma on and lie back on that uncomfortable sofa that only seated two people.

Raks thought about his own place, and the independence he had. He performed most nights, so used his flat as a place to sleep and iron clothes before going out for meals and waiting for the rushing call of the stage. He never cooked in the kitchen. He had two acoustic guitars and that unread series of *Game of Thrones* books and his Sky box, recording things he'd never watch.

She had told him, just before she died, to find their maternal grandmother. He planned this trip to do just that, as well as dispose of the ashes.

He came up against endless Kenyan bureaucracy in his attempts to trace his maternal grandmother at the central records office in Mombasa.

She did not exist, according to the government. He had the address of her house, where they had sent letters, but a visit in a tuk-tuk brought him to a new building, where you could change currency.

His trail at a dead end, frustrated, he decided to come to Lamu.

He is exhausted after his confession. We slip into silence.

The promenade is bright. The sun reflects off the clothing of most of the passers-by. People wear white on this island. It's hot.

The white also makes things a lot brighter for Raks, who has no sunglasses. He squints as I lead him along the waterfront, the high street that runs the length of the island. We walk past donkeys and tourists and beach boys. The water flares with silver reflections of the sun.

'Thank you for listening to me,' Raks says quietly. 'It was like as soon as I started talking, I couldn't stop. I've been travelling a lot, learning a lot, thinking a lot.'

'Your sister's died,' I say. 'It's okay. You have a whole heap to think about.'

'It's more than that,' he assures me, pointing out to the water. 'I've spent my adult life with my sole focus being my career, becoming a legend. But the last few months, I've come back home.'

'How do you mean?' I ask, looking at my hands, freckled and pink and dry. I sidestep a donkey and hold on to Raks to steady myself. I feel him flinch so I let go.

'I don't know yet. I've come home. I don't know what that means. I finally don't have an answer for everything. It's strangely comforting.'

We walk in silence. Raks is close to me. His arm brushes mine. It's funny – he hasn't talked properly to anyone in days but I realize, as our arms touch, I have not had any human contact either. I talk to an unknown force in my room every night. It is benevolent and formless, there only to make me feel as though I am not facing the future alone.

Someone offers us a romantic boat ride. I hold up a firm hand to say, no thanks.

'How long have you been in Lamu?' he asks.

'Two weeks,' I say. 'I have been here for two weeks.'

'Local expert.'

'Somewhat. I'm on autopilot.'

'Are you travelling?'

'Not any more,' I say. 'I'm happy here.'

'Me too,' Raks says. 'I'm not sure I could live here, though. I worry I'd get bored.'

'It's nice not having to work, isn't it? I haven't had to work in three weeks now. Not since I left for Kenya. I mean, the beauty of this country is majestic. Everything in its right place at its own speed with its own wings of flight,' I say. '*Pole-pole.*'

'You're talking about us, right? As tourists?'

I stop and look at him.

'We're not tourists,' I say, pointing at his chest.

I can see the change in his squinting eyes. He's thinking, oh no, I've befriended one of those hippy-traveller types who eats, prays and loves around the world, in order to find some spiritual respite.

'Look at everyone,' I say. 'They seem so happy with the nothing they have. That's why they smile. They don't care about wi-fi.'

Raks keeps smiling but I know inside he wants to call me an eat-pray-lover.

I burst out laughing.

'What?' he says.

'I know what you're thinking. You're thinking I'm one of those problematic white tourists who comes to an exotic place to find herself before going back to her grotesquely privileged life.'

'I did, for a second.'

'First-World problems...'

'Just because we're out here in this traveller bubble and we see everyone smiling because they want us to buy something from them, doesn't mean they don't have connectivity issues. That's the trouble with the idea of First-World problems,' Raks says. 'The First World thinks they are its own particular problem. People are complex enough to want money for food and medicine, and have a strong wi-fi signal as well.'

'It's just a saying.'

I turn away from Raks and look to the houses we are passing. He walks ahead of me. He has dark circles under his eyes and his beard is unruly. He looks sad and bloated, as though he has travelled so far in such a short space of time that he needs a moment of rest. This is what happened to me when I arrived. It took me so long to get here, took so much of the little energy I have, but that first moment, in the water, everything was washed away. I was between worlds. Between the living and the dead. Between my old and my new life. Between the things that weighed on me and the things that could set me free. I want to strip all of that away for him in the same way it was stripped away for me.

'Come on, then,' I say.

'Where are you taking me?' he asks, smiling nervously.

'That is definitely a secret.' I pause. 'Are you with anyone?'

'How do you mean? A girlfriend? No. Not me. No time. You?'

'No. I mean, are you travelling alone?'

'Yes,' he says. 'My dad is joining me in Mombasa in a few days. He wants to show me where he grew up. He's very excited about coming home. When I told him I was doing this, he said that the expectation was that he would come back to live out his retirement. That is the immigrant dream. To go to England, make his fortune, and come back to die near the sea. But for the longest time, this hasn't been the plan – he's wanted to be British. After my sister died, though, he thought maybe he should come home. He's considering it, anyway.'

We take a right off the main strip on to a side street. The houses here are close together. It feels European with its higgledy-piggledy white-and-beige building fronts.

I see him shudder and look around furtively. I wonder if he's feeling he should have exercised caution when going off with a strange woman, maybe paid a little attention to the direction she has led him in. But she seemed so benevolent and kind. He doesn't need to be paranoid.

'My dad filled my head with advice before I left. He was like, keep your money in your shoes and your pants. Don't wear a watch or the thick silver chain he knows I'm partial to. He was actually horrified when he found out I wear boxers, making it impossible to keep money in them. He told me not to carry my wallet or take my phone out. Everyone has phones now. Why would anyone want mine? It's two models old.'

I laugh.

'What did you say to that?'

'"Just listen to me, these are my people," he said, like, really pissed off. I was like, "You haven't lived in Kenya for over forty years. Places change."'

'People don't.'

'Yes, you're right – and that's what he said. I was like, your opinions are still from the sixties.'

'He's just worrying. He's already lost one child.'

'I know, but he doesn't need to start paying attention now.'

'I'm sorry about your sister.'

'Thanks. She was annoying when she was alive. Really annoying. But we grew up together, and I miss her so much. You forget to always appreciate what a constant people are for you.'

'I don't know what it is to lose anyone so close to you. I've been lucky.'

I remember something from the day before.

'I read this story in a children's book in my Airbnb and I can't get it out of my head,' I say. 'About how in the beginning there was no death. And when someone dies and you dispose of the corpse, you must remember to say, man die and come back again, moon die and stay away. But man, being man, forgot to say it and so that's why they say death came about, because the man in the story forgot to ask for his friend to return, and instead asked for the moon. And that is why up to this day when a man dies he does not return, but when the moon dies, it always comes back again.'

Raks smiles. 'My dad used to tell me something similar but he'd put his finger to his lips and say, tell no one. We're Hindu, not Kikuyu.'

'The Maasai don't say a person is dead. They say they are asleep. I like that. The idea of a big snooze.'

'My sister never slept. She'd stay awake all night drinking and watching *Star Trek*.'

'How did your mother take it?'

'My mum's dead. She died when we were babies, of the same thing that killed my sister.'

I smile. 'I like the romance of that. Generations apart and yet brought together.'

'It's not romantic.'

He thinks I am being flippant. He does not know.

I lead Raks through an archway. We are on sand now. Flecks of dried seaweed circle the ground, caught on the wind. Palm trees hiss.

I take off my shoes and hold them. Raks stares at my feet. The nails were painted red months ago. They're chipped with usage.

'You interested in my feet?' I say, laughing.

He shakes his head.

'I'm not. Ever since I was a kid, I check people's feet to see how friendly they are. You can tell a lot about someone from their toes. It's just a weird thing I do. I don't want to fuck anyone's feet.'

The swear word hangs in the air as we reach the top of the dune. The beach is immaculate. It's empty, the sea is silver, and the untrodden sand looks like an inviting duvet.

'What do mine tell you?'

'You're worn out,' Raks says.

I laugh. 'You're so right.'

I run backwards down the incline of the dune, watching as Raks, removing his shoes, follows, plunging his own feet deep into the sand.

He runs down the incline, hands aloft, his backpack bouncing up and down. If he had troubles, they are blasted in the face by the warm sea breeze that greets his momentum. Hot sand scatters like buckshot across our calves, toes melting into the cool clusters underneath. I tear off my clothes as I run. I'm wearing a bikini underneath my long-sleeved T-shirt and linen trousers. I pull off my bandana and let my hair explode over my shoulders.

I dive into the water, am underneath for ten long seconds and swim out into the cooling refreshing sea. I beckon to him. Raks stops running at the water's edge. Its shallows caress his toes. The water is warm.

'Come on in,' I shout, beckoning with splashes. 'You won't regret it.'

Raks rubs at his hair and takes off his T-shirt and shorts. He puts his belongings on top of his bag and runs in, just wearing his white boxers. He keeps turning his head back to his things, hoping they won't be taken. There's not a lot he can do if they are.

He dives into the water. It's warm and cooling at the same time, like swimming in bathwater. He isn't a strong swimmer – his kick is the problem and he paddles his way to me. We look back at the coast.

'No one ever comes here,' I say.

'Why not? It's beautiful.'

I point to the ruins of a castle to his left, the fringes of the town to his right.

'There was a shark-sighting years ago. Now it's deserted.'

'The Indian Ocean's too warm for sharks, right?'

'That's why I come here.'

Raks wades closer to me, our fingers and limbs close enough to touch as we tread water in sync. He faces me as I continue to look at the beach.

'Please,' I say. 'That isn't what this is.'

I pull off the wig to show him my bald head. There are wisps of red hair where it's tried to grow back but the hair is gone and my scalp is white – there is a thick tan line between my face and hairline. It's bumpy and you can almost see the blood pumping underneath its alabaster cling film around my crown. I smile at Raks. He shakes his head, his curly hair wildly tossing with each turn. He stops and looks at me, then hesitates, submerging slightly and swallowing water in surprise.

'How far along are you?'

'Well, I had months left months ago, so now I wait.'

'Why aren't you at home?'

'It's complicated.'

'Everything's complicated. It's simple too,' Raks says.

'Okay, well, it's none of your business.'

'What are you doing?'

'Out here? I'm living in paradise. With the donkeys and the beautiful people, eating fresh mangoes and avocados, relaxing, whatever I choose. I am a donkey.'

'But you're by yourself.'

'On all roads we are alone,' I say and lie back so my ears are covered by the bobbing water and I am floating.

'I'm sorry,' he says.

'Don't be. I'm in paradise and I am happy,' I tell him.

It's true. I had to come here to be in the moment of what was happening to me. Back home was noise. Here, I cannot be a burden and I can come to terms with it.

'Just before I got here,' Raks says, 'I fucked up my career. I said a thing I shouldn't have, on television. And my community eviscerated me for it. So while I'm here for my sister, I'm also hiding a bit. And what you're going through is…'

'Don't compare yourself to me, Raks,' I say. 'That's patronizing. What is happening to me is mine alone. What did you say?'

'I sold my people out. The irony is, up until I did, I didn't really embrace them as my people.'

'So you have to find a way back to them?'

'Yes,' he says. 'I do. But for the moment, being here, in this water, with the sun on my back and my toes being nibbled by fish, is the only place in the world I want to be. Thank you. This is a blessing.'

'I know. And you will find your way back.'

'Yes, I will. It's my destiny.'

He laughs.

'What's funny?'

'I'm just laughing at my own entitlement. It's stupid.'

He swims backwards and then forwards towards me.

'What will you do?' he asks.

I close my eyes and lay my head back in the water, kicking away from him.

'In what way?' I ask.

'While you're here. Is there nothing else you can do?'

I shake my head.

'I am waiting for him,' I say.

'Who?'

'Death. And I'm okay with that.'

When we wade out of the water, our bodies heavy with gravity, we are in silence. He has to get a bus back to Mombasa. I have dinner plans with a local book group. We are to discuss Ngũgĩ wa Thiong'o's *Wizard of the Crow.* A quote sticks with me: Your own actions are a better mirror of your life than the actions of all your enemies put together.

Though my life here is dictated by inaction, that in itself is a conscious choice: inaction is still an act.

'Try not to beat yourself up over whatever you did,' I say. 'Thank you for today.'

'I won't. And, look, good luck.'

'Pole-pole,' I say. He repeats it.

I tell him the Thiong'o quote by way of comfort, and he smiles, writing it in the notes on his phone.

He looks down at his feet, the imprinted contours they've made in the sand. Bobbing next to them is a lump of hair. It makes him jump and he moves away from it, thinking it an animal. It's my wig. It's lifeless now and though it may have been sun-streaked by excessive blasts of light in this paradise, now it is a wig without a place to call home. I pick it up and wrap it in my towel.

At a loss for anything to do, Raks takes his phone out of his pocket and checks it absently. As he stares at the screen, he sings to himself.

La-la salama. Sleep well soon.

Kenya, 1988

I am not ready for my destiny.

Saraswati Mehta

I Heard that People Bear the Pain of Being Away

The twins look at me quizzically as I sit between them and the radio, playing Rafi, always Rafi, and I place the bowl on the floor, clamping it between my two big toes to steady it before bringing the stone pestle down on to the cumin and dragging it across the surface of the mortar.

I curse Mukesh for bringing them to me. I came here for solitude. I came here to forget. And he has brought me these children, to disrupt my preparations.

Another song comes on, more up-tempo, Lata, doing disco.

Ye hum kyaa jaane, ye wahee jaane, jisane likhaa hain sab kaa naseeb.

I translate the words as I grind the cumin seeds. What do I know, only he knows, the one who has written the destiny of all.

Neither child looks up. She is rereading an old *Star Trek* comic she has brought with her and he is staring into space, smiling.

I let them ignore me.

I crumble some grit between my fingers and flick it down towards the floor.

It is going to be a long week. Definitely a long week.

You can see a droplet of sea from here. I look at it, hoping for a dance of sunlight. I can hear the frangipani tree swish. Soft music. Listening to the music helps the long days, the long weeks. I do not know why time is stubborn.

I'm not sure of my purpose any more. It is not to be a babysitter. I long for death.

These children have no energy. I say to them, go and play? They ignore me. Go and eat? They sit still, as one.

It reminds me of when Angrezi people talked in uniform. We are one, they would say. We belong to the King, the Queen, goodbye. Stare at my accomplishments on my chest. Tell me why you stand before me. The Beatles are good.

It reminds me of Keighley. How still people were. How inert. Walking to the battery factory, the shirt factory, with heavy shoulders. My God. How I longed to come home.

What did I come home for?

You stayed there.

Scattered in the Worth. A British man to the end. Cremated in your Sunday best, with your china teacup.

I do not remember you in colour any more.

Our photographs stopped before the end of black-and-white.

Why did you not want to come home with me?

I look at our grandchildren and wonder what destiny has written for them. Nisha, when she visited the Bradford Baba, she got him to look into their futures. She never showed me. It is for us, she said. I imagined she was disappointed, otherwise she would have shared their futures with me. Perhaps it felt too much for her, to be shown who her children would become. It would serve as a cruel reminder that she perhaps might not live long enough to bear witness. Destiny is not always what we hope.

The Bradford Baba, a tricky character. Often seen drinking in the places where only Angrezi people went. He did not want to drink with us, in the pubs that were friendly to the coloureds. He was a scam artist. He once asked me to hold a rolled-up piece of card for him while he meditated. It was a blessing, he said. It was actually a mat. For a lager. From a pub where only Angrezi people went.

I had seen him once a year since we arrived in Keighley. But after this, I stopped going.

Because he did not tell me my destiny.

To outlive you, my husband: expected. To outlive our youngest child: expected. To outlive your eldest child who treated his body like a sugar factory: expected.

We knew it was coming.

Genes.

The problem is genes.

We come from bad stock. Bad hearts, bad lungs, bad immune systems, bad tolerance to sugar. We are walking dead.

Nisha, the last thing she said to me, on the phone, I remember it.

Don't make them believe in destiny, I beg you. They cannot see what is coming. I let her say this to me because she needed to say it, and I said Hahn-ji, because I knew she needed to hear this. All my life, I wanted to take responsibility for my actions. Alas, if these things are pre-written, if we have no control of what is ahead, then we must try to make the most of what is coming. My grandchildren should know what that is. It will help them navigate the time between now and then.

Me? Everything that was destined for me has happened to

me and been taken from me. I wait for it all to be over.

All my life, I only wanted to take responsibility for my actions.

I have no role in my grandchildren's lives. Either of them. Twins. So connected. So different. So the same.

Both act as though they are the only ones in the room.

I am not needed. We do not speak the same language. Mukesh failed. Teach them Gujarati, I begged of him. Speak to them in Gujarati, I pleaded. Yes, Amee, sure, Amee, anything, Amee, he said. I wrote them letters in Gujarati derived from the English script, and I spoke to them in Gujarati and English. I gave them all the tools.

No one understood me at any juncture.

It is important. The language of your forefathers is important.

When the cumin is a coarse powder, I lift the bowl up and tap the contents into a cupped fold of my saree. I stand up and walk towards the bowl where I do the vaghar.

She does not eat spicy food, Mukesh told me.

She will, I think. We have one week till he is back from visiting his mummy.

One week to break you both, I think.

Before you can fix something, it must first be broken.

Rakesh interrupts his staring competition with the wall when I cross the room and he stands up. Neha stays where she is. She is transfixed by a panel of Spock trying to stay alive.

Rakesh walks over to where I stand at my bowl, hand-mixing the grains of spices together by grabbing a fist's worth and sieving through my fingers so the grains separate.

Bhook lage che? I ask, rubbing my stomach, hoping they will learn through forced repetition.

He shakes his head as he watches what I am doing. Neither of them has eaten anything since they've arrived - only a packet of Parle-G biscuits between them for each meal. Mukesh warned me they had difficult dietary requirements.

Who is going to cook them home food? he asked. Me? Who has the time to learn? I already do everything for them.

You hide behind your dead girlfriend too much, I told him.

I knew as soon as I said it that I was driving him away, back to England with closure in his heart. They had booked the wedding. They had booked the taxis. She had bought the saree. I kept it. I kept everything.

Sugar rotli? I ask. Rakesh looks confused. I repeat myself. Two or three times. He smiles at me as though I am talking two different languages. I make him one. I take a cold rotli glistening with ghee out of the steel dubba and I sprinkle sugar on to it, roll it into a tube and hand it to him.

Sugar rotli, I say.

He repeats it.

Shoo-gur rot-lee, he says, understanding.

Sugar rotli, I repeat. He parrots my syllables. I cannot hear the difference. I was born on a dhow. I cannot hear accents. I was born in the sea.

He chomps on it. He is confused at first, and takes a few nibbles before finishing the whole thing in one bite. I laugh at his enthusiasm.

I make him two more.

It is a small victory.

He eats both sugar rotlis within a minute.

His sister does not look up.

I was like her until I discovered a copy of *Lady Chatterley's Lover* in a bookshop on Salim Road. I thought the book was banned. In England, maybe. In Mombasa, you could find anything if you had the money.

My neighbour asks, why are they so quiet, why have you not seen them since they were babies? She does not need to know that after losing my daughter, my husband, knowing I would lose my son too, I came home. Shut up, Mrs Chatterjee, you shit. Your son likes women's feet too much. I see him sniffing chappals. He thinks, because I'm old I don't understand.

I am awake. D. H. Lawrence, I am awake.

I don't want to tell her, my son-in-law forgot to teach his children Gujarati. My son-in-law forgot to feed his children Gujarati food. My son-in-law isn't even my son-in-law. He is the sperm that carried on my bloodline.

My Gujarati bloodline.

God, now Mrs Chatterjee is inside my brain. I think she is evil. She tells my cleaner I do not mind if she washes her sheets. She has opened a letter from my bank. She likes lager. I like lager too but in private. She likes lager like the neighbourhood sharabi.

That night I read Neha and Rakesh a bedtime story. It is about the moon and about death and why people die. When Nisha died I read it to Chumchee, even though he was a grown man. Because it helped him understand why we mourn and why these things happen.

Before they fall asleep, I ask Rakesh and Neha what they want for breakfast.

Sugar rotli, Rakesh says.

Neha looks through me, uninterested.

Tomorrow, I think, I will find something to connect me to her. Rakesh's stomach has been reached.

I make us go for a walk.

My darling, I want to show them where you taught our daughter to swim. She was so young when we took her to England, that she quickly forgot where she came from. I did not. I remember everything. I see the ghosts of our every footstep on these streets.

They should see these shrines to her, proof that she existed, examples of who she was, beyond the confines of photographs.

Jonathan makes a sudden gurgling sound as we pass him. He is sitting against the wall as he always does, where the green of the bush masks the green of his clothes, the green in his matted hair, the green around his face. The sudden noise frightens Neha – she leaps into Rakesh, who stumbles and yelps in pain. Jonathan leaps towards Rakesh and catches him before he falls. He moves oddly, wildly, splaying his arms and legs as he gathers Rakesh in to his chest.

Rakesh barks in fear. Jonathan looks at his leg, grunts fiercely into Rakesh's eye and he touches down the leg till he reaches the ankle. He clutches it tight. I'm frozen too. I do not intervene. I trust Jonathan's instincts, so still and primal now. I know him, you see. When I first saw him there, against the wall, I asked him what he was doing. He sits and he waits for death, he told me. Why? I asked. Because death is the only destiny, he replied. The next day, when I walked past him again, I saw that what he was doing was strangely beautiful. He was trying to disappear in plain sight. He didn't want anything from anyone and the easiest way to do that was to cease to exist. I watched as he ground leaves and soil together, kneading them in a well in his long tunic, till they became muddy and off-green, finding spilt atoms of moisture to help make the mixture wet enough to apply. He daubed himself over the course of three days, becoming greener and greener. The rest of the month was about the art of keeping still.

He massages Rakesh's leg, looking at me through his hair. Rakesh squeezes his eyes closed and waits for it to be over. Jonathan smells like duttee and dirt. Neha places a hand on his shoulder as he continues to grip Rakesh's ankle. He does this for a minute and then lifts Rakesh to standing.

Rakesh twirls his foot around. He nods and looks at me. It doesn't hurt? my eyes ask. He shakes his head. Then he looks at Jonathan. It's as though he hasn't moved – he sits, legs akimbo, arms folded, staring into the distance, as still as he can manage. You cannot even trace an outline of shifted dirt.

I stare at him for a while, trying to understand why he broke his cover for my grandson. Neha walks towards him. Jonathan continues to look at me. For a second, he breaks his stare to look at Neha, then back to me. Neha shows no fear now but stands in front of Jonathan and takes the *Star Trek* comic out of her back pocket. I asked her to leave it at home but she tucked it into the waistband of her jeans and pulled her T-shirt down over it. She unrolls the comic and holds it up to Jonathan's face. Not so close that it's intrusive but close enough not to be ignored.

She holds it there for him to read the cover.

I watch them both. He neither moves nor takes his eyes off me. Frustrated, she lifts up and down on her heels.

She gets bored and drops the comic into his lap.

Thank you, she says quietly. Thank you for not hurting my brother.

Jonathan picks up the comic book and surveys the front page.

He tears at it and shoves the cover into his mouth.

Neha cries. She turns to me. I try to usher her away but she stands there for a few more seconds before following me. I pause to let her catch up, and cast an eye back to Jonathan. The comic has been flung away from him and he is back in position. Disappeared against the wall.

I tell them a story of their mummy while we walk to a bookshop that sells comic books. In Gujarati. I have a plan.

The shop is always open.

I stand in the doorway and let the children walk in.

It is a chaotic mess. This shop has no structure to it. Books find their way on to shelves without categories – there is no reason for school books to be next to romance, no reason for me to find *Lady Chatterley's Lover* next to a cookery book.

I watch as these two walk to the back of the shop. It is small enough for me not to lose sight of them.

Neither Neha nor Rakesh know what to do. It is funny watching them react to freedom. Mr Shukla, the owner of the shop, does not even look up from a ledger he is annotating. I run my fingers along a shelf near the door, gathering a thick skin of dust. I lick at it and it tastes fermented on my tongue.

Neha picks up a stack of what looks to her like comics and flicks through them. They are Amar Chitra Katha books, comic strips about Hindu deities, Jātaka folk tales, Buddhist parables. I want to buy a stack for her, replace Spock with Hanuman.

Rakesh disappears from view but I do not worry. I am standing by the only way in and out of this dim dusty box of a room.

Mr Shukla continues to ignore us.

I cannot see myself in these grandchildren of mine.

Neither of them knows what they want. They cannot do. Not at this age. It will take years of them chasing what they don't want before they get tired and acquiesce to their destinies. I have no interest in their future, no investment in their destiny. And yet, here they are, against my wishes.

I tried to have sex with Jonathan.

One night, it was hot, sticky, I could not sleep. He was on my mind. It was a Sunday. I knew there was nothing outside – no Kenyans, no Indians, no British, no market, no drunks. Nothing.

I had not felt this way since I left London. I remember fragments of the end of my time there: your cremation, my darling. Scattering your ashes in the Thames, so you could be an Englishman for ever. I sat with Nisha towards the end, while Mukesh looked after the babies. We watched Bollywood films, with her head in my lap. I massaged coconut oil in her hair. Mukesh, beleaguered with the twins in a pram, pushing them around the park until they slept. I remember the day Nisha died. We were watching a film, and a mummy yelled naheeeeee because her child had died. I laughed and did the same. Naheeeeeee, I called out, clutching at your daughter's head. But she had passed. I left soon after this because I could not be there any longer. I remember that first year back here. People were so desperate for me to remarry, they kept introducing me to men. I was mourning you and Nisha, and missing my Chumchee, and instead of giving myself to this, I was meeting people, not as a mother or a masi, but as an eligible widow looking for companionship. I felt this stirring again that night. Not for any specific reason. There was no catalyst for the chemistry in my body other than the fact that I had not been touched in years. Decades. I wanted to feel something.

I went for a walk. To walk off these tingles. Push them into the mud of the streets.

Sea breeze. It blows things out of your brain.

I saw Jonathan because the light bleeding from the moon highlighted the hulk of his body against the wall. In the dark, he didn't look green any more. The orb of moon glinted off his eyeball. I stopped, then moved towards him. He didn't move. Everything was static around us. Frozen. I moved closer. He neither flinched nor moved to accommodate me. He just sat there, staring…

I sat next to him.

I shuffled back, uncomfortably sticky in my saree, till my back was against the wall.

I could not even hear him breathing.

For a second I thought he was dead though I knew he wasn't.

I could feel the warmth inside him throbbing on his skin.

He was still. He did not move.

I felt the throb beat harder.

I put my hand in the air in front of me, feeling the cool sea against my fingertips.

Then I put my hand on his thigh.

I wanted.

I could feel his bones. There was no fat left on him. He had wasted away.

I didn't dare move my hand until he showed a response. I didn't know what to do. I expected him to stink of rotting and wasting and disintegration and street dirt. Instead he smelled of musty fungal growth, almost earthy. Like the dust in Mr Shukla's bookshop. I started inching my little finger towards his penis, hoping for it to stir something in him.

My finger curved and extended, millimetres closer and closer to his lap, where who knew what lay underneath his tattered clothing.

He shifted.

He placed his hand on mine, forcing it down on to his thigh so I couldn't move it. Then he turned to me.

No, he whispered, without looking at me. No.

He released my hand and I removed it, brushing it off as though he had covered it in sand.

Why do you do this? I asked. Why do you sit here?

He turned and looked at me through the matt of coarse unkempt hair falling on to his face.

You have a weakness in you. The women in your family will be cursed by it, the men by their own weakness. Who has cursed you? he said. He repeated the question, looking ahead once more. Who has cursed you?

Then he went still again, as though he had never moved.

How did he know about Nisha's disease? My bad genes, the ones I gave her.

Why did it take my daughter? I asked him, crying, thinking about the reality of her for the first time in a year. Why not me? Why am I stuck here?

I am not God, he whispered. I can only see in front of me. I can only see what is going to happen, not why it will happen. I cannot see the patterns that thread everything together.

I walked home and slumped on to my doorstep. I watched the sun rise, hoping for an epiphany. I felt tired the rest of the week.

Rakesh walks towards me with a book thrust out in front of him. *101 Jokes*, it says on the cover. I smile and hold it for him.

May I have it? he asks.

I nod. I'm starting to forget that I told Mukesh I would pretend to be unable to speak English.

Neha comes back towards me. She has found a Batman book which she holds out. I smile and put it on the shelf, then pick up three or four Amar Chitra Katha books to show her, but she shakes her head and points at the Batman comic.

I pick it up and place it in a pile with the joke book and the Amar Chitra Katha comics. It occurs to me that our stories, your story and mine, will die with me, because who will tell our histories? Mukesh? It must be me. I must tell them about their mother, their bapuji, their family.

If they must be here, to pass the time, I will tell them your history and mine. Our history.

Over dinner, I watch Rakesh and Neha sit in silence. I fear they are communicating with each other in their minds. They eat nothing. They are not difficult about it and do not cry, but they both look around the room, waiting for dinner time to be filed as defeat. I persist, eating slowly, tearing off shards of rotli and scooping up delicious oily bateta shaak into my mouth. I chew slowly, and wait till they are looking at me before swallowing.

The radio is on. Playing Mohd. Rafi. Always Rafi.

It is a song about how young people wander about, hopeless. I look at my grandchildren, who are still.

I sing along.

Neha stands up.

Sit down, I say, motioning for her to remain where she is. We are eating.

I'm not hungry, she whispers, then looks at Rakesh.

I am eating, I say in English. It is rude to leave the table when someone else is eating. You have to ask to be excused.

It's strange talking in English. I never do it any longer and have forgotten more than I remember. I had to relearn Swahili. Being here, it's essential to preserve things. Everyone wants to learn English and letting them know you speak it means you lose part of yourself. You will always converse in English. They may have given us our country back but they have left us their ways. We want that British passport and to be able to move around, be free. The world has been given to us. I am here now. English is a functional language with no poetry. When I hear a good Rafi line on the radio and translate it into English, it sounds flat. My world – it is not flat. The globe is not flat. We exist in tiny clusters. Now we have been given a burden. We were enslaved, then freed but still with shackles. Like the English language – and bone-china teacups, and politeness, and gratefulness. The English want us to be grateful. The English for please and thank you comes much easier to the tongue than abhara and shukriya, tafadali and asante.

I came home because I could not pretend to like people any more.

I am comfortable here.

I am not required to speak in English.

Why do you not speak in English? she asks.

I nod.

I do, I reply.

No, she says. You speak in Gujarati, which we do not know. Sometimes you speak in English.

Gujarati is our family language, I tell her.

It is not my language, she shouts.

It is the language your mummy and I spoke, I say, smiling and lifting my arms out to cuddle her.

She is dead, Neha shouts.

She thinks about it, then turns and bolts for the door. I continue sitting.

Rakesh turns to her. Neha, man, come back, he says limply.

She cannot open the door because I have locked it.

Neha tugs at the door, kicks it, rattles it as aggressively as she can, shouting in frustration. Rakesh sits, looking at me, daring me to intervene. She drowns out Rafi. I finish everything on my plate as slowly as I can. I take two rotlis from the dubba and put them on to my plate. I pinch sugar from the pot on the table in my dhal-smeared fingers and sprinkle down the spine of one. I roll the rotli into a cylinder and offer it to Rakesh.

Neha stops rattling the door and looks at her brother.

Don't, she says. Don't eat it.

I hold it aloft. His eyes are drawn to it.

Don't you see what she's doing? She's buying you. We can escape. Go and find Dad, go home, like we talked about. Don't eat it.

Rakesh tells me he is hungry. Neha is fuelled by the need to be right, by anger. Rakesh has baser needs. Food and, in the future, girls, money, compliments – these are the things that will make him do anything for ever more.

When I was clearing away Nisha's things, I found her handbag. Darling, I did not tell you. Going through it, throwing away all the dirty tissues and shopping lists and hairpins, I found the notes she had written when she went to see the fortune teller. That was when these children were still very young, only days before her death.

Neha: egotist, hard-working, stubborn, avoid these numbers: 16, 12, 9, 22.

Rakesh: clown, needs validation, lazy, avoid these numbers: 3, 13, 14, 22.

I took them because I didn't want Mukesh to throw them away, thinking things like this didn't matter.

I took them so that the children had a record of their destiny. And it comforted me to have these bits of paper with me here. It kept these children at a distance.

Mukesh should want to hold on to these things.

Rakesh can't decide whether he wants my approval or Neha's. Neha is still angry with me for saying that chips were for goras when she asked me to cook them for her on the first day.

I look at the time. It's 9.21 p.m.

Rakesh takes the sugar rotli from my hands. Neha tuts and goes back to rattling the door as loudly as she can, begging for escape. The neighbours will not care. Be quiet, child, they'll think, if they understand the cries in English for escape.

Rakesh stands up and walks towards Neha, who is getting into a frenzy. He puts a hand on her shoulder without saying anything. He talks to her in their minds and it makes her stop.

Rakesh tears the sugar rotli in two and hands half to his sister.

The moment is so still and beautiful that I realize what's been missing in this room the entire time. I thought it was Nisha. I realize now, it was me.

I have been missing.

I smile at my two grandchildren, eating their halves of the sugar rotli, Neha with her back turned to me so I won't be able to see what she deems a defeat.

In that brief minute, my grandchildren and I no longer feel like strangers.

The Bed Will Form the Heart of the Garden

Watching Neha hold Rakesh's hand as we amble around the museum, I think about our daughter and how she used to do the same for Chumchee.

Do you remember, darling? How Chumchee did not have the confidence to go to places he had never been before. How he had so many anxieties that taught him to be cautious. We thought he would die from stress or from a heart attack, the way he seemed to panic and then eat and then panic and then eat. He was picking up a hot dog he'd dropped to the ground when the bus hit him. I cannot lay any of the blame on you. But you, specifically – I keep wondering how much of what happened was because you wanted it to happen. Maybe it was your fault. Maybe it was how you died, the way you weren't around any more. Maybe it was that Indian restaurant. Everything started with that Indian restaurant. When you lost your job.

Remember that man who would come in, wearing a pinstriped suit. The man with a red face who had no interest in those beneath him. You didn't know what he did. Instead, you just knew him as Mr Landry. Mr Landry would call you Smiley.

Whenever you saw him, he'd say, hey, Smiley, what's happening tonight? What's making you smile?

It was benign – he probably meant nothing behind it. But you hated it, being called Smiley. Mr Landry came in often enough that we didn't ever think he was a racist. He loved Indian food and tipped generously in a culture that doesn't generally give tips for good service, unlike America. Still, the Smiley nickname would stick in your stomach like an ulcer. You told me you did not understand it.

I have to repeat these stories to you so neither of us forgets our histories when we are together again.

Hey, Smiley, what are the specials?

Hey, Smiley, more poppadoms.

Hey, Smiley, what's the score? Have you got the radio on?

Smiley, you're looking extra smiley today. I can see all of your teeth.

Smiley, with that dark complexion, your teeth really shine.

One day, you served Mr Landry the bill and as he took out his wallet to pay for it while you waited, counting out the money, you said, My name is Vijay. Not Smiley.

I know. But you are very Smiley. It makes me happy to see.

Not all Indian people are smiley, sir.

Mr Landry stopped, looked at you and smiled. Then, glancing at the wedge of money he was holding, he put it in the metal plate on the table for change.

It's not like I called you a wog, is it? he said.

You were asked to leave by the owner.

We do not talk back in this country, he told you. It is important to be grateful.

This comment stuck with you. You wanted to be accepted here, live here as a British man. This is why we came. But after you were let go, for speaking your mind, you told me you were going to change, because you could not do anything further to jeopardize us being here.

Compliant, you told me. I shall be compliant.

And so you became the worst kind of immigrant. You talked of the good old days. You compared the prices and outside temperatures of everything to Kenya. You cursed the influx of immigrants as my cousins and I flocked around you in a ready-made community. You would even go as far as to quote Margaret Thatcher. To think that you, an immigrant yourself who had been hard done by her and those who came before, used her to score points against the next wave. I loved you still but you became difficult to live with. You switched from drinking to chewing tobacco although you didn't actually chew it. You would keep it in the front of your mouth and stare off at the wall. You held it there until dinner time at 11 p.m. and then you ate a piece of fruit or half an onion, anything other than the thing that had been cooked for you. You had none of your charm left. You talked in a mixture of Caine from *Kung Fu*, Sun Tzu and Bruce Lee. You had an attic shelf filled with books on martial arts and Zen, but though you threw the quotes about spirituality in our faces, you didn't seem to understand them.

When you lost your job, you spent hours with those books, reading up on meditation, stretches and fighting stances. You broke your leg in our garden at one of our world-famous barbecues, showing Mukesh and Chumchee how to execute a flying kick. You landed in the splits and shattered your shin bone. Apart from the critical landing, it was a smart-looking flying kick.

I begged you to take me out. We have no money, you told

me. I longed for us to have fun but you were adamant that we stay indoors. I was a brat, I know this now. I demanded that you treat me like somebody you loved and take me out. And then, with perfect timing, there was a new James Bond film.

Nothing made you feel more English than watching a new James Bond film at a cinema in the West End. Nothing made you feel more like a part of society than Bond, James Bond, shaken not stirred. Silly bevakoofs, you and him.

We left Nisha and Mukesh at home, with Chumchee as their chaperone, hoping he would help them plan their wedding. All they needed to do was set a date. That was the last thing. The only job they had was to look at the calendar and select a date.

You were still on crutches but insisted we go.

You leaned on my shoulder and I helped you to the street. Once there, you held on to me and used your crutch to shimmy yourself along towards the bus stop, which was only twenty feet from our front door – one of the reasons you had chosen the house in the first place. You were in such pain, I could feel you crying against me, making my saree damp. You looked at me and said sorry. Sorry for all the difficulties.

At the bus stop there were three people waiting. When they saw us approach, they let you go to the front of the queue.

You smiled at them and they smiled back. The bus arrived at the stop and you hobbled towards it to get on. It was busy with the post-work trudge home and there was standing room only.

I'm sure someone will let you sit down, said a woman behind us in the queue. She said it slowly and loudly, a chasm between each word.

I smiled at her. We boarded the bus, I paid the fares and we squeezed down as far as we could to let as many people on as possible.

No one offered you a seat. They either shrugged or avoided eye contact. Even so, nothing could beat your buzz. The prospect of a new James Bond film had returned a joy and a charm to your life. Being without a seat would normally have made you intensely angry, but there was something quiet and unassuming about your happiness.

I propped you up while you stood against a pole. The ticket conductor smiled at you as if to say, sorry mate, and you smiled back, holding on to the pole as the bus pulled away. You were shaken off balance and fell forward, putting your hand out to break your fall. This happened too quickly for me to reach out and steady you. Your crutch fell to the floor and I bent down to pick it up.

Don't push me, a man shouted.

I'm sorry, you said. I've injured my leg and...

Expect special treatment, do you? Just because you've hurt yourself?

Mortified, you apologized once more. You could see the tips of his ears go red with anger.

I'm so sorry, you said again.

That's enough, settle down, the ticket conductor said.

The man stood up. He was shorter than you and me, pink-faced, greying at his temples. He was wearing a suit jacket and jeans with a white shirt buttoned up to the top even though he had no tie on. There was this intensity to him as though he was looking for a reason to stand up and shout.

I'm sick of this, he announced to the bus.

People shushed him but he continued, getting louder and hoarser.

We are supposed to tread lightly around the likes of you. We've opened up our gates and look at you – you push me around the bus like you own it.

I picked up your crutch as you straightened, placing myself between you and this man. He reached out and tried to clip your ear but I was in the way. I felt a churn in my stomach – of all the times we had not been accepted, of all the times I had been treated as a sub-human, of all the regret and disappointment and humiliation. We were finally happy and unified and we had our lives and this was pushing us to the edge. Know your place, it screamed. Know your place. I batted his hand away.

He started shouting at me. Calling me names. Wog. Paki. Wog. Paki. Again, and again. Like a barrage of punches.

There were gasps and complaints. He stepped forward, this man. You were flailing, trying to stay upright, wincing in pain as you were forced to put weight on your hurt leg.

You were yelling at him to stop, and the bus was eerily quiet except for the conductor shouting for us to calm down. The bus came to a halt. I fell backwards.

I felt a hand on my shoulder. It was you, standing there.

Stop shouting, you begged. Please stop. What will the Angrezi think of you? Please be quiet.

We belong here, I sobbed.

The people in the gangway had parted and the conductor stood by the door.

Off, he said. Get off my bus.

Exactly, the man said. And take your peg leg with you.

You too, Barry, the conductor said. I can't have that kind of language on my bus. It's your stop anyway. Go home, sleep it off.

I helped you towards the door and you hopped behind me while Barry argued with the conductor. I could feel the stares of disappointment and admonishment around me, and I could tell that you felt all eyes were on us, not Barry. That we were in the wrong. I didn't dare make eye contact with anyone because I knew you wanted not to be seen. I jumped down from the bus and eased you off with me.

I belong here, I thought.

Barry followed us.

Fucking pakis, he was muttering under his breath.

It was a time when using this word was like second nature.

People used it so casually. To refer to the paki shop where they bought milk. To call the place where they bought the curries modelled to their tastes rather than our own the paki kitchen.

People did not care about keeping these words under their breath. So Barry said them. And you were acting calm. For once I was the angry one, the one with the fire inside me.

We stood at the bus stop. Barry was ready to walk away from our confrontation and head home for the evening but I could not let it go. I could not be the bigger person, so I turned around and said to him, we are people too, sir. Please treat us with respect.

Sorry, I don't speak paki, he replied.

How dare, I mean, how dare you... how can you say that?

Barry started to walk away from me and I did the worst thing possible. I touched his arm as he turned his back on me, to stop him, make him face me while I spoke to him. Why did I do that? I run this scenario through my head every time I have two or three lagers now; before, it used to be every single night and I think to myself, why did I touch his arm? Why did I not just walk away? Leave it. Because that is what I should have done.

He started screaming at me.

How dare you touch me? Who do you think you are?

As he shouted all these things a crowd started to form around us, wanting to see what I was doing to him. People mistook me for the problem, thinking that I was the person causing all the trouble. I got annoyed. I don't lose my temper – I have never lost my temper since. Because of what happened next I am a changed person.

I hit him.

I hit him in the mouth with the flat of my palm. He was so shocked he fell backwards into a rubbish bin, and people rushed to help him. I was shouting, no! and you were holding my shoulders to steady me and calm me down.

Shaanti, shaanti, you kept saying.

I was screaming, who do you think you are? Eh? You think you are somebody but you are not. You are nobody. You think you are better than me but you are nobody. I am a person. I am a person, I kept shouting that. I am a person.

I remember those words, how they rolled off the tongue, how they felt around my lips. I remember the rush of wind, the slight breeze against my teeth. Everything appears in slow motion and when I see myself say all these things, it does not feel like me. It no longer feels like my mouth or my teeth or the sound of my voice. It sounds and feels and looks like a film, as though I am watching myself make the biggest mistake I have made in my life, and now knowing what it cost me, what it cost your mummy, what it costs you to this day.

I heard you scream and I turned as glass shattered over my shirt and hair.

I remember the night in the church hall, when you gave Mukesh your shoes and we ran to safety as that racist group gathered to beat our bodies.

I remember them yelling for us to go home. I remember you shouting, this is my home, benchods.

I remember the night we had duttee shoved through our letter-box.

I remember you crying and telling me, this is our home. You were so desperate for this to be our home.

You fell against me, dropping your crutch. Someone had smashed a bottle over your head. I could hear the fizz of the soda as the little bubbles bounced off your skull. You had been smiling a calming smile when you were struck and your face contorted into a horrified look of pain. You were too shocked to cry out. I looked at the face of the man who had done this. I caught his eye and he grinned at me. One of his front teeth was missing; he had thin lips, eyes filled with wrinkled rage and laughter. It was a type of hysteria that only came with his brand of craziness.

I retell us these moments so we do not forget.

As I caught you in my arms, the man aimed his booted foot at your back, cracking something, because I heard it splitting, like a haroomph, all over your body. The weight of that kick. The way he smiled as he split you.

It was like a tear in space.

It was like a coffee cup falling off a table.

It was like a bullet through a windscreen.

It was like a chair in a Western, broken over a cowboy's back.

I could see all the splinters and all that remained was you. Helpless. You fell on to me. I turned to Barry to intervene but he was no longer there. I looked in the eyes of those gathered around us and I knew.

You bounced off me and fell to the ground. I felt something behind me, arms locking around my stomach and then curling around my armpits. I felt the savage wrench of something bigger than me hold me tight against its taut body. I couldn't move. I couldn't speak. There was only you, with a shower raining down on him. A shower of black boots. No sound.

I left Great Britain because I was afraid of white men.

The way they assembled over our beaten bodies and struck us more, with no remorse. I could not live side by side with these men and call them my neighbours.

They kept kicking and finally I found my voice. I screamed for help. There were three of them. My eyes pulled into focus. Three men. As blue lights flickered across their white T-shirts and I saw people arrive on the scene, my eardrums burst with the sound of their sirens. The men stopped what they were doing and whoever held me let me go so that I fell to the ground.

As they ran off I shouted at others to help.

I couldn't see your chest moving. All I could see was that smile on your face. You were scarred with it.

You were gone.

I retell you these stories again and again, staring into the darkness of my home, because I have to remember everything. I want to feel that pain. I need to feel something.

I want you to remember.

I will never forget.

My grandchildren live amongst these white men now, and I worry that nothing has changed and their bodies are close to a similar fate.

I am lost in these memories as we walk through the museum, looking at dolls representing different countries, different cultures. The museum is empty. The only sound is the flap of the chappal against the heel of my foot. I look at these two grandchildren now, walking in front of me, holding each other's hands just as my own two children used to, and I do not know why I am here.

Why is history repeating itself?

I cannot look anywhere else. I cannot look at these children. They are ghosts.

Neha turns to me and asks for a drink. I give her the water bottle I have packed for the three of us.

I can see her mouth grimace, so I shake my head at her and wipe the nozzle with my fingers.

She does the same.

She looks like her mum so much as she makes that face.

Patterns.

So many patterns.

We look at dolls sent from around the African continent. By white people, surely. These dolls, dressed up to represent our world, are viewed through the lens of the aggressor. I stare at the tribal masks framing black bodies dancing with one leg up, lifting spears. I try to remember when I have seen such things.

I have not.

Neha and Rakesh have stopped walking. They are staring into a cabinet labelled Kenya.

I look to see how my country has decided to remember itself.

British soldiers stand in a circle, holding rifles pointed at black boys, in rags, on their knees, their spears on the ground. The title of the cabinet is *British Quell Mau Mau Rebels.*

The British still paint themselves as the victors, despite the bloodshed they caused.

The British think they saved black Kenyans with railways and religion. They think that colonialism was positive. Benevolent enslavement, that is what they thought. And when they needed people to build things, they looked outside Kenya. Every day we must be thankful for railways and religion. My family were brought over as indentured labourers to help build the Uganda railway. We stayed and eventually I was born. I am a stranger in my own country because I left and tried to be British. I could not be a double immigrant. When that failed, I came back here – it was always home, here. Alas, I cannot escape the things I ran away from in England, so wherever I lay my head, that is my purgatory.

Who are these people? Neha asks. Why are they on their knees?

Because they spoke up, I tell her. They wanted their freedom but they paid with their lives. It was not enough.

You know, I tell my grandchildren, I know these brave men and women.

One night, back in 1953 during the state of emergency, when

your mother was two, I tell them, three Mau Mau soldiers came in the darkness, asking us to give them food and a bed for the night in the factory that belonged to your grandfather and his brothers. They were being hunted by the British, who were close. Our factory was on the outskirts of Nairobi, and your grandfather, the youngest, knew that his brothers would say no. So he waited, and when they all left for the day, he gave these three soldiers beds in the factory, and a bag of maize, and I cooked for them.

One of them joked with your mummy and teased her. She was very shy back then. It was a quiet night. We heard shots in the distance and trees rustling. We heard the lives of others. Every single noise made us think it would be the end.

One of the men told us, you will not die tonight. At worst, you will be imprisoned. Only people fighting for a cause should die for a cause. You are not.

But we support you, your grandfather told the man.

Support is all you can give and that's all that we want. This one – he pointed to your mother. Is she healthy?

I nodded. Why? I asked.

There are small black spots on her fingernails. Get them checked immediately.

That is how we knew. It was in our blood. Some things we cannot chase and some things we cannot escape.

Before we leave the museum, I watch Neha approach the table where a visitors' book sits. She picks up a pencil, stares upwards at the wall for a few seconds and then writes, her tongue between her lips as she presses the pencil to the page. It reminds me of our daughter.

Rakesh slips his hand into mine because Neha has let go. So needy, this one.

He looks up at me, imploringly. He is hungry, wants his sugar rotli. I smile and rub at the back of his neck lightly, watching my granddaughter write something.

I can see Nisha in her so much. She is singularly our daughter. Rakesh feels like an amalgamation. He is sometimes Nisha, sometimes Chumchee, sometimes separately, sometimes simultaneously. Other times he is just like his bevakoof father. But mostly, Neha reminds me of her mother, in that she is stubborn and headstrong and never happy about anything. And Rakesh is just like Mukesh, in that he is always doing something to make you look at him. He wants everyone to laugh at him, but he does not know what to do with the attention when he has it.

The more I am with them, the more they remind me of what I have lost.

Rakesh shakes at my hand and calls out to his sister who holds up a palm to say, don't hurry me.

She finishes and walks back to us.

I did not like the Kenya display, she says. There was too much fighting.

Come bedtime, the children are sitting on the bed, watching me fold their clothes. Rakesh has not spoken for most of the day. He is quiet. Needy. A chumchee. Neha has not stopped talking since we arrived at home. This museum, it has unlocked something within her.

The world is so big and everything is so different, she says. Why would we want to go anywhere different? I cannot wait to go home. Why do you stay here?

I shake my head and shrug.

Nowhere I go feels like home to me, I tell her. I understand myself here.

Do you not miss England?

No, I say. It reminds me too much of everything that I have lost. Here, I feel most like myself. It is familiar.

Neha cries.

What is wrong? I ask her.

I miss Daddy. I don't want to be here.

Of course. He will return. Until then, we are stuck with each other.

Rakesh holds his sister's hand in solidarity. I wonder if they realize I will never see them again after this. I will never return to the UK, a country that doesn't want me. And I cannot leave this country. Not while I wait for destiny to come and collect me. Or is it death? Are they sometimes the same?

Will you make me lots of sugar rotlis before I go? Rakesh asks.

I could show you how to make them, I say. That way, whenever you eat one, you will be here. With me.

That is not the same, Neha says.

She jumps off the bed and runs into the kitchen, sitting on the floor with her back to me.

I go to the kitchen and sit down next to her, taking great pains to cross my legs.

I put an arm around her.

Your destiny is not with me, I tell her. But I will always guide you when I can. Do you miss her?

Who? Neha says.

Your mummy.

No, she says.

Why not? I whisper, trying to calm her, feeling the tension across her shoulders.

She was never my mummy.

I turn away so that she does not see my tears. I have not cried since I came home and realized I was alone, except for the stories I tell you.

She will not see me cry.

I can hear Rakesh sleeping and Neha squirming about next to him. She insists on wearing trousers to bed as she is worried about mosquitoes, but they make her knees sweat. I lie with my back turned to them both, on the double mattress we all share in the middle of my one-room house, staring at the text on the page – none of the Mills & Boon book enters my brain. Their presence is an irritation. Every time one of them breathes, I can feel the room get hotter, and when they shift on the mattress, the fat rolls on my stomach shake. I tremble with irritation and tut loudly at their every infraction. I look down my body to my grey toenails, remembering when I could wear chappals and not feel embarrassed. Now I wear socks so no one can see that my body is beginning to crack, starting with my feet.

Go to sleep, I whisper to Neha, without looking at her.

No, she replies.

What's wrong?

Did you know my mummy was going to die? she asks softly.

No.

Rakesh mutters something in his sleep. Gibberish.

No, I say. I didn't know any of them would die. Not before me. I did not think about it.

I sit up, and turn to face Neha on the mattress. She stares at me passively. Her eyes have dark circles under them and they are red from where she has scratched her tears away. I sit cross-legged and she does the same, facing me.

I did not think about death till it came to find my family, I say. I only knew about destiny.

What is destiny?

Destiny is…cruel. Destiny does not send us heralds. She is too wise or too cruel – Oscar Wilde said that. I read it on some toilet paper in a hotel I stayed in with your bapuji and I remembered it. It is not my place to question destiny. Everything is pre-written, pre-judged. Why fight it?

Does that mean it is decided how I will die?

I nod, conscious that, years later, I am going against my daughter's dying wish. Yes, I say softly. There is comfort in that. To know that it is beyond your control. Live your life. The wind is blowing; those vessels whose sails are unfurled catch it, and go forward on their way, but those that have their sails furled do not catch the wind. Is that the fault of the wind? I smile. Bedtime, I say.

I'm scared, Neha says.

Of what?

I cannot control anything.

No, I say. I have lost enough people to find this comforting. Your daddy, you know? He moved to England to be with my nephew, Sailesh. He was going to live in London, working in clubs, earning money as a juggler, a clown. And your daddy was going to come with him, to study. So he came, because he got the visa quicker. And he lived in Keighley, because he could not find anywhere in England that would accept darkies, like you and me. And if he hadn't gone to Keighley, he would not have met your mother. Is that coincidence? Or is it destiny? If his friend, Sailesh, had not died, your daddy might have moved quickly from Keighley to London, and he might not have started a relationship with your mummy. You can believe it is coincidence. Or it is fate, destiny? But you can control neither.

Maybe she would still be alive if he hadn't met her, Neha says. Maybe I would have a mummy.

Maybe. But if he hadn't met her, then you wouldn't have been born. It is not for us to question the one who writes destiny, only to honour their wishes.

Who is the one who writes destiny?

Some say he is the cousin of death. Others say he is the accountant of our life, sitting there, making note of everything we do, checking it against a balance sheet.

I do not understand.

You are young, I tell her.

It's not because I'm young, she hisses. It's because you talk in funny riddles.

Neha lies down, turning to face Rakesh. She closes her eyes.

That night, I tell her softly, in the maize factory, while we waited for the British never to arrive, your bapuji asked me if I believed in fate. I said no. He told me, fate is comfort. And your bapuji, he knew more than anyone. I remember talking to one of the soldiers, who walked and walked all day to get to us. He told me, a man's actions are more important than his ancestry. Your DNA, your genes, you worry too much about them.

Worry about what you do in life. Please. Do not worry about anything other than what you do with the time you have. Me? I have done everything I wanted to. I've lost everything. Now, I'm just waiting to die, to be reunited with my three loves. And then you two come into my life, and I can see your amee and your papa and your mama in you. And it makes me angry because I look at you both and all I can think about is what I have lost. But I should not be this way. You are children. You are my grandchildren. Please, do not worry about anything other than what you do.

Neha is snoring.

I look back at my book and whisper the lines of dialogue to myself.

Rakesh is already awake when I sit up.

Neha is lying in bed reading one of the comics I bought for her. When she sees me, she drops it and pretends to be asleep.

On the other side of the room, Rakesh is standing over one of my steel mixing bowls. He is cupping his hands full of flour and dropping it into the bowl, spilling grains all over the floor. He looks up at me and smiles, then lifts a cup of water.

Only enough to bind the flour, I say. Just a little. And even though I say it in English, I can still hear my mother saying this to me, me saying it to Nisha, and imagining Nisha saying it to her children.

He pours in a large drop and smiles, expectantly.

Now knead, I say. I stand up. I kick Neha with a foot and she opens one eye. Sugar rotlis for breakfast? Made by your brother?

She rolls her eyes, but I know she's hungry.

God Knows My Past, but Not Today's Separation

My mother told me what it was like to give birth on a dhow.

She said, she cared not for privacy. She waited for the waves to be hypnotic, for the ebb and flow of the horizon to be calming, for the cool breeze to soothe her nerves.

I was her first child and so she did not know how I would emerge. Despite being a small baby, I came out with a hand over my face, shielding myself from the world. She nearly bled to death because my elbow tore at her like a metal rod.

She said I was quiet. She said I was alert very early on and that I watched everything. She also said it was the first time she'd appreciated that she would always be closer in age to her first-born than to her husband. She was a teenager when she had me, a teenager when I was conceived, barely out of childhood when she was married.

Sometimes I think, if I had not moved to the West, would I have accepted that as custom and tradition? Tradition is very important, it upholds structure. But it is static.

I try to picture this dhow birth.

I want to tell these children about their family. They find the way I live hard. They are not used to the lack of space inside when there is an abundance of space outside. We live in one room, it houses part of a kitchen. The toilet is outside, the bath is a cup and a bucket wherever you can find space. I have no television, I wear two sarees. Most of the space in my house is taken up by their suitcases. Even so, I do not want to be seen as a savage.

Neha and I surface at the same time the next day. I know she's awake because I can hear her shuffling about under the sheet.

I roll over to face her. She is lying on her back, staring at the ceiling, and does not notice that I am awake. Her entire body is straight and stiff.

Raks snores.

Pani? I ask.

She turns her head to me and nods.

Pani, she repeats.

If they leave with one lesson, it's the lesson of nouns for proper things. Pani, gadi, gadhero, keree, chumchee, for starters.

I remember when our Chumchee died. I had already lost you and Nisha. I was there, in the hospital with him. I sat with him while he stared out of the window, held his hands and read the Gita to him. His body never recovered from the collision. I tried to rescue his mind but he was slipping away from the moment of that accident.

Dehino'smin yatha deha kaumaram yauvanam jara tatha dehantara praptir dhiras tatra na muhyati.

Just as in the physical body of the embodied being is the process of childhood, youth, old age; similarly in the transmigration from one body to another the wise are never deluded, I whispered – in case he had forgotten how to speak properly.

Na jayate mriyate va kadacin nayam bhutva bhavita

va na bhuyah ajo nityah sasvato yam purano na hanyate hanyamane.

The soul never takes birth and never dies at any time, nor does it come into being again when the body is created. The soul is birthless, eternal, imperishable and timeless and is never terminated when the body is terminated.

Jatasya hi dhruvo mrtyur dhruvam janma mrtasya ca tasmad apariharye'rthe na tvam socitum arhasi.

For one who has taken birth, death is certain, and for one who has died, birth is certain. Therefore in an inevitable situation understanding should prevail.

I repeated my favourite bit to myself.

The soul is indestructible, the soul is incombustible, insoluble and unwitherable. The soul is eternal, all-pervasive, unmodifiable, immovable and primordial.

Acchedyo'yam adahyo'yam akledya'sosya eva ca nityah sarva-gatah sthanur acalo'yam sanatanah.

I do not know at what point he died, but I know when I realized he had. I pretended I had not noticed, not until I had finished reading. Years later, I was able to admit to myself that I had noted the point at which he was no longer with me and decided, consciously but with the overriding feeling of subconsciousness, to ignore this and carry on reading the Gitas to the end.

I did not cry when Chumchee died. I was prepared for the loss of another child. Nisha I never recovered from.

Neha looks like her mother.

When Nisha died, I was sitting next to her, quietly. I had been sitting up with her all night. She told me she could see her father, her grandmother, her grandfather whom she had never met before, her cousin Sailesh, and she was talking to them – in tongues. It wasn't Gujarati and it wasn't English but it seemed like a pleasant conversation. I sat next to her and watched. I called for Mukesh and he came into the room and held her hand. It went limp early on but he stayed holding it for as long as she wanted to talk.

When she was finished, she smiled at him and closed her eyes.

I spent much of that time just quietly watching her. I wish I had let her know it was okay, that victims of cancer had a good reincarnation in front of them. That it was all going to be okay. Whether I believed it or not, I needed for there to be that option.

Most of them did not even know she had cancer till afterwards.

They blamed me.

It was Mukesh's decision to not tell anyone. Why should we let people know our business? he said to me. Your family is filled with hypochondriacs. They all play that game with each other. I am ill. No, I am more ill. My son has a cold, my daughter has typhoid, my cousin has dengue fever, my mother has malaria, I am dead. Why should we subject Nisha to this scrutiny? She had years longer than we thought she would have. We lived knowing this day would come. It's not a surprise.

This is the fallacy of our family. We play league games with our health. It is the only status we can afford – and instead of banking good health, we want to be the ones with the most suffering. So we count out maladies like coins and play card games to see who has been through the most, who has suffered the most, who requires the most sympathy.

Nisha hated this way.

She told me off when she found out I had idly given away her diagnosis to her mami and mama, because my brother's wife had been diagnosed with lupus. I wanted them to know that I understood the struggle.

We make life difficult for ourselves in order to relate to each other. We live miles away from each other, often in different countries. We don't have cars or degrees or kitchens that look like the pages of catalogues. We have health. Health can be measured.

We see suffering as karma. To suffer is to gain something in the next life.

We walk together in a line.

The fruit market is busy at this time of day.

It should smell like magic but instead, it smells like rotting mounds of discarded fruit. I squeeze mangos and mclons, look at papayas. Each one is decaying, dying. Like me.

I buy Rakesh and Neha a mango each. It is a luxury. I show them both how to eat the fruit without cutting it up into pieces.

We sit on the steps of the fruit market as I squeeze one of the mangos in its skin. I squeeze and squeeze until I can feel the mango meat underneath getting softer and juicier.

When it feels as though the flesh has been loosened and pulped underneath my warm hands, I tear off the top of the mango and pass it to Neha. I tell her to suck it, and push with her fingers, so that the pulp erupts straight into her mouth like squeezing toothpaste.

The look of pleasure on her face is worth it.

She is tasting mango the way it should be eaten. She

squeezes till the flesh is spilling out on to her fingers, over her mouth, down towards her chin. I wipe her with my hand.

Rakesh does the same as I did. He smiles at her.

I have done something right.

We watch the world go by and I notice an old Indian man, bald, wearing round glasses, his dhoti folded up into itself so it looks like pants.

He stands next to a little boy who is looking around, bemused at what is happening to him as the old man stands with one hand on the crown of his head. His other hand stretches up, cupping the sky, straining for water, or sunshine, or something.

His eyes are closed. He mutters silently.

He is in a trance.

The boy is bewildered by what he's doing.

The old man opens his eyes - they are glassy - and looks at me. He does not break the stride of his muttering.

He smiles, revealing separated teeth, mostly white, a front one missing. It gives his face an impish look.

He smiles by trapping his top lip behind the erratic arrangement of his bottom teeth and waggles his head.

I turn away, back to Rakesh and Neha. She has finished half of her fruit, a sated mess. He is eating as quickly as he can, as if someone is about to take mangos away from him for life.

Daddy says we cannot buy these at home, Neha says. This is the last one I will eat.

What is that man doing? Rakesh says, lifting the mango from his mouth; a dumping of flesh falls into his lap.

The old man is walking towards us, smiling.

Jay Shree Krishna, he says, as he approaches. Gujarati?

Swahili, I reply.

I was never born in Gujarat.

Gujarati bole che?

I nod, down once, then up, to ask what he wants.

Su? I say.

The old man holds his hand out to Neha who looks at me, confused.

Take it, he says. Take it.

I put my hand under his and gesture for him to drop whatever he is offering into my palm.

What do you want? I ask.

Beek lage che? he asks. Don't be frightened. I am not to be feared.

I keep my hand there, waiting for him to drop the object into my hand.

He swivels his hand around and shows me. It is one petal of a bougainvillea plant, faded pink like his palm.

What is this? I ask.

I see sadness in you. All of you.

Thank you, sahib. We are going home now, I say.

I usher Neha and Rakesh to stand up. They both do, lazily, as though their limbs are stuck to the floor. It is midday now and the sun is streaking down in waves of unbelievable heat. I want us all to stay here until it cools down.

I have not eaten today, he says, holding out his hands. Please.

I wave my hand at him, to say no. I am not unkind. I make and serve food at the mandhir where they offer meals to everybody, Hindu or no. He can go there. I walk past him and turn to chivvy Neha and Rakesh to hurry up. He reminds me of something – I can't quite picture what in my head. It is a photograph I have seen. I turn to watch as Rakesh, and then Neha, place their half-finished mangos in his hands and walk towards me. Neha slips her hand into mine and Rakesh grabs hers. Her hand is sticky and moist. Instinctively, I squeeze it.

The old man smiles at me, sucking at some mango skin, and winks.

I am annoyed. Why did you do that? I ask.

He was hungry.

That was your mango, I say, squeezing her hand tight till I feel her resistance, trying to pull it away. I clutch her hand tighter to stop her from squirming.

I say to her, I give you my food. You eat my food. I give him my food. He eats my food. You do not give anyone my food. That is for me to decide, not you. Okay? Do you understand me?

Neha nods.

I do not know why I am angry.

We walk home in silence. It is hot and by the time we get to the house, my back is slick with rivers of sweat. I wet a cloth and place it on my head as I sit down on a chair and close my eyes.

I open my eyes to stillness.

My body becomes alert and aware that I am surrounded by quiet. There is no movement in the room. I sit up and look around. Rakesh, Neha, neither of them is in sight. The chair crunches against the ground as I stand up.

I call their names but there is nothing – only the clammy hand of heat and stillness in my ears. I look in the kitchen. Neither of them is there. I look out of the back door to the toilet.

Neither of them is there, nor are they playing in the courtyard outside my house. Not that either of these two sluggish children would be doing what normal children do, running around and playing chase. No, they sit and they read and they stare and they eat. They are lazy. They are mine. Children after my own heart. I do not move unless I have to, which is rare when these two are not here.

I call their names again.

Kantha, who lives across the road from me, walks past the house. I shout her name, and ask if she has seen my grandchildren. She does not stop walking as she turns to me and she shakes her head. I calmly step outside and look around.

Dogs tear at nappies strewn across the waste ground next to Kantha's house.

A car splutters goodbye as it judders off into the distance but I cannot hear any human voices, least of all any children playing.

My stomach churns, as though I'm turning over ghee, again and again.

I step out of the house and shout Rakesh's name, then Neha's, then Rakesh's again. All I can hear is the hushed roar of the sea.

I don't know where to go, whether towards the shore, or into town or through the wasteland to where they used to have a race track when the British were here. I don't know. I just don't know.

These pagal chokrao.

I picture the old man for a second. Maybe he – no, who is he?

I decide to head back towards the town and walk as fast as I can with my knees and my gout.

I lead with my head. Stopping. Panting. Walking. Towards the town. Where there are people.

I begin to run, but my body is slowed by age and weakened by inactivity. Adrenaline drills at my brain and I push myself faster.

All of this was supposed to be easier than it is. What is life, if it is constantly grieving for you, and for Nisha, and for Chumchee? What is life, if it is trying to ensure none of you are ever forgotten? What is life, if I am the one who outlives you all – who am I? Am I the one who writes destiny for our family? A scribe, who records all these things, in order that they hold our family to account? No. I do not control any of this. I do not control our destiny. I am like the rusty car that will not die, the cockroach which cannot be killed. I am the moment in time when you can see neither ahead nor behind, only down to your feet. I live on my knees. And they are worn.

Desperate, I call for my grandchildren. I cannot outlive them. I cannot see their bodies put into the ground, cannot be the one who remembers them for ever. Is my destiny to be a record of our family's suffering? Is my destiny to be the memory banks for who we were and what we could have done? I do not want this for life. I want to live again. I want to take everything we can achieve and throw it into the sky. I want to be a person again.

I call their names.

I remember when Nisha died, and Chumchee, and you; when Papa and Amee died – I knew of one thing only. I knew this would all happen. There, in the factory, that one long night, watching as those men played cards with us, and joked with you, and one of them looked at me and said, she carries the weight of the world in her eyes. She never forgets a thing, that one. It will be the death of her.

And I said, you can talk to me as an equal. You do not talk about me as though I am not in this room. Women are not servants and spectres.

The man laughed, and said, I'm sorry. You remind me of Martha. St Martha.

Who is she? I asked.

As Jesus and his disciples were out walking, they came to a village where a woman named Martha opened her home to them. She had a sister called Mary, who sat at the Lord's feet listening to what he said. But Martha was distracted by all the preparations that had to be made. She came to him and asked, Lord, don't you care that my sister has left me to do the work by myself? Tell her to help me. Martha, Martha, the Lord answered, you are worried and upset about many things, but only one thing is needed. Mary has chosen what is better, and it will not be taken away from her. Luke chapter ten, verses thirty-eight to forty-two. She is the patron saint of servants and cooks.

What a beautiful example for women everywhere, I told him, as I poured out some tea.

He laughed.

I laughed with him. The situation itself was ridiculous. It seemed like the wrong time for us to descend into arguments about the roles we must inherit.

He kept looking at me. When you were helping some of the other men make beds, he said – his name was John – when you remember all this, it's important not just to remember our names, but to try and take something of who we are.

I asked what he meant.

He said, you will remember all this. You will look out on to the ashes of everyone you loved and wonder how you outlived them. Do not question why. Just remember them. That is their right and your duty. Your daughter will find love. Briefly, but she will find it. Tragedy is a community, not a singularity. A community. A man without a donkey is a donkey. This is your burden.

He smiled. I told him I was tired and he said, we all are. I understood. And I hated the know-it-all.

By the time I woke up in the morning, ready to tell John where all the things for breakfast were so that he and his friends could make it themselves, they had already tidied up after themselves and left.

He did tell me this would all happen.

Tragedy.

This was my burden, my destiny. Both, hand in hand. In bed together, lying naked next to each other. Tragedy and destiny, the strange bedfellows of my life.

I reach the fruit market and look around, wildly, for my children. My babies.

I want to live again.

I listen. I cannot hear them.

Mtoto, I shout. Watoto. Wako wapi watoto wangu? Nisaidie.

People gather around me.

I ask them, Wajukuu zangu kuwa na kukimbia mbali. Msaada mimi kupata yao.

Apart from the odd word, the odd noun, the odd thing I need, I do not speak Swahili. I do not speak English except to my grandchildren. I do not speak Gujarati except to you. I do not speak at all in this world. My mouth is dry.

Nisaidie, I say again, strained. Desperate.

I give a brief description in a mixture of English, Swahili and Gujarati, all of my tongues, and people smile and nod and disappear into the streets, calling out their names. Rakesh. Neha. Rakesh, the lord of the full-moon day, and Neha, love. Where are you?

I walk around the perimeter of the fruit market. It has been packed away now. It is empty and I can see through the space. The stalls and tables have been moved to the edges, making it easier to clean away the rotten fruit on the ground. Not that anyone does this.

I walk and I walk and I seem to get lost in the streets I've known since I was born. Each one looks exactly the same. Emptying out as the evening approaches and people retreat home to sit, and wait for the sea breeze to cool off a hot day.

I am lost.

The house is dark. There are no lights on. The door is still open from when I ran out earlier.

I turn on the single bulb for the main room and call out Neha and Rakesh's names. I hear nothing.

I stand outside my door, under the wooden awning, and wait.

I fix my stare on a single point in the distance – it's the gap between the trees behind my across-the-road neighbour's house where you can see the sea. I watch it as the dusk grows and feel an ache in my stomach. I am hungry but this does not feel like the time to be eating. Nor preparing food. Who am I preparing food for?

The children have gone.

Everybody leaves me.

When I hear the man's voice I don't know how long I have been standing there watching the darkness descend over a single spot of sea. That man. I know his voice. I can hear him in the distance.

Those who remember me at the time of death will come to me. Do not doubt this. Whatever occupies the mind at the time of death determines the destination of the dying; always they will tend towards that state of being.

He is reciting Gitas. I look for him in the darkness.

His dhoti, now unfolded down to his ankles, gleams at me.

He holds the hands of Neha and Rakesh.

I run to them both, screaming, my hand aloft ready for a severe thapad.

Undur ja! I scream at them both. Get inside.

Neha and Rakesh release themselves from the old man and disappear into the house, holding each other's hands.

I slap the air behind Rakesh's head with the back of my hand and turn to the man.

What did you do with them? I hiss.

Auntie, he says, even though he is at least ten years older than me, Auntie, they come to me when they need me the most. When their hurt is so great that they cannot contain it any more. I give them what they need. And they help me get closer to God.

Who are you? I ask.

I step closer to him to show I am not afraid. Except here we are. In the dark. In front of my house. A man who is mostly muscle despite his age, half-naked, and me. I barely move. I am scared but he must not know this. He adjusts his round glasses.

Do not be afraid, he tells me. This was supposed to happen. You knew this day would come.

What are you talking about?

Princess, you see me only by the power of your prayer and fasting. I am Yama, god of death. Now is the time I must take the spirit of Satyavan.

I stare at him and take a step backwards, turning away from his eyes. He has come for me. Finally, death has come for me.

Did you hurt them? I ask, edging quietly back towards the door.

Why would I hurt them? I am not ready for them. I whispered to them when I would come for them. Then I took them swimming. You know, neither of those two children knows how to swim. You should teach them while you can.

I am not ready to come with you, I whisper.

I can feel everything around us slow down. Every sound is a muffled cacophony. Everything in my view fades into darkness as I try to focus on his face, to remember it. Where have I seen him before?

Happiness awaits you in my kingdom, he says, smiling.

His mouth, open, shows not teeth but a black empty hole. He smiles, and his mouth is wider, bigger than his face, for a second, just for a fragment of a second. I am dreaming still, I think. I must be. I realize that my feet are throbbing with all the blood pumping around my body. I turn around to face the house, to check on my babies, make sure they are okay, but the house has faded into darkness.

You leave them alone, I tell him.

I am not ready for them.

Please, I need more time, I beg.

Princess, even love must bend to fate. Still, I admire your devotion. I will grant you a favour.

I need more time, I tell him. I need more time.

I hear snarling. Dogs, I think. I check for the number of their eyes.

Yes, this the Immortals seek of thee with longing, progeny of the sole existing mortal.

He smiles, and he nods.

Please, I say again. Please.

This time when he smiles, he has teeth. He nods.

I will see you soon, Mrs Mehta. I will see you soon.

He turns and walks slowly away. Everything seems to get lighter as he does so. I hear dogs growling in the wasteland and I can see their eyes glint off the lamp on my porch. Only two eyes. I breathe quietly, slowing my breath.

He has come for me, to bring me to you. Finally. But I am not ready for him. I am not ready to see you yet. All these years, to come back to you is all I have wanted to do. But now I am not ready.

I turn and rush into the house to gather my two babies up and give them valis that will last into their adult years. What did he whisper to them?

When will he come for me?

I rush in to find that Neha has curled up into Rakesh's arm and they are both asleep, on the gadi, next to where I lie. They are tired but they look fine and breathe deeply, peaceful in their sleep.

It is a cruel realization, as I watch them both sleeping, that I am not ready for him. I am not ready for my destiny. All this time I have been static and waiting, and now it is undone by these two children. When they came into my life, I wanted nothing more than for them to be gone. But they are here, for a few more days, and I want that time with them. I want them to know me, and our family, and this country. This country that is so significant to our history. I have been waiting for him for so long, and now he has come for me, I don't feel ready. I do not feel ready.

We need to go from here. We need to escape, to get out of Mombasa. I cannot be in the same place as him, now that he is waiting for me.

We will go to Lamu, I think. I have a cousin there. We have not seen each other for years and I barely remember him, but he is family. These children should meet him. When I am gone, he will be their connection here.

When I am gone. I shudder. I have waited so long for this but now it is close, I feel nothing but fear.

I lock the children in the house and go to a phone kiosk. I have my cousin's telephone number written down at the top of a letter he sent me, thanking me for the rakhri I send every year without fail.

He seems happy to hear from me. Of course, he says. Come and stay. Bring the children.

He sounds so friendly on the phone, not like the cousin I remember as cruel and quick-tempered. But he is family.

I rush home. I am nervous, watching for him everywhere, for the one who wrote destiny.

I unlock the door and enter my small house. My grandchildren, my beautiful grandchildren, are still asleep and I burst into tears at the sight of them. They know only loss and absence.

I walk to my mixing bowl and pour out flour, making sugar rotlis for the morning.

We have a long journey ahead.

Walking, Walking

They fall about the coach seats, laughing. The joke has a strange effect on me, of being funny, then really funny, then not funny, then tedious, then funny again.

They shake hands.

Good. Bye, Neha says firmly. Good. Bye. One day you will die. Until then, good. Bye.

Rakesh shakes her hand back.

Goodbye, he replies, giggling. When I die, I'm bringing you down with me. Goodbye.

They fall all about their seats on the coach. We've been travelling for over a day and we are all feeling a little crazy.

But this is torture.

They giggle.

They look at each other.

They shake hands.

Good. Bye, Neha says firmly. Good. Bye. One day you will die. Until then, good. Bye.

Rakesh shakes her hand back.

Goodbye, he replies, giggling. When I die, I'm bringing you down with me. Goodbye.

Neha shows affection to a donkey and it surprises me.

She does not like hugs, is not tactile, will not hold my hand.

She rarely shows her brother any affection, is not very good at acknowledging other people in the room, and backs away from neighbourhood cats and dogs.

There is a donkey tied up outside the house we are staying in. It belongs to my cousin – the house and the donkey.

My cousin, Ajay, lives in a small house with a big gate in front of it. Though there are two bedrooms, they all sleep on mattresses in his room: Ajay, his wife, their baby and their two-year-old. Their children are both silent and immobile, and neither is offered to play with Rakesh and Neha. Ajay's wife, Seema, keeps them with her in the bedroom until mealtimes, when they emerge, smiling and obliging. Seema seems too young for my cousin, and with a two-year-old as well.

My cousin has got fatter but is largely the same: short, frowning, tense. As soon as we arrived, I remembered why I have not seen him for so long. All the way to Lamu, I convinced myself that he would protect me from the one who writes destiny. For all his anger and temper, I am family and thus under his protection.

But on arrival, it appears that we are an imposition. I can tell because of how Seema bends over backgrounds to accommodate our simple needs. As we sit down to refresh ourselves from the long journey, we are offered water, which she tops up from a jug each time one of us takes a sip. After that, we do not see her again till the mealtime. Whenever one of us enters from outside and takes our sandals off, Ajay straightens them. Each time it is done with the right amount of annoyance and aggression, a tut and a tense small act, all to remind me we are strangers. It feels entirely consistent with my cousin and I start to regret bringing our children here. Then there is the donkey.

Neha spends the whole first day sitting cross-legged in front of it. The only time she leaves it is when she runs in for a glass of limbu pani and to ask the animal's name. She is horrified when she is told it doesn't have one. It's a donkey. She suggests Spock but the way my cousin pronounces the name, Spack, ruins it. Then she suggests Vijay. She looks at me and tells me she is naming it after you.

I'm naming him after your husband, she tells me. He looks like the photo you showed me. Same nose.

We already have a Vijay, my cousin tells her in Gujarati. He looks at me. Sorry, sister. Had a Vijay. God rest his soul. Does she know it is a girl donkey?

She runs out of the house and sits down opposite Vijay.

She even eats her dinner out there, feeding sugar rotlis to a nonplussed donkey.

Rakesh wakes in the middle of the night, calling for his daddy. It is pitch black and I am sleeping between him and Neha.

I rub at his hair but it does nothing to stop the screaming. His eyes are closed and he is still fast asleep. I try talking to him, reassuring him.

Beta, I say. Beta, beta, beta.

But it is not enough.

The light is switched on, making me squint.

Neha crosses over to Rakesh's side of the bed. She rubs at his back and then whacks him across the shoulder blades.

Rakesh gasps, opens his eyes for a few seconds and looks at me.

Neha looks at me too.

Then Rakesh closes his eyes again.

Neha walks over to the light switch again, turns it off. I feel her shuffling back into bed.

He needs somebody to show him he is okay, she tells me quietly.

I tell her to go to sleep.

I thought I would be comforted by the stillness and the blackness that come from being on this island. The whoosh and rush of the sea in the background.

Instead I feel as though I am waiting for something.

I'm waiting for Mukesh to come home, to take these children away from me.

I'm waiting for Yama. I do not know how long my reprieve is. I'm waiting to see you.

Neha asks if she can ride the donkey.

I have called him Little Vijay, she says. He is younger than Vijay mama.

I look at my cousin for his approval of the name, but Ajay tuts and flings his hands up as if to say, this conversation is not appropriate. The donkey is ill, which is why it's not working. There are no vehicles on the island. Donkeys are transportation and couriers.

The donkey has back problems, he tells me in Gujarati. Soon it will no longer be with us.

I tell Neha about the back problem.

He seems bored, she replies.

I know, I say.

I take Rakesh to the beach. Neha insists on staying with Vijay.

It is quiet here. My cousin told me as we left that the locals tell the tourists that sharks feed there. It keeps the beach free for the Kenyans. The dunes make me feel small. I imagine myself sinking into them and disappearing.

Rakesh splashes in the water and I read the book I have brought with me. On page 67, I raise an eyebrow and look around me. There is nobody else on the beach, luckily. They cannot see what I am reading.

I am fucking you, Tania, so that you'll stay fucked. And if you are afraid of being fucked publicly I will fuck you privately. I will bite your clitoris and spit out two francs.

I close the book. This should shock me. Or arouse me. It should make me feel something. I have not felt anything since that night with Jonathan.

How a man can wander about all day on an empty stomach, and even get an erection once in a while, is one of those mysteries which are all too easily explained.

How, indeed? Ask only men about men, I think.

Rakesh trips and falls into the water. He looks up at me and cries, so I stand and walk over. When I help him to get up he hugs me and manages to get sand between my saree and skin.

As he wades out into the water again, I walk back to where I've left our things.

The book has gone.

I can see the imprint of it in the sand but it is not there. I can see the shaal I sat on, and the tiffin with the samosas and tamarind chutney. Not the book.

I look around. I cannot see any footprints other than my own leading to and from this point.

Help, I hear. Help.

Rakesh has caught a wave straight in his face. I stand him up in the water and ask if he is okay.

Am I okay? he asks.

Drowning, cancer, these things run in our family.

Ba, Rakesh asks me, holding up the book he chose at Shukla's shop. Can I tell you a joke?

Neha has untied Little Vijay and is walking her around in a circle in front of the house when we get home.

Inside, my cousin is standing by the door, slurping masala chai loudly and watching her. I can tell by how upright he is that he is not happy.

She has untied him, he says. Why are you not telling off your child?

Even though Rakesh cannot understand Gujarati, I know he understands tone. I tell him to go and wash off the salt water and get himself clean for dinner.

Bhai, I tell him. She is a child.

Does not matter. It is my donkey. She has given it a name. She is ruining its back, making it feel like part of the family. Shall my wife set a place for it for dinner?

I walk outside, silently.

Without explanation, I take the rope from Neha's hand and pull the donkey, as delicately as I can, back towards the fence. Neha sits on the ground and cries loudly. Finally, I think, she is behaving like a child. I look back towards the house. My cousin has disappeared from view.

I hate how much I am intimidated by him and yet he is my family.

You only met him once. At our wedding. He bruised my

wrist, squeezing it too hard as I went to touch his feet and he reached to stop me.

I look at Neha and debate between telling her off so she doesn't untie the donkey again – we are guests, after all – and trying to explain to her what the problem is. I'm not sure I know, other than a sense of property. I try not to understand a cousin I have not seen since I came back to Kenya and who, as a child, would beat me and my brother with sticks and call it playing. I try to understand his second family. He tried again. After his wife died of cancer. Years later, he got what he always wanted. A family. And yet they seem like actors he has hired for my benefit.

When Seema emerges from the bedroom, her baby is silent and does not cry, and the toddler is silent and does not want to play. They compliantly sit with her, as she cooks for us. When she requires two hands to roll out chapattis, I offer to help, but she tells me to sit. I suggest taking the baby but she says it is okay. I am fine. I walk outside and watch my grandchildren instead. I cannot keep watching Seema struggle. Rakesh reads his joke book to himself and falls about laughing. Neha is talking to this donkey, always talking to this donkey.

Neha does not come for dinner when she is called. She sits in protest where I have left her but we can all hear her talking to the donkey in a high-pitched voice. Rakesh goes out to speak to her even though, he tells me, she won't change her mind. I go out and tell her that dinner is getting cold. She ignores me and carries on talking to the donkey.

Inside, I can see my cousin, his wife, their children and Rakesh all sitting at the table, their food uneaten. My cousin has been complaining about how hungry he is since he arrived home.

He told me that snacks are for the rich. He is a worker. He eats two big meals a day because that is what he works hard to provide. Snacking is a luxury he cannot afford. He moved to Lamu because there was rumour of it becoming a tourist resort, with a big hotel, beach parties, maybe even discos. However, the lack of vehicles on the small island, the abundance of infrastructure needed, makes it very unlikely. I ask if he ever plans to come back to Mombasa. Or even go to Nairobi.

No, he says.

My cousin has seemed on edge since our arrival. This is such a different reaction from when I phoned him that night and he said he was so happy to hear from me. It would be exciting to meet his London family. He had not seen or heard from me for years but Seema always tied his rakhri on when I sent it. He called me beta, as though I was his dearest young sister. I even got excited at the prospect of seeing him.

He will keep us safe, I thought. While I spend time with my grandchildren. While we grow to know each other.

He will offer me refuge.

When we arrived, the gate was locked. He let us into his compound and immediately locked the gate behind him again. He is a worse version of the person I remember. And though I feel a duty to introduce family members to each other, as soon as I saw him, I knew I had made a mistake in bringing my babies to him. He does not socialize. Every door must be locked, every gate, every fence barbed. He is living in his compound, scared to go outside, but outside he must go in order to provide two big meals a day.

A cup of masala chai and a single Parle-G biscuit for breakfast. Every day.

I wish I had not brought my children here. I wanted to show them paradise. I wish I had not suppressed memories of what a bully my cousin is.

Please start, I tell them, coming back into the house.

Is she coming? he asks.

She will come in her own time.

Bloody bastard, he says in English, standing up and edging away from the table.

He thumps his feet. His children recoil.

I stand in his way, dumbly, frozen. He makes me still.

He walks outside, grumbling about his hunger.

I run to the door.

He picks Neha up off the ground and as she shouts in protest, I call for him to stop.

He hisses, Choop, at me and smacks her bottom hard three times, chewing at his lip.

There is something in his eyes. A glint.

She cries.

He hits her again and tells her to be quiet as he enters the house, then puts her in the chair.

She is crying.

Eat, he shouts. I have worked hard for this meal. You will eat. Eat.

I stand in the doorway, frozen.

He looks up at me.

Why does he have this power still?

He gestures at my empty seat and smiles with a mouth only.

I sit down.

I watch as he tears a mouthful of chapatti, dunks it into the dhal and shoves it into Neha's crying mouth. It falls back out on to her lap.

He grabs a fistful of khichdi and thrusts it towards her.

Stop, I scream, getting to my feet.

I pick Neha up and I grab Rakesh's hand, greasy with ghee from the sugar rotli. And I pull them both towards our bedroom.

We lie in the dark.

I have massaged lotion into Neha's sore bottom, which caused hilarity for Raks. I have fed them both theplas and Parle-G biscuits squirrelled away for the long journey. They're so hungry, they do not fuss.

We lie there.

He told us not to love you because soon you will be gone, Neha says, breaking the darkness with a whisper.

Who told you that? I ask, trying to not show concern in my voice.

A man.

I prod her for more information, but she remains quiet. I know who she means. He is preparing me. He is preparing my family to be without me.

I am sorry for my cousin, I say. That was cruel.

Neha turns to me. I do not like that he keeps Little Vijay tied up. Little Vijay should be free. I love him.

Sometimes, we marvel at a child's capacity to forget. Sometimes, we marvel at what they remember and retain.

I am sorry about the food.

I love Little Vijay, she says sleepily. He is my friend.

We have not left the room.

Rakesh has urinated in a water glass and I have emptied it out of the window. Neha wants to see Little Vijay, to make sure the donkey is okay.

I say, we have one more day here tomorrow. We need to keep out of people's way.

I leave our bedroom to go and find water.

As soon as I open the door and see the light on, I realize my mistake. My cousin is sitting, with a whisky, upright in a chair. He looks at me and swirls his drink.

Get yourself a glass, he says. Join me.

He slurs. He is drunk. His eyes are half-closed.

I walk to the kitchen and pick a steel cup off the side, bring it to where he sits and hold it out. He pours me some whisky. I sit down opposite him and put my feet on his glass table so that my toes are on the edge, pinching. I sip.

I have not tasted hard alcohol since I left England. Beer, yes, but not harsh and acrid like this whisky.

I have not missed it. Until this taste. It is delicious. It burns. I cough.

Good, na? he says.

Ha, I say. Reminds me of when Bhai was alive.

I think I hear him snore. I do not know if Ajay is awake.

My darling, my dearest, I have so many memories in this whisky that tastes like your breath.

You are different now, he says suddenly, with his eyes closed. I do not know you. You are not my cousin.

I have not seen you since my wedding.

You did not come to either of my weddings, he says.

England was so far away. I thought of you, I reassure him.

I cannot see that girl in you any more, he says, snarling. You have come back to Kenya changed. You are not African now.

I am nowhere, I reply. I am nowhere.

We sit in silence. I let that hang in the air and sip from the whisky. Then I see a jug of water on the table in front of me and reach for it but the movement stirs him and he jerks his body forward to move it out of reach.

This is my house, he says. I decide who gets what.

That was cruel, what you did to Neha, I say calmly.

He opens his eyes and sits forward.

Who are you to tell me? You will go home and leave me here. She will too. To England. This is my house.

I gulp down the rest of the whisky and stand up. I am wobbly. I want to be out of this home again and look at him sadly. He did not grow up into himself, I realize now, decades later. He grew into an older version of what he always was.

When I phoned you, you seemed so happy to hear from me, I say, backing away from him.

He stands up and holds a hand out to me.

I am happy, he says. You are family. You are always welcome here. We grew up together.

I wanted to tell my grandchildren good memories of us from childhood but all I could remember was that you used to beat me with sticks.

Why did you come, little sister? he asks, smiling.

You were so happy, I tell him. And I had not heard from my family for so long that I forgot. But now I remember what you did. I think I am supposed to say thank you, for turning me into this. I cannot feel pain. You say I am changed, that I am different. You beat Kenya out of me and I left. And now that I'm back, all I think about is another place at another time. You cannot scare me. I have stared death in the eyes and we are friends now. You are just a bully.

He laughs.

Cousin, he says. Never question a man in his own house. Especially when you do not know where you are.

Big brother, I say, sarcastically. I know where I am. I am in between worlds and you talk to me about houses. You think too small.

Why did you come? he asks, opening his eyes suddenly as they have been slowly closing. If I am such a bully.

Because I needed your protection, I say. From death.

I do not understand, he says, flopping back into his seat, shutting his eyes and putting his palm over them.

You do not need to, I tell him. Being here has given me the time I need with my grandchildren. You, it was you, I smile. You who made me love them. Who knew your cruelty could bring people together.

I laugh.

I edge back into my bedroom, smiling into the darkness, hoping you will hold my hand and guide me away from this place. I am nearly ready to see you, my darling.

I leave him there, asleep, and walk back into the pitch black of our bedroom. I shift Neha and Rakesh into my arms and cuddle them both. I love them and I am ready to let them both go. I am ready to go home and face what I was waiting for.

I waited for so long that when it came, I got scared.

I love you, I whisper to my grandchildren. I always will.

*

We wake to bleats and brays, wild and unnerving.

Neha springs out of bed.

Little Vijay, she says, running to the door.

Rakesh is slower to wake. I sit up and stretch, dab at the sweat in my armpits and blink the sleep from my eyes.

Neha struggles violently with the door, pulling at it till it opens, then runs out of the room.

I follow her with quick strides through the house.

She screams when she reaches the front door and I hurry in time to hold her back. Ajay squats over Little Vijay, whose legs are bound in thick rope.

What are you doing? Neha screams.

Take her back inside, Ajay says firmly.

He picks up a big panga and places a knee on Little Vijay's stomach.

Go back inside the house, I tell my child.

She looks up at me with pain in her eyes. I cannot comfort her.

Please, she says. Little Vijay.

My cousin holds up the panga.

I tell her again, firmly, go back inside.

I feel Rakesh take her hand and pull her. She resists at first but then allows him to lead her away.

Walking towards Ajay, I thrust my hands out in confusion.

What are you doing? I ask.

This donkey is no good to me now. It will not work. Go back inside. Tonight we barbecue – a celebration for your last night.

Stop, I say. Stop, please stop.

My cousin stands up. He throws the panga to the ground, leaving Little Vijay to struggle and squirm. Expecting me to retreat, he stomps towards me, but I do not. He thinks he can own my body, show me what space is mine, because this is his house.

But I do not live in this world any more.

I wait for him to approach. I have been sitting by myself for too long now, but I understand the frailty of men. He wants me to be defined by him. My reaction to him should be one of fear.

But I do not live in this world any more. I will deliver these children to their father the day after next.

I have decided to die.

My brain is a list of names of those I have lost. I want to be with my family again. I want to see you.

My cousin stops walking towards me. He places his hand behind his back and looks over my shoulder to where Neha and Rakesh stand in the doorway of our bedroom. I turn to them and ask them to close the door.

Rakesh shakes his head but Neha listens to me.

Cousin, I say. You can punish the donkey but you will not punish my granddaughter. She has lost more than you so young.

We have all lost someone, cousin, he tells me. None of this is written in destiny. It is a kidology to believe this nonsense. None of this is happening because it needs to – it happens because it does.

He stops.

She is a child, I tell him.

So was I when...He stops and smiles. Do not think you can abandon us here and go and live in England like a gora, then come back and expect me to bow to you.

Men like my cousin give themselves to one god. And that is the amount of their own father they have in them. My cousin's father was an angry man.

Cousin, he tells me.

I listen. I let him say his words. Words are nothing to the dead. They mean that little to me now.

He says, you expect to bring Angrezi politics back home? You must know where you belong.

He has come for me, cousin, I tell him. I speak quietly. Destiny has called for me.

My cousin laughs. He actually laughs.

Cousin, he says, through guffaws. You are superstitious.

I take my purse from my bra and pull out what shillings I have left with me.

Stop, I say. Ajay bhai, stop. Here. Take this.

This is my property, he shouts.

I hold out the wad of shillings. I do not own much and I do not need much. Not where I am going.

Have it, bhai, I say. We will take Little Vijay with us.

He laughs. Cousin, he says, are you dizzy? Have you lost your mind? How will you get this donkey to the mainland? Is she going to take it back to England on a plane? This is silly. Now, leave me to do my business.

He picks up the panga and raises it once more. I run towards him and as he drops his arm, I catch it with all my might. The force of his blow knocks me over but it is enough to make him hesitate. He throws the panga down again and it clangs on the ground. He raises his free hand to me.

You attack your own brother.

Ajay, bhai, money is more useful than a donkey carcass.

Take it, I say, picking myself up.

I look towards the door. Neha is watching us and though I gesture for her to go back inside, she stands still and watches, frowning.

You raised your hand to me, he says. I should beat you here and send you home.

We will leave, I say, standing up and squaring my chest to his. He used to be bigger than me. Now we are both old and slower and roughly the same size. And we will go home safely, taking Little Vijay with us. And you will never touch me again. Cousin.

I drop the shillings at his feet and kneel down to pat the donkey, who I imagine is confused. As I stroke her, Neha runs out to us, blowing on Little Vijay's nose as she approaches. She hugs her neck and smiles at me.

Thank you, she says.

Ajay marches back into the house, shouting for chai as he enters.

We must leave, I say. Immediately.

I have rewritten Little Vijay's destiny, I think.

When we leave, I untie Little Vijay on the way. When we leave, my cousin is nowhere to be seen. When we leave, there are no goodbyes, only a handkerchief containing theplas, and one aloo paratha for me, left on the floor near our chappals. I nearly step on it as I walk out of the door.

We progress silently along the waterfront, Rakesh holding on to my hand, Neha to a rope around Little Vijay's neck. The donkey is slow, for she is old and her back is not in good condition. We walk in silence.

As we approach the docks where the ferries leave from, I point to a pace of donkeys, each one vying for food on a small patch of grass. There are ten of them. Donkeys roam freely here and Little Vijay can be free. I untie the rope from her neck.

Time to say goodbye, I tell Neha.

I do not want to.

We have to go, we have arrangements. Your daddy will be waiting when we arrive back, I assure her.

I need to know Little Vijay is okay. I love him.

I can hear the hurt in her voice.

I promise you, I tell her. Wherever she is, it is the best place for her to be. And look, she will be amongst her own. This is what is written for her now.

I don't want to say goodbye, she says.

I rub at her back and stroke above Little Vijay's eye.

We stand in silence.

It is time, I say, fighting back tears.

Neha cuddles Little Vijay. Tears fall from her face on to Little Vijay's cheek and I cannot contain my emotions: I cry too.

Rakesh squeezes my hand while Neha leads Little Vijay to the pace of donkeys.

Good. Bye, she says. One day you will die. Until then, good. Bye.

Goodbye, I hear Rakesh whisper, standing next to me. When I die, I'm bringing you down with me. Goodbye.

She walks back to us and we watch Little Vijay put her nose down into the muddle of heads trying to find food on this tiny patch of grass. We stand in silence.

Want to hear a joke? Rakesh says. I read it in my joke book.

Yes.

How do oceans say hello to each other? he asks. They wave.

We all laugh, each one straining to make the moment less painful.

As the bus slowly navigates the bumpy road, feeling car sick I turn to my babies and hold out my hand to Rakesh to shake. He looks at Neha, puzzled, and then back at me but reaches his hand out to mine.

Goodbye, until you are dead, I say.

No, Neha screams, laughing. You're doing it wrong.

I do it wrong again and again, until they are frustrated with me.

I do it right once, for the relief, and Neha gives me a big hug. The next time, I do it wrong. And we fall about laughing on the bus.

Everyone Disperses – One by One They All Leave

The beach is as I remember. Shards of palm trees try to lacerate my feet as I walk along, barefoot. The reef is jagged and treacherous but you can go a mile on to it when the tide is out.

I see something silver glinting in the sand. It looks like a coin but when I pick it up it's a piece of dagger-sharp glass, so I drop it back into the sand and step over it. I've left all my money at home, all my possessions. I'm wearing the saree I wore the day you died. I can see the blood stained into it, still hear the prathna we held in that tiny terraced house in Harrow.

I made everyone sing the Hanuman Chalisa because it was your favourite, and I remember wiping the tears streaming from my face with another saree, one of your cousins' floral ones. Nisha, just home from work, wore a miniskirt and a white shirt. She lay in Mukesh's arms and disengaged from the room.

Months later she would be pregnant. Pregnant, cancerous.

This saree is stained with memories. It is stained with you. It seems fitting to wear it now.

The emptiness of my house in the weeks after the twins leave is confusing. When they arrived I felt as though my life of static and solitude had been upturned. Then they showed me joy. Now they are gone, I fail to find instant comfort in the quiet. Instead I feel restless and clear out everything I don't want.

I take all my clothes to the temple but leave the kitchen as it is. It feels used, as though someone has been here. I leave my copies of *Lady Chatterley* and *Tropic of Cancer* on Mrs Chatterjee's doorstep, with no explanation. It amuses me that she will be shocked and outraged long after I am gone. I have nothing else. I do not have any money to speak of, any books, or any luxury items. My radio I give to the children who play in the street, the ones who come and sit near my veranda when I am listening to cricket.

I look at my room.

All I have left is myself.

I am ready for you.

I did not bring letters or photographs back with me – I gave them to Mukesh to give to the children. He can live with these ghosts, not me. I long to be one myself. I left photographs of you and Nisha and Chumchee because I could not look at you all any more.

When it comes time to say goodbye to Neha and Rakesh, I give Neha a picture of a donkey that I bought in Lamu, a postcard.

There is post for you, I say.

She takes it and looks at the picture, turning it over to see what I have written: *THANK YOU FOR SAVING ME AND FOR LOVING ME I AM HAPPY WITH MY FRIENDS LOVE LITTLE VIJAY.*

This is not real, she says.

Are you sure?

Rakesh is talking Mukesh through his joke book and Mukesh is doing his best to laugh. Neha steps out of my home on to the front step. I watch her watching the day pass by and then go out and stand next to her.

I will miss you, I say.

Will we see you again? she asks.

No. I am old, too old to travel now. And I am tired.

I will come back and visit, she says. I want to.

I hope you will. You remind me so much of your mother, I add. You know your own mind like her. Never think that anyone knows it better than you. The world is filled with average white men. You have to be twice as good as them. Okay?

I give her two small pieces of paper.

What are these? she asks, looking down at them. Written in our daughter's hand are some words. Every time I see her handwriting, I remember everything about her, as though she is still here.

Neha: egotist, hard-working, stubborn, avoid these numbers: 16, 12, 9, 22.

Rakesh: clown, needs validation, lazy, avoid these numbers: 3, 13, 14, 22.

She screws up her nose when she reads them.

She is so much like our daughter. I miss our daughter. I miss when we were together.

I don't understand, she says.

I tell her about the Bradford Baba and how our daughter asked him to write down the destiny of her children, so that she could know them in some way, what they would become, so she could feel a part of their lives.

What is an egotist? Neha asks.

It means you know your own mind. These are your destinies, the ones your mother knew you would have when she died. She was so sad not to be able to see what you would become. Whatever happens, whatever heartbreak you feel, whatever pain, whatever loss, it was meant to happen. Whatever love, happiness or joy, it was always meant to be. There is a comfort in this. Knowing your destiny is helpful so you are prepared for whatever comes.

Daddy said destiny is not as important as science. Science is real.

That is because destiny is written by people we cannot see.

I don't want to know what will happen, she says.

Our destiny determines who we are, what we achieve, what we suffer, what we feel. Everything happens according to destiny. We can't escape from what we have to face in life, no matter how hard we try.

What is your destiny? she asks.

As I hold her I feel myself breaking into tears.

It is to love my family whatever happens, at all costs. I walk towards my destiny with my head held high. I pause. I love you, I add.

I love you too, she whispers, looking over my shoulder.

Rakesh cries when I say goodbye, the poor boy. He wears his emotions like badges. I said to him, embrace your nature, your desire to please. Do something with that. Do not care what others think.

I look at Mukesh and extend my hand to him. He tries to hug me.

We are concluding a business transaction, not saying a tearful goodbye of two loved ones, I tell him.

I want to laugh, saying that the look on his face makes me shiver. As he walks away, I remember my first impression of the boy, setting fire to our toilet door. Chaos follows him.

I reach a mound of jagged rocks slick with sea spray and put my chappals back on, in order to clamber over them, as I have done many times in the past. The trick is to embrace the slipperiness of your chappals and move quickly, use the sliding inertia to push yourself up on to the initial rock. Once you are there, you can get over the rest of them. I try to summon up the strength in my tired legs but I cannot do it. My knees have not been the same since returning here. They feel swollen and inflamed with every move. I have to stand and walk with them bent ever so slightly, to ensure they are not locked in place.

With no reason to go back, unable to move forward, I sing something tuneless, just so there is noise.

There he is, standing next to me, an orange shawl draped over his shoulders to hide his feathered body. He wears those round glasses. At first I think it is him, from the market, Yama, come for me. But now, in the stillness of the moment, I realize that he looks just like you. It is you. It is you who has been waiting for me all this time.

I smile at you.

I am ready now, I say, to break the silence after what feels like a lifetime of waiting.

The clouds close in, black and fuzzy, like a wisp of beard.

I know, you say. That is why I am here.

I have missed you so much.

I have missed you too. I am glad you came home and chose

to come here to meet me. I was wrong to be left in England. I missed this.

Our grandchildren are beautiful, I tell you. They have bright futures ahead of them.

Whatever is written for their destiny is what is written. That is how it should be.

I realized something, darling, I tell you. Something I had not realized before about destiny. When I was leading our grandchildren from Ajay's house, it came to me. The present moment is the only thing that actually exists and so when we have to be fully engaged in what is happening right this second, we have the power to change our future, to change the world. All change comes from this moment.

There is free will and there is destiny, you tell me. They coexist. Some things we write, some things are written for us. Fate is our sanskara. We created some of it in the past, which gives us the experiences we are having now, but we can change what our future self will be experiencing by our choices right now. That is all destiny is: the consequences of choices.

I did not know this before, I say. I know it now.

I walk towards the water. It is cold around my toes. I wade in until it comes to my waist and I feel my chappals slip off my feet, stuck in the muddy sand.

I fall into the water and swim.

I never wanted to be a mother. It was thrust on me. I was told it was my destiny and I accepted this, feeling I had no choice. It was my role, what I was destined to do. There were days I felt I had lost any sense of myself other than being a mother. In my dark moments, I thought perhaps I had killed my children, and punished my husband for impregnating me. The whole time I have been here, in solitude, I punished myself because I thought that I had written their destinies for them. That which was meant for me had consequences for my family.

My mother drowned.

There was too much fluid in Nisha's lungs when she died.

She drowned.

It feels romantic. How our destinies are intertwined. I smile.

I swim until I feel faint, letting the waves wash over me as the tide ebbs away. You stand on the shore and you watch.

I wave to you. I am happy to see you.

I sing to myself, that song that is always on the radio, and I picture my family, my Chumchee, my Nisha, Neha and Rakesh, and you, and I close my eyes. I am so tired, and I am, finally, so happy. I bob in the water, watching the shore. You are standing still and watching me, waiting for me. I smile and close my eyes.

Ye hum kyaa jaane, ye wahee jaane, jisane likhaa hain sab kaa naseeb.

What do I know, only he knows, the one who has written the destiny of all.

Acknowledgments

Firstly, thank you to James Roxburgh for being a wise, careful and generous editor. Thank you to everyone at Atlantic Books. Thank you to Margaret Stead, also. Thanks for the unwavering support, Julia Kingsford. Thank you to early readers Chimene Suleyman and James Smythe for their insights.

Thank you to Mahesh mama for bringing that case under the Race Relations Act in 1968; to Miss L for running the Casting Call Woe blog (where I plucked some of Laila's casting calls); to Josie Long and Nish Kumar for insights into the life of a stand-up comedian; to Bahul for his CV, which is Neha's CV (and I still don't quite get what either of them do); to Wei Ming Kam, Charlie Morris and Liz Wawrykow for advice; thank you to women of colour for absolutely everything.

Thank you to Coco, who for the first few months of her life would only sleep on me in a sling for entire nights, which gave me the necessary time to edit this. Thank you to Sunnie for telling me you want to read this one day.

Thank you to Jo, Gigi and Katie for a memorable journey to Lamu forever ago. Thank you to Emma-Lee Moss for a tour of New York coffee spots once.

Thank you to the Arts Council for their time to write a grant. I've been lucky to receive a few of these over the years and each time, the work I did, the characters and stories I developed got me closer to writing this book. It's not often, these days, as a writer, that you get time to play and experiment and nurture and be creative and try things out, but these Arts Council grants are invaluable in providing this time. So thank you to them for continuing to make these opportunities available in spite of our current government's war on the arts.

You can adopt the real Little Vijay at the Donkey Sanctuary in East Devon.

Thank you to the Arvon Foundation centre at Lumb Bank, where I did some work on this in between workshops.

Thank you to Salena Godden and Niven Govinden for mentoring me and giving me time, support and love when I needed it the most.

Thank you to all the contributors to *The Good Immigrant*, which is a book that has changed my life.

An earlier version of Raks' chapter, *A Man, Without A Donkey*, was longlisted for the London Short Story Prize.

Save libraries.

I miss you mum.

Katie, I love you so very much.